PRAISE FOR MARSHALL HARRISON AND HIS ACCLAIMED VIETNAM MEMOIR, *A LONELY KIND OF WAR*...

"One of the best to come out of the Vietnam era."
—*Marine Corps Gazette*

"A well-written, fast-moving account."
—*Rocky Mountain News*

"Reads like a novel and has the ring of truth, as can be told only by one who has been there."
—*Wings of Gold*

"An instant classic—the best book about the air war over Vietnam in more than a decade . . . This is a real-time look at war in 1969—close up and personal."
—*The Topeka Capital-Journal*

"Harrison brings surprise, suspense, excitement and even some humor to his memoirs."
—*The San Diego Union*

"This may be the best account written of air combat during the Vietnam War, fiction or nonfiction . . . Harrison has a tremendous talent."
—*Monterey Sunday Herald*

"A gripping tale . . . well worth reading."
—Department of Defense,
The Friday Review of Defense Literature

MARSHALL HARRISON is a retired Air Force officer who served three tours in Vietnam. He now lives in Lubbock, Texas.

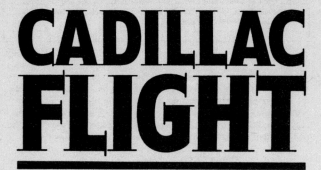

CADILLAC FLIGHT

MARSHALL HARRISON

JOVE BOOKS, NEW YORK

This is a novel. The characters and military organizations are an invention of the author, except where they can be identified historically, and are intended to depict no real persons or organizations. Any resemblance to actual persons, living or dead, is purely coincidental. Likewise, names, dialogue, and opinions expressed are products of the author's imagination and should not be interpreted as real.

This Jove Book contains the complete
text of the original hardcover edition.
It has been completely reset in a typeface
designed for easy reading and was printed
from new film.

CADILLAC FLIGHT

A Jove Book / published by arrangement with
Presidio Press

PRINTING HISTORY
Presidio Press edition published 1991
Jove edition / December 1993

ISBN: 0-515-11232-1

A JOVE BOOK®
Jove Books are published by The Berkley Publishing Group,
200 Madison Avenue, New York, New York 10016.
JOVE and the "J" design are trademarks
belonging to Jove Publications, Inc.

PRINTED IN THE UNITED STATES OF AMERICA

10 9 8 7 6 5 4 3 2 1

This book is dedicated to those military and naval attack pilots who flew into the hornets' nest of the North Vietnamese air defense system. Especially to those who carried the early load for the USAF, many of whom never returned—the F-105 Thunderchief pilots. As in the old fighter pilot toast to the missing: "To our comrades up north!"

and

To Mary Ann, as always.

So, stand by your glasses steady,
This world is a world of lies.
Here's a toast to the dead already;
Hurrah for the next man who dies!

World War I pilots'
drinking song

ACKNOWLEDGMENTS

I owe a special thanks to Col. Ken Hite and other pilots who flew the F-105 Thunderchief into combat over North Vietnam. All were generous with their time in providing me advice on tactics and systems. Any mistakes belong solely to the author.

A very special thanks to Joan Griffin, Senior Editor at Presidio Press. Her objectivity and sensitive handling of a writer struggling for coherency has been a class act.

GLOSSARY

AAA   Antiaircraft artillery.

Barrel roll   A maneuver in which an aircraft makes a complete rotation around the longitudinal axis.

Blood chit   A piece of nylon measuring 10 inches by 20 inches with an American flag printed on it and a request for assistance written in several local languages and dialects. A reward for assistance is promised by the U.S. government. Each chit is controlled by a serial number so that the carrier may be identified.

CAP   Combat air patrol. Provides cover for strike aircraft.

FAC   Forward air controller. A low-flying pilot who directs attack aircraft.

Frag orders   The daily plan for the number, type of aircraft, and ordnance loads to be launched against specific targets. Fragments of the complete Seventh Air Force plan were sent to the operational wings.

GCI   Ground-controlled intercept.

Immelmann turn   A complete change in direction accomplished by completing half of a loop.

Jink   To maneuver an aircraft sharply and continuously to avoid ground fire.

Jolly Green Giants   Nickname for the Sikorsky HH-3E helicopter modified for rescue service.

MIA   Missing in action.

MiGCAP   Combat air patrol designed specifically to defend the strike force from the MiG interceptors.

MER   Multiple ejector racks.

Pickle   Pilot slang for releasing the aircraft's bomb load by depressing a button on the control stick.

POL   Petroleum-oil-lubricants.

REMF   Rear-echelon motherfucker. The name given to everyone not actually in combat.

RESCAP   Combat air patrol for rescue operations.
RHAW   Radar homing and warning gear.
RP   Rendezvous point.
RTU   Replacement training unit.
SAR   Search and rescue.
Twix   A military cablegram.
VFR   Visual flight rules. A flight conducted free of the clouds.
Yankee Station   An area 100 miles east of Danang in the South China Sea where U.S. naval carriers cruised as they launched their attack aircraft against Vietnamese and Laotian targets.

Prologue, 1986

"Would you like a last cup of coffee, General? We're just about ready to start our descent."

The lean, middle-aged officer turned from the window of the Air Force C-141 transport to smile and shake his head at the sergeant before returning his gaze to the countryside sliding beneath them. The sergeant thought he looked to be a thousand miles away.

In fact, the general's thoughts were distant, but not quite as far as the sergeant had guessed. They were focused approximately 30,000 feet below and north of the aircraft's flight path onto a group of rough limestone hills some fifty-odd miles northwest of Hanoi, Democratic Republic of Vietnam. His fascination was not geologic but a more personal association from a time long past, when reaching that sanctuary could literally mean life or death.

The dark blue eyes searched the tree-covered slopes in detail, seeking out familiar ravines and knolls. With some amusement he realized he'd never learned the proper name for the karst formations. He'd never heard them called anything other than the nickname coined by the American pilots who used them to mask their approaches to targets in the Hanoi area many years before. Thud Ridge, the hills had been called.

The area looked the same, even after twenty years, as he compared it to the image burned indelibly into his memory.

1

His eyes moved southeasterly from the last of the hills to the broadening floodplain of the Red River valley. Old antiaircraft gun sites stood naked, easily seen amongst the verdant rice paddies. He caught his breath as he saw the familiar circle of a surface-to-air missile ring. It too stood empty except for what appeared to be a small group of water buffalo. At least this trip he need not be concerned with deadly missiles. Nevertheless, his pulse quickened as the aircraft approached the city, much as it had done so many years before. Just like Pavlov's dog, he thought; ring the bell and watch me salivate.

"Better get a move on, General. We'll be on the ground in a few minutes and I'll want us to start deplaning immediately."

The general turned from the window and glanced at the back of the already retreating young State Department officer. He remained silent, just managing to conceal his irritation at the abrupt manner of the Recovery Team chief. With any luck the Vietnamese would have the bones ready and the team would have to spend only minimum time in Hanoi before they could leave with their grisly cargo for the Joint Resolution Center in Honolulu. Minimum time in Hanoi would suit him perfectly, especially since he hadn't wanted to make the trip in the first place. And now, he had to contend with this officious young ass from State, who seemed determined to prod him into saying something he'd end up regretting. The team could leave him out of their socializing with the Viets. He'd spent a significant part of his life trying to kill the little buggers or trying to keep them from doing the same to him, and damned if he felt like drinking tea and making small talk with them.

The aircraft banked slightly to the left and for the first time the general was able to get a view of the city, apparently unchanged from the last time he'd seen it twenty years before. He picked up the Red River as it meandered through a broad valley on its way to the sea, followed it eastward to the Paul Doumer bridge, and watched it disappear into the haze. Of course, it was now the Long Bien bridge, its builder having been relegated by the victors to history's garbage dump. Whatever its name, the structure retained the brooding, solid look it had when it was one of his wing's targets.

Farther east, he recognized the runway pattern of their destination, the Gia Lam airport, but his thoughts remained with the bridge. Throughout the long war, it had been a prime target of the American fighter-bombers and had become a symbol of tenacity to both sides. Spans were dropped, only to be quickly rebuilt; aircraft were shot down and ground gunners were blown from their pits—move and countermove. More than likely some of the remains that the team was picking up had come as a result of attacks against the bridge. Never the airfields, though. They had not been attacked until near the end, when it was too late, despite the deadly little MiG interceptors revetted there within full sight of the attacking forces but immune from harm by governmental decree. It had seemed insane then and it seemed insane today. How many pilots had fallen to their deaths because of stupid targeting decisions? Not that it really mattered anymore. Dead was dead, and trying to fix the blame wasn't going to bring any of them back.

The general leaned out into the aisle and looked forward to where the team chief was putting on the jacket to his lightweight suit. The general could well imagine someone just like that little twit making asinine targeting decisions that could only put men in unnecessary jeopardy.

The familiar knot of anger formed in his stomach as the thought of the last team meeting replayed in his mind. Everyone acted as if this were some sort of poker game, using the bones of the missing American pilots as chips. The Vietnamese had withheld the remains until the American players somehow sweetened the pot, then suddenly discovered that perhaps there were a few dead American pilots around after all. The Americans were just as bad. They acted as if the remains of their countrymen who had died fighting in this foreign land on their government's orders had become a prize to be wrested from the Vietnamese by superior bargaining rather than objects of veneration to be brought home honorably. Both groups made him sick to his stomach.

He knew, however, that no matter how odious the game, it had to be played if these pilots were ever to rest in their homeland. After all, the little folks had won the war and could call the shots with the few chips they had available. But the Vietnamese had found to their dismay that the world

had lost interest in them and their victory; it had left them
to their battered and ruined economy, forsaken for the most
part by their former suppliers. Indeed, they were almost
in a state of war with the giant to the north, whose rail
lines and highways had kept them afloat for the duration
of the hostilities. Now, they found themselves reduced to
haggling over bones found in their decimated countryside,
even trying occasionally to slip in some Vietnamese dead
in their desperation to increase the worth of their only
export.

The landing gear extended with a jarring thump and the
flap motors whined as the transport pilot positioned his huge
aircraft onto the final approach course. There was a last flap
setting and the silver transport settled gently to the concrete.
The thrust reversers were brought in so smoothly that the
general was hardly aware he was being pushed against the
restraining lap belt.

The C-141 swung onto the main parking ramp, and the
general was able to see the Vietnamese delegation—mostly
civilian, but a few in uniform—formed into a line to greet
them. As the aircraft braked gently to a stop, the general rose
and slipped into his uniform blouse, still feeling something
of an imposter as he glanced at the two silver stars on each
shoulder. He still didn't *feel* like a general. He wasn't even
sure he wanted to. He'd really like to feel like the fighter pilot
he'd once been. He stood patiently for the queue to form.

The engines whined to a stop and the master sergeant
immediately opened the entry door. The miasma of Southeast
Asia assaulted the cabin—that combination of humus, night
soil, charcoal smoke, and God knows what, which mixed
and convoluted until it seemed as though it could be chewed.
Once in the nostrils, it was stamped there forever, available
for immediate recall.

As the Americans deplaned in the order decreed by the
protocol of the State Department, the general was partially
amused, partially annoyed, to find himself behind three
of the younger men. Actually, there had been earlier
suggestions that the military members of the team wear
civilian clothing so as not to offend their hosts. Instant
and unanimous opposition from the Joint Chiefs of Staff
eventually convinced the State Department that this move
would be not only unwise but insulting to the remains that

were to be borne to friendlier climes. After all, there were no civilian bones in those wooden boxes. If it had been left to me, he thought, there would have been a full color guard and a band to escort them, and screw what the Vietnamese thought.

The Viet reception line had formed near the aircraft's stairwell, and each American had to negotiate a sea of smiling faces as he came down the stairs, pausing briefly before shaking hands, then moving to the next figure. The general was struck again by the youthful appearance of his late adversaries; most of the faces were wrinkle-free and smooth, although there was a great deal of white hair among them. He knew that most had to be his age or older. Both groups wore name tags pinned to their left breast. The general could feel the sweat start to trickle down his back beneath the blue blouse and wished the team chief would get the lead out and move the troops into the shade. There had been little point in not allowing them to wear their short-sleeved uniforms. Some of the Viets wore suits but the majority were in their shirtsleeves. They seemed to be completely unaffected by the withering heat.

The general looked around the airfield as he waited, still on the airstairs, while the team leader continued to trade pleasantries with the Vietnamese. Away from the terminal the distinctive tails of MiG-21s rose above the revetments. His eyes swept down the row, consciously counting them for the intelligence debrief he knew they would all get on their return to Washington. The old birds had been around a long time, he thought wryly, almost as long as some of ours. They looked to be in good condition from what he could see. The maintenance areas were neat and well kept.

The knot suddenly formed again in the general's stomach as his eyes raked over one of the small fighters; the tail poking above the revetment wall was a distinctive red color. Then he was pushed forward into the line of smiling delegates and his view of the aircraft was cut off.

He waded through the line of limp handshakes favored by the Vietnamese, barely looking at their faces. What he really wanted was an icy beer and some time alone to think about that red-tailed fighter. At the end of the line he found himself being closely scrutinized by a short, stocky man in uniform. This one was not smiling. He was heavy for a Viet and looked, the general thought, just a little silly in his uniform. On his chest was a Vietnamese pilot badge, placed just above three rows of metal ribbons. The shorter man—his name tag read NGUYEN THI MINH—studied the five rows of ribbons and command pilot badge on the general's chest. Then their eyes met.

"Perhaps we might have met before, General? In another time?" He spoke in heavily accented but very passable English. A small smile slightly twisted his mouth.

"I believe it could be entirely possible, Colonel."

Their eyes held until pressure from the others in the line forced them apart.

Captain James Evelyn Broussard

There is absolutely no way I can do this ninety-eight more times, Jim Broussard thought as the dirty gray smoke of the flak sought their flight level. One hundred completed missions seemed a preposterous notion at the moment; for that matter, *two* completed missions seemed impossible, since the flight entered what was probably the most heavily defended area in the world.

Broussard had no idea who had been responsible for determining that fighter-bomber pilots could rotate stateside after reaching the hundred-mission goal, but whoever he was he had obviously never been into Route Package Six, the area encompassing Hanoi-Haiphong. Broussard's stomach churned as the shock waves from two flak bursts jarred his aircraft.

Yesterday's mission over Route Package One, the southernmost part of North Vietnam, had been exciting with the knowledge that hostile eyes and guns were following his flight's movements. But he had been told that while overflying that area the Vietnamese gunners would leave you alone provided you showed them the same courtesy. And they had. There had been no hostile reaction to their flight, even when their bombs had been dropped on an unseen target so heavily blanketed by foliage that even the experienced pilots of the flight couldn't tell whether or not the truck park had been destroyed. But this! This was

7

the most terrifying thing he'd ever done. The fear was like
a small animal gnawing at his belly, and he realized that
he was a heartbeat from real panic for the first time in his
life. He had never imagined it could be this bad.

One lousy ride, he thought, then right into the big one: the
Hanoi suburbs! Dodge City itself! Downtown! Broussard
shrugged his shoulders against the constraining straps of the
ejection seat and parachute harness, consciously trying to
loosen his muscles and become the calm, confident fighter
pilot he was supposed to be. It didn't work. He saw that
he was drifting slowly back from his left wing position and
tried to push the throttle forward, attempting to overtake the
flight leader. The throttle was already against the quadrant
stops, and unless he moved it outboard into afterburner,
there was little chance of him regaining his proper position.
If he did go into burner he'd probably accelerate right past
the lead ship and find himself in the unintentional position
of Cadillac Flight leader—one who had no idea where he
was! Not a comforting thought on his second mission,
experiencing for the first time the sensation that someone
was seriously trying to kill him. No, he'd just have to accept
that his aircraft was a little slower than Lead's and hope that
Donkey would take notice of his predicament.

Jim watched the lead aircraft creep farther away and tried
to decide what the best course of action would be. He could
call Lead, but Donkey would be at his busiest now, trying
to find the target in the perpetual haze of North Vietnam,
and he wouldn't appreciate the distraction. Jim considered
checking the two fighters of the second element but didn't
dare take his eyes from Lead even for a moment. The last
thing he wanted to do was find himself lost and alone in
this area. He flinched as small balls of orange antiaircraft
fire tracked the flight, then fell by the wayside as the aircraft
outdistanced them.

Jim reviewed his options. He could go to burner, but
the fuel consumption would be so high that he might not
be able to make the tanker on recovery—not that he was
convinced he would live that long anyway. And he had no
desire to suddenly become the new unannounced leader of
Cadillac Flight. Scrub that one. He could radio a request for
a slower airspeed, but he wasn't sure it would get through
to Donkey over the congested radio frequency—the strike

net was jammed with radio calls, and the RHAW (radar homing and warning) gear was screeching like souls in hell into his headset as it identified tracking radars. Jim decided to soldier on and follow as best he could, hoping he didn't lose sight of the leader.

Suddenly, the lead ship turned from the IP (initial point) and began the sprint toward the target, an oil refinery, which was to be attacked from a left roll-in for the dive-bombing pass. The high-pitched warbling grew in intensity and frequency as they neared the target. Jim's hands scurried around the cockpit, flipping the switches necessary to release the armed bombs. Last, he rechecked the master bomb arm to the on position. By the time he raised his head from the cockpit, he had fallen even farther behind.

There would be minimum evasive action from the IP to the roll-in point: electronic countermeasures and prayer would be their only defense until the dive toward the target had been completed and the ordnance released. Only then would they stroke the afterburner and make a low-level break toward the sanctuary of the sheltering hills northwest of the city. On the way out, the planes would again have to run the gauntlet of small-arms fire, flak, and SAM (surface-to-air missile) batteries they had faced coming in. Also, Jim remembered that the flight was now in the backyard of the agile little MiG-17s and -21s, which could be radar directed against them. Yes, there were truly exciting differences between Route Packs Six and One.

Over the strike net Jim heard the excited voices of the flak-suppression aircraft already engaging the ground defenses. His aircraft rocked again as a flak cloud appeared almost directly in front of him—the center of the dirty gray mass was a glowing red. He thought he heard metal fragments hit the fuselage, but the tight-fitting crash helmet and the high-pitched warble of the radar detector made this unlikely. He was through the cloud quickly, before his hand could twitch the control stick. Streams of exploding orange balls from a 37- or 57mm gun cut between him and his flight leader. This time, his hand involuntarily jerked the aircraft away from the deadly flow.

He tried to ignore the orange balls tracking the flight, but his peripheral vision had a will of its own and insisted upon closely watching the balls float directly at the aircraft, then veer away sharply at the last moment. More of the dirty-gray balls erupted at one o'clock, level, close enough that the fireball contained in each cloud was outlined in red. The airspeed indicator, when he was finally able to pull his eyes away from the flak, showed almost 600 knots over the ground. The lead fighter continued to pull slowly away from him. Cadillac Flight was going about as fast as its birds could go with slabs of ordnance hanging beneath them.

Jim followed through a course correction and again lowered his eyes for a quick scan of the instrument tapes. At that moment the lead fighter elected to begin his dive-bomb attack, almost losing Jim completely. The huge lead fighter rolled nearly inverted and hung there for several seconds while Donkey searched for the target through the haze, then hurtled toward the ground with Cadillac Two— Jim Broussard—in wild pursuit.

A quick glance at the altimeter showed that they were already down to 9,000 feet, and although Jim's position in relation to the lead aircraft had improved slightly, he was still far from being where he was supposed to be. Suddenly, it hit him—9,000 feet! Christ! They were briefed to drop at 6,000 and he hadn't even looked for the target!

Frantically, he clicked his eyes from Cadillac Lead to the ground and back again, just in time to see all six 750-pound bombs leave Donkey's aircraft. He didn't have a clue where the briefed target was supposed to be, so he quickly hit the pickle button on the control stick, immediately feeling the aircraft lighten as the bombs left.

His world turned gray from the g forces as he tried to match Donkey's pullout; consequently, Jim was late noticing that the other aircraft had gone into afterburner and was rapidly pulling away. He slammed the throttle outboard and felt the kick in the pants from the extra power. Both aircraft leveled at 500 feet. Broussard tried to anticipate Donkey's wild jinking, but he wasn't very successful at that either: When he thought the lead bird would turn in one direction, it usually went the other way.

The aircraft were now close enough to the ground that the farmers with their shiny new Russian rifles could have their turn at them. The peasants blasted directly up into an area of the sky assigned to them by the North Vietnamese Defense Command and hoped that the Yankee air pirates would run into one of their small projectiles, as deadly as a flak shell if it struck the aircraft in the right area. Jim sincerely hoped that the rifle bullets would expend their energy, untouched by the fragile skin of his aircraft, and fall directly back down on their heads.

White bursts of 23- and 37mm guns continued to track them at low level, looking quite different from the black clouds of the exploding 85- and 100mm guns he had seen at altitude. Jim felt numb, as if someone else was flying the aircraft and he was a disinterested observer along for the ride. His hands and feet reacted without thought on his part. He was brought back to reality by the voice of Donkey, the flight leader. It was the first he'd heard from him since before they hit the IP. Cadillac Lead was not happy with the newest member of his flight.

"Cadillac Two," Donkey called from the lead ship, "if I have to come outta burner to let you catch up, I'm going to kick your ass right up into your helmet when we get back. Get back in here and stop horsing around."

Christ, Jim said to himself, watching the tracers track his ship, we're doing better than Mach 1 at 500 feet over the trees with everybody and his brother trying to kill us and he's got time to look over his shoulder and do a critique. Jim's aircraft bucked again and he fought it back to level flight before he answered. "Roger, Cadillac Lead. I'm trying to get back in." There was nothing else to say.

Then they were away from the suburban sprawl and nudging up to start the high-speed climb over the rough, tree-covered limestone hills called Thud Ridge in the briefing. No one seemed to know the reason for the name except that the area had become a sanctuary of sorts for the strike birds egressing the Hanoi area. The terrain was too rough and eroded to serve as a satisfactory launching site for the SAMs, the trees decreased the tracking time for any antiaircraft artillery emplaced there, and the elevation somewhat masked the Viet radars. The story went that if you could make it to the ridge, you had a pretty good chance of living through another mission. That is, unless the MiGs happened to be in the area that day, or you just happened to stray a few too many miles north toward the Yen Bai area, where the gunners and missileers were known to be particularly testy.

Cadillac Lead stayed low for another couple of minutes, nudging the flight right or left away from the strings of light automatic weapon fire probing for them, then began a slow climb to the briefed egress altitude of 20,000 feet. Jim Broussard was right with Donkey when he came out of burner. Can't keep fooling the kid all the time, Jim thought, and glanced quickly to his right as his element leveled. There were both aircraft of the second element of the flight, exactly where they should be.

"Cadillac Flight, this is Cadillac Lead," Donkey called over the radio, now saturated by the other flights of strike aircraft beginning their turn in the barrel. "Let's go flight manual, and spread it out for a drink break." Using flight manual, a radio frequency used exclusively by his flight, would clear the airways of a lot of unwanted chatter. "Cadillac Two," he continued, "you want to come in and take a quick look at me? I think I took something coming off target. Felt like it was in the aft part of the fuselage."

While the flight checked in on the new radio frequency, Jim hurriedly gulped from the hose connected to the cockpit water bottle and began to move in on his leader. A new voice came over the radio.

"Lead, this is Cadillac Three. Do you want me to look you over, Donkey?" It was Capt. Andrew Pritchard, the second element leader.

Apparently, he doesn't think I'm good enough to fly that kind of a formation, Jim thought.

"Negative, Three. You go ahead and take your drink break. Even a new guy ought to be able to tell if a hole in the fuselage is natural or not."

Broussard hurriedly reclipped his oxygen mask and punched the mic button on the throttle. "Lead, Two's moving in." Almost imperceptibly, he moved the control stick to the right and nudged the right rudder with his toe. The F-105 responded instantly to the command and began to slide gently toward the other aircraft. He reversed the control movements to stop the rightward movement, then stabilized just aft and below the lead ship. From his trail position Jim could look up slightly and see the inferno inside the tail pipe of the huge jet engine, its airflow making the controls buffet beneath his hands and feet as it rushed over the tail surfaces of his aircraft. Several small, jagged holes were readily visible on the belly of the lead aircraft. Manipulating the controls once again, he moved in a complete circle around the lead ship, then back into the left wing position.

"Cadillac Lead, this is Two. It looks like you've got ten to twelve small shrapnel holes on the bottom aft of your fuselage, about a meter in past the speed brakes. No other damage or leaks observed."

"OK, thanks Two. All my gauges are reading normal, so I guess the big bastard will get me home."

Broussard allowed his thoughts to drift as the flight cruised over the relatively peaceful highlands of western North Vietnam. Had he been lucky or cursed in his F-105 assignment? The "Thud," as it was known throughout the Air Force, was nothing at all like the nimble, speedy little T-38 jet trainers he'd flown for the last four years as a Training Command instructor pilot. It was like comparing an Arabian horse with a Percheron. Each had been built for a specific assignment. The Talon performed as if it looked forward to and relished whatever maneuver was requested. It was light and delicate on the controls and forgiving of mistakes by ham-fisted students just beginning to find their way about in the aeronautical wilderness.

The Thud, on the other hand, had been designed and built during an era when the only sort of aerial combat anticipated was a nuclear war. Gone, supposedly, were the days of rat races through the sky against an airborne opponent and dropping iron bombs in close proximity to friendly forces. The Thunderchief, as it was officially named, had been designed for tremendous straight-and-level speeds and huge carrying capacities where survival depended upon its ability to outdistance an interceptor while carrying one huge bomb. It could still perform all the fighter type of maneuvers, albeit more grudgingly, but its real strength came in straight-and-level flight. It remained the fastest operational aircraft in the world. And it did haul six tons of ordnance, a feat unmatched by any other attack aircraft. But the huge size of the monster fighter put it at a decided disadvantage when dodging SAMs and dueling with the smaller, more agile MiGs.

The Thud—rumor had it that the nickname derived from the sound the aircraft made as it crashed into the ground— had several other advantages over other operational aircraft in the U.S. inventory. First, the pilots who did live to complete their hundred required missions in the aircraft swore by its ruggedness. The Thud would bring them home after sustaining battle damage that would have put another aircraft into the weeds. The big kicker, of course, was the fact that the Air Force had about a zillion of the things in stock, left over from the plane's nuke role when it was the mainstay of TAC (Tactical Air Command). Not a bad reason for using it as the primary strike aircraft if you planned to fly into the world's most heavily defended area and make the natives angry by dropping bombs on them.

Broussard liked the idea of going home, and if this was the aircraft that could bring him through his hundred missions, then he was delighted to be sitting in its cockpit. On the other hand, if he had to fly a hundred missions like the one today simply because that was what this particular airplane did, then he would have been more delighted to be in the front office of a C-123 hauling trash around South Vietnam. This job was no stepping-stone to higher rank for him. He wanted nothing more out of the Air Force than himself—to be allowed to go home, take off his uniform, and get down to some serious discussions with a major airline. In his heart, he knew he was no live-on-the-edge fighter pilot, just a civilian who happened to be wearing a uniform and flying jets for the United States Air Force for the last few years.

He looked down through the left side of his canopy and matched the Black River to the line on the map spread askew in his lap. The map had started the mission as a neat, folded packet, but now it looked like the Sunday papers after the dog was through playing with them. He scrunched the map into manageable shape, and was mildly pleased with himself when he used it to correctly anticipate Donkey's southerly turn to avoid the heavy flak batteries in the Dien Bien Phu valley. Within minutes they would be across the border into Laos, where there would be little danger from ground fire as long as they remained at high altitude.

"Cadillac Flight, this is Lead. Fuel check."

Quickly, Broussard checked his tank readings and reported the total to the lead ship. He listened attentively as the two aircraft of the other element reported in sequence.

It was embarrassing to hear that he had considerably less fuel than the other members of the flight, telling the world, or at least anyone who might be listening, that he had been throttle-jockeying in an attempt to maintain his position in the formation. To an astute observer, that would mean he was either new or inept. Possibly both.

"OK, Two," Donkey transmitted, "you'll be the first on the tanker, followed by Four, Three, then Lead. Let's go refueling frequency."

The aircraft with the low fuel in the flight normally got first crack at the tanker in case fuel wouldn't transfer for some reason. This gave him a shot at getting to an alternate base before fuel exhaustion. It was inevitable that the low-fuel aircraft would be one of the wingmen, since they had to fly position on the element leader.

As Donkey lowered the nose of his aircraft during the descent to their refueling altitude of 15,000 feet, Jim matched the flight leader's attitude with his own ship. Just over the border into Thailand, the tanker would be flying an orbital pattern along "anchors," or refueling tracks. Donkey made it easy for Jim to maintain formation position by flying a smooth lead. Jim tried to relax by using only his fingertips to move the button-festooned control stick and throttle. He had little trouble with formation under normal circumstances, having been an instructor who had taught many students to fly in close proximity to another aircraft. He realized that his earlier problems in maintaining position during the strike had come about because he had a slower aircraft and had not correctly anticipated what his leader was doing in the combat situation. These factors would have little influence now that they had slowed to a cruising speed.

Good formation technique was really all that was needed to get fuel from the huge KC-135 tanker. But, flying a good formation over the plains of western Texas and doing it under the belly of an aluminum overcast in eastern Thailand were two different things. Here, he had to hold position or he'd be trying to walk back to home plate. None of the aircraft had sufficient fuel to reach an alternate base.

Another factor would also come into play now. The other pilots of the flight would have a close and unobstructed view of his flying techniques as they perched near the tanker, awaiting their turn at the nozzle. It was not a good situation if you happened to be the type who became nervous while performing for an audience or was intimidated by a public bathroom.

"Red Anchor Two One, this is Cadillac Lead," Donkey called the tanker orbiting at the preplanned RZ (rendezvous point). The response from the large aerial gas station was immediate.

"Cadillac Lead, this is Red Anchor Two One. You're loud and clear. We're in a left orbit at this time. Would you transmit for a fix?"

"Rog. This is Cadillac Lead with a short count. One, two, three, four, five, four, three, two, one. Cadillac Lead."

"OK, Cadillac. Steer one five degrees left. We also have a positive ID on your beacon. Go ahead with your lineup."

"Rog. First on the boom will be Cadillac Two, followed by Four; then Three; finally, Lead. We'd like a full top-off but don't require cycling off, if you can spare it."

"No problem, Lead. We've got plenty today."

The flight of four F-105s leveled at refueling altitude. Jim didn't bother searching for the tanker but concentrated on maintaining his position within the flight. Donkey dipped a wing sharply to the right, kicking them into an echelon formation, right. Jim reduced power slightly and blended in a combination of rudder and aileron to slip beneath the lead aircraft into the open slot the other element had made for him. Each ship now had the one ahead of him at a forty-five-degree angle to his left front.

"Red Anchor Two One, this is Cadillac Lead. I've got an eyeball on you at twelve o'clock. We'll do this radio silence."

"Roger, we're turning down track at this time. Understand you'll want radio silence during the refueling."

There wasn't any particular need to conduct the refueling operation using radio silence techniques, Broussard thought, except that Donkey Sheehan wanted to check out the flying abilities of his new wingman. After all, if the dinks had wanted to know how many Thuds had been bombing them that day, all they had to do was step outside and count them as they flew over.

The flight was quickly into the observation position, a point some hundred feet aft and about fifty feet low on the tanker. They stabilized and Jim began to edge his aircraft slowly toward the belly of the larger plane. He tried to forget that the other pilots were watching and evaluating, and concentrated only on moving forward smoothly. His eyes darted toward the fuel panel to ensure that the fuel switches were in the proper position to receive fuel. Just in time he noted that he hadn't opened the door to his refueling receptacle, and hurriedly corrected his mistake. Christ! What would Donkey have said if the boomer waved him away because he'd forgotten that!

Carefully, he inched the throttle forward, then quickly retarded it as the fighter began to slide forward, making every effort to keep his movements small and his attitude matched to that of the tanker. Lights were installed on the belly of the tanker to help the pilot of the receiver aircraft maintain the proper refueling position. The forward light was now blinking at him, attempting to help steer him into the refueling envelope. He ignored it, concentrating instead on simply flying a good, tight formation on the larger aircraft. His experience in the RTU (Replacement Training Unit) had shown him that the lights tended to confuse him more than they helped. Probably in a larger aircraft such as the B-52 they were more useful.

The boom operator, lying face down on his contoured couch in the bulbous pod beneath the tail of the tanker, peered at him through the plexiglass and unhinged the metal polelike refueling boom anchored beneath the tail. Using his set of pilot-type controls, he literally flew the boom toward the fighter's receptacle.

Jim moved into the final position beneath the tail of the tanker and tried to ignore the refueling boom as it flew directly at him. That, however, was like trying to ignore a punch coming straight at his face. The boom stabilized over the nose cone of the fighter, then quickly extended and seated itself into the receptacle with a jarring thump. There was something blatantly sexual about the process, like two huge birds copulating in flight.

Even with his oxygen regulator set on one hundred percent, he could still smell the raw fumes of the JP-4 jet fuel starting to transfer. Minutes passed and the controls of the aircraft began to grow heavy and sluggish beneath his gloved hand as he took on more and more of the life-giving kerosene derivative that made up the diet of his aircraft.

Small wonder the plane felt heavy, he thought, considering that jet fuel weighs almost seven pounds per gallon. The fuel often outweighed the ordnance tonnage of the Thud. He kept adding power to compensate for the extra weight, until finally the boom popped free of the receptacle and swung away from his line of sight, telling him he had his required load.

He reduced power, slowly moving back from the tanker until he regained his place in the formation. Cadillac Four, Bob Packard, moved forward as soon as he had elbowroom. More relaxed now that he had fuel enough to reach almost any base in Southeast Asia, Jim watched the other fighters move in and away as they replenished their tanks. As soon as they were all back into formation, Donkey broke the radio silence.

"Red Anchor Two One, this is Cadillac Lead. You folks do good work. We'll see you again another day. Adios."

"Adios, Cadillac Flight. We're glad to see that you all came out today. See you later."

Forty minutes later the long concrete runway of Takhli Royal Thailand Air Force Base, home of the 318th Tactical Fighter Wing and Cadillac Flight, was visible in the verdant countryside. Again, Donkey kicked the flight into an echelon right formation for the pitchout and 360-degree overhead pattern favored by fighter pilots. The aircraft snuggled closely to one another on the initial approach as they flew straight down the runway at traffic pattern altitude, knowing that every pilot on the base would automatically look up when they heard aircraft.

Major Delbert "Donkey" Sheehan

Donkey grunted against the knot of pain in his back aggravated by clambering down the ladder from the cockpit. On the tarmac he hobbled in a small semicircle, trying to restore some sensitivity to his numbed legs and feet. He felt all of his forty-two years. His feet were swollen inside the combat boots, an affliction noticeable only during the last year and in particular after long flights. Twenty-eight more of these fuckers and I won't have to worry about it anymore, he thought grimly, mentally chalking up another mark on his internal mission board.

Donkey glanced across the taxiway to where Jim Broussard was gathering his gear. The newest member of Cadillac Flight looked drained and wan, his feet dragging as he and his crew chief stepped around the large fighter. Kid, Donkey thought, you don't know what tired really is. He stamped his feet in an attempt to get the circulation moving again.

Still hobbling, he wandered to the rear of the revetment. Christ! Pain had won over numbness, and his feet felt as though they had been frostbitten—unlikely, however, with the temperature nudging the hundred-degree mark and the humidity in the same percentile. With all this moisture in the air, the monsoons couldn't be too far off. He walked to the revetment wall, unzipped his flight suit, and stood urinating against the wall, grinning at the young crew chief

scowling at him. He knew that the young sergeant was
annoyed because he wouldn't use the flight line latrine
only fifty yards away. What the sergeant didn't understand
was that Donkey continued the ritual only because it did
annoy him. A small strike for middle-aged men everywhere
against the youth of the world.

He zipped up and stamped his feet again. The circulation
seemed to be returning, and the knot of pain in his back
had eased a bit. He began a slow stroll around the aircraft,
joined by the sour-looking crew chief, who shook his head
as he stared at the great wet splotch on the revetment wall.
Donkey smiled benignly and bent to critically inspect the
battle damage below the engine tail pipe. He wiped the
sweat from his squarish forehead, which was losing its
fight to a receding hairline, and peered closely at the small,
jagged holes in the fuselage. The sergeant's dour expression
deepened as he saw the new holes in his aircraft. Like crew
chiefs everywhere, he considered pilots as only a necessary
evil; he would have been delighted to have the authority to
restrict their flying to the immediate local area and then
only under his control.

After several moments of intense study, Donkey straightened and, with both hands on his back, groaned, then patted
the huge fighter's fuselage as if it were a horse that had done
particularly well by its rider. And it had. Seventy-two good
rides it, or another just like it, had given him during his tour
of duty at Takhli. The plane had taken him over some of
the most heavily defended real estate in the world and had
always brought him home. Big baby, just twenty-eight more
and they can put you out to pasture as far as I'm concerned,
because I'll be home free! King's X! Tax exempt! Do not
remove under penalty of law! By the time I'm eligible for
another tour over here, he mused, I'll have my twenty in
and it'll be retirement on half pay and maybe some cushy
corporate flying job for beer money.

Donkey gave another grin and a wink to the scowling
crew chief and walked to the front of the aircraft to pick up
his helmet and map bag, then across the taxiway to where
Jim Broussard stood unzipping his g suit. Good-looking kid,
Donkey thought, but then who the hell wasn't at twenty-five
with feet that didn't feel like two pools of pus after a long
flight. The kid flew a pretty good wing for a new guy,

except for the time he fell behind over the target. He should have let me know he couldn't keep up. Sometimes there's just not a damned thing you can do about it. Some aircraft are simply slower than others and no one can figure out why. Maybe just slightly out of rig, or something as simple as an accumulation of grime and dust that had seeped into the bowels of the fuselage over the years and added a little extra weight. Perhaps just a general flabbiness of the engine or airframe close to the end of its useful life.

It probably hadn't been apparent to his new wingman, but Donkey had given him several opportunities to regain his position. He'd just have to learn to anticipate his flight leader's movements when he found himself in a slower bird, then cut the necessary corners, or he'd be sucking hind tit for the entire flight. He'd learn, though; of that, Donkey was positive. Having flown nearly every operational fighter that the Air Force had deployed over the past twenty years, and having been around a great many fighter pilots, he knew that with a little fine tuning Jim Broussard would be good. Maybe very good. Such praise Donkey did not give lightly, for flying fighters had been his profession for nearly twenty years and all of his adult life. He was no longer easily impressed.

For sure, the kid was better than most of the new arrivals that the wing had been getting in replacement levies. Some of them had only the seventy hours of fighter time they'd received in transition school. Many, such as Broussard, had never been in a fighter until they were assigned to the F-105 transition course, but at least they had been flying high-performance aircraft of different types. Others came from the Air Training Command or the Air Defense Command. There were few problems with the replacement pilots who in their previous jobs had been required to think in the three-dimensional world of the fighter pilot. They normally became adequate at their assigned job—to deliver bombs against targets in North Vietnam—but even they could hardly be considered seasoned fighter pilots.

Unfortunately, more and more of the replacements were coming to the air war with a background of multiengine flying and the few hours received in the F-105 school. Some became good, but others were unable to hack the program and had to be shuttled off into ground jobs in the already-bloated headquarters staffs. Donkey had nothing personal against multiengine, heavy-iron drivers, provided he needn't have anything to do with them and they knew their place at the club.

"Jimbo," he boomed over the roar of the jet engines farther down the flight line. "What do ya' think of the carefree life of flying fighters like a real pilot instead of waiting around for some asshole student to kill you?"

Broussard gave him a small smile and a weary shake of his head. His face was pale, and a steady stream of sweat dribbled in rivulets from his short brown hair. He was tall for a fighter pilot, at least two inches over six feet, and lean.

"As my new wingman and the newest member of Cadillac Flight, you may have the privilege of buying me my first beer after debriefing," Donkey continued, "and, remember, don't sweat this small shit. Today is as bad as it gets. It's all downhill from now on."

Yeah, downhill, Donkey thought, barely able to get the lie out of his mouth. In fact, this mission had been a goddamned cakewalk compared to some of them in Pack Six. Today, the poor dumb-assed kid hadn't even seen most of the bad stuff that had been flung at the pilots, because he'd been too busy trying to hold position. Maybe it was a good thing that the new guys weren't able to take it all in the first time. Shit, they just might never go back again. Just wait until Jim had been around long enough to actually see all the SAMs, the radar-controlled flak, the MiGs, and every damned farmer in North Vietnam blasting away with his rifle as soon as he hears an aircraft. Yeah, it gets worse. It could get a lot worse. But he'd have to find that out for himself, if he lived long enough. No reason to worry him now; there'd be plenty of time for that.

Donkey noticed the ground crew huddled on the far side of Broussard's aircraft. He left the young pilot and walked to the group to inspect the battle damage. His opinion of his new wingman went up another notch. He hadn't mentioned a goddamned word about the shrapnel.

"Looks like our newbie got his cherry popped," a voice said over his shoulder. He glanced up into the chiseled, handsome face of Capt. Andrew Pritchard, leader of the second element of the flight. They were joined by Lt. Bob

Packard, Pritchard's wingman, who flew in the number four
slot. The deep marks from the oxygen masks provided a
channel for the sweat dribbling from their matted hair.
Their flight suits—light green one-piece cotton coveralls—
were almost blackened with sweat beneath their parachutes,
survival vests, and g suits.

"Yeah," Donkey replied, looking at Pritchard, "I just
found out about it from the crew chief." He was satisfied
that the significance of the words was not lost on the other
pilots. Pritchard and Broussard had been bristling at each
other like a pair of strange dogs since their first meeting a
week earlier. Actually, Donkey felt that Pritchard had been
the more hostile of the two, and he didn't like squabbling
in his flight.

He watched Andy Pritchard lean in to look more closely
at the shrapnel holes. He is one good-looking dude, Donkey
thought. Probably has to beat 'em off with a stick back in
the States. Even with his hair all mussed up and sweat
pouring off his face, he still looks like a recruiting poster.
Or like an NFL quarterback coming off the field after
throwing a seventy-yard touchdown pass. Calm, confident,
and just the least bit mussed, so that you know he's been
involved in a strenuous game. The rest of us look like
offensive linemen who've just allowed the third sack of
the day. Still, with Andy, you get exactly what you see.
He is calm and confident, and a hell of a good pilot. God
knows why he's up Broussard's nose, for it certainly isn't
like him to snipe at anyone. What the hell, Donkey thought,
as long as it doesn't affect their jobs. I'm not their damned
keeper.

"Well, there's the crew truck," he said. "Let's get
debriefing over with so we can get outside a few cold
ones. I don't know about you folks, but my beer low-level
light just came on."

"Our leader," Pritchard said to Bob Packard, "has never
met a beer he didn't like."

"True," Donkey responded, "but I've never met all of
them, although I'm doing my best to change that."

Still wearing their flight gear, they clambered onto the
back of the truck for the ride to PE (personal equipment)
and the ops building. The younger pilots stuck their faces
in the breeze trying to beat the late afternoon heat, but

Donkey was too tired to make the effort. He watched as
Pritchard and Packard quipped and smirked at each other,
finding camaraderie in their survival of another flight over
North Vietnam. Even Broussard was drawn into the edges
of the banter.

God! He had fifteen years on the oldest of them and
he felt every one of those years. Donkey knuckled his
eyes, burning from three hours of staring into the sun
and at distant horizons for hostile flak and aircraft. Lately,
he'd secretly begun wearing cheap magnification glasses
that he'd picked up in Bangkok for reading in his room.
Fortunately, his annual flight physical examination was
waived for the time the pilots were in the combat zone. He
wasn't sure he could stand the "old man" jokes that would
begin as soon as he appeared publicly in prescription lenses.
Maybe he could get a pair from the hospital while he was on
leave and before reporting to his new duty assignment back
in the States. That way, perhaps no one would comment
on them.

Donkey leaned forward and shoved his palms beneath
his parachute, massaging his back. Christ, he thought, it's
getting to the point where I can hardly get out of the
cockpit after a long flight. Look at those young assholes
laughing and giggling like a bunch of schoolgirls. They've
already shaken off the stiffness and bounced back. Hell! At
forty-two most people are just getting good at their jobs
and I'm already used up and ready to be thrown down the
crapper.

At the PE hootch the pilots bounded from the back of the
truck; Donkey followed at a more sedate pace, looking like
a geriatric turtle. Helmets, map cases, parachutes, g suits,
and survival vests went onto their personal racks; pistols
and blood chits were turned in to the PE sergeant. Donkey
looked disgustedly at Bob Packard, who, while keeping his
legs straight, bent over to touch the palms of his hands to the
floor to stretch his tightened muscles. Thirstily, they took
turns at the drinking fountain. The air-conditioned building
felt frigid after the hot sun outside.

"Let's get the rest of this crap over with," Donkey said,
and led the way to the ops building for debriefing. Water
stained the walls of the building where window air con-
ditioners vainly attempted to squeeze the moisture from

the humid air. Pilots from other flights on the raid were arriving, ambling from the PE section, cigarettes hanging from their mouths. Conversations and gestures were still muted by exhaustion and, in some cases, sheer disbelief that they had survived yet another run Downtown. Inside, the talk became increasingly raucous as relief from the afternoon's tensions grew more evident. The young men were, for the most part, naturally healthy and optimistic, or they wouldn't be doing what they were, and nothing less than death or a physical maiming could long suppress their natural animation.

An intelligence lieutenant waved Cadillac Flight toward his table as he finished with another flight. The men slumped into chairs as the lieutenant produced his list of canned questions, from which he would skillfully draw as accurate a picture of the raid as possible. After the strike crews had debriefed, he and the other intelligence people would compile the individual debriefs into a composite, to be forwarded to Seventh Air Force in Saigon and PACAF (Pacific Air Forces) in Hawaii. By then, the frag orders for the following day's strikes would be coming in, and they would begin laying the groundwork for the next day's flights. They slept when they could.

Donkey answered most of the questions. The other pilots, Broussard excepted, chimed in when they had something to add that would amplify Donkey's statement.

"Going in, we were hit with Spoonrest search radar at least five minutes earlier than we were on the last mission up that way. It may have been boosted, or additional sites may have been located farther west. Fansongs started tracking us about here," he said, pointing to a spot on the map on the table. "I never saw any launches from this area, though." Fansong was the NATO code name for the guidance radar of the SA-2 Guideline surface-to-air missile. Donkey looked at the other pilots, noting that only Broussard didn't nod in confirmation.

"From the color of the flak bursts," he continued, "it looks like the gooners have moved some 100mm guns closer to Thud Ridge. They were tracking us pretty good after we left it, and they bracketed us damned quick. And about the same time, Crown was yelling about a MiG launch from Phuc Yen, and between him and that dipshit MiGCAP they

managed to keep the strike frequency blocked for about five
minutes while they discussed recipes and whatever. I never
saw any MiGs, but there were two SAMs launched from
about here," he pointed to another place on the map. "They
probably came outta this new site they've put in since our
last trip, but in any event they were tracking some other
flight, so I didn't pay a lot of attention to them after I
made sure it wasn't us they were after. Coming out, I saw
a single launch about here, just before we got to the ridge,
but it was tracking away as well." He looked expectantly
at the other pilots. "Any of you see anything else?"

Lieutenant Bob Packard, who flew the number four position on Pritchard's wing, pointed to an area on the map
just north of Thud Ridge. "There were two SAMs airborne
about here. Looked like they may have launched from that
site there, just south of Yen Bai, where the Weasels were
working."

The Wild Weasels were the F-105 flights dedicated to
SAM suppression. The flight of four was normally led by
an F-105F two-seater version of the standard warplane. The
crew member in the aft cockpit was not a pilot but an
ECM (electronic countermeasures) officer, affectionately
nicknamed "The Bear." His job was to locate a missile
with his black boxes, and jam its signal until it could be
destroyed by one of the standard single-seated F-105Ds in
the flight, or until the strike force was by it and it was no
longer a threat. Since the surface-to-air missile had a much
greater effective range than did the weapons used by the
attacking Weasel, the ground missileers had the advantage.
Only the aggressiveness of the Weasel Flight evened the
odds. Even so, dueling head to head with SAMs was not
a job for the nervous or fainthearted.

"Yeah, I saw those," Pritchard broke in, "only it looked
like there were three of them in the air. Almost as if they'd
salvoed them."

"How about you, Captain? Anything to add?" the intelligence officer asked, looking at Broussard.

Donkey watched Broussard shake his head slowly, eyes
on the floor. He didn't see crap, Donkey thought. Second
mission, and the first one to Hanoi. Naw. He'd be lucky to
tell the intelligence puke which country he'd been flying
over. Damnit! How'd we get so shorthanded that we can't

give the new people a little seasoning where it's not so hot before we throw 'em right into Pack Six? Christ! We used to be able to give every new guy at least ten sorties into Laos or Pack One before they had to go up there. When I first got here, he thought, we had at least six or seven guys in every flight, just the way you're supposed to. Now, for God's sake, if half the wing weenies don't fly, we can't even put up all our aircraft. Where the hell did all the pilots go?

"That's it then, gentlemen. Thanks very much for your time, and I'm glad to see that all of you came home today." As they rose, the debriefer was already waving forward the pilots of another flight.

"Let's get some beer," said Donkey, leading the men in a fast trot toward the officers' club. His feet and backache were forgotten as he thought of frosty cans of lager being pulled from a chest and popped open with ice still clinging to the tops of the cans.

The bar was filling rapidly with predinner drinkers, some in loud, boisterous groups standing together or sitting in chairs pulled around the tables. Others talked and drank in pairs or triples along the bar. Their conversations and tones tended to be more sedate. Interspersed among them were the solitary drinkers who grimly emptied their glasses and stared at nothing. Donkey had no use for these introspective killjoys who died a hundred times in inventive ways before each mission.

Isolated more by circumstances than physical distance was another group of flight-suited figures. These men sat idly flipping through old magazines, sipping soft drinks or coffee, remote from the conversations and songs of the others—part of the clan but not participating members at this time. They had yet to earn their bread for the day. They were the night fliers, and soon would be leaving to fly interdiction missions along the Ho Chi Minh trail in Laos and North Vietnam. Their beer would come at about sunrise, when they too could unwind from the rigors of combat flying.

Donkey led his flight toward a group of a dozen pilots lounging around a large table. Its surface supported a small mountain of beer cans. Smoke from cigars and cigarettes had turned the air blue, circling outboard and up in the feeble currents of the old overhead fan. Breathing was difficult. Most of the pilots had the zippers of their flight suits drawn down to their navels in an attempt to cool themselves in the late afternoon heat. They all seemed to be talking at once, their language incomprehensible to an outsider. Their hands flew as maneuvers and attack procedures were explained to an audience that would rather have talked than listened.

Donkey plowed through the crowd toward the table, the remainder of his flight in tow. Shouts and insults greeted him as he approached the table. Many of the fliers had known each other for years at one TAC base or another. And many were on their second combat tour in Southeast Asia, for these were the professionals—the backbone of the Tactical Air Command. Most were in their early to mid thirties and had flown every tactical fighter aircraft that had been operational in the U.S. inventory. Except for their age, they were indistinguishable from the other pilots at the table, more recent acquisitions in the fighter pilot trade. They all wore the familiar green cotton flying suit—"the bag." Most of them still showed the sweat stains from parachutes and survival vests. Donkey had served with more than half of them before.

He traded good-natured insults with some of the group before turning questioning eyes to the members of his own flight clustered about him. They nodded and he held up four fingers as he shouted over the noise to the small, harassed Thai waitress. She smiled and nodded and headed to the bar for their beer. Donkey turned to Broussard.

"Well, Jimbo, how do you fancy life in the fast lane now? Not much like instructing over West Texas, is it?" The decibel level was becoming painful as more pilots entered the club and filled the vacant spaces.

"I'll be honest, Donkey," Broussard answered with a tired smile, "I don't really know if I'm cut out for this. I didn't see a single one of those missiles you guys were talking about, and for that matter I didn't even see the damned target. How can you miss anything that big? I ended up just pickling off my load when I saw you drop. I didn't hear the missile or gun-tracking radars. I didn't even hear that call from Crown that there were MiGs airborne. I was out of position the whole time. Everything just ran together on me, and if I hadn't been following you I probably wouldn't have been able to find the tanker either." He lowered his voice when he saw Pritchard casually listening, pretending not to. "All in all, I'd have to say that today was pretty much a washout for me, and I sure as hell wouldn't want to fly with anybody as dumb as me."

The beer arrived and was distributed. Bobby Packard and Andy Pritchard were engaged in conversation by a large major sitting at the table.

Broussard went on: "And I've never been so scared in my life. I mean I was puckering from the time we left the tankers, inbound." His shoulders sagged. "I just don't know if I can do this or not."

Donkey looked at him speculatively before he spoke. "Well, you don't have to, you know," he said in a neutral voice. "About all you've got to do is go to the squadron commander and tell him you can't cut it, and they'll find something else for you to do. It ain't as if you'll be the first one."

Broussard's eyes were suddenly staring into his with an intensity that startled Donkey. The transition from a mild-mannered, dejected young man to someone about to poke his lights out had been jarring. Broussard didn't blink. "I can hack it."

Donkey saw a knot in his jaw that hadn't been there before. He realized that the younger pilot was only a breath away from releasing some of his frustrations of the day. He grinned and held his hand up.

"Don't sweat it, kid. You did fine for a first trip Downtown. That dollar ride we gave you yesterday into Route Package One doesn't really mean shit when you look at Hanoi for the first time. I mean, part of the country really isn't all that different from South Vietnam. And down there, unless you do something pretty stupid or you're unlucky, a fighter pilot won't get hurt all that bad. Let's face it. Hell, they have helicopters and C-123s flying all over the place down there. Can you imagine how long they'd last where you've been today? Naw, going into Pack Six is a real ball breaker if you're new and don't know half of what's going on. Come to think of it, it ain't all that damned great if you do know what's going on."

The young pilot, Donkey noticed with relief, had dropped his pugnacious stare and relaxed as he listened to his flight leader.

"Christ," he continued, signaling the waitress for more beer, "talk about not knowing what's going on! We got jumped by MiGs my first mission in Korea up over the Yalu, and I almost got my ass shot out of the sky because I got buck fever and punched the wrong button when my flight leader told us to dump our drop tanks. Had me a MiG at my six o'clock for damned near half an hour, or at least what felt like it, with me twisting and turning and yelling for somebody to come shoot him off. But my element leader was laughing so hard at what I'd done and what I was yelling that he couldn't keep the pipper centered on the MiG. Everybody thought it was damned funny except me."

Donkey saw that Broussard was now grinning at him.

"Naw, you did OK," he continued. "It's just that you've got to learn to anticipate what I'm going to do before I even think about doing it. Sounds right difficult, doesn't it? Well, it damned well is! Flying a good wing is the hardest job in the world. But, it's just like with those students you used to instruct. You learned to anticipate their mistakes before they even knew they were going to make them. Same thing here. And it won't happen in a day, but I'll guarantee you, Jimbo, if you want it, it will come. And I suspect that in your case it won't be too long.

"Things'll slow down after you get a few missions under your belt. Besides, today was pretty unusual. Normally, a new pilot gets ten sorties or so into the easier areas, and we let him get a little seasoning before taking him Downtown. Right now, though, we're pretty skoshi on pilots, and all we've got assigned to the flight are just us four little injuns. At least at this rate you'll get your tour over with pretty quickly; that is, unless Seventh Air Force decides to make it a straight year's tour rather than a hundred counters over North Vietnam."

Jim looked up with alarm. Donkey could read his thoughts. A hundred missions seemed almost too formidable to think about. A year doing this was inconceivable. "Do you think they'll do that?"

"Who knows what those assholes around the flagpole will do. That particular rumor makes the rounds about every month, and so far nothing's come of it."

Broussard pondered this information solemnly, then asked Donkey, "Do you think we'll go out again tomorrow?"

"Does a bear crap in the woods?" He grinned. "Yeah, we'll probably go, and since there's only the four of us in Cadillac Flight right now, it figures that you'll go as well. You can find out if you want to stay up late enough for the staff to break out the frag order from Seventh Air Force. Personally, I'd just kick back and enjoy myself and not sweat it. If we're on, they'll let us know in plenty of time. There's no sense worrying about it, since there ain't a damned thing any of us can do about it anyway. My advice is to relax and enjoy the war. Hell, if they kill you, you won't know about it anyway . . . More beer?"

Lieutenant Aspirant
Nguyen Thi Minh

As the pilots of Cadillac Flight drank their beer, to the northeast almost six hundred miles as the crow flies, Lieutenant Aspirant Nguyen Thi Minh embraced the floor with his belly, legs, and elbows, his hands clasped over his head in a futile gesture to ward off danger. Another ripple of explosions, which seemed closer than the last, jarred him free from the floor of the camouflaged radar van. He landed with a thump as the pull of gravity overcame the lift provided by the bomb explosions. He tried to move under one of the vacated radar consoles, propelling himself only by his fingertips and toes and still keeping his belly button in contact with the reed rug.

He gained the sanctuary and curled into a tight ball as the radar van was tilted sharply by another explosion. The van settled back onto all four wheels with a jar that hurt his clenched teeth. He could smell smoke, and added a fiery death trapped in the trailer to his list of major concerns. He waited tensely for flames to appear at the door or windows, but they did not. So he focused his concerns where they rightfully belonged—on the bombs falling around him.

"What *are* we doing here?" Minh heard his best friend, Lieutenant Aspirant Trach, mumble from beneath an adjoining desk. Trach had reacted with admirable speed when the first bombs began to fall and had beaten Minh to the more desirable desk—twice as long as the other one. It had a deeper kneehole and a buffer of electronic equipment surrounding it as well. On the other hand, electrocution from the stacks of electronic boxes could not be ruled out. Perhaps Trach had acted too hastily.

Another salvo of bombs erupted and stunned the trailer's occupants almost into insensibility. Minh looked wide-eyed around the trailer, seeking a possible escape route. The windows were too small; the door appeared to be the only way out. Trach was still mumbling and couldn't be seen in the darkened recess beneath the technician's desk. The three permanent members of the trailer's duty crew were twined together like kittens beneath a shelter made of old mattresses piled onto a metal bed frame. They were not moving. Minh turned his attention to a flurry of dust motes visible in a column of sunlight coming from a new hole in the roof of the trailer. He could smell the dust now, shaken loose from where it had been entombed for years. It may even have been Siberian dust, for the radar van had been in service in the Soviet Union for a number of years before the PAVN (People's Army of Vietnam) received it. He sneezed as the particles drifted into his nose. The mundane act of forcefully expelling air from his lungs helped put things into proper perspective. Minh even began to see some humor in their situation as the bombs momentarily stopped.

Here were six newly arrived fighter pilots of the 17th Air Defense Regiment cowering beneath any protection they could find from the attacks by the American fighter-bombers. Will we die aloft in aerial combat, defending our homeland against the Yankee air pirates? No, more than likely we're going to die in this damned radar van before we ever get airborne. And all because of some stupid training requirement that insists that all new interceptor pilots returning from training abroad must undergo yet another dry and tedious lecture by Senior GCI (ground control intercept) Controller Capt. Nguyen Lin Bo before becoming fully qualified.

Minh found Captain Bo an officious ass and thought the whole situation would have been extremely humorous if it had not been so frightening. In the middle of the captain's lecture on ground radar guidance techniques, an American missile-fighting warplane had launched an antiradiation missile, which homed in on the captain's tracking radar and blew the antenna almost all the way to the Gulf of Tonkin. The other aircraft in the flight were carrying bombs and began attacking the site's general area. Minh doubted that the attackers could see much of the actual radar gear or vans and living quarters, for they were hidden extremely well.

No bombs had fallen for several minutes, and Minh cautiously stuck his head from beneath the console. He found himself nose to nose with Trach, who looked like a turtle with its head sticking out of its shell. The comparison was heightened by Trach's long, skinny neck. His wide eyes met Minh's and focused on him.

"My friend," Trach stage-whispered, "just between you and me, I think this is the shits. I really would like to live long enough to get into aerial combat and not die under this evil apparatus." He gestured toward the humming and complaining electronic racks. Several were sizzling, and with a great popping noise, one blanked out and went dead.

In spite of his fear, Minh forced a smile, then cocked an ear to determine if the air attack was going to be renewed. He could hear shouts and commands coming from outside the van. Someone was moaning close to the door. There was definitely a fire burning somewhere, because he could hear its roar and smell the smoke. He inched out a little farther, as did Trach. The captain and his two controllers still lay together under their improvised shelter. One of them began moving cautiously, checking to see that all his parts were still intact.

Captain Nguyen Lin Bo finally rolled from beneath the bed, walked directly to the radar console, and studied it for a moment. He began to swear. Minh and Trach took that as a sign to crawl from beneath their shelters. Bo ignored them and continued cursing the malfunctioning equipment. A tiny column of smoke rose from the electronic rack.

"Let's see if we can help outside," Minh whispered to Trach, who nodded in agreement.

The door had to be forced open, accomplished with a smart shove of Trach's shoulder. The frame of the trailer-van had been twisted as the bombs rocked it.

Outside, though the antenna van burned lustily, most of the remaining equipment had been spared severe damage. It was the antenna van that had attracted the missile; the dummy site erected south of the real control site had drawn most of the bombs from the attacking F-105s. Minh and Trach started across the open space in front of the van to offer their assistance in fighting the fire. Three of the fledgling pilots from their group were already separating the burning parts in an effort to stop the smoke, which would only attract other American fighters.

Twenty meters from the burning antenna van, the working group erupted in a combination of body parts and dirt as some unseen force tore them apart. A ripping sound, like cloth being torn, came a moment later. The F-105 went over the carnage at 200 meters, smoke from his Gatling gun trailing behind him. His aim had been good, and few rounds missed impacting in the target area.

Minh found himself on his belly again, with Trach lying beside him. He had no memory of falling; he was just suddenly there, with his head buried beneath his arms once more. Hearing the afterburner of the attacking aircraft cut in with a loud roar, he peeped from beneath his protecting arms. The fighter was in a maximum rate climb. Minh's professional calculation was that he had to be light on fuel to get that sort of acceleration and climb performance. The aircraft disappeared as it climbed through a middle stratus layer. Minh turned to face what had been the group fighting the fire.

The bodies lay tumbled about, the three fledgling pilots from the fighter company joined with their ground brethren in the grotesque postures of violent death. Had there been anything worth salvaging in the radar antenna van before the last attack, there certainly was nothing now.

Minh was stunned at the destruction wreaked in a moment's gunfire by the American aircraft. Almost casually, it had snuffed out the life of ten to twelve people, the accumulated experience and emotions of two hundred years. The future of perhaps ten families had been altered indelibly by this one act of an American pilot who saw a target of opportunity. Of course, that was the very nature of war, Minh knew. He and Trach climbed slowly to their feet and started toward the place where the bodies lay in such absurd positions.

They stooped to help the radar site cadre gather the macabre remnants, placing them gently and quickly into

plastic bags. This was the major problem he'd always had
with war on the ground; you were always much too close
to its victims to feel comfortable. In the air, a pilot was
far removed from any destruction he might create. Minh
preferred it that way.

"If this doesn't keep those damned fools at headquarters
from making us take these asinine field trips, then nothing
will," Trach said as he bagged the arm of one of his flight
mates. "If I'm to die, I don't want it to be like this."

"It probably will be if you don't learn to fly a tighter wing
position," Minh said with a small smile, trying to ease the
tension.

Trach was ready for the mood to be lightened. "My
limited experience has shown that often the problem in
maintaining a good formation comes because the leader
is incapable of flying a smooth enough platform for his
wingman to formate properly."

It was a bantering talk they'd had many times since Minh
had been placed in position of flight leader of the two when
they stood cockpit alert. Of course, they'd never actually
taken off on a hot intercept; always they were reserves
while the experienced pilots scrambled to what seemed a
whimsical schedule by the air defense headquarters. The
pilots had long since grown weary of trying to determine
what constituted a raid in which they'd be launched and
one in which they'd watch the F-105s overfly Hanoi and
its suburbs.

The civilian bus that took them back to the airfield
was gaily painted in bright colors, which indeed was the
primary reason for the young pilots to be aboard it. Any
vehicle that looked even remotely military stood an excellent chance of being blasted from the road by the American
air force and navy attack planes. Even beneath this vehicle's bright red and green top, the pilots would be uneasy
until they reached the built-up environs of the city. Thus
far, the Americans had refrained from bombing the city
proper, although the inhabitants always took precautions.
They headed for the shelters when the raids commenced
early in the morning, returning to them at intervals during
the day as new formations of enemy aircraft attacked targets in the suburbs. Most casualties in the city came from

expended rounds of antiaircraft fire falling back to earth. The tinkle and crash of metal fragments could be heard striking the buildings and streets for minutes after the last bombers left.

The bus pulled through the guarded gate and deposited the pilots at their company headquarters. Minh and Trach filed inside with the others and listened to the senior pilot explain to their company commander the loss of three of his men. The commander shook his head and kicked his desk, turning his back to them as they stood at attention. He scrubbed his face with his hands. When he turned back toward his depleted group, his face was flushed and his eyes were red. Minh couldn't tell whether he was angry or sad. The commander's voice didn't reveal his emotions either. His voice was always soft and well modulated, even when he gave vent to his frustrations by kicking his desk or waste can.

"That's all for the day. Check tomorrow's alert schedule before you leave," was all the commander said before he walked away. As he left the room, he stopped in the doorway and smiled back at them. "And try to stay sober. Who knows? One of these days they may actually launch you!"

As usual, Minh found himself on cockpit alert with Trach listed as his wingman. There were six aircraft scheduled for launch before his flight. He brightened. That was only three flights if they launched them in pairs.

" 'Stay sober,' the man said!" Trach fussed as they walked to the small restaurant outside the gate where the management let the pilots buy liter bottles of beer at reduced prices. "I couldn't drink too much if I wanted to. How much money do you have?"

They counted their pooled resources in the falling dusk and saw that they had the choice of two liters of beer and a light dinner at the restaurant or four liter bottles and the horrible food of the mess hall. It took little discussion. They opted for the beer.

The tables in the dimly lit restaurant were packed with aviation personnel. The alert pilots for the day were easy to spot as they sat and quietly drank and smoked in a group. Each had a strained look and seemed to have difficulty focusing his thoughts. They talked little for the most part.

Several of their faces still showed the indentations of the oxygen mask, indicating that they had had at least one launch that day.

"How much longer before we get promoted?" Trach was grumbling. "There's no way a man can live on this aspirant pay. I thought that when we returned to Vietnam after training, the promotions would have been made. We've been back quite awhile now, so where are the damned promotions?"

"They're probably holding yours up until you learn to fly properly," Minh said with a straight face.

"Hah!" said Trach. "If that were the case, half the flight leaders would still be aspirants. Seriously, I need more money. I don't make enough to even go out with a girl unless she pays for the beer and food. That's embarrassing. I haven't been to the cinema since we were in Russia, and I'll tell you, my short-assed friend, no girl is going to be enticed into letting you into her bed if all you can offer her is a walk through Patriots' Park and a tour of the relics from Dien Bien Phu. It's been so long since I've been with a woman that even those huge, hairy Russian women are turning up in my dreams. I'm a desperate man!"

"Surely not *that* desperate," said Minh, remembering the doughy women of the north with a shudder.

"I am! I mean it! You know, I think we really were screwed properly when we went to Russia for training. Those who went to the Arab countries came home with enough black-market materials to last them through this war, if they're careful. And the stuff was given to them! Didn't have to put out a dong of their own money, I've heard. Watches, pens, cigarette lighters. Everything! One pilot I know who trained in Iraq was even given his own personal leather flying jacket. What did we get in Russia? Nothing but borscht and insults."

"That's because they don't have those things themselves," explained Minh. It was not the first time they'd had this discussion.

"So what? They could have broken loose with a few things. Like maybe some of those great fur coats and stoles. With just one sable coat I could be comfortable with what I made from it until my flying days are over. But, did you see anyone offer? Of course not! Russians!"

"You have to admit," Minh said, "that you probably got better training there than if you'd been sent to Iraq."

Trach snorted. "Yes, if you don't consider that half our training hours were spent in strafing tank mock-ups. We'll be in great shape if we ever decide to invade Germany."

Minh laughed. He could seldom stay serious around Trach for very long. "Well, nobody knows for sure. Maybe you'll have your chance against the Yankees and their tanks if they ever decide to come north."

"Puh! If they were going to invade us, they'd have done it long before this. The government in Saigon is happy with things just the way they are. Their generals take turns leading the government just long enough to put a fortune in gold into the Swiss banks, then someone else takes over so that he can get his share. If the Americans come, it will be alone."

"Given your knowledge of geopolitics, I'm sure you're correct in your assumptions," Minh teased. "Seriously, why do you think they haven't hit the airfields or dikes? And they've wasted hundreds of sorties trying to blow bridges but ignored the stacked cargoes sitting in the open just inside the city. What do you suppose their thinking is?"

"I really don't know," Trach said, his open countenance baffled. "It doesn't make sense, but few things they do seem to. One thing I do know, however. I've talked to enough of the older pilots in the regiment to know that we'd better have everything together if we go against them head to head. This stuff they put into the newspaper about one Vietnamese pilot being able to handle two or three Americans because of superior training and aircraft is crap. Major Hoa told me they're damned good. Much better than the Russians were and much more aggressive. I think I'll take his word for it."

Minh only smiled. He had his own private thoughts on the subject. He stretched and looked into the dark velvet night. The warm, moist breezes from the Gulf of Tonkin felt wonderful as they licked his face. It was good to be back in Hanoi after the intense Russian winter that he and the other pilot trainees had endured at the training base just east of the Urals. Even the Russian summer had felt cool to the Vietnamese. He shuddered convulsively as he thought of the snow being whipped into a frenzy by the large cyclonic systems pushing south from the Arctic.

It had been an odd but productive eighteen months for the Vietnamese students. The twenty-five of them who had graduated from the pilot course were the remnants of nearly sixty handpicked volunteers his country had sent to the Soviet Union for training. This training was unavailable at home for the primary reason that the Yankees were no respecters of training sorties and happily shot from the sky every Vietnamese aircraft they could find. Understandably, this made the instructors somewhat nervous, and they tended to pay more attention to their six o'clock than to evaluating their students' mistakes. The Soviets, who supplied the aircraft to the Vietnamese in any event, had extended the invitation for a limited number of students to attend their training academies. Other socialist countries had done the same.

Another good reason to train abroad had been the chronic lack of fuel. Since the American aircraft had begun their attacks on the POL yards, there had scarcely been enough petrol available to supply truck convoys heading down the long trail to South Vietnam or for the active air defense fighter aircraft. Their refinery capacity had, for the most part, been destroyed, and fuel had to be imported in ready-to-use form.

The eighteen months provided many disillusions for Minh and the other trainees. Their disqualification rate had been very high for such a handpicked group, almost as if the Soviet instructors were deliberately trying to prove the inferiority of the visitors. And there was scarcely concealed contempt from most of the Russians. The senior Vietnamese captain had reminded his men to remain silent in the face of the insults, reiterating the obvious fact that their country desperately needed the training as well as the Soviet aircraft. They held their tongues and learned the needed skills, and most had learned them well.

But, for God's sake, Minh thought, why couldn't we have been allied with someone like the French rather than those joyless Russians? Minh felt a certain kinship with the French, because his father had been a minor bureaucrat working for the colonial forces until their departure. Of course, he'd also been a minor bureaucrat in the Viet Minh sub-structure, and surprisingly enough, a Catholic.

After the armistice with the French, his father had elected not to relocate to the south, as the majority of Catholics had done. Ho Chi Minh, who could be ruthless as well as benevolent, had kept the family in suspense for more than a month while he pondered their fate. In the end, the services that Minh's father had provided to Uncle Ho during the war had swayed him to let the family remain unharmed in the north and to retain their religion as long as they made no show of overt practice. The family had become the token Catholics for the regime.

Minh had left the church immediately after his father's death. He had always considered himself a socialist, and with the French departed he became an ardent nationalist as well. It was common sense that the two artificially created Vietnams were, in reality, meant to be one country. Of course, the corrupt government in the south resisted the unification; the bureaucrats had everything to lose, although the people had everything to gain. Minh was truly confused when he tried to reason why the Americans were backing the puppets in Saigon. It was unseemly conduct from a nation whose own origins were revolutionary. Indeed, the Vietnamese constitution was almost a direct copy of the one written by the Americans many years ago. Very confusing.

Trach gave a mighty belch and scowled at the near emptied beer bottle. "When do you think we'll get replacements for those we lost today?"

Minh shrugged. "I don't think there's much of a hurry. They seem to want only the experienced pilots to launch during a raid. The problem is that the less they let us fly, the more we lose our edge. I know that some of the older pilots are launching three and four times a day."

"Well," said Trach, "I'm ready to fly if it will speed up my promotion. A man could starve to death as an Aspirant."

Captain James Evelyn Broussard

The coterie of pilots were attracted to Donkey like moths to
a flame. They gathered around him in animated discussion,
allowing Jim to make his way to the bar through wildly
flailing arms. Jim had not let Donkey see his full concern
with the possibility of flying missions over North Vietnam
for an entire year. The crescendo at the table inhibited
further private conversation, for which he was suddenly
glad. He found an empty slot and slipped into it, ordering
another beer from the Thai bartender. He paid and leaned
back against the bar, watching his flight leader's virtuoso
performance. It wasn't just a show, however. The man was
made for this all-male ritual at the end of a battle or hunt.
These were the men Donkey felt comfortable with, and it
was as much a part of his life as mowing the lawn was to
a suburban husband.

Jim watched tears of laughter squeeze from Donkey's
eyes as another major yelled something indecipherable. His
body vibrated with continuous movement as he twisted first
one way, then the other. It was a fighter pilot's body. Short,
stocky. More able to withstand the forces of gravity than a
taller man, whose blood had farther to travel to the brain.
His jaw was thrust forward, unconsciously pugnacious, and
sweat beaded on his wide forehead. His dark hair was
shoved straight back, revealing a severe widow's peak.
He'd probably be bald in a few years, but now it distracted

42

little from the Irish-looking face.

A year! The thought kept popping back into Jim's mind like an aching tooth he couldn't ignore. Christ. He'd figured on six months maximum. A year of missions like today's was unthinkable. Jim had never thought of himself as a coward. Just the opposite. But he admitted to himself that he'd never been as frightened in his life as he had been over Hanoi this afternoon.

"Nothing like a nice, quiet evening of relaxation at your friendly club," a voice said at his left shoulder.

Broussard turned and saw Andy Pritchard grinning sardonically at Donkey's ever-growing crowd. Jim hadn't seen him leave the group. Donkey was yelling the punch line of his latest joke: "And they say an optimist is a Thud driver who quits smoking because he's afraid it's hazardous to his health!" The group roared its approval. Jim swallowed hard at the mordant humor.

"Well," Pritchard said, "I figure the beer fights will be starting in five or ten minutes, and I'm cutting out of here for some chow before I get drafted into them."

"Want some company?" Jim asked without thinking, then winced, though he didn't allow it to reach his face.

Pritchard's dark blue eyes surveyed him as if he were a specimen and Andy was thoughtfully deciding where to stick the pin. "Suit yourself," he said as he pushed himself away from the bar and began to walk purposely toward the dining room, not looking back to see if he were being followed. Jim trailed him stiffly, feeling like a fool and angry with himself for asking to join the element leader. Who needed another put-down? He considered turning away from the dining room door, but they were joined by Bob Packard. Good, thought Broussard. That spares me half an hour alone with Mister Charm.

Bob looked as if he'd been waiting for someone to break away so he could join them. He, too, was short, with a medium build, and looked much too young to be flying warplanes in combat. Actually, Jim thought, he looked as if he'd be much more at home in the tenor section of a Methodist youth choir than in the cockpit of an F-105. They chose a table as far from the noise of the bar as possible.

"So tell me," Jim said to the young lieutenant after they were seated, "how did such a terrible person as yourself manage to get to a nice place like this?"

Bob Packard grinned at him as he lifted his eyes from the typed menu of the night's horrors. "Oh, it's an old story and one that you've heard a million times. Boy goes to college to avoid draft and finds that on graduation the war is still going on. Boy goes to Air Force Officer Candidate School, since it appears that an officer has a much smaller chance of being dinged than a draftee. Boy becomes a second lieutenant and finds that the war is *still* going on, much to his horror, so he volunteers for flight training, hoping that these durned fools will have it settled by the time he gets out. Well, they don't and boy finds himself in the Thud RTU. The war continues and finally boy can't think of another thing to volunteer for to keep his ass out of it. They ship his precious young body way the hell and gone out here in the wilds of Thailand, where they make him fly over all sorts of terrible people doing their damnedest to keep him from reaching his promised biblical span of seven score. I tell you, it's enough to make you lose patience entirely with the way this whole thing is being run. Personally, I feel, deep down inside, that it's some kind of Yankee plot to get as many of us Alabama studs out of the way as possible, knowing how we tend to monopolize women wherever we go."

"Bobby," Pritchard cut in, "I doubt seriously if any of you southern ridge runners would know what to do with a female even if you ever did catch one. Unless she happened to be blood kin, of course."

"Now, Andy," he complained dolefully, "you know that's a vicious lie. We almost never have intimate relations with anybody closer than a first cousin, unless it's just kind of a test flight." They grinned at each other, their affection obvious to Jim, who felt left out of their circle.

"How about you, Jim?" asked Bob Packard. "How did you get to be among Uncle Lyndon's finest?"

"About the same as you, I guess. I sure didn't plan on a shooting war when I went through pilot training. I figured I'd do the four years I owed the Air Force in the Training Command, build up some jet time, and apply to one of the airlines. It almost worked. I had only a little more than a year of active duty to go when they nailed me for 105s. They had me in the pipeline so quickly that I had time to complete the Thud repple-depple and still get over here for a full tour before my discharge date."

"How terrible for you," Pritchard said in a flat voice. "Imagine that. Expecting you to give up an airline job to fight their silly war for them, and after they've given you only about two million dollars' worth of training and experience. How tacky. I don't know if I'd put up with that kind of injustice or not. Maybe you ought to write to your pet congressman, for I'm sure you have one. Your type usually does."

"Hey!" Jim said through clenched teeth, his temper flaring, "I didn't say I blamed the Air Force. But, even if I had, it's nothing that half the people over here wouldn't say if they got the chance. How many people actually want to be here? Bob just said they had to drag him out to Southeast Asia kicking and squealing. It's not exactly like I headed for Canada or something. All I did was to obey orders, and when they said 'Go,' I went. I just didn't volunteer for it."

"Actually, Bob did volunteer for Thuds," Pritchard said quietly. "Forget all that crap he was just spewing."

Jim turned to look at the lieutenant and saw it was true. The boyish face had it written all over it. Jim silently cursed himself for letting Pritchard get to him again. He took a deep breath and turned to face the man.

"Look," he said, "I'm sorry if I'm not everybody's idea of what a fighter pilot should be. If you're expecting me to join that mob scene at the bar, well, I'm just not your man. I like a party as well as the next guy but not every night. I'll do my job, though."

"What the hell do you think that bunch at the bar has to do with being a fighter pilot? Bob and I aren't out there, are we? That's the way some of the guys work off their tensions, but don't think everybody does it that way. Flying fighters is as much an attitude as anything else. But every man out at that bar is convinced that he's the best damn pilot in the wing, if not the Air Force. If he didn't think that, he shouldn't be in the cockpit of an F-105. And if you don't believe it, I'll guarantee that you'll end up getting your ass waxed or somebody else hurt. We lose people, but that's luck. There's nothing anybody can do about that where we fly. But, the first time you whimper to one of those guys out there that you don't think you should be over here or that you're scared, he'll laugh in your face, and that's the same as laughing in the face of every pilot in Cadillac Flight. Let the old man hear about it and you'll be out of the cockpit so fast you won't know what happened. We've had a few other guys who slipped through, and when they got here they found they had an aversion to flying up north. As soon as the wing commander found out about it, they were on their way to Saigon or back to the States or anyplace he could get them off the base just as quick as he could. And for your information, Broussard, these birds are called fighters because they fight. You should have chosen another line of work if you don't like what they do."

"Listen," Jim flared, "if you like this shit so well, why don't *you* volunteer for another tour. I'm sure they'd be glad to have a real experienced fighter pilot hang around for another hundred missions."

There was a long moment of silence before Bob broke it in an embarrassed voice. "Ah, actually Andy is on his second tour. He flew a hundred with an RF-101 recce outfit out of Ubon before he volunteered for 105s. He managed to pick up two Hearts and a Silver Star."

"Forget it, Bobby," Pritchard snapped. "Nobody has to explain me to this fucking new guy who's got all the answers."

Broussard could feel himself start to choke on the foot in his mouth. He dropped his eyes from Pritchard's stare, desperately trying to think of something conciliatory to say. Something that would put everything right. Christ. How had he gotten himself into this position?

"Look," he stammered, "I'm sorry I spouted off. I shouldn't have—"

"Forget it," Pritchard said coldly as he moved his eyes to the mystery meat of the day the waitress set before him. He obviously was not prepared to kiss and make up.

Bob attempted small talk through the remainder of the meal, but the mood was strained, with Jim contributing little, Pritchard, nothing except comments such as "pass the salt." His eyes remained fixed on his plate.

As quickly as he could do so without allowing the other pilots to think he'd been driven from the table, Broussard excused himself and headed back to his spartan quarters.

Going out through the bar, he saw that Donkey's group had grown to something the size of a rock concert.

Those palm trees that had survived the new construction on the base drooped lethargically in the hot night air, their fronds still and silent in the windless calm. Sweat immediately formed on Jim's forehead, and his armpits felt sticky. He knew his body odor was ripe, with a new layer of perspiration adding to the older one.

The canals running through the base were fetid as they awaited the cleansing monsoonal rains, the water now so low that it barely moved. Jim tried to stay on the lighted walkway as much as possible, afraid of the cobras and kraits that he'd been told still inhabited the weeds. Being bitten by a goddamned snake on the way to my bunk would make my day complete, he thought.

He trudged up the steps to his hootch, finally feeling his exhaustion. The place seemed deserted and probably was; there was little to do in the primitive building. In his room he stripped off the soggy flight suit and threw it into a far corner to be collected by the hootch girl tomorrow. Socks and underwear followed. He sat naked in the straight chair, feet propped on the small wooden desk directly under the wheezing air conditioner. There was little cool air coming from its stained vents, but he was grateful for the slight drop in temperature it provided.

He thought about Pritchard's remarks. Who the hell was that guy to be jumping up his nose that way? Just because he was the new boy? Did his admission that he had not volunteered for combat duty give justification to the cutting remarks? Jim shook his head angrily. Well, too bad if it offended Pritchard's patriotic sensibilities. But he hadn't cut and run, and if he had little desire to drop bombs on a bunch of foreigners who meant little to him one way or the other, what the hell difference should it make to Pritchard? Still, though, realistically he had to live and fly with the guy. Well, he'd worry about it another time.

Jim showered and brushed his teeth in the lukewarm water of the community latrine and decided to shave in case he had to fly early the next morning. Clean and moving slowly so as not to work up a new sweat, he stretched out on his cot and turned off the weak light on the desk. He stacked two pillows behind his head and thought of Helen.

They had been together for almost a year when the orders for F-105 transition school arrived. Jim had been only a bit surprised; many of the other instructor pilots had already received orders for combat aircraft. He hadn't mentioned the possibility to Helen only because in a vague sort of way he felt that if he didn't talk about it, it wouldn't happen. But, it had, and Helen hadn't taken it at all well.

That final week she had presented a thoughtful, well-organized denunciation of the war, which he could only feebly defend. All he had known for sure was that the Air Force had said he was going to war and there was damned little he could do about it. Helen was emphatic and knowledgeable in her views; Jim felt as if he was one of the Three Stooges. After she had left, as he had known inevitably that she would, he had seriously thought for the first time about the business of killing. He realized that his knowledge of the affair going on in Southeast Asia was less than complete. He was reasonably sure that Vietnam was in the Eastern Hemisphere and would have even bet money that it was located somewhere on the continent of Asia and was not an island. Ho Chi Minh had something to do with the conflict or was against it or something of the sort.

The one thing he knew about it clearly was that he did not want to participate in the lunacy. That made as little difference in the long run as his lack of knowledge on the subject, for he was caught up in the computer dragnet that TAC employed to keep their fighting machines filled. He tried to feel sorry for himself over the fact that Helen was gone forever but could not. Being completely honest with himself, he had known all along that love was not the bond in their relationship. It had been more of a friendly mutual lusting.

Jim sat up and turned on the light, his sweat glands immediately beginning to ooze with the exertion as the air conditioner continued its losing battle with the moisture-laden outside air. Suddenly, he was no longer sleepy. He thought briefly of taking another shower but knew that would only open his pores. He needed to buy an electric fan, as most of the other pilots in the hootch had done. He'd do that the next time he was at the base exchange. He knew he wasn't being honest with himself. It wasn't the heat that kept his eyes open or moving rapidly beneath the lids when he tried to keep them closed. It was the probability of another mission in only a few hours.

He sat on his bunk and stared into the mirror on the far wall. His reflection stared back in the pale illumination of the desk light. Mister Average, Helen had teased him. She thought all military men looked the same in their uniforms and short hair. He supposed that they did. He looked at his reflection again. Hair-colored hair, eye-colored eyes, nose-shaped nose, face-shaped face. Yes, sir, he had it all.

But we're not all the same, he thought. Already there was one thing that set him apart from just about everyone else on the planet: the afternoon raid against Hanoi. There had been other milestones in his life: his first solo; the first time he'd had sex; graduation from high school and college, then from flight training. But nothing had been as intense as today's experiences. He'd read that having a baby changed a woman's perspective forever, that anything short of death would always be secondary to that event. Maybe today's mission had been like that. He had the certain knowledge that if he should be lucky enough to survive the next fifty-odd years of life that should be his, absolutely nothing could dull the memories he'd gathered on his first mission up north.

Jim walked to the thermos and poured a glass of tepid water, his mind pulling back to his immediate problem. What the hell was he going to do about the friction between himself and Pritchard? There had to be some sort of resolution, and soon, or one or the other would be transferred to another flight to keep the peace. And he was sure who that would be. But, damnit, he wanted to stay where he was. He liked Donkey and Bob and knew he could learn much from them, perhaps even enough to survive. He'd just have to back away from Pritchard and hope that the man had the good sense to do the same. He'd have to try to relax and be cool and learn to do his job the very best he could.

Still not sleepy, Jim thought of slipping on his flight suit and boots and walking over to the ops building to see if the frag orders had been broken down and the crew schedule posted for the next day. He rejected the idea immediately, knowing that the staff pukes would find it amusing that a rookie pilot just happened to be sauntering by at 2200. He decided instead to write a few lines to his parents in Santa Fe, normally a soporific event. And so it proved, for by the end of the first page, which was written with extralarge script to take up space on the paper, the weariness of the afternoon flight had returned. He shoved the unfinished letter into the desk drawer, crawled back onto the bed, and turned out the light.

It was odd that Helen wouldn't stop shaking him by the shoulder, considering that he'd just stripped the silken teddy from her lean body and was running his hands sinuously over her smooth flanks.

"Goddamnit, Captain! Wake up! It's 0330 and you've got forty-five minutes before briefing and I'm not coming back to wake you up again."

He peered fuzzily at the lieutenant wearing the OD (officer of the day) arm band and glaring down at him with both hands on his hips. The lieutenant turned quickly and stomped from the room and in moments Jim could hear him swearing at someone else. Suddenly, he was wide awake, as what the lieutenant had said penetrated his sleep-sludged mind. They were going!

He sprang quickly from the bed and grabbed his toothbrush and a towel, glad now that he'd showered and shaved the night before. Of course they were going, he thought, just as Donkey had said. What else could be expected if you were assigned to a fighter-bomber unit in a war zone.

The only other occupant of the latrine was a captain Jim knew only slightly, who was staring with disgust at his face in the mirror. Jim quickly scrubbed the gunk from his teeth and tried to slick back his short hair, heart already beginning to pound with anticipation. He didn't feel frightened. Not yet, in any event. Just terribly alert, although he'd slept fewer than five hours.

Back in his room, Jim Broussard slipped his military ID card into a flight suit pocket and hung his identity tags around his neck, then locked his wallet in the wall locker and pocketed the key. The fresh flight suit smelled vaguely of washing detergent as he slipped it on over one of his newer sets of cotton drawers. He wore the new underclothing on Donkey's advice that if he were shot down and captured he might have to go a long time on one set of GI boxer shorts. Finally, he buckled on the air force-issue watch, his good one locked in the wall locker with his wallet. No sense in making the gomers a present of his college graduation present if he got bagged. The thought sent a sudden chill down his back, making him shiver involuntarily. A rabbit running over his grave, his grandfather used to say.

His stomach felt queasy as he made his way to the club, and the thought of food made his innards churn. But he knew that it was going to be a long day and he should eat something. The dining room was already filled with other pilots going on the early strike, and Jim realized that he must have been one of the last to be awakened. He hurried toward a table where members of Cadillac Flight sat with two other majors, drinking coffee from heavy china mugs. Remnants of breakfast were solidified on the plates, making Jim realize that his stomach was in no condition to take on any food. On the table, was a large platter of burned toast, butter and jelly, and a coffeepot.

"Sit down, bright eyes," Donkey told him with a grin, showing no signs of wear from the night's party. "Here, better have some of this coffee and toast."

Donkey poured him a steaming mug of thick black coffee, and Jim began to gnaw halfheartedly on a piece of cold toast. Pritchard had a half smile on his face as if he were enjoying Jim's discomfort. Chewing the toast was difficult, for Jim found that his mouth had unaccountably gone dry. He tried isolating small lumps of the doughy mixture with his tongue and washing them down with hot coffee.

Bob Packard looked more like a Norman Rockwell painting than usual, with his cowlick sticking up in back and him lapping up cold cereal and milk like a kid getting ready for his paper route. Jim finally gave up on the toast and settled for the harsh GI coffee. He noticed that the Thai waitress tiptoed around the men as if they were already dead and she was dealing with ghosts. The pilots ignored her.

Donkey watched with ill-concealed amusement as Bob tilted the cereal bowl to his mouth to swallow the last of the powdered milk. "Well," Donkey said to the table at large, "looks like Bobby's finished, so it must be about that time."

The pilots of Cadillac Flight sat together in the large wing briefing room, along with the members of Ford, Chevy, and Lincoln flights. Lincoln Flight, from one of the other squadrons in the wing, would be leading the sixteen bombing aircraft on the raid. The bombing aircraft were outnumbered by support birds of all types, most of which would launch from other airfields in response to the Seventh Air Force frag order. These would include the flak suppression aircraft, F-100s and F-4s from Cam Rahn Bay and Danang in South Vietnam; pre- and poststrike recce flown by RF-101s out of Tan Son Nhut in Saigon; tankers from the SAC (Strategic Air Command) detachment in U-Tapao in Thailand; and an F-4 MiGCAP out of Ubon. In addition, there would be A-1s and Jolly Green rescue helicopters standing ground alert if they were needed.

It takes an awful lot of expensive hardware to get a few bombs on a jungle road, Broussard thought. The briefers had his full attention, for the target had a forbidding reputation.

The Met officer was passing the weather forecast for the target area—the Mu Gia Pass, a choke point on the Ho Chi Minh trail lying almost astradle the Laos-North Vietnamese border. At least it isn't Hanoi again, Jim thought with some relief, although Mu Gia was bad enough. He'd talked to pilots who had flown against it several times and knew it was heavily defended. Not the defense in depth found in the Hanoi area, but still not a milk run.

"Clouds should be broken around four thousand feet," the weather briefer continued, "and I would remind you gentlemen that means there's a real possibility the mountaintops will be obscured. The forecast winds remain as given to you on your target cards, except that this large low-pressure system has begun to move into the South China Sea and looks like it's going to be veering toward the south. If you're delayed in reaching the target at the briefed time, you may find that the winds have increased significantly and shifted to a more easterly direction. Weather for home plate should remain VFR through your arrival times. Questions? . . . Thank you, gentlemen, and good luck."

The bespectacled wing intelligence officer walked to the small stage, picked up a clicker, and punched a picture onto the screen. He turned to face the waiting pilots. "A lot of you have been to Mu Gia before, so you know that it's one of the more heavily defended choke points along the trail.

That shows the importance Uncle Ho places on it, with good reason." His clicker brought up an aerial photo of the target area.

"With its heavily mountainous terrain, Mu Gia is one of the few areas in which the Viets have had trouble finding an alternative roadway and truck parks. There simply isn't room in those narrow valleys for them to do much except drive straight through. Obviously, they don't do it much during the day, or they'd risk being caught in the open. No, it's mostly a nighttime operation, both driving through and repairing the road. Without major excavations, the Viets are pretty much stuck with what they've got. And that, of course, is why Seventh Air Force keeps sending you back. Interdict the trail here and you can significantly slow the movement of trucks and troops to South Vietnam."

Jim looked around the briefing room. Some eyes were beginning to glaze over and several pilots were yawning. Obviously these pilots didn't give a damn *why* they had to bomb a target.

"Your aiming points," the debriefer continued, "will be the roadways or the high embankments on either side of the roads, attempting to create mud and dirt slides. Please double-check your bomb fusing for maximum delay, because we want to dig a hole as deep as we can. We doubt that you'll actually see any rolling stock; road-watch teams report that all of last night's convoys have cleared the pass and are well down country. The next traffic probably won't attempt the pass before total darkness."

Another aerial photograph flashed onto the screen. This one had red circles drawn on it. "So," the captain continued happily, "we'll be delighted if you're just able to crater the road enough to stop the traffic for a few nights. You'll notice the importance they put on Mu Gia by checking this last picture. Note the new antiaircraft weapons they've emplaced there since the wing struck it two weeks ago."

Is that the reason they've put in the new guns? Jim wondered. Or is it because we think it's important and keep coming back at it? Cause or effect?

"In addition," the intelligence officer concluded, "along with the new 100mm gun sites, there are now at least three confirmed SAM sites in the area. Here, here, and here. We don't know if these sites are active or just available. No

radar emissions have been picked up from there, but that
doesn't mean that old Luke the Gook isn't being cagey until the time is ripe to use them. Any questions, gents . . . ?
Good luck."

The lanky wing operations officer, a lieutenant colonel,
ambled toward the podium. Jim was having trouble deciding whether he should be taking down everything that had
been said. There was so much of it to remember. He felt
tired and very nervous. He noticed Pritchard looking at him
with an amused smile and felt himself flush. Well, anyone
in his right mind *ought* to be nervous.

The ops officer grinned at the mumbling pilots, regaining
their attention. "I'll be leading the gaggle with Lincoln
Flight, and we'll hit White Anchor refueling track going
in and off the target. You don't have to write down the
coordinates," he explained patiently to the newer pilots who
were scribbling furiously. "It's all there on your nav card.
All the tanker rendezvous coordinates, times, frequencies,
and call signs are listed there. But, flight leaders, make
damned sure that all of your people, and especially the
new sports, know where all the refueling tracks are in case
they get separated. The one in the gulf as well. Make sure
that everybody cycles off the tankers for a complete top-off
before you leave them. They should have been briefed on
that, but let's don't take chances on a screwup.

"They've given us two tankers for the four strike flights,
so everybody try to make his rendezvous time as close
as possible so you don't foul up the following flight. If
anybody has trouble taking fuel, flight leaders get 'em the
hell out of the way and have 'em jettison weapons safe over
Laos before they come home. It's up to you whether you
have the other aircraft in the element accompany them or
go as a three-shipper.

"Y'all know that you don't have many options when we
go against these passes, especially this one. It's gotta be
right down the valley if you expect to see the mother, so
let's do it the usual way and angle the bombs across the
road. Even if you don't crater it, you're bound to get some
good slides. Double check your bomb fusing and let's do
this right.

"Anybody hit hard, try to get a call out so we know
what the hell's going on, and get your bird pointed away

from the pass. You all know there's not a chance in hell of successfully completing a rescue right there, and the gomers are going to be highly pissed at anybody they catch who's been dropping bombs on their sorry asses. If you're not hit too hard, consider the option of trying to make Danang or NKP. If you think you can make it to the sea, you'll be a hell of a lot better off than punching out over rain forest.

"You new people, don't be shy about letting your flight leaders know what the hell's going on. If you're hit, let him know. But otherwise keep off the radio. This wing has lost too many people and aircraft because some pilot didn't want to bother his lead with something as trivial as a 37mm round through the cockpit." The pilots grinned at one another. The last thing any of them would do was declare over the radio that he had a problem unless it was a damned serious problem.

"If you do have to punch out, stay put if you can. Hide. Make like a tree. Do not contact the locals. Assume they're all working for the other side, and most of them are."

The ops officer didn't elaborate, but Jim had heard enough stories to believe him. Apparently the Pathet Lao Communist troops would summarily execute any American flier who fell into their hands.

"Let's try to keep the frequencies clear of all the bullshit today," the ops officer continued. "We're beginning to sound like a bunch of navy pilots. Plan your drops for no lower than sixty-five hundred feet, and for Christ's sake remember how high those mountaintops are. Don't try to stay low and jink around them unless you have the peaks in sight."

When the wing commander took the podium for the next pep talk, Jim let his mind drift. This strike would make number three, since Mu Gia was a "counter." Most of the strikes into Laos were not. To be counted toward the hundred missions needed for a complete tour, the flight had to be targeted into North Vietnam. Strange, for many parts of the trail in Laos were said to be more heavily defended than much of southern North Vietnam. Actually, the golden beebee, that lucky shot by a Viet gunner aiming an SA-2 missile or a single-shot rifle, could find you anywhere. And either could scatter the big jet over the countryside if it connected in the right place. It was just such a dichotomy that made Jim uneasy, for there didn't seem to be any consistent rules to the game. Jet fighters were meant to be combatted by modern, sophisticated weapons, not a scrawny farmer firing a vintage French rifle. Yet the farmer could be just as deadly.

The colonel was finally finished and the pilots were dismissed to complete their mission planning. Jim watched Pritchard nudge the apparently comatose Donkey from his nap. Jim knew that his flight leader must have absorbed all that was necessary from the briefing. God knows how many of these things he must have sat through in his lifetime. He must assimilate it by osmosis, however, for the gentle snores had been unmistakable.

Donkey stretched and yawned hugely, winked at Broussard, and ambled for the exit. From the briefing room they all headed back to their individual squadrons to complete the mission planning. Other members of the wing joined Donkey and his flight for the slow stroll through the early morning tropical air. There was still no hint of a sunrise. Just being around Donkey made Jim feel as if everything was going to be all right. The flight leader acted as though flying against an enemy and dropping bombs on them was the most normal thing a pilot could do.

In the squadron, the pilots clustered around the long, high tables, drawing the mundane lines on their charts and placing dull-appearing figures on their nav cards. The width of a pencil line, however, could mean that a flight would enter the lethal zone of a SAM ring rather than passing it by with no more than the rattlesnake buzz of its tracking radar in their headsets. As usual, Donkey passed the detail work on to Andy Pritchard and amused himself by talking to the other flight leaders. He glanced only casually at the finished product.

The pilots of Cadillac Flight then walked together to the PE building to gather the equipment and paraphernalia unique to their profession. The scene was usually quiet going out, most of the pilots showing some degree of tenseness, anticipating the challenges and dangers of the coming hours.

Each pilot wiggled into his tight-fitting g suit, remarkably like a pair of sleek cowboy chaps but containing inflatable bladders. These bladders filled with compressed air during high-speed maneuvers and squeezed the legs and abdomen, assisting the blood on its journey to the brain, thus helping to prevent blackout. An umbilical-like hose hung from the side of the g suit to be connected to a pneumatic source within the airplane.

The mesh survival vest was worn over the flight coveralls and under the parachute. The vest contained myriad pockets to store a small URC-10 survival radio, flares, a compass, a signal mirror, and a tree-lowering device—a small pulley and length of strong strap that a downed aviator could use to lower himself to the ground in the event his parachute canopy snagged in the top of a tree. Other pockets in the vest contained fishhooks, a whistle, emergency rations, a small quantity of water, and tracer ammunition for the .38 Special revolver carried in a leather holster attached to the vest. Other small items included additions that each individual considered appropriate to meet minimum survival needs. One optimist included a dozen condoms.

Finally, the fifty-pound parachute, equipped with underarm flotation packets, was strapped over the vest after the chute had been carefully checked for re-pack currency and to see that the restraining pins were straight. Each chute was individually sized for wear by only one pilot. Helmets, map cases, knives, and gloves were taken from pegs above the chutes. Pistols, blood chits, and gold coins were signed out by the PE sergeant.

Jim waited his turn to complete the last chore before leaving the PE section, filling three plastic baby bottles with water from the fountain. He carefully tightened the tops and fitted them into one of the billowing pockets of his g suit. The pilots had tried different canisters to hold their survival water; none had proven as effective as the plastic bottles. Each aircraft contained a water supply, but unfortunately it stayed with the aircraft if the pilot ejected. Jim wondered what the stateside base exchange procurement officer must have thought when the large requisition for baby bottles in the combat zone reached his desk. Probably thought the pilots had knocked up every Thai whore in the countryside.

The routine finally complete, the pilots of Cadillac Flight, each wearing and carrying more than eighty pounds of gear, waddled to the waiting truck for the short ride to the flight line. There they would be deposited by their individual aircraft. Like most flight leaders, Donkey used this time in the truck to pass on his special instructions. He directed them primarily toward Broussard.

"The important thing," he was saying, "is to stick to my ass like ugly on an ape, 'cause the dinkers know which way we'll have to come in and which way we'll have to go out. There just ain't that many choices in the mountains, particularly if the weather puke is right and the tops are obscured. We're the third flight in, so it ain't going to take a fucking genius to be able to figure out their tracking problem. It ought to be right easy for them. You can also bet your ass that they'll know the exact elevation of the lowest cloud deck and have their guns fused to detonate right about there. So, we'll go through it in a hurry. Andy, you take your element and go for the northern part of the pass unless it looks like one of the earlier flights has already done a number on it. Jimbo and me'll rain shit on 'em in the south.

"I'd be real surprised to see any trucks, but you never know, so keep your eyes open. Just make sure your fusing is right and you drop 'em in train at an angle across the roadbed. Hell, they'll probably use all this fresh dirt we're making for 'em to keep Uncle Ho's trail in good repair, but that's not our worry. Let's just do our job right."

Donkey looked intently at Broussard before continuing. "Stay with me on this one, Jimbo, because I'm going to be jinking hard coming off target and I don't want to have to worry about running into you as well as one of those goddamned mountains. And here's the last thing. There's going to be umpteen airplanes compressed down into a mighty small amount of airspace beneath those clouds, so let's everybody keep his head outta his ass and the old eyeballs clicking. These TOTs are swell, but it'll be a damned miracle if everybody manages to roll in at just the right moment and especially in the right place. So, look around. Let's do her right, OK?"

His briefing completed, Donkey collapsed once more into a shapeless bag of equipment and clothing, closed his eyes, and immediately began to snore for the remainder of the trip to the flight line. How does he do it? Jim wondered.

The truck made its first stop by Donkey's aircraft, where the young crew chief was awaiting his arrival. The flight leader clambered from the rear of the truck, already grinning at the sergeant and picking his spot on the revetment wall on which he would relieve his bladder in what he called "the last nervous piss."

Broussard's revetment was next down the line. He returned the sergeant's salute crisply and together they talked their way through the aircraft's maintenance record and the few discrepancies that had not been cleared from its last flight. His preflight inspection was thorough, particularly compared to Donkey's, who figured that the crew chief had a better opportunity to find anything out of kilter than he did in the dark shadows of the revetment.

Jim carefully checked the 750-pound bombs and shackles, ensuring that safing clips and wires were intact and that the fusing was properly set. Satisfied, he trudged up the ladder under his heavy load and wedged himself into the ejection seat. With the chief's assistance, he secured the belts and straps that held him firmly against the seat. He carefully stowed his nav cards and maps and buckled his kneeboard around his left thigh. Methodically, he placed the tools of his trade in their customary position, so he could find them with minimum fuss even in a darkened cockpit. The bomb run, he'd found out, was not the place to be searching for a misplaced item.

He plugged his g-suit hose into the internal connector and checked it, then made certain that the oxygen system was full and operational. The opened checklist lay on his clipboard, and he checked off each item on the prestart list. Satisfied, he settled his helmet comfortably onto his head and made sure that the stopwatch was synchronized to the correct time.

As the second hand on the watch nudged the exact start engines time, Jim thrust his hand overhead out of the cockpit. He made a twirling motion with his finger until he received an answering nod from the crew chief, now wearing a noise-deadening headset plugged into a receptacle on the fuselage. Simultaneously, Jim engaged the starter and felt the black-powdered cartridge fire, providing initial spin-up RPMs for the engine. The huge engine rumbled slowly but steadily into a deep, full-throated roar. He extended his hand sharply, index finger pointing away from the aircraft, and a ground crew member disengaged the APU (auxiliary power unit) as Jim brought the internal power onto the line.

Methodically, Jim went through the dozens of checklist items, the list still opened on his kneeboard. The checks he did from memory but backed them up with a quick scan of the printed items. He saw Donkey's aircraft nosing from its revetment and heard his radio call simultaneously.

"Cadillac Flight, check in."

"Two," Broussard responded.

"Three," came Pritchard's quick call.

"Four," radioed Bob Packard.

"Takhli Ground Control, this is Cadillac Lead. Taxi four Thuds, operational."

The ground controller answered with taxi directions to the active runway, and Jim watched the lead aircraft pull from its revetment. He advanced power as Donkey passed his position. Jet engines used prodigious amounts of fuel on the ground, and extensive runups and general vacillation was discouraged. A multiengine aircraft might take half an hour from taxi to takeoff. Fighters normally took less than ten minutes.

Jim raised both fists to shoulder height as the J-75 engine spooled up, holding the toe brakes firmly against the increasing thrust, then extended both thumbs and jerked them outboard. In well-trained movements, two airmen leapt beneath the aircraft and pulled the wheel chocks, then straightened up until the pilot could see them. Jim advanced the throttle another half inch so that the heavily laden aircraft would gain forward momentum, then retarded it abruptly to the idle position after it was moving. He had to hit the left rudder and brake hard to negotiate the ninety-degree left turn onto the taxiway. The crew chief marshaled him away from the tight area, then came to rigid attention and snapped his sharpest salute. Broussard returned it and gave him a thumbs-up signal.

Jim glanced quickly over his shoulder as the aircraft accelerated to taxi speed, and saw Andy.Pritchard's aircraft pulling from its revetment. Bob Packard fell in behind him. Jim moved in closer to Donkey. In moments the four aircraft of Cadillac Flight had pulled together and taxied as a formation to the arming and last-chance area adjacent to the active runway.

The ground crew stood stoically, arms folded, to one side of the arming area, where they would remain until all four pilots raised both hands into plain view. A signal from the senior sergeant and they dashed forward to remove the safing devices from the weapons. Another crew of specialists made a careful exterior inspection of each aircraft, checking for leaks and damage.

Eventually, one man stood in front of each aircraft and displayed the safing pins as if they were hunting trophies, holding them in position until each pilot responded by displaying his own ejection seat safing pins and streamers. Everyone counted everyone's pins and then, satisfied, the flight taxied toward the active runway. No spares would be needed today. Jim noticed that the sky to the east was beginning to turn pink. Cadillac Flight was going to war.

Major Delbert "Donkey" Sheehan

"Tower, this is Cadillac Lead. Ready to go with a flight of four Thuds. Operational," Donkey called over the radio.

"Roger, Cadillac Lead. You're cleared for takeoff. Winds are one seven zero at zero five. Altimeter is two niner niner one. Good luck."

"Thank you, Tower."

Donkey pulled his aircraft onto the left center of the runway, allowing Jim ample space to taxi behind him and align his aircraft slightly to the left and aft of the lead ship. He held his brakes and watched Cadillac Three and Four move into a similar alignment to his right. The sunlight was just beginning to become noticeable and the outside air temperature gauge had already reached eighty degrees. The air-conditioning outlet spit moisture into Donkey's face as it struggled to overcome the humid air. He quickly lowered the tinted helmet visor and let his eyes roam to the other aircraft. Fighters would normally depart in pairs, but safety considerations for the F-105 strike aircraft dictated single takeoffs. Hopefully, this would prevent the loss of more than one aircraft should a bomb come free during the takeoff roll.

Donkey cocked his head over his right shoulder and received nods from Three and Four, then turned toward Jim Broussard, a wide grin on his face. Jim responded quickly with a nod of his own, indicating that he was

ready for takeoff. Donkey drew his head back into the
cockpit for another quick scan of the instrument panel,
punched the stopwatch sweep-second hand, and released
the brakes.

The aircraft began to slowly lurch down the runway, and
Donkey firmly moved the throttle outboard into maximum
afterburner. A sheet of flame shot from the tail pipe as
the burner kicked in, and the large aircraft quickened its
acceleration. Black smoke from the water injection system
intermingled with the jet fumes as the aircraft shifted into
maximum performance, fighting gravity and drag as it lumbered down the runway. Above the roar of his own engine,
Donkey could hear the number two aircraft start to spool
up its engines.

As Donkey broke ground, he tipped his aircraft slightly to
the left and glanced back at the runway. Jim in the number
two slot was well into his roll, having started precisely ten
seconds after the initial movement of the lead ship. The
last two aircraft, just now into the early moments of their
takeoffs, moved along like doddering old men, then came to
life as the burners, then the water injection, cut in. Twenty
seconds and more than a mile down the runway, the last
heavily ladened Thud consented to fly.

Donkey held the nose of his aircraft down, allowing it
to quickly accelerate to 300 knots, then eased in a slight
back pressure on the stick to begin his climb. The briefed
procedure was for the flight leader to fly on the runway
heading for about three miles, then make a lazy reversing
turn toward the initial flight-planned heading. Using this
technique, the rest of the flight could cut him off and gain
their formation positions with a minimum of fuss and delay.
As he brought the throttle out of burner, Donkey made
a careful check of all his instruments, paying particular
attention to the Doppler navigation gear. He passed over
the airfield in the reversing turn and checked it against the
coordinates of the runway. The clever but neurotic little box
seemed to be working for the moment.

Donkey shifted his attention and watched Jim Broussard
cut the angle of his turn. He really made it look easy, but
Donkey knew that years of practice had gone into making
that rendezvous seem simple. Many people never learned
it. The young captain promised to be an excellent pilot. The

number two aircraft stabilized, then moved into his slot on Donkey's left wing.

Filled with fuel and a maximum weapon load, the F-105 flew with all the characteristics of an airborne turd. It demanded that the pilot constantly manipulate the throttle and controls to maintain position. Donkey attempted to fly smoothly in order to give his flight as stable a platform as possible.

Very soon, the two aircraft of the second element slid into position on the right side of the lead ship. Donkey didn't even bother turning his head to watch their join-up, a silent compliment to the formating skills of Andy and Bobby. When they settled onto their initial heading, Donkey did glance casually at the remainder of his flight to ensure they were all properly tucked in and that a spare wouldn't be needed. He relayed this to the ground by the radio and bumped each rudder to fishtail his aircraft, signaling the flight to move into a loose combat spread. Close formation flying was tiring, and most of their workday still lay ahead of them.

Donkey reached for his neatly folded maps and began to match checkpoints on the ground with the Doppler readout, verifying their progress toward the air refueling rendezvous point. A ground radar controller had already given them the precise heading to that same point, but Donkey had one major rule for survival in aerial combat: Take nothing for granted. Radios and navigational systems fail; pilots become separated from their flights; plans change. Everyone, friend and foe alike, seems unified in an attempt to kill them. The wary combatant just might stay alive; the nonchalant will eventually be hurt.

Donkey watched the verdant hills of eastern Thailand slide easily beneath their wings. The other aircraft stood out starkly against the impossibly green backdrop despite mottled green camouflage paint. The early morning air was smooth and silky, with none of the thermals and clear air turbulence that would accompany the heat of the afternoon. His aircraft had settled down in the smooth air like a recalcitrant pack animal that had felt obliged to react toward the load at the beginning of a day but was now enjoying the experience. The aircraft stayed almost effortlessly where his hand put it. Pilots called it "good air." "Bad air," which they could expect on the return trip, made the aircraft sulky and rebellious. The planes would refuse to make coordinated turns and would be consistently out of trim. Bad air produced a little wiggle in the aircraft that a pilot could feel in his bottom as his plane serpentined through the sky, constantly bobbing and weaving with small yawing and pitching motions.

"Cadillac Flight, this is Lead. Gimme your fuel status."

Donkey knew he had caught Jim dreaming when he was slow to answer. Anything other than an immediate response to a lead query was considered slack in fighter circles and would inevitably invite censure. The pilots of the second element snapped their replies as Jim's tardy voice cleared the airways.

Donkey turned in his cockpit and gave Jim a long stare. "You *will* pull your head outta your ass today, won't you, Jimbo?"

Jim must have assumed it to be a rhetorical question, for he chose to remain silent. Donkey grinned beneath the mask, knowing that the rebuke would produce immediate responses in the future. It was a small embarrassment to get a promising young pilot up to speed. With scarcely a pause, Donkey continued: "Refueling lineup will be Two, Four, Three, then Lead. Cadillac Flight, let's go refueling frequency."

The check-in on the new frequency was brisk and immediate. Donkey called the tanker, White One One. The tanker pilot confirmed that each fighter could refuel and then cycle off for a final topping of his tank to replenish fuel that had been burned while the others refueled. This ensured that each strike aircraft would have a maximum fuel load before leaving the tanker. With full tanks, a malfunctioning aircraft could make almost any base in Southeast Asia.

Donkey dipped a wing and placed the flight into an echelon formation, then began the descent to the tanker. "Got you in sight, One One," he called.

The fighters rapidly overtook the large KC-135 aerial tanker and stabilized in the observation position, about a hundred feet aft and below the tanker. Jim had first crack at the refueling and moved forward quickly. The forty-seven-foot retractable boom nodded up and down, beckoning him. Donkey watched critically. The pilot had to concentrate on keeping his position in the refueling envelope, a parcel of air some twenty feet aft and fifteen feet below the tanker's belly. The heavy fighter would be sluggish and critically close to its stall speed.

The boom extended sharply and thrust into the refueling receptacle. Donkey watched Jim compensate with a slight addition of power to overcome the disruptive break in the smooth airflow over the fighter's fuselage. Donkey felt an almost paternal pride at the skill of the latest addition to Cadillac Flight.

When the flying boom popped free from the nose receptacle of Jim's F-105, the residual fuel in the boom drenched his windscreen. As the tiny windscreen wiper worked frantically to clear it away, Jim moved slowly back into his position within the formation, and Cadillac Four moved in like a suckling calf that had spotted its mother.

Each aircraft of Cadillac Flight refueled with a minimum of fuss, making it look easy. Then each moved forward once more to top their tanks before departing the refueling track.

"White One One," Donkey called as his flight moved away, "mucho thanks for the petrol and we'll see you coming out."

"You bet, Cadillac Lead. Good luck to you folks and we'll see you later."

Donkey led the flight into a gentle turn toward the target some thirty minutes away, then kicked them again into a combat spread. In the distance he could just see the Troung Son mountains in the haze. The Doppler indicated the target was dead ahead at twelve o'clock, located in one of the deep valleys between craggy peaks. The weather puke had been right; most of the mountaintops were obscured by clouds. Donkey pressed the mike button on the throttle.

"Cadillac Flight, this is Lead. Let's clean 'em up and green 'em up." He twisted in the cockpit toward Jim as he spoke. "Two, keep your head out and stick with me real close. Cadillac Flight, let's go strike frequency."

Donkey checked the cockpit for potential projectiles; any loose items needed to be stored so they wouldn't end up in his face during the attack and recovery. He was very deliberate with the arming switches for the bombs; all nine of them had to be positioned to successfully release the weapons during a dive-bombing run. Last, he turned the master switch to the on position. He double-checked each switch again. There were no electronic jammer switches to flip, because Cadillac Flight carried no ECM pods. A chronic shortage had precluded their use by any missions except those targeted into the Hanoi area. He switched to the strike frequency on the UHF radio. "Cadillac Flight, check in."

"Two," Jim responded quickly. Donkey chuckled to himself. Probably didn't want another ass-chewing over the airwaves.

"Three."

"Four."

Cadillac Flight followed Donkey as he nosed his aircraft down toward the roll-in altitude of 13,000 feet. Normally, they would have gone in much lower, then popped up to their roll-in altitude. At Mu Gia, however, they did not have to negotiate an extended gauntlet of guns and missiles. The mountainous terrain worked against the defenders in this instance, and the briefers had insisted that there would be only minimal opposition until the flights reached their IPs.

The flak suppressors were already at work; some of their voices were shrill with excitement, others sounded almost bored. Donkey scanned the air to their front and saw deadly little puffs of white smoke as the Vietnamese gunners ranged their weapons against the striking aircraft. Streams of 12.7mm fire poured in a green fury from the sides of the mountains, some even directed downward at the flak suppressors and the first strike flights as they weaved down the valley. Cadillac Flight increased speed to more than 500 knots over the surface of the ground.

Warbles from the radar warning system filled Donkey's helmet, then they were overridden by a new high-pitched squeal. Recognition came instantly. It was the emergency beeper, which automatically activates whenever a pilot ejects from a stricken aircraft. Someone was down!

The flak bursts were much closer—some dark gray, others almost white. Strings of orange balls seemed to stretch toward them as they came within range of the deadly missiles. Green tracers laced up from the sides of the mountains, veering away from the aircraft at seemingly only the last moment. Donkey realized that his breathing was becoming faster and faster. Things would start happening rapidly now. Often they happened so quickly that it was difficult to assimilate and adjust to them. Cadillac Flight continued its inexorable route.

"Lincoln Three is down," came a laconic voice over the strike net.

"This is Lincoln Lead. Is that you calling, Four? Where did he go in?"

"Yeah, Lead, this is Lincoln Four. He was hit just as we came off target. He's got a good chute, but it looks like he's going to land damned near on top of a gun site."

"OK, Lincoln Flight, this is Lead. Let's move out to the west and orbit at fifteen thou until the rest of the strike force has expended, then we'll see if there's anything we can do. Crown Control, did you monitor that Lincoln Three is down almost over the target?"

"Affirmative," a new voice said over the radio. "We're standing by until you decide whether we should launch the SAR." Crown was the airborne command post orbiting over eastern Thailand. It was staffed by controllers who monitored the strike nets and radars. Senior officers aboard were supposedly capable of making astute decisions, but Donkey was not convinced he wanted those weenies making life or death calls for him or his flight.

The radio transmissions, which moments before had been bubbling over the ether, dried quickly as the strike force pilots realized that one of their number was in deep shit. The warbling of the emergency beacon continued to make any communications difficult. Donkey was simultaneously conscious of the beeper's screech, the radar warning system crackling in his headset like a demented rattlesnake, and his own rapid breathing into his headset inside the helmet. Would Crown call off the strike to support a rescue attempt? What would be the point? Stop worrying about it and do your damned job! A quick glance at the instrument panel told him that they were barreling across the ground at close to 600 knots, about the maximum speed they could achieve with the bombs dragging beneath them.

A dozen or more black clouds dotted their two o'clock less than a triple wingspan distance away. Donkey's eyes were involuntarily drawn to the bright red glow within their ragged borders. His lips thinned into a grimace within the oxygen mask, and he could feel his heart pounding. He quickly scanned the ground for the target. The haze and clouds made everything indistinct.

Then he saw it between the breaks in the undercast, just as the emergency beeper went suddenly silent. Donkey slammed the stick to the right side of the cockpit and stood on the rudder, determined that he wouldn't lose sight of the target. He rolled almost inverted and pulled the nose down through the horizon, eyes never leaving the spot. Fighting the urge to look back and see if his wingman was still with him, he instead pulled his eyes away from the ground long enough for a three-second instrument scan, then aimed them back at the target. He righted the aircraft in a sixty-degree dive and stabilized. Only then did he spare a quick glance at where his wingman should be. He was still there. Good boy! They dived through a cloud layer, and the guns were waiting as they reappeared. Donkey tried to ignore them. The dive angle was a steady sixty degrees and the airspeed was good. He stared at the ground rushing toward him, trying to pick out anything that looked familiar from the briefing photos. Nothing looked at all like the recce pictures. Where was the road?

Then he picked it up again. The narrow, red dirt track snaked through the mountains, looking much smaller than it had on the briefing photographs. He made a small, quick adjustment to his flight path so that the lighted reticle in the windscreen was lined up just short of the near side of the road. The sight drifted away from his aim point, and he nudged the rudder and aileron slightly until it was back where he wanted it. The damned briefed winds were wrong. He hoped Jim would adjust for it. He knew Andy would. They'd be coming across the road at a slight angle, hoping to walk the bombs across it. One last quick check of the flight parameters. Airspeed and dive angle still good; no pressure on the controls. He felt the bombs begin to kick off, driven by small explosive charges. He punched his thumb firmly onto the pickle button on the control stick, backing up the automatic sequence, and felt the lurch as the 750-pounders rippled off, one at a time. The ground was coming up at an alarming rate.

Donkey began his pull off target before the last of Jim's bombs left the aircraft. His vision grayed from the g forces as he pulled hard against the control stick. He could feel his bottom jaw sag with the force, and drool begin to leak from the corner of his mouth. The accelerometer was pointing at the six-g figure, and he felt as if he were being pressed through the seat back. At that moment he weighed almost 1,200 pounds. The bladders of his g suit were fully inflated and tightened against his legs and abdomen, trying to force the blood in his body back in its correct path.

Donkey was nearly immobile but was able to stroke the throttle outboard to bring in the burner. Gaily colored flak clouds erupted directly to their front. Donkey put the aircraft on one wing tip, then the other, as he tried to outguess the gunners. Together the element flew through the converging streams of flak; and somehow emerged unscathed.

Donkey leveled the element at full throttle and burner just above the sparse trees. He jinked hard left, then right, and left again. He knew Jim would have a hard time staying with him. Anyone would. Nevertheless, the wingman was hanging on, despite the gyrations. Donkey threaded his way down a heavily eroded valley, seemingly in a constant turn.

To an untrained eye, the path ahead appeared to be completely blocked in all quadrants by mountains, but this was not Donkey's first visit to Mu Gia. Somehow Cadillac Lead found an opening and dragged his wingman through it. Suddenly, Donkey pulled his aircraft into a near vertical zoom climb, and together they entered the overcast.

The steep climb took them quickly back to 20,000 feet. For the first time since the attack began, Donkey was able to turn his head and look for the two aircraft in the second element. They were slightly aft and sticking to the first element like an aluminum growth. Donkey didn't turn the flight directly toward the tanker rendezvous but swung back to the west of the target, where Lincoln Flight circled forlornly, now short one of their aircraft. Only the larger flak guns could reach the aircraft at this distance, but the gunners seemed more interested in the last flight now in for the attack. Through the broken cloud deck Donkey could see the explosions of their bombs, which all seemed to be on target. More dirt moved around. What a war!

"Lincoln Lead, this is Cadillac Lead. Y'all have anything on your downed bird yet?"

"Yeah," came the wooden voice of the ops officer who had elected to lead Lincoln Flight. "Forget it. We just made a low-level swing over the target and saw them take him. There's nothing we can do without getting him hurt. Let's head on back to the tankers. Did you copy, Crown?"

"Roger, Crown copies," the airborne command post replied immediately. "Sorry 'bout that."

"Yeah," said Lincoln Lead.

Donkey kicked the flight back into a spread formation and gave them the opportunity to grab their water tubes. He took stock. His flight suit was completely darkened with sweat, but the huge aircraft was purring contentedly. Broussard had done OK. Hung in there real good. So had Andy's element, but he expected that of him. Old Jimbo just might make a fighter pilot yet.

Donkey shrugged his shoulders, trying to release the tension that had built up. He tried to recall the sequence of events. The flight had been over the target area from the IP to the roll-in point for maybe five minutes or less. The attack itself had taken no more than a minute. There had been maybe three to four minutes coming out. They had been under fire for no more than about ten minutes altogether. Christ! It had seemed longer than that.

Lieutenant Aspirant
Nguyen Thi Minh

"Do you think we'll get a chance to launch today?" asked Lieutenant Aspirant Trach, pulling his antigravity suit from his locker. "It seems like all we've done since we've been home is sit cockpit alert and watch the Yankees fly around Hanoi as if they were wanting to buy real estate. One of these days they're going to change their minds about not attacking airfields and we're going to find ourselves sitting there in the arming area with a three-hundred-kilo bomb on our asses."

"Now, Comrade Trach," Minh said mockingly while trying to keep a grin from his face. He turned from the window toward his best friend. "You must remember that our leaders know what is best for us. Didn't General Giap defeat the French, and have they never grown tired of telling us about it? The good general is probably waiting until we have enough aircraft so that we can surround the Americans, as he did with his artillery at Dien Bien Phu."

"Well," Trach grumbled, "if he doesn't get off his short ass and get us some more aircraft, it just might work the other way around. The only pilots getting enough flying time to stay competent these days are those large-butted Russian 'advisers.' And I notice they never seem to need an aircraft when the Yankees are inbound. Then they always seem to have pressing duties someplace else. The only thing they know what to advise on is the best black-market prices."

"I've noticed that myself. I think they're really here to make sure we're not selling their aircraft and equipment to the Americans, like those shits in the south would do. Either that or as a reward for some service that allows them to get out of that damned cold-weather factory they live in. Sometimes I think we'll have more trouble getting rid of the Ivans than the Americans."

Trach laughed as an enlisted man burst through the door to the equipment area. "Orders just came down from Sector Control. You're both to go to cockpit alert immediately. An American attack force has been radar identified inbound from the west."

"So what else is new?" Trach said. "Now, we'll get to go out and sit in our aircraft and watch them practice their bombing techniques again. I'm beginning to feel more like a ground observer than a fighter pilot."

"Just remember," Minh told his friend, smiling at his bellicosity as they crawled into the rear of the small truck that would take them to the flight line, "it's better than carrying an assault rifle. Anyway, being a fighter pilot is a state of mind."

"So the major tells me. But I notice that he manages to put a new dent in his desk with his boot every time we waste a morning sitting out there watching the F-105s destroy the suburbs."

The MiG-21 fighter airplane gleamed an uninterrupted streak of silver in the early morning sun, broken only by the red identification numbers on the forward fuselage and the red and gold star farther aft. It was in its usual meticulous condition. The NCO in charge of the ground crew greeted Minh and followed him in his inspection around the aircraft. Both paid particular attention to the twin-barreled 23mm guns and four air-to-air rockets. It was all correct, as Minh knew it would be. He complimented the ground crew, aware that their hard work was too often unappreciated by the pilots. He knew this for he had once been in their position before pilot training, maintaining a vintage MiG-15, which had accumulated thousands of flying hours before the Soviets released it to the Vietnamese.

The NCO assisted him up the ladder of the modern jet fighter and helped with the parachute harness and restraining straps. Minh adjusted the rudder pedals, flushing with resentment as he always did when he remembered the amusement of the Russian instructors when they found the pedals had to be extended to accommodate the shorter legs of the Vietnamese. As if physical size had anything to do with the quality of a fighter pilot. And he *was* a fighter pilot.

The MiG-21, called the Fishbed in the West, was the top line fighter of the North Vietnamese defense forces. Minh knew it was a real honor to be allowed to fight in it. The aircraft was capable of Mach 2 speeds at sea level, and its swept wings and light airframe made it more than a match for the larger American attack aircraft, certainly against the bomb-laden F-105s carrying the brunt of the raids into the country. His training had taught him, however, that it was often the pilot, not the aircraft, that made the difference in an aerial engagement. Only after he had matched himself against the Americans would he truly know his effectiveness and that of his aircraft as a weapons system.

Perhaps he should say *if* he was matched against the Americans. Thus far, his days had been spent watching the bastards overfly the area, trapped helplessly in the cockpit on five-minute alert. He'd engaged in but a single combat launch and had participated in no action that day.

Minh was confident of his flying abilities, admitting only to himself that beneath the confidence there was also an edge of apprehension and concern. Not fear, exactly; more the fear of the unknown. In simulated combat, he'd been beaten only once, and that time by a Soviet instructor with more than 2,000 flying hours in the MiG-21. He had confidence in his ability to fly the aircraft well, but he was also wise enough to realize that simulated dogfights meant little in the dizzying world of aerial combat.

Minh flicked two switches on the side panel, closing a relay that allowed power from the auxiliary power unit to reach the aircraft electrical bus and warm the avionics. The radios hissed and crackled as they came to life. His thumb punched the radio transmit button on the throttle to call control with his status. "Dragon Control, this is Dragon One Five. Ready for engine start."

"Dragon One Five, this is Dragon Control. Understood. Stand by for instructions."

He listened as Trach in Dragon One Six called in his status and received the same standby orders. Above the chatter on the radio he heard the wailing of the sirens warning of an impending raid. As far as he knew, the Americans had never struck an airfield. Strange, he thought. We sit here like brooding hens while they overfly us as if we didn't exist. They must know that they could destroy eighty percent of our capability with one successful raid on each field. He felt very vulnerable. Perhaps there were some things it was best not to think about.

Minh shielded his eyes from the sunlight, which had managed to break through a near-solid overcast, and looked northwest toward the limestone karst hills. That would be the way they would come. They almost always did, because the gunners had difficulty siting their weapons in the rugged terrain and the attackers could use the hills to radar mask their approach for part of the inbound leg. But the flatlands of the Red River valley and delta lay between the hills and the targets. Minh knew that the antiaircraft defenses were solid from the hills eastward to the sea. Surely their mission planners could be more imaginative than that. After the losses their F-105s had taken, common sense should suggest that alternate entry routes would be advisable. But if the fools wanted to continue their predictability, it was certainly all right with the defenders.

"Dragon One Five and Dragon One Six," came the voice of the controller over the radio. Minh's heart leapt as he quickly turned up the volume to override the noise of the APU. "Start engines. Repeat, start engines."

"Dragon One Five, starting engines!"

"Dragon One Six, starting engines!"

They're really going to launch us, Minh thought excitedly. Surely they wouldn't have us start engines if they weren't going to launch us. He hit the starter button and at twelve percent RPMs brought the throttle from stopcock to idle, watching the tail pipe temperature begin to rise quickly. He scanned the other instruments, checking that the oil pressure was alive and hydraulic pressure was coming up. He quickly ran through his prelaunch checklist and waved away the wheel chocks and external power cart. Glancing at Trach's revetment directly across the taxiway, he saw that the APU was still plugged into the fuselage.

Trach was fun but he was slow. He reached to the ejection seat and removed the safing pins, momentarily displaying them to the NCO on the ground, then checked his armament panel safe.

"Dragon One Five and One Six, this is Dragon Control. Taxi to runway zero seven. You're cleared for immediate takeoff. Repeat, you're cleared for immediate takeoff. Switch to Hanoi Sector Control when airborne on channel B. Repeat, channel B."

Minh's aircraft was rolling before he received the entire transmission; he was ahead of Trach by more than a hundred meters by the time he reached the end of the active runway. He didn't slow while he made the ninety-degree turn onto the runway, spooling the engine up during the turn so that by the time he had correct alignment, he was also at one hundred percent power. The interceptor's response was immediate and gratifying as Minh moved the throttle into the afterburner range. The new acceleration shoved him back into the ejection seat.

He raised the nose of the aircraft and almost immediately felt the main gear leave the runway, then he slammed the gear handle into the up position. He held the nose at only ten degrees climbing attitude until he reached 450 kilometers, then gave the agile aircraft its head for the climb toward the base of the clouds. He would wait until Trach was airborne before he called Hanoi Sector to avoid them having to repeat the instructions.

He quickly reached the base of the overcast, where he pushed the nose down so he could retain visual reference until he received the controller's instructions. The acceleration was more noticeable now that he had the clouds as a reference. He did love this aircraft! He'd flown only two other jets during his training; compared to this little speedster they'd been water buffalo. He put the aircraft ninety degrees onto its wing and saw that Trach was finally airborne. Minh waited a long moment for Trach to clean up the cockpit before he radioed.

"Hanoi Control, this is Dragon One Five and One Six. Airborne and climbing through six hundred meters on runway heading. Standing by for instructions."

"Dragon One Five and One Six, this is Control. We have positive radar identification on both your aircraft. Climb to five hundred meters on a heading of three five zero degrees. Report level-off."

"Dragon One Five and One Six will comply," Minh responded, falling into the formalized pilot-controller jargon they had picked up from the Soviets. Actually, the stylized manner of airborne communications worked very well, since theirs was a tonal language easily distorted by the radio. He watched as Trach put his aircraft on an interception course that would place him in the proper formation position.

He's not a bad pilot, thought Minh, as he watched his friend slide into position alongside him. And he's certainly not without courage. But that probably won't be enough if some Yankee Phantom catches him alone, for Minh knew that his friend had no real aptitude for the three-dimensional world of the fighter pilot. He simply lacked the feel for the aircraft and tended to fly it in a mechanical fashion. They had once fought each other over the wintery plains of Russia, and in the first moments of simulated combat he knew that he could have dispatched Trach within two or three hard maneuvers. Instead, he'd made it look like a real fight, almost to the point that he'd been afraid he'd overdone the charade.

That night, while drinking the heavy Russian beer, Trach had confessed in an embarrassed manner that he'd never even ridden in a motorized vehicle until he was fifteen years of age. He knew that Minh had not pressed his advantage, saving his face in front of the Soviet instructors. Minh suspected that Trach had little idea how hard he had worked not to demonstrate his own prowess. Still, if the system worked the way it should, there was little danger of Trach being caught alone, for they were under constant friendly radar coverage.

"Hanoi Sector, this is Dragon One Five and Dragon One Six. Level at five thousand meters. Heading three five zero degrees."

"Dragon One Five and One Six," said a new voice over the radio, "this is your final director. Sixteen enemy aircraft in flights of four are approaching at your eleven o'clock position, sixty miles. Each flight is approximately three minutes apart. This will be a parallel approach to an angle-off attack with a low-altitude disengagement to the north. Do you understand?"

"One Five understands."

"One Six understands." Trach answered for himself rather than letting Minh do it for them both, since they would no longer be handled as a flight but rather as individual aircraft, with independent instructions issued by different controllers.

"Dragon One Six, fly a heading of one nine zero degrees and maintain five thousand meters."

Minh watched Trach give him a thumbs-up and turn abruptly to the south, where he would be vectored into an attack position on the other side of the American formations. He listened as the director switched his friend to channel C on the radio, to minimize the chance of communication confusion between them. He fiddled with his radar set as he continued northward, adjusting the gain until the picture on the tube was as clear as he could get it. It would be useful only during the attack phase and then only as a backup in the event of communications failure between the controller and the aircraft. He turned the selector switch back to the standby position, knowing that its radiation might pinpoint his position to enemy electronic warfare aircraft.

"Dragon One Five, this is Hanoi Sector. Turn left to a new heading of three one five degrees. Maintain five thousand meters."

Minh acknowledged and tried to work out the intercept problem in his head. He was flying northwest toward the attacking force but offset to the north by some ten to twelve miles. At the appropriate time, the controller would turn him about 180 degrees to parallel their track, flying a very loose formation with them but well out of their sight and slightly in front. He and the controller knew with almost certainty that the enemy aircraft would be F-105s with a monopulse radar system capable of only the crudest airborne detection. The effective scan was only ten miles or so, and with his position established well to their side he had little fear of early detection. With the haze and clouds it would be only in the last few miles of the attack that he need fear visual identification by the Americans. The fighter CAP that normally accompanied the strike force must not be in a position to interfere or the controller would have told him.

When both he and Trach were properly positioned, they would be given turn instructions to place them in a quartering tail attack, so that either the 23mm guns or the heat-seeking missiles could be used. Minh knew that the controller would permit only a single attack by each aircraft before moving them out of the way of retaliatory danger. The reasoning was understandable but humiliating: They could ill afford to lose aircraft or trained pilots in a head-to-head duel with the American fighters. He wondered what it would be like to go against them pilot to pilot. How well would his training stand up to actual dogfighting? No doubt this method was effective, but it hardly tested a fighter pilot.

"Dragon One Five, this is Hanoi Sector. Turn left immediately to one three zero degrees. On roll-out, enemy aircraft will be at your five o'clock position, approximately twelve miles distance. Confirm instructions."

"Control, this is One Five. I understand." The game was beginning, and Minh's heart rate began to accelerate. Please, he prayed, just let me have one shot at them. He felt a tick in his right cheek under the mask. He raised his hand to rub the mask against it, then stared at the hand for a long moment. It was steady.

He rolled the aircraft onto its new vector. Just as he thought the controller was going to allow him his choice of weapons, the radio came alive again.

"Dragon One Five, this is Hanoi Sector. Attack with cannon only. Repeat. Attack with cannon only. Confirm."

"Hanoi Control, this is One Five. Understand. Guns only."

He was disappointed as he flipped the switches for the 23mm guns. He would have had a much better chance of a kill with the heat seekers. But he understood. Obviously Trach's position on the other side of the attackers would make him vulnerable to the heat-seeking missiles as well.

All right, then. A gun pass was less sure, but he had no desire to splash old Trach. A gun pass would do just fine, provided he could close enough before the Americans sighted him. But if they saw him, jettisoned their loads, and turned on him, he realized he could be in very deep trouble. The huge fighter-bombers could be formidable opponents without the drag of their ordnance. He adjusted the brightness of the gun-sight reticle and the mil setting, then turned his attention outside the cockpit. The final turn should be coming very soon.

"Dragon One Five, turn right immediately to a heading of two two zero degrees. Descend to forty-five hundred meters. Increase airspeed to military rated. Multiple targets are at your five o'clock position, twelve miles distance. They'll be crossing right to left. Plan on a one-two-zero-degree angle-off firing pass. On roll-out the targets will be at your twelve o'clock. Attempt to close as near as possible unless detected. After attack, turn right immediately to a heading of three four zero degrees and descend to one thousand meters using afterburner. You are cleared to fire!"

"Control, this is One Five. I understand the instructions and I am cleared to fire." Minh peered through the haze and occasional cloud trying to pick up the enemy aircraft. Under the mask he licked his lips; his mouth had gone dry. He found himself mumbling a half-forgotten Catholic prayer from his childhood.

He *couldn't* miss them. He knew he'd been placed on the proper course and altitude. Where the hell were they? This damned haze made it almost impossible to pick up anything more than a couple of miles away. What if they flew right by him undetected and unloaded their bombs as if he hadn't even been there? What would the controller say? What would his friends think when they heard about it? Big Fighter Pilot! God!

The explosion pinpointed their position when it rocked their formation with a near miss. Probably one of Trach's heat seekers. How could it have missed them? The aircraft stood out starkly against a lower cloud layer. The missiles were usually fired in pairs, so the other must have been a dud. Soviet technology! Shit!

There were four F-105s, flying in loose combat formation. As Minh closed rapidly, he was able to distinguish the bulging shapes of the bombs beneath the wings. The explosion in their midst hadn't made them jettison their ordnance. Perhaps they didn't realize that they were under attack by an aircraft and had mistakenly thought the missile was flak from one of the antiaircraft sites. Good! Maybe they'd be looking at the ground rather than for aircraft.

The company commander had told them that causing the attackers to jettison their bomb loads short of the targets was almost as effective as knocking one of them down. Neither Minh nor any of the other pilots believed that nonsense. Neither did the company commander, he suspected, for no awards were given for making a Yankee dump his bombs on a rice paddy.

Minh made a slight left turn and placed his lighted gun sight well ahead of the last aircraft in the flight. There would be time for only one good, long burst, because the F-105s were undoubtedly approaching 600 knots and would pull quickly away from him with their heading. As the targets grew larger he was astounded. The size of that brute! He had known it was a large aircraft, but this monster looked to be the size of a bomber.

As Minh approached the firing point, the F-105 quickly filled his gun sight. Minh carefully wrapped his finger around the trigger on the control stick, almost caressing it. As his finger tightened, he saw the American pilot turn his face toward him. He held down the trigger before the other pilot could react, and watched the tracers snake out toward the aircraft. His heart pounding, he watched them lick between the last two aircraft, then slide the length of the last ship. Parts of the fuselage and canopy were torn from the stricken ship as the cannon fire ripped it apart. The aircraft wobbled, then pitched nose high, one wing slowly pointing toward the ground.

Minh disregarded the controller's instructions and turned to follow the American aircraft, trying to keep them in sight in the haze. He had to know if he'd been successful. At that moment he would have cheerfully disregarded a direct order from Ho Chi Minh to break away. He saw the wounded aircraft slowly roll inverted and nose toward the earth as if a dead man's hand was on the control stick. The pilot didn't eject.

Suddenly, as if realizing for the first time that one of their number had been hurt, the remaining three enemy aircraft jettisoned their bomb loads and turned hard toward Minh. He had almost forgotten about them in the suspense of watching his first kill. He became aware of the controller's strident voice over the radio.

"Dragon One Five, this is Hanoi Sector Control. If you read me, turn immediately to a heading of three five zero degrees and descend to one thousand meters. Maximum speed. Do you understand?"

"Control, Dragon One Five. I understand, be advised that one F-105 has definitely been destroyed and the remaining three have jettisoned ordnance and need no longer be considered capable of ground attack. However, they do appear to be intent on attacking me. Instructions, please."

"One Five, this is Control. Thank you for your report," came the sarcastic voice in reply. "Perhaps if you'd have obeyed your attack and withdrawal instructions, you might not find yourself in this position. In the future, if Control tells you to turn *immediately* to a new heading, I suggest that you consider it to be an order rather than a recommendation. It might just save your life and one of our aircraft."

"Believe me, I do understand," Minh said anxiously, looking over his shoulder at the three aircraft bearing down on him. He knew these were the fastest operational fighters in the world, and with three of them there was little chance to use the better maneuverability of his aircraft.

"Uhh, Control, if you have any suggestion that might help, I'd be very appreciative. The other three aircraft are getting quite close to me."

"Oh, One Five? Have you decided that perhaps Control might be necessary after all?"

"Ah, yes, Control. I definitely see your point of view now."

"In that case," said the triumphant controller, "turn *immediately* to three zero zero degrees and descend to five hundred meters. That should put you well into the cloud deck and I doubt the Yankees will chase you into that. In fact, their returns indicate they're going back to the position of the kill."

Minh turned hard to the northwest and left the throttle in afterburner, deciding not to take the controller's word that the Americans had broken off the chase. They might be bombless, but they were certainly not toothless. Not with those Gatling guns. The g forces drove the blood from his brain, temporarily depriving him of his eyesight. He released some of the back pressure on the stick, allowing the nose to slip below the horizon. Looking back, he could see that the American warplanes had set up a protective CAP over their stricken comrade. There was a bright orange glow where it had hit the ground.

Minh carefully followed the controller's instructions and flew a box pattern well north of the city. The controller took obvious delight in telling him that he was being kept out of the way until the strike against the steel works south of the river was over. He had sufficient fuel for another intercept, but he knew it would not come that day. The controller had a point to make.

He wondered if he had killed the American pilot with his burst of gunfire. It seemed likely, considering the large chunks of canopy that had been blown away. The adrenaline was leaving his system and he felt weary. He glanced at his watch. Barely nine o'clock in the morning. He wondered what it must have felt like to suddenly turn as the American had done and see the gunfire coming at you. What would it be like in the final seconds knowing you were about to die?

Eventually, the controller relented and vectored him toward the airfield, his flying apparently over for the day. Just north of the city his canopy starred crazily as what had to be a small arms bullet crashed through the plexiglass. Violently, he jerked the aircraft around into a series of jinking turns to avoid the ground fire. Stupid, fucking farmers! Can't tell a friendly aircraft from a Yankee! Grimly, he explained what had happened to the controller, who seemed to find the incident amusing, and then accepted a new vector to the airfield.

The pressurized air of the cockpit whistled as it escaped through the small hole in the canopy. Minh stared at it and wondered again if his victim had time for rational thought before the 23mm slugs burst into the cockpit. He was probably dead before that. Minh decided he preferred to think of it that way. His natural ebullience returned as he flew into the traffic pattern. He had scored! Wait until he told Trach! Tonight he'd buy him all the beer he could hold.

Captain James Evelyn Broussard

Things were going well. There had been no ground or air
aborts, and the twelve aircraft of the strike force, eight
flak suppressors, and eight MiGCAP aircraft had taken
fuel without incident or delay along Green Anchor route.
Jim Broussard felt wide-awake and vibrant, as though he'd
had a good twelve hours of sleep rather than the solid
four he'd managed to squeeze in. The strike force was
on course and on time. It would have made the mission
planners proud. They might have known it was going to
go to hell in a hurry.

The attacking force had flown across the narrow southern
panhandle of North Vietnam, coasting out into the Gulf of
Tonkin, then turned abruptly north, staying well clear of
the coastline and out of range of the guns emplaced there.
Jim could hear the warbling of the Fansong search radar
in the earphones of his helmet, but the searchers had no
way of knowing when the attacking aircraft would turn
inland. They, therefore, had to keep their entire defense
force alerted. The targets were the POL sites south of Vinh,
in Route Package Three. The khaki-clad mission planners
in Saigon must consider this a daring plan, since Route
Package Three was normally bombed only by naval planes
from Yankee Station in the South China Sea. That it was
about to be struck by air force aircraft was a monument to
either interservice cooperation or divine guidance. To the

combat pilots it all seemed to be a large load of horseshit, since they distinguished the areas of North Vietnam as easy or bad, and it seemed to be pretty evenly split between the sea- and land-based forces.

Broussard was on his sixth mission into North Vietnam and was beginning to feel better about his ability to keep track of what was happening. But then he hadn't been back to Hanoi, either.

"Ring Tail, Ring Tail, this is Lead," came the voice of the mission commander, who also led the first flight. "Let's go strike frequency."

The flight check-in was crisp and clear and took only seconds. Jim watched the flak suppressors, then the first attack flight break hard toward the beach. At two-minute intervals other flights broke for the target, leaving Cadillac, next to the last of the strike force, still churning northward.

The radio discipline of the inbound flight had evaporated as the early flights in front of Cadillac approached the target. Jim could hear the voices of the pilots as the flak suppressors positioned their aircraft for the run against the heaviest ground fire. With no warning Donkey suddenly broke hard westward toward the fight. Jim fought to maintain his position, then looked directly ahead at the lush green landscape with the small fringe of white beach. Donkey took them down until they were skimming the water, literally having to lift over the small boats in their path. Fishermen, Jim supposed. Guess the people couldn't stop eating just because a war was going on.

Inland he could see a growing number of small, dirty, gray puffs put out by the radar-controlled guns protecting the fuel dump. More strident voices could be heard on the radio frequency now as the first flight of attack aircraft fought its way over the target. "SAMs airborne!" an excited voice called over the strike net. "Apple Flight, this is Apple Lead. Looks like they're heading for us! Jettison your ordnance and take evasive action."

From the North Vietnamese viewpoint, the principal advantage of the SAM was that it forced the attacking American planes to either jettison the bomb load or take evasive action that would put the aircraft in a lower environment, within easy range of the antiaircraft guns. At this point, the heavy warplane would be in the difficult position of being out of altitude and maybe airspeed, and the pilot was likely to be fresh out of ideas. The Viets moved the missile sites regularly, and it was difficult to see if one was occupied until it was too late to matter.

"Cadillac Flight, let's clean 'em up, green 'em up, and start the music." Donkey concluded his preattack liturgy by turning hard toward the target, Jim hanging onto his wing. The g forces caused his mask to sag on his face. He hurriedly flipped the nine switches that put the Thud into the attack configuration, then rechecked them and went about his business of trying to stay with Donkey during his acceleration to the run-in altitude.

Chaff corridors, strips of metal foil designed to confuse the Vietnamese radars, had been laid to mask the approach. It made little difference to Cadillac Flight, however, since any hope of surprise had been lost when the first aircraft appeared over the fuel dump.

"Apple Two is down!" an excited voice cried. The SAM had been aimed for Apple Flight. Maybe Two had tried to hang onto his leader rather than dueling the missile. Perhaps he hadn't been able to pick up the SAM visually. Maybe, hell! There could be a thousand reasons. Jim could feel the hair prickling on the back of his neck as Donkey sagged the flight down until they were kicking up a spray of water, now doing 600 knots and trying for more. The rapid, high-pitched squealing of the gun and SAM attack radars washed over him like a wave, blotting out rational thought. Directly ahead he could see a man-made cloud, the residue of the explosions left by the flak guns, forming an almost solid overcast above the target area. They lifted slightly as the aircraft flashed directly over a fishing boat. The beach was approaching rapidly.

"SAMs airborne!" God! he thought. Don't they ever run out of those things? They were close enough to see the individual strings of tracers arcing skyward, seemingly from every point on the ground. Airbursts from the larger weapons were huge.

"Peach Lead is down! Peach Lead is down!"

"This is Peach Three. Where did he go in?"

"This is Peach Two. There was negative chute. Negative chute. He just exploded!"

"OK, Peach Two, this is Peach Three. Take it easy. We've got you in sight. You're at our seven o'clock, low. Join up with us as soon as we're over water."

Christ, this was starting to sound expensive! Solid ground suddenly flashed beneath them, and Donkey was pulling the flight upward into a pop-up maneuver designed to gain altitude quickly. As they shoved their noses over at 13,000 feet and the negative g forces tried to lift him from his seat, Jim almost lost what little food was in his stomach. The seconds hung like minutes as they twisted toward the target, now partially hidden by billowing black clouds of smoke from the other strikes.

"SAM launch!" came the call again. The radar signals were deafening, and Peach Three was still trying to get what was left of his flight together over the sea. Somewhere a rescue beeper added to the cacophonous stew coming over Jim's headset. A Wild Weasel flight was attacking a SAM site, and the flak suppression aircraft from the other wing were calling gun locations to each other as they continued to attack the flak sites. Overhead, the F-4 MiGCAP pilots were discussing something, while Hillsboro, the airborne command post, continued to call missile launches minutes after the actual occurrence. It had become an audio nightmare.

Frantically, Jim swung his head back and forth trying to locate the latest missile launch, and from somewhere in the ether another emergency beeper began to wail—was it from one of the aircraft hit earlier or was someone else in trouble?

Cadillac Lead bored straight ahead to the target, now all but obscured by smoke. It rolled inverted and pointed its nose straight down into the smoke. Jim still hadn't located the airborne missile, but he followed Donkey into his dive, hoping the SAM would be absorbed by some other flight.

The POL tanks were burning at either end of the installation, and Cadillac Flight aimed toward its center. Jim picked one large metal tank for an aiming point and tried to forget about the hell that was going on around him. Concentration was difficult as the flak ranged and bumped them from their chosen targets with near misses. He squeezed the aileron and rudder to the right to put the sight directly on the tank. The aircraft bucked as it flew through a fresh flak cloud, momentarily causing him to lose sight of the ground. God, I'm dead! he thought, feeling close to panic as he emerged from the cloud and reacquired the tank. 8,000, 7,000! Pickle and pull. Afterburner! Donkey was already in a hard climbing turn to the left. Jim grunted with the forces of the g's, watching his vision go gray. His aircraft bucked with another near miss. More likely a near hit, he thought giddily. He rolled upright, forcing the throttle outboard, though he knew he was already in maximum afterburner and had all the power the engine could supply.

"Cadillac Lead, this is Cadillac Four. I'm hit!"

God! thought Jim, that was Bobby Packard flying Pritchard's wing.

"OK, Four. This is Cadillac Lead. Will it still fly?" Donkey's voice had to fight its way through the radio chatter, now a little quieter with someone new in trouble, but annoying nevertheless.

"It's still flying, but I've got problems with the controls. It's just not responding."

"Can you get to the water, Bobby?"

"Negative. The spoilers and ailerons don't answer, and the elevators are porpoising me all over the place. I'm keeping it upright with the rudders and trim, but they're kicking like hell. I think I can keep it going in the direction I'm headed."

"You're losing fuel, too, Bob," Pritchard broke in, having returned after the distress call by his wingman. "Lead," he continued, "we're heading almost due west from the target area."

"I think I'd better get outta this thing!" Packard said, his voice beginning to sound a little shrill.

"Now, let's not rush off into the heat of the day," Donkey said soothingly. "You're still flying and we're coming to join up, so let's don't do anything hastylike just yet. Where are you, Cadillac Three?"

"About ten west of the smoke," Pritchard answered, "descending through nine thousand feet."

"OK, we're coming your way."

Donkey put the first element into a tight, gut-wrenching turn to the west, trying to stay south of the target area. Even so, the heavy guns tried to track them. The flak was uncomfortably close to their altitude. Broussard could feel his sphincter tighten as the orange balls of 37- and 57mm shells bracketed his aircraft. And let's not forget, he thought grimly, old Nguyen, the farmer, firing his rifle blindly overhead and hoping someone would run into it, thereby gaining his merit badge or whatever it was that Uncle Ho gave for that sort of thing. He hunched his shoulders under the restraining straps, as if that would make him less a target.

Cadillac Four was easy to spot. The plume of fuel spewing from either a ruptured tank or fuel line showed in good contrast to the verdant jungle below him. If that wasn't enough to catch the eye, then the spectacular porpoising of the aircraft surely did. The nose of the stricken Thud would rise suddenly and the aircraft would gain several thousand feet, then lurch and fall into a sickening stall, dropping all the altitude gained and more before it regained flying speed, only to repeat the cycle. Every cycle brought the aircraft closer to the threatening jungle below. Pritchard had tried to stay with his wingman but gave it up as a bad job; he moved out and stabilized some fifty yards away.

Donkey brought the first element of Cadillac Flight toward them in full burner until they were less than a mile behind; then he reduced power, calling a single command over the radio: "Speed brakes!" It caught Broussard unprepared. He almost overflew his leader before he could hit the switch to extend the clover-leaf metal sections that made up the last three feet of the fuselage and tail pipe. The speed brakes allowed the pilots to slow their aircraft swiftly.

The other element was proceeding forward very slowly. Packard was attempting to keep his aircraft airborne and upright through use of the throttle and electric trim switch on his control stick.

Donkey called: "Bobby, how's your hydraulic pressure?"

"I've got no hydraulic pressure," answered Cadillac Four at the apogee of a porpoise.

"Do you mean both primary and secondary are gone?"

"That's right, as well as the utility pressure."

That does it, thought Jim. He's out of everything. There were three hydraulic systems, redundant in part, but with colocated lines so that one piece of shrapnel could take out all of them. Most systems of the Thud worked by hydraulics. Hell, Packard couldn't even go into burner. Not that it much mattered, for the large fuel plume promised that soon he wouldn't have power to do anything. Thank God the ejection system worked independently of everything else.

"Bobby, can you go to flight manual?" asked Donkey. He needed to separate his stricken flight member from the background noise of the remainder of the force, who were still having their own problems. Flight manual was a discrete radio frequency, which could be used by Cadillac Flight alone.

"Rog. I'll try."

"OK, Cadillac Flight, let's go flight manual." They checked in after the frequency change, in sequence, as if it were a normal mission.

As Jim watched the lurching aircraft, he was suddenly aware that they had left the ground fire behind them. The intensity of his attention had been such that the exploding balls of death had simply taken on a dreamlike quality that had no bearing on their present tragic circumstances. It was obvious now that the stricken F-105 would not make the safety of the Thailand border. Or even Laos. The oscillations were becoming worse and precious little fuel could remain. Cadillac Four was going to come to roost soon, one way or another. A fact not to be ignored was that at any moment the spilling jet fuel might ignite and make him a large torch. Cadillac Four had obviously been giving some thought to the same scenario.

"Donkey, I'm getting out of this thing. I've got almost no control left and fuel is reading zero pounds!" Bob's voice was tense, like a spring that had been overwound. He knows he's had it, thought Jim. Even if he could make it to a tanker, there's absolutely no way he could take on fuel with those control problems. Probably the tanker wouldn't even let him try. And without additional fuel he couldn't possibly get to safe countryside before ejecting.

"Now, Bobby, let's don't be in too much of a hurry. You're not on fire and you've still got some altitude. Let's see if we can't get a little closer to the border, or at least away from this place, before we do anything drastic. I'm leaving frequency for one to call Crown and see about getting a SAR cranked up. Try not to do anything until I get back with you, OK?"

"OK, but hurry," Bob answered.

Jim suspected that the reason Donkey himself made the call to the airborne command post, rather than having him or Pritchard do it, was so Bob couldn't talk to him for a few minutes. Donkey knew his troops well enough to know that Bob wouldn't eject, unless he simply had no choice, without telling him of the decision. Donkey was doing his best to delay the ejection until they had reached an area more suitable for rescue. The heavily populated area of the coastal plain was not the best choice.

Jim could see the hazy outline of the Annam Cordillera in the distance. He glanced back to Donkey in time to see him wave toward the other element, then put his head down into the cockpit, switching radio channels for the call to Crown. Jim nudged his aircraft toward the struggling fighter. Pritchard was stabilized off the right wing as Jim slowly crept into position on the left, giving himself plenty of room to maneuver away from the wildly pitching and oscillating aircraft. In close, he could see that the damage and control problems were even more severe than he had first thought. He could see the many gaping holes in the fuselage and wing root. But Bob must have had a little rudder control, because he was keeping the aircraft approximately on a heading line to the west.

"I think we'd better move out a little," radioed Pritchard.

He's right, thought Jim. If that fuel ignites it could take out all three of us. He wondered how that transmission had made Bob Packard feel. Pritchard could be a cold son of a bitch. Still, Jim took the advice and moved his aircraft out to a point where he figured an explosion wouldn't affect him.

"Cadillac Four, this is Lead back with you. Can you go Guard channel, Bobby?"

"Yeah, I can do that," Bob replied, the strain of trying to keep the heavy fighter in the air showing in his voice.

Broussard glanced at his altimeter. The flight was down to 6,000 feet. They'd never be able to clear the range of mountains in front of them.

"OK, Cadillac Four," said Donkey on Guard channel, the emergency frequency monitored by all aircraft and search teams. "We're almost to the railroad, and when we're by it we'll be coming into some more-sparsely populated areas."

He's way ahead of me, Jim thought. I'd forgotten about the railroad. There would be people and guns along a rail line. He quickly pulled out his map from under his leg and flipped it over to show the proper section of North Vietnam. The railroad was the major trunk line between Hanoi in the north and the DMZ in the south. Of course it would be shoulder to shoulder with people. If Bobby was to have a chance at rescue, they would have to get beyond it.

"The Sandies," Donkey continued, "are launching and busting ass toward us, so I want you to make sure that you're strapped in really tight. Pull your chute straps until they hurt. And make sure that everything is stowed. OK?"

"Rog."

"You're doing real good, Bobby. If you can, after everything is stowed, make sure that your baby bottles of water are in your g-suit pocket and it's zipped up. Unplug all your connectors except for the radio. OK, we're coming up on the rail line now. We'll make sure we've got lots of distance away from it before you go."

Bob didn't answer. Flak began probing the flight from several sites positioned along the rail line. Some of the bursts were very close, but Cadillac Four was pitching so badly that at least his aircraft was relatively safe from the gunners aiming at them. It would have taken an uncanny eye to track his movements. They probably think he's practicing some new type of Yankee evasive maneuver, thought Jim, staring at the flak burst, still feeling disconnected from the situation.

He returned his attention to the failing jet, no longer able to look with equanimity at the ground fire. The pitch-ups were clearly worsening; soon there would be no room to recover when the aircraft stalled to a nose-low attitude. Donkey was cutting it close.

Then the flak was gone and they had passed the populated farming area along the railroad tracks. They were overflying the dark green foothills leading to the mountain range bordering North Vietnam and Laos. Jim thought they'd done well—or rather Bobby and Donkey had done well—to get this far from the target.

"Are you about ready, Bobby?" Donkey asked quietly over the radio.

"As ready as I'll ever get, I guess." His voice was still tight but seemed more under control now that a course of action had been decided. "Besides, I can't have more than a minute or so of fuel left. I really don't know what this hog is running on."

"All right, buddy. Whenever you're ready. We'll CAP you till the Sandies get here. Get on your survival radio and give us a status report just as soon as you can. And turn off the emergency beeper on your chute right away. We'll know where you are, and there's no sense in letting the rest of the world in on it. We'll have the beer cold for you when they bring your sorry ass back to Thailand. Good luck, boy!"

"Thanks. See ya, guys. I'm outta here!"

Jim watched the ejection seat fire high above the aircraft as it reached the top of what was to be its last climb. There was a good chute and the emergency beacon immediately began to sob. Bob must have been ready, for it was silenced after only a few seconds. Without the pilot's thumb on the trim button, the stricken F-105 never recovered from its last stall. It plowed straight ahead into the ground, falling off on one wing just before impact.

They circled nose to tail, close as they dared to the dangling stick figure hanging beneath the chute. There were tense moments as the figure did not respond but hung motionless beneath the nylon. Then, as if clearing his head of the vapor lock caused by the ejection, Bob waved at the circling aircraft.

Jim watched him land like a bundle of wet newspapers, lie there for long moments to think it over, then rise to gather the now-limp parachute and scamper for the wood line. Sooner than Jim expected, Bobby's voice came over the emergency channel, sounding harsh, as though he were holding the small radio too close to his mouth. His breathing was ragged and rapid.

"Cadillac Lead, this is Four." Although he was on the ground, Bob still considered himself a member of the flight and continued using his regular call sign. "I'm OK and hiding in some bushes just inside the tree line north of that opening where I landed. How do you read?"

"We've got you five square, Cadillac Four." Donkey let Bob know immediately that he was still an integral member of the flight. "I'm sending Two and Three out to Green Anchor for a quick refueling, but I'll be here until they get back. Hang in there, kid, and let me know if your situation changes in any way. Cadillac Three, you take Two and shag ass for a tanker. Make it as quick as you can,'cause I'm not too fat on fuel myself. I'm going to hang around here to make sure old Bobby doesn't get bored. I've even got a few jokes I don't think he's heard, and now I've got him as a captive audience."

"Rog, Lead. Come on, Two. Let's move out. Switch to refueling frequency."

Jim eased his throttle forward and switched to the common tanker frequency, slid onto Pritchard's left wing, and listened while he called the tanker.

"Green tanker, this is Cadillac Three. Emergency." The response was immediate.

"Cadillac Three, this is Green Two Zero. May we be of assistance?"

"Rog, Two Zero. We're two Thuds inbound to the refueling track. About fifteen minutes out. We have one bird from the flight down, which Cadillac Lead is capping. We need a quick transfer so we can get back in and let him come out before we have two of them down back there. Can you help?"

"You bet! Transmit with a short count for a DF steer." Broussard listened as Pritchard counted slowly to five, then back to one again.

"Cadillac Three, this is Green Two Zero. Turn right two five degrees. We're leaving orbit at this time and proceeding in your direction."

"Thanks, Green Two Zero. We sure do appreciate it."

It took a moment for the gears in Jim's mind to shift sufficiently to realize the impact of the tanker's transmission. He was leaving his orbital position over the safety of Thailand and was now flying his airliner-sized aircraft over the hostile countryside of Laos to save them a few precious minutes of flying time. Jim had never cared for SAC, the parent unit of the tanker. The crew members of the bombers and tankers had always seemed middle-aged and stuffy, given more to mowing the lawn than engaging in the pursuits in which most of the younger air force pilots delighted. But these guys were hanging it all out, directly disobeying the standing SAC order stating that their unarmed aircraft would not overfly hostile territory, even in emergencies. The tanker speed would be less than half that of the Thuds, but it could still cut the time needed to effect the rendezvous by nearly half.

After long minutes, they heard the voice of the tanker pilot: "Cadillac, if you'll start a standard rate turn to the left, I think you'll be in pretty close to the observation position when you roll out."

Neither Pritchard nor Broussard had picked up the tanker until they were almost halfway through their reversing turn. Then, the sun reflected from the shiny fuselage as the KC-135 popped out from behind a shallow cloud deck. The Cadillac element moved quickly into refueling position, first Pritchard, then Broussard. Time was too critical to worry about the niceties of who had the least fuel. Jim was surprised that after Pritchard's hookup the large tanker didn't start a turn back toward their assigned refueling track but instead plowed straight ahead toward North Vietnam and their downed flight mate and Donkey.

"Does this heading look about right to you, Cadillac Three?" asked the tanker pilot.

"About ten degrees left would be even better," responded Pritchard.

"You've got it."

The strange procession continued eastward across the Laotian panhandle. Each fighter took only half loads and then disconnected, so as to hustle back toward the crash site. Jim knew that Donkey must be getting very low on fuel at this point, since at low level the large Pratt & Whitney engine gulped it with a voracious appetite. He glanced over his shoulder and was amazed to see the distant shape of the unarmed tanker still doggedly lumbering in their wake toward the North Vietnamese border. I'd like to think I had the balls to do that, he thought. But he wasn't sure he did.

"Cadillac Two, this is Three. Let's you and me and anybody else who's interested go back to Guard channel." So Pritchard had spotted their ponderous escort as well, but he didn't want to compromise him anymore than necessary, hoping that anonymity would serve as some measure of protection if he were caught in prohibited country.

Ahead, Jim could just make out the smoke from Bob Packard's still-smoldering aircraft. And so could every

NVA in the area, he thought. Perhaps another five minutes. Pritchard called Donkey.

"Cadillac Lead, this is Three. We've got you in sight and a big friend is right behind us. What's the story?"

"Howdy, Three. Bob says he can hear people now but hasn't been able to spot them. He thinks they're at least half a mile or so away. The Sandies and Jolly Green are due in here in about fifteen. What's this about somebody following you?"

"Don't know. Guess he just got lost or something. Call sign is Something or Other Two Zero if you'd like to talk to him."

Donkey chuckled over the radio as he called the tanker. "Well, Something or Other Two Zero, this is Cadillac Lead. Understand you're lost over here across the fence."

"I reckon, Cadillac Lead. I'm having a little trouble following those two boys of yours, since they're just a skosh faster than we are. But I'd guess that we're about ten miles behind 'em, and if you'd be so kind as to come on over and join up on us, we'd like to get some fuel transferred and get the hell back where we belong. I've already got the crew writing out statements for our court-martial in case SAC headquarters ever finds out about this."

"Well, if you need a character witness, just have them give Cadillac Flight a call," said Pritchard.

"Jesus! That's all we need to really seal our fate, putting a bunch of perverted fighter pukes on the stand as character witnesses."

"Well, if that won't work," said Donkey, "we'll be glad to take all of you into the Tactical Air Command. I've got you in sight now, Green Two Zero, and not a moment too soon. I'm down to seven hundred pounds so I'll be moving straight in."

Jim calculated that meant Donkey had only five to six minutes of flying time before he, too, had to punch out. If the tanker hadn't been following them, well . . . Moments passed, then he heard: "Fuel is transferring and we're starting our turn to the west." The KC-135 was heading back to his orbit and possibly trouble for the aircraft commander should the radar controllers in Crown decide to press the issue. The bunch of them should be getting medals for this,

Jim thought, but they'll probably be lucky to get out with a stiff ass-chewing.

Broussard and Pritchard continued to circle the crash site, trying to stay away from Bob but still include his position within their orbit, hoping to not give him away. When Donkey returned with topped tanks, Broussard and Pritchard chased down the tanker and replenished their fuel once more. Afterward, they returned to the orbit.

As they pulled into trail position behind Donkey, Jim heard the A-1 Sandy flight check in. Now that they were on station, their leader would control the rescue attempt from his slow-moving Korean War–vintage prop plane. The large single-engine aircraft could haul an incredible amount of ordnance, as well as deliver it with precision. In addition, should it become necessary, the plane could loiter for hours and provide protection from flak sites that might try to take out the Jolly Green Giant rescue helicopters.

Donkey raised the Thud orbit to give the Sandies room to maneuver, but he remained close enough to provide suppressive fire in the event the A-1s bit off more than they could chew. Cadillac had no bombs, but there remained the full load of 20mm ammo for the internal Vulcan cannon, an awesome weapon.

"Sandy Lead, this is Cadillac Four," Bob's hoarse whisper came over the radio. "I think they must know where I am, because the voices are much louder and they sound as if they're coming directly at me."

"Roger, Four. This is Sandy Lead. Do you think you could use your compass to give me a bearing to them from your position? We're unable to pick them up visually. If you can do that, maybe we can discourage them."

"Well, I hear voices almost due west through northwest, less than half a mile I'd say, because they're not yelling that loud and I can still pick out their words pretty well. I'm right at the edge of the tree line, about fifteen meters from a real tall tree along the edge of the opening."

There's obviously a very large difference in our perspectives, thought Jim. At his orbiting altitude he could see at least a thousand trees that would have to be considered "real tall." From Bob's position on the ground, however, there was little doubt that one stood out from the others within his limited visual field.

"Four, this is Sandy Lead. Rog. We've got a good fix on you and we're going to start working the gomers now. Keep your head down and let me know if the ordnance sounds as if it's in the right spot or if it's coming too close to you."

Perched above, Cadillac Flight watched the A-1 pilots pick their targets and roll inverted, with the large dive brakes flared to prevent excessive speed. Their reputation for accurate bombing was legendary. With the steep dive angle they used, even if they were off a few degrees it had little effect on the placement of the bomb. More importantly, the Sandy pilots had been trained to deliver their weapons within close proximity to friendly troops. Their 250-pound antipersonnel bombs were designed for just such purposes as rescue.

The ground gunners began to make themselves known as the attack progressed and there was no longer any point in trying to keep their presence a secret. Most of the ground fire seemed to be 12.7mm guns, which were directing streams of greenish tracers toward the working Sandies. The smaller tracers of the AK-47 assault rifles of the NVA infantry joined the fight. Jim hoped they didn't have anything down there larger than the highly mobile 12.7mm guns. After all, it was unlikely they'd have large guns just sitting there in the jungle.

The intensity of the fire increased. My God, thought Jim as he watched the A-1s being savaged below them, how could so many of those bullets miss? Only one out of five was a tracer round, yet even the visible ones seemed to weave an impenetrable web through which nothing could fly unscathed. Apparently he was correct. The doughty Sandies were eventually driven away, but only after each had taken numerous hits.

"Cadillac Lead, this is Sandy Lead. We have to get some of that stuff suppressed if we're going to have a chance in hell of effecting a helicopter pickup. The Jolly Greens wouldn't have a prayer down there right now."

At that moment, the airborne rescue command post broke into the transmission. "Sandy Lead, this is Crown. Suggest you utilize Cadillac Flight's Vulcan guns to help the flak suppression."

"Well, thank you, Crown," Sandy Lead said dryly. "That's just about what I was going to suggest before you felt obliged to tell me how to run the operation. Now, unless you have anything else of equal importance, I'd like to get back to my job."

There was silence from Crown, and the Sandy leader continued: "Now then, Cadillac Lead. As I was saying, it looks like the heaviest concentration is in the tree line of that next little clearing north of Cadillac Four. If you fast movers could work that area to hold 'em back, old Sandy Two and I will try to clear a path through here for the chopper. Think you could help out if—"

"Sandy Lead, this is Crown. Be advised that Sandy Three and Four are inbound to your area escorting Jolly Green Two. ETA approximately twenty-five minutes. Time now 1245 Hotel. Crown, out."

"Crown, this is Sandy Lead. Now, that's mighty interesting, but as it happens I already knew it because I'd been talking to them on my other radio. And I don't give a shit what time it is. Now get off and *stay* off the fucking frequency unless you've got something sensible to add to the conversation."

There was silence from Crown. Sandy Lead continued his talk with Donkey. "As I was saying, Cadillac Lead, if you people can work the tree lines in that north clearing, we two will try to blow a hole through for the Jollies. Any problem with that?"

"Nope," answered Donkey. "You heard the man, Cadillac Flight. Let's arm up the guns and take position."

Jim eased back his throttle to give himself a little more space behind the lead ship, widening his pattern for the gun run. He flipped the gun arming switches and then the master arm, pointing his index finger out stiffly, away from the trigger on the front of the control stick handle. It would not only be embarrassing if he allowed his finger to curl normally around the stick, where he might inadvertently squeeze the trigger, but it just might also piss off Donkey to see 20mm rounds zipping by his cockpit. He concentrated on keeping him and the target in sight.

He watched as Donkey rolled into a more shallow dive than he had become accustomed to when they dive-bombed. He had almost forgotten until then that Donkey was not a shake and bake instant fighter pilot, as so many of them were, but one of the old hands who had flown almost every jet fighter TAC had ever acquired. Many of the Thud pilots had very little training in close air support, but it was soon apparent that he was watching a pilot who did.

Donkey made a turning dive toward the target, waiting until the last moment to set the Thud upright, which complicated the gunners' tracking problems. A well-aimed, two-second burst of 20mm cannon fire chewed up the tree line. Then, he was off hard left in a jinking, steep, climbing turn. Streams of green tracers followed him. Most of them seemed to fall well behind the twisting aircraft.

Jim came in next. He tried to emulate the lead ship but rolled out with his nose pointed at the target much sooner than Donkey had. He needed the extra seconds to wrestle with the aircraft, trying to find the proper parameters for the strafe. Until that moment, his attacks had always begun at 12,000 to 13,000 feet, flying about as fast as the bird would go without resorting to afterburner. The pullouts from their dive-bomb runs had been initiated at 6,500 feet or so. Now he was trying to shoot from a 400-knot, twenty-degree dive at 1,500 feet. It gave him a completely different sight picture.

The gun-sight pipper settled on the tree line just north of the dust still rising from Donkey's attack. It looked as good a place as any and he gently squeezed the trigger, counting one thousand and one, one thousand and two. Then he released the trigger. He tried to ignore the ground fire; it was hard to do.

There was, he realized, something satisfying about firing guns. A fighter pilot doesn't normally get to see the explosion of his bombs and rockets, because he is involved in pulling off the target and trying not to be caught in his own blast. During a normal dive-bombing run, the only sensation a pilot feels as he thumbs the bombs is the massive weight leave the aircraft; he then immediately begins the gut-wrenching pull on the stick, trying for the safety of higher altitude. Jim now found the effects of the gun hypnotic. The stick vibrated, and he could hear the noise of the rapid-firing Vulcan through the confines of his crash helmet. There was also the instant gratification of watching the exploding 20mm slugs tearing up everything in their path. Even small trees burst apart in the onslaught and flew into the air. It was like watching a madman with a giant scythe tearing through the jungle foliage.

A string of tracers laced in front of him as he released the trigger to begin a jinking left turn off target. Before he could react to them, the aircraft was through the deadly green stream. It looked like a good in-trail formation by a gaggle of fireflies. His left foot was suddenly pushed violently from the rudder pedal, and something clawed at his leg. Hell of a time to be getting a cramp, he thought, his hands automatically adjusting the aircraft into the pattern with little conscious thought. He watched Pritchard complete his run before investigating the cramp.

His toes in the left flying boot seemed to be sweating a great deal. He wriggled them about in the confines of the boot and found it squishy, as though he'd been barefoot in the barnyard and had stepped in something unpleasant. He rolled onto the base leg, the perch from where he would begin another attack, and tried to peer down into the confines of the cockpit. It was virtually impossible, since he could move only his head, his body cinched tightly to the seat at the shoulders and waist by the restraining straps. In any event his legs were stretched out in front of him under the instrument panel like a racing car driver and were out of sight for all practical purposes. There was something definitely wrong, though.

Then he saw the dark brown stain seeping through the canvas shell of his g suit. His left thigh was beginning to tingle and feel as though it had been pinched. My God! he thought, I've been shot! That's blood! Stupid. What had he been expecting—maple syrup? His head was spinning. He'd have to tell Donkey immediately. No. Wait until he pulls out of this firing pass and then tell him.

Jim's mind was on his wound but his hands and feet obeyed instinctively the memory of 3,000 hours of flight time, continuing to fly the aircraft in the gunnery pattern. Unconsciously they placed the aircraft into the proper dive and adjusted the plane's parameters for the strafe pass. His thumb was reaching for the radio mike button as he realized that he was once again in a twenty-degree dive and aiming the guns. He'd wait until he went through on this pass; then he'd tell Donkey.

The tracers no longer looked like fireflies to Jim. They were ugly hornets, and he physically flinched away as they sought him. He bottomed from the dive at 1,000 feet, pulling hard on the control stick and momentarily blacking out. The inflation of the g suit was painful as it squeezed his thigh.

Once more on the downwind leg, he tried to examine the wound, and inadvertently extended the pattern as he fumbled with the g suit. When he looked up for the target, it was almost out of sight.

"Goddamnit, Cadillac Two! Pull your head outta your ass and close it up," Donkey called.

To hell with it, Jim thought. He shoved violently on the stick, preparing for another pass. He couldn't be hurt too badly. There was feeling in the foot and more in the thigh. The blood had probably just seeped into the boot. Besides, he was prepared to bleed to death rather than make a fool of himself by announcing that he was wounded and having it turn out to be a minor scratch. He found a fresh piece of woods to blow away, but before he could squeeze the trigger, Bob Packard called over the emergency radio.

"Oh, crap! Donkey, it looks like they're here." His voice was flat and subdued. "Sorry, guys. Nice try. I'm going to try and destroy the radio and beeper now. Good luck. This is Cadillac Four. Out."

The remaining F-105s and a pair of A-1s circled helplessly over the downed pilot. No one was paying a great deal of attention to the heavier gunfire being flung at them. Each pilot knew that further attacks by them would only put Bob Packard in more jeopardy. It wasn't clear whether he had actually been able to destroy his radio, but Donkey said it for them all: "Good luck, kid!"

It became quickly apparent that no miracle would occur this day, and the A-1 flight departed, taking the Jolly Green Giant helicopter with them. It had been lurking on the periphery of the battle area, away from the shooting.

"Sandy Lead, this is Cadillac Lead. Thanks for your effort."

"Rog, Cadillac Lead. This was a tough one to lose. You folks take care, and if you're ever at NKP, give us a call. So long."

Jim watched the Sandies depart, then responded to Donkey's signal and rejoined on his left wing as Pritchard slid smoothly onto his right. Donkey led the three-ship formation in one last circuit, then set course for the tanker rendezvous. Jim still couldn't believe that they were really leaving Bobby Packard on the ground. And, he hadn't yet found the opportunity to tell his flight leader about his leg. Actually, he'd almost forgotten about it in the anxiety over Bob's capture.

He hunkered down as far as he could, and by loosening his shoulder straps he could see that blood had overflowed from the boot onto the floor of the cockpit. The wound itself seemed to have self-sealed. The tight-fitting g suit may have been just what was needed to help stop the blood flow. The pain was no worse than a lot of minor cuts he'd had, and, anyway, how could he answer Donkey's obvious question if he should report it to him now: How bad was it? He had no idea. Besides, what could anyone do about it? There was no one to take over and refuel and land the plane for him. Maybe he could let Donkey know after they'd hit the tanker and he'd gotten his fuel.

The fuel transfer went smoothly, perhaps due to all the practice he'd had that day. The blood on the g suit had dried and was now getting crusty. The leg was starting to ache like hell; still he had no difficulty moving it during fuel transfer. Hell, he thought, I might as well wait until we're back on the ground. It can't make any difference now and it's only some forty-odd minutes back to the field.

It was less than that, for Donkey kept the aircraft at full throttle until the concrete runways were in sight. They made the usual stop in the de-arming area, then taxied to the squadron area to be marshaled into their parking slots. Jim noticed as they taxied that the ground personnel had become still except for those involved in the actual recovery of the aircraft. They were well aware that a three-ship formation could only mean that one was missing. The men watched intently, hands shading their eyes from the bright sun, trying to determine which aircraft it was.

Jim opened the canopy as the engine and gyros spooled down, removed his helmet, and punched the stopwatch on the panel. They had been airborne for more than five hours. Christ! No wonder he felt stiff and sore, leg notwithstanding. The crew chief moved the metal ladder to the side of the cockpit so Jim could crawl down. He made no move to get out of the cockpit and the young sergeant called up to him.

"Who didn't make it back, Captain Broussard?"

"Lieutenant Packard," he answered. The sergeant stared at him, not wanting to ask the next question. "Captured," Jim continued. "I don't think he was hurt."

The sergeant shook his head and looked toward the revetment where Packard's aircraft was usually parked. There, the ground crew of the missing aircraft wandered around the empty space, looking at everything except each other. One of the bare-chested men viciously kicked the wall of the revetment.

Broussard still hadn't made a move to get out of the cockpit. The sergeant was starting up the ladder to help him when one of his assistants touched his arm, pointing beneath the aircraft. The sergeant stepped quickly to the ground and peered intently at the belly of the aircraft, then turned and scampered up the ladder. At the edge of the cockpit he looked into Broussard's face, now wrinkled like a prune after being bound for more than five hours by the oxygen mask. The sergeant had a tight grin on his face.

"Jesus, Captain! Did you know that you took a hit?"

Jim leaned over the edge of the cockpit and looked down into the side of the fuselage, then back at the crew chief. "Well, uh, I guess actually I did, Sarge. Does it look bad?"

"Shit, yes, it looks bad! There are a couple of holes down there I could put my fist through. You're just damned lucky they didn't come all the way into the cockpit."

"Uh, actually, I think some did. In fact, I think I got myself a little bit wounded or something." Oh, great! Jim thought. Why don't you do your Mortimer Snerd act and let everyone see your stupid man imitation. He felt acutely embarrassed, though he didn't know why. It wasn't as if he'd done anything wrong. Maybe he was supposed to feel heroic. All he could think of was that his bladder was full to the bursting point.

He could feel himself start to blush as the sergeant lifted his inquiring eyes from his precious airplane and quickly pulled himself the rest of the way up the ladder. He looked closely into Jim's face, as though expecting to see a large gaping hole.

"I really don't think it's that bad," Jim stammered as he pointed toward the dark stain on the left leg of his g suit. In truth, it really didn't look that bad, with the blood dried now to nothing more than a smear on the floor of the cockpit.

The sergeant wasn't having any of *that*, however. *His* pilot and airplane were wounded and, by God, everybody was going to know about it. He turned and bellowed at the top of his lungs to one of his mechanical henchmen: "This pilot is wounded! Get an ambulance out here right now!"

Jim tried to slink down in the cockpit to avoid the stares of all the line personnel within earshot, who now began to move toward them. The assistant on the ground left little vortices of dust as he went from a standing start to full speed, sprinting toward the telephone in the line shack.

Jim's full bladder finally won over his pride, and he allowed the sergeant to assist him from the cockpit. He felt doubly foolish about the attention he was getting when he considered what Bobby Packard was probably going through at this moment. With both feet firmly on the ground, he turned to hobble behind the aircraft to relieve himself when he heard Donkey calling. He and Pritchard were jogging toward him as well as they could under the weight of their flight gear. They had been alerted by the shouts of the crew chief. Donkey was hobbling as if he had cramps in his legs. Crap, thought Jim, his legs probably hurt worse than mine.

"What's wrong, kid," Donkey puffed as he pulled up with Pritchard in his wake, probably positioned there to assist in the event that Donkey passed out from all the unaccustomed exercise. Donkey took a quick look at the stains on the leg and boot and began reaching for the zippers of the g suit.

"Uh, Donkey," Jim said, trying to brush away the hands. "Before we do anything I've really got to take a leak."

Donkey straightened. "So, do it, and then let's get that pair of high-speed jeans off you."

Jim waded through the crowd that had formed around them and limped to the rear of the aircraft. Unzipping the front of his flight suit, he felt eyes upon him and turned to find that the crowd, including Donkey and Pritchard, had followed and were watching. Jim's bladder froze. He looked away and thought of something else, trying to trick the bladder into believing they were alone. His bladder knew better. Minutes passed with no result but the crowd wasn't restive. They appeared to be fascinated. Pritchard, he noticed, had a half smile on his face, as if this were a story to be relished tonight at the bar.

Jim pursed his lips and whistled a tuneless little song, gazing up at a pair of hawks soaring overhead. Oh, for God's sake! This was getting ridiculous. He peered coyly over his shoulder and found that his crowd, rather than diminishing, had grown by a substantial number. That did it! He turned to shriek at them just as his bladder relaxed, spraying a thick, yellow stream in their direction. The crowd flinched backward, then began to applaud. Jim couldn't have stopped on direct orders from the president.

He zipped, his face bright red, as Donkey stepped up and smiled. Without a word, he bent forward and loosened the left leg of the g suit. There was a small jagged tear in the fabric of the flight suit, the edges of which had dried to the wound. Donkey immediately ripped the leg of the flight suit to the bottom hem, exposing the leg. A small wave of nausea grew in Jim's belly as he looked at the blood-encrusted gash some five inches long, running vertically up his leg. He'd always hated the sight of his own blood. More than that, he realized how close he'd been to death. Holes in the aircraft were one thing. Holes in his body were something else.

Donkey upended a baby bottle of water on the gash and scrubbed away none too gently with a grimy handkerchief. Cleansed, the wound didn't look that serious, even to Jim. Just an irregular tear in the flesh of the thigh, the edges of the wound now puckered and swollen looking. As he tried to hobble a step forward, new blood began to ooze, following the path toward his boot.

Donkey straightened from his crouch and looked at Pritchard: "Go with him to the hospital," he said. "I'll take care of the debriefing and see him over there later."

Pritchard looked at Donkey. "What can I do at the hospital? They probably won't even let me in."

"Just go, Andy. We've lost a good man today. And damned if I'm going to let a member of Cadillac Flight hobble into the hospital by himself like nobody cares."

The ambulance made a Hollywood production of arriving at the flight line, doubtlessly expecting something a little more dramatic than the picture presented by Jim. Nevertheless, he crawled into the back, still wearing his flight gear, feeling more embarrassed than hurt. Pritchard followed him in. The ambulance crew was sensitive enough not to turn on the siren on the way to the hospital.

First Lieutenant
Katherine Elaine Johnson

Kate was bored. She had imagined many things about being in a combat zone, but boredom was not one of them. Now that she thought about it, she'd been wrong on several other significant counts. The exotic east was about as exotic as Matamoros, Mexico, which was less than a score of miles from where she had grown up on the coastal plains of Texas. There were in fact, many similarities between the two areas. The high temperatures and humidity were much the same, and though she knew that primary, triple-canopy jungle existed a short distance away, there was a definite paucity of other than scrub trees around the air base. The larger trees, she had been told, had long since vanished under the charcoal makers' axes. All the place needed to make it look like the Rio Grande valley were some larger farms and citrus groves.

Then there was the red dust as thick as that found on a south Texas dirt road after a drought. She gazed out of the small window at the weeds growing rampantly alongside the walkway. Tiny Thai women periodically tried to hack them to a more manageable height in an attempt to deny the cobras and kraits this part of their ancestral homeland. Several airmen had already been rushed to the hospital for treatment after being careless about where they put their hands and feet. But even that didn't seem unusual to Kate. More times than she could remember, she'd seen migrant and local farm workers brought into the emergency room after an encounter with a coral or rattlesnake in the vegetable and cotton fields of the valley.

Kate wasn't exactly sure what she had expected of Takhli, Thailand, her first permanent duty station, but she knew it was not the life she was presently living. The base really didn't look all that different from the one on which she had trained in San Antonio, except the buildings were made of tropical hardwoods and there was, in general, a more seedy air about it. There was a movie theater, a well-stocked base exchange, a library, and even a bowling alley. There were two officers' clubs—three, if you counted the Thai club across the field. The base, she knew, was really Thai property, but the Americans, as they tended to do everywhere, had attempted to remake it into a replica of what they were accustomed to in the States.

She sighed and scratched her short, auburn hair under the crisp white nursing cap. A year ago she never would have thought that working in Brownsville Memorial would seem exciting when compared to a tour in Thailand. But, at least there, you could always count on the usual flotsam from automobile accidents and knife fights. While that experience may not have been exactly uplifting, at least it had made the shift hurry by.

After graduation, she'd lasted almost two years in the ER before succumbing to the blandishment of the air force nurse recruiter, who had been surprised at how little selling he'd had to do. Almost immediately, she'd become a first lieutenant and had spent some not disagreeable weeks at the San Antonio base, where the staff attempted to teach her and dozens of young women that they didn't have to salute the gray-haired senior master sergeant teaching them the complexities of close-order drill, even though he was twenty years their elder. They knew their profession, but they had to learn how to wear their uniforms, shine their shoes, and do the thousands of other peculiarities dear to the heart of the military.

Kate took to it like a duck to water. Her natural vivaciousness brought her quickly to the attention of the training cadre and she soon had been made the student leader of her flight. Her enthusiasm was infectious, and in the end, her flight had far outstripped the others to win the military achievement award. The professional courses had been routine and were mostly concerned with helping the nurses adjust to the military methods of health care. At the end of the course, in a fit of patriotism, Kate had applied for duty in Vietnam. The Air Force decided instead that she was needed more in Thailand.

At Takhli, she found that, though the odd patient was brought into the ER with a mangled hand from carelessness around a bomb hoist or with a snakebite, many of the complaints ran more to broken noses and lacerated faces of overenthusiastic drinkers, who had let their judgment seep away in the heat of the tropical nights. By far the most common medical complaint was venereal disease, contracted from one of the girls plying their ancient trade in the village that had grown with the base.

For a population of the size of the military presence on the base, there were surprisingly few sick men. Surprising until one realized that most of these men were between eighteen and thirty-five years of age and had been in near-perfect health when they left the States.

Kate had seen none of the trauma she had always associated with medical duties in a so-called war zone. She realized now that duty in Takhli, Thailand, differed little from duty at Tinker Air Force Base in Oklahoma. She was acutely aware of the fighter aircraft taking off and landing twenty-four hours a day, but other than that she was almost totally insulated from the war.

She had become accustomed to the throaty rumbles of the aircraft taking off, and of their shrieking landing approaches, and although she had seen some of the young pilots around the base, readily identifiable in their baggy green flight suits, she knew none of them. Nor did she think she was likely to, unless she broke out of the pattern she had set for herself. Immediately following her day's shift, she, along with almost every other officer medic in the hospital, stopped by the Medical Club for happy hour drinks. Then, it was back to her room to change into her bathing suit for a couple of hours in the pool and some sun. Once more back to her room for another change for dinner at the club with the other nurses or with a mixed group, which normally included some of the doctors. The routine varied only when she changed to a late shift, which meant that she did her sunning in the morning or early afternoon and had breakfast and lunch, rather than dinner, with her friends.

It was pleasant enough, but she was beginning to feel completely boxed in. After a month, the conversation was becoming stale, and it was increasingly difficult to keep the more persistent doctors at bay. Invariably, they were married, and although Kate didn't feel that she was a prude, she had been shocked at the open liaisons between some of the doctors and nurses.

Kate had talked to several friends who had gone to what had come to be called the "fighter" club, most had returned bewildered by the antics that occurred there. The doctors looked at these visits with ill-concealed disapproval, though Kate was more than a little amused by their newfound propriety. She suspected that what they really disliked was the fighter pilots poaching into their "private preserve."

With that excellent peripheral vision developed by all attractive women, she had felt the medical duty officer checking out her legs. They'd worked several nights together and had now rotated so their shifts would again be matched for a few days. More and more, he'd been openly observing her; she knew the opening moves wouldn't be long in coming. She hadn't decided what her reaction to them would be. She knew he was married, for he hadn't bothered to remove his ring, as so many of them had, men and women alike. Kate was a healthy young woman, and although the need for physical intimacy was not overwhelming, she would not ignore it if the right man came along. After all, she wasn't hunting a husband. Had she been, there was no shortage of possibilities before she came to Thailand. Realistically, she still had almost eleven months of her tour to complete, and that seemed a long time to be strictly in the company of other women. But it was the need to interact with men on a social level that she missed most. The gentle flirtation, the eye contact with unspoken promises and questions, the casual but lingering touch of a hand on hers. You're still a romantic, Kate Johnson, she thought and laughed to herself.

She'd be eligible for an R and R to Bangkok in a few weeks. Perhaps a few days of shopping and sight-seeing would release her from her doldrums. Or perhaps she could get a few friends together and they'd be able to take a short tour of the country doing tourist kinds of things. And there was always the chance of a trip to Hong Kong or even Hawaii. She brightened at the thought.

"Lieutenant, do you have a first name?"

Here it comes, she thought, turning to smile at the doctor now leaning on the counter next to where she was preparing her paperwork.

"Why, of course, Doctor." She put just a little emphasis on his title. "It's Katherine. Kate, really."

"Mine's Roger," he smiled, "and I don't see that it would completely destroy military discipline if we used them when none of the enlisted people were around. Do you?"

"Of course not, Roger." A little short and stocky, but not bad looking. Nice eyes, but thinning hair. Very tan.

"Fine, Kate it is. I've seen you around the club a few times and someone told me that you were fairly new over here. What do you think of Thailand so far?"

"Well, I've only been here for about a month and in the Air Force for less than four months, and I was just thinking how much I'd like to have that Medical Corps recruiter here with me right now so that we could discuss some of the differences between the picture he painted for me and reality."

Roger laughed. "I know what you mean, but for me, there really wasn't any choice. They drafted me after my residency and it was either this or some MASH in Vietnam. It's boring as hell out here, but you don't really have anything to worry about as long as your liver continues to make friendly fluids out of the contents of a liquor bottle."

"I don't know; it's just that nothing ever seems to happen here. If this were an ER back in the States, we'd have at least twenty-five customers lined up outside, waiting to get in. In the time I've been here I think I've seen about that many total, not counting those coming in to get jabbed in the butt for their VD."

"Yeah," Roger said, "and it's worse on the wards. If it weren't for the VD, half the staff here wouldn't have anything to do. But, you've got to realize that you're deal-ing with one of the healthiest populations you'll ever see and—"

"Hey, Doctor," a corpsman called from the small office, "there's a WIA inbound from the flight line. One of the fighter pilots has got himself a leg wound."

Kate and Roger straightened from leaning on the counter, professional relations established once more. Saved by the bell, she thought, knowing that this had been only round one and that it was not going to be easy to brush Roger away. She wasn't sure she wanted to. He seemed nice enough.

Kate yelled for the corpsman to bring the medical cart, then matched Roger's stride through the automatic door of the emergency room. Away from that air-conditioned room, she was hit by the full fury of the pressure-cooker heat of the Thai afternoon. It was like Houston in August. She could feel the sweat trickling down the back of her exposed tanned neck. One of the first things she had done after arriving in Thailand was to have her thick mass of auburn hair trimmed. She thought that the Thai girl who had cut it was going to weep as she scissored into the heavy mane. It might not be stylish, Kate thought, but it sure dried easily in this heavy air.

She stood by Roger and squinted into the sunlight as the ambulance turned into the emergency room drive, moving fast but without the blaring siren.

Roger noted the silence. "Well, the patient is either dead or not too badly hurt. They've got the sound and light off."

A corpsman hopped from the cab as the blue ambulance backed into the loading dock; he opened the rear doors, then reached a hand inside to steady someone. The green-clad occupant ignored the hand and clambered awkwardly from the rear of the vehicle. At least he's ambulatory, Kate thought. He can't be too bad or the corpsman would never have let him get out by himself. Behind the first man, another emerged carrying two crash helmets. Each pilot still wore a parachute and other mountains of gear.

"Take that stuff off him and get him into a chair," Roger ordered, already kneeling to examine the pilot's leg wound. The medical corpsman walked slowly around the patient, trying to figure out how to remove the parachute, survival vest, and g suit.

Kate was astounded. She'd given little, if any, thought to how the pilots dressed to fly their airplanes. Her experience with pilots was limited to the second officer on a Delta 727 trying out his moves on her between Houston and Atlanta. He'd worn a uniform, all right, but nothing like this. These two were dressed as if they were going to the moon.

Under what had to be the parachute, Kate saw that the pilot was wearing a green mesh canvas vest with many pockets containing odd-shaped devices. He was also festooned with knives, guns, and bandoliers of ammunition. The pistol looked to Kate much like the .38 Special her father had taught her to fire as a girl.

She saw immediately that the wound was not serious. In her old stateside ER they would have had the patient cleaned, stitched, and Blue Crossed in less than half an hour. For the first time she looked directly into the face of the wounded pilot as he stood patiently with one side of his "chaps" unzipped. He was watching the corpsman walk warily around him as though he might find the proper string to pull so that the encumbrances would fall away. He has a good-looking, pleasant face, she thought. Probably one that could grow on you. Not outrageously handsome, but with a good-natured expression. She was taken back by his youth, more pronounced with his hair hanging onto his forehead. He couldn't have been much older than she.

Kate took her eyes from the injured pilot to glance at the other man. She caught her breath. My God! He's gorgeous! She let her glance linger on his face for just a moment, then looked back to the patient. Unable to resist, she returned her gaze to the other man once more. He caught her and his eyes locked onto hers in a level gaze as a small smile tugged at the corner of his mouth. She forced her eyes back to the injured man, who seemed embarrassed by the attention he was getting. Finally, he motioned the fumbling corpsman back with a wave of his hand and quickly unbuckled the parachute and swung it from his shoulders. It was followed in turn by the survival vest, g suit, and shoulder-holstered pistol.

Without his gear, Kate saw that his flight suit was blackened with sweat. The little leather name tag on his left chest showed a silver-embossed pair of pilot wings and the name Captain Jim Broussard. Carefully, the corpsman helped him into the wheelchair, his injured leg braced and stuck straight out in front of him as if it were in a cast.

The corpsman pushed the chair into the cool interior of the emergency room. The other pilot gathered all the equipment and followed them.

With a detached sort of interest, Kate watched Roger clean and stitch the puckered lips of the wound. He had a good touch, she thought. As he worked, she slipped another glance at the standing pilot, who stared intently at the medical procedure. She let her eyes roam at leisure this time, taking in as much of him as she could. There were deeply etched lines marking his face, which she assumed came from wearing the oxygen mask dangling from the helmet in his hand. His short hair was matted with sweat and still damp enough that she couldn't really tell its color except that it was dark. His nose was straight and narrow under heavy dark brows, knitted now in concentration. No one feature seemed exceptional until the face was viewed as a whole; then the features fit together and the masculine face was very good-looking.

The long, heavy lashes suddenly flickered up as if he'd felt her gaze, and once again she found herself staring directly into his dark blue eyes. Immediately, she looked back to where the doctor's nimble fingers were putting the finishing touches on the torn flesh. Her face was hot and she knew she was flushing. My God! she thought. I'm acting like a fifteen-year-old who's just been spoken to in the hallway by the senior quarterback. The doctor's voice brought her back to reality.

"OK, Captain," he told the young pilot on the table, "we're going to give you a tetanus booster and something for the pain. You'd better plan on spending the night with us just to play it safe. But it's a clean wound, and those tight-fitting things you wear around your belly and legs did a good job of preventing you from losing much blood, not that you would have anyway. In a few hours it's going to start letting you know it's there, but you ought to be flying again within the week, provided the flight surgeon agrees. We'll need to get some information from you, but Lieutenant Johnson here can do that after we've got you tucked into bed."

"Thanks, Doctor," the pilot answered. He really does look young, Kate thought, and a little lost, like most healthy folks when faced with a hospital stay. She and the corpsman helped him into the wheelchair and he turned to look inquiringly at his companion, now shouldering all the equipment.

"Give me your blood chit," his friend said, "and I'll turn it in for you along with your gear."

Captain Broussard fumbled in one of the leg pockets of his flight suit and handed a small plastic-wrapped package to his companion. He took it and turned to the corpsman: "How about a ride over to my squadron?"

The corpsman looked at the doctor, who nodded his agreement, already engrossed in filling out his paperwork. The dark-haired pilot turned to the man in the wheelchair: "Donkey and I'll be back after chow tonight."

"Thanks, Andy." Not a bad name, mused Kate. Broussard continued: "I'm sorry about Bobby."

A flat stare, then "Yeah," as he turned and strode to the door, motioning the ambulance driver to follow.

Roger touched Kate's elbow. "Lieutenant, would you see that Captain Broussard gets to the ward all right? And get any information we need from him. You know, make sure his hospitalization insurance is paid up—that sort of thing." He patted Broussard on the shoulder. "I'm going to grab a bite of chow, but give me a call if you need me. Otherwise, somebody will be checking on you later. Don't worry. It's not bad. We just want to make sure you don't pick up an infection."

"I'll take good care of him, Doctor," said Kate. She telephoned the ward nurse to alert her for a patient and found there were plenty of rooms available in the officers' section. The only other patient was a middle-aged colonel waiting to have his hemorrhoids surgically purged the following morning and the assistant base civil engineering officer, who had acquired a skin disease that had so far defied definition. The corpsman pushed Captain Broussard from the ER while she gathered the myriad forms to be completed before his entry into the hospital was official.

Kate gave him half an hour to let the ward nurse and corpsman get him bathed, inoculated, and settled into bed before she walked briskly down the hall to his room, long legs eating up the yards. She wondered if the same pilots flew together all the time. Maybe there'd be an opportunity to do some subtle probing about Captain Andy Whoever.

Subtle, hell. She grinned at the thought. She was prepared to stick her GI pen into this guy's wound if he didn't volunteer the information she wanted.

He had been bathed, for his hair was slicked back, and he was sitting on the bed, which had been cranked upright. His injured leg lay straight out on the sheets. His blue eyes were solemnly staring at his toes but switched to her as she approached and pulled the straight chair next to his bed.

"Well, then, Captain Broussard. How are you feeling now? One thing for sure, you certainly smell better than you did earlier. Are you up to answering a few questions?"

"I guess so," he said listlessly.

What *is* his problem, she wondered. Certainly, it couldn't be that dinky little wound in his leg. All that could mean was a couple of days break from flying. She looked at him closely as he turned to stare out of the window at two Thai women hacking at the tall grass in the never-ending battle against snakes.

"Well," she said brightly, "let's get this over with and then I can leave you to get some rest."

He nodded but continued to stare out of the window, his blank gaze telling her that his mind was elsewhere. Her antenna buzzed sharply. Something definitely wasn't right here. Even a happily married man didn't react to her in this manner, particularly if she deliberately gave him an opening. Kate was not a conceited woman, and she wasn't stupid. She had known that she was good-looking, close to beautiful, since she was fifteen. She also knew how men reacted to her looks; she expected it and handled it in a manner appropriate for the moment. What she did not expect was no reaction at all.

"OK, Dorothy, it's time for you and Toto to head back to Kansas now," she joked.

He turned his gaze back to her, flat and level. Only then did she see the muscles in his jaw quivering with tension. Puzzled, she pressed ahead with the questions, to which he gave curt answers, volunteering nothing. Finally, they were finished and she tamped the papers into a neat square and made ready to leave. Captain Broussard didn't look as if he cared one way or the other.

"You know, you're the first pilot I've met since I've been here," she said on impulse, "though I don't know if you could actually call it a meeting, since I've had to pull every word out of you. Are all of you guys this talky?" she teased.

A corner of his mouth turned up quickly into what could have been either an attempt at a smile or a grimace. He shrugged, and she could barely hear the "sorry" he spoke so softly. OK, buddy, she thought and mentally hitched up her pants, I'm going to get your lips moving if I have to do a strip right here. It was for a good cause, since she did want information about Captain Andy. Besides, this was becoming intriguing.

She tried again. "You know, I think you're the first pilot to come into the hospital with a wound since I've been here and that's been almost a month. How did you get so lucky? Do the others land somewhere else?"

Instinctively, she knew she'd said the wrong thing, but it was too late to take back the words. He turned from the window and stared at her, jaw muscles working furiously. He's lost it, she thought, then noticed the moisture in his eyes. My God! He's liable to bust out bawling at any moment, thought Kate. She was no stranger to dismay and tragedy. No one could spend two years in emergency room nursing and not rub shoulders with it every day.

"I doubt it," he finally answered. "Maybe I was just the lucky one."

Now, what the hell did that mean? Truly curious now, and her interest no longer feigned she asked: "Sorry, I guess I just don't get it. What do you mean? Where do they usually land if they don't come here?"

His flat stare turned to one of pure astonishment, then anger. She could see it seeping into his eyes. He no longer looked like a little boy ready to cry but a hard, tough young man. He was a lot better looking than she had first supposed, she thought absently, staring at the metamorphosis happening before her.

"Don't you people have the foggiest, fucking idea about what's going on all around you?" he demanded. "Aren't you just the teeniest bit curious about those airplanes that take off and land twenty-four hours a day? Doesn't anyone give the smallest thought where they might be going or what they might be doing? What the hell does everyone think they're doing? Playing war games?"

The profanity shocked her. It was like hearing your favorite minister blaspheme. "Well, of course I know they're going out to bomb something, but I . . . we don't really have any way to know what's going on over there. Most of us don't talk about it and I haven't really been here very long, but I think someone would have said something if . . . you know." It sounded stupid in her ears but she couldn't think of anything else. "I'm really sorry if I've said anything that's hurt your feelings. If I have, I do apologize, Captain Broussard." She was more than ready to leave the room now, but his voice held her.

"How's this for something you people can talk about tonight, Lieutenant? Our wing, *your* wing, lost four, maybe five aircraft today, and one of them happened to be a member of my flight. A guy I happen to have liked pretty well. And today wasn't anything all that unusual. And we know that all the REMFs complain about the pilots going to the head of the line in the movie and BX. And every officer on the base complains about the noise in the club without stopping to think that it might be the last beer that some of those jocks will ever drink. Crap! Everybody feels that it's just something they have to put up with for a year while we barbarians keep them from getting their beauty rest. If you looked real close you might just see that not all those barbarians stick around too long. Like Bobby Packard, our number four man. Not a name that anybody on this whole damned base would recognize outside his wing." The animation had gone from his voice now. "We saw him led off with a rope around his neck, and there wasn't a damned thing we could do about it. Go play your games with someone else, Lieutenant Johnson."

She sat stunned and speechless from his outburst. Somehow, she had been made into the bad guy and she didn't think that she was, unless it was through ignorance of the circumstances. Her temper flared momentarily, then she saw Broussard lie back and put his arm over his eyes. She sat in silence, thinking about what he had said. True enough, there was little talk of the war in their club and among the medical staff. But that didn't mean they didn't care. Or did it? To survive in frontline medicine, a person had to build up a veneer of objectivity. Not get too wrapped up in a patient if they were to survive emotionally. Was that what they were doing, or was it that they just couldn't be bothered with lives other than their own?

"How many missions have you flown?" she asked softly.

He snorted at the question, arm still over his face, but he did answer. "Only six, with ninety-four more to go. A piece of cake."

"Are they very bad?"

He removed his arm from across his face and stared at her as if she'd asked if it hurt when you stuck a knife into your belly. "Bad enough."

"Then why do you do it?"

A small smile cracked his face. "I think most of us do it for the combat pay. After all, we get an extra two dollars and sixteen cents a day for doing it, you know."

She returned the smile. "Tell me about it. Where do you fly? What do you do? I suddenly feel like a real fool for not knowing any more about it than I do. You guys obviously live in a different world from the rest of us."

A full natural smile lit his face now that he had vented his anger. "I surely imagine that we do, unless you folks are in the habit of taking your R and Rs to the Red River valley. Let's just say that things do get interesting when your neighbors don't like you. Incidentally, I'm sorry for spouting off that way. It wasn't very fighter pilot of me."

Kate's radar twitched. She could detect his interest in her picking up. About damned time, she thought, or I'd have figured that one of us was in trouble. "Tell me about a mission."

"They're really pretty simple. You take off and fly to North Vietnam. Drop your bombs. They get mad and start shooting, and, if you're lucky, you come home."

"How do you do it?" she asked. "How do any of you do it?"

"Hey, I've only done it six times. Some of those guys are into their second hundred missions. Better ask them."

"How about that other pilot who was in here with you today? Do you often fly with him?"

"Yeah, that's Andy Pritchard. We've flown all of my missions together, though he's got lots more of them than I do. It was his wingman that the gomers got today."

"So, the same pilots always fly together?"

"Well, you do if you're as shorthanded as we are right now. The element leader and his wingman make up half the flight, and they're like cops who are partners. They look after each other. You don't have to particularly like the other guy but you sure as hell have to trust him. Do that for a while and an element leader and his wingie can get pretty tight, or so they tell me. I'm just an instant fighter pilot. I'd only flown trainers until a few months ago."

"Who'll be Captain Pritchard's wingman now?"

"I really don't know how that's going to work. I imagine he'll get somebody pretty new, since they don't like to put all the old, experienced fighter heads together in the same flight. It's supposed to weaken the rest of the flights if they have too many new guys like me in it." The smile disappeared from his face as he continued. "Why do I get the feeling, Lieutenant Johnson, that it isn't idle curiosity causing you to ask questions about Andy." His face was dejected as he lowered his eyes. "He is a good-looking devil, isn't he? And the hell of it is, he's a pretty decent guy as well, though we don't seem to get along so hot together."

"And just what is it, Captain Broussard, that makes you think it's not *you* I'm interested in finding out about?" she answered with a wide smile. She patted him gently on the shoulder as she stood up to leave. "Get some rest now, Captain, or I'll tell everyone what your middle name is."

He threw up his hands as if to ward off a threat.

"Maybe I can drop by after chow tonight," she continued, "and we can chat for a while. If that's OK with you and you're not too tired or anything."

"That would be great," he said, looking very much as if he meant it.

"By the way," she said, "what was that you called us? An REMF? What does that mean?"

"I think I'd better wait until I know you better to explain it," he grinned.

Captain James Evelyn Broussard

He watched her stride briskly from the room, long, shapely legs mostly hidden by the starched whites but flashing enough to show their sleekness. Her body fought the good fight against the nurse's uniform as well. Perhaps not the voluptuousness of a centerfold but everything was in the right place, as far as he could tell. He felt a powerful attraction to her and thought he'd felt her interest in him. He'd always found it difficult to tell with women, though. For the most part they'd remained a dark mystery to him.

It was unfortunate that he'd snapped at her, but he'd been close to weeping as he thought of Bob Packard and the hopelessness in his voice as the NVA advanced upon him. Her questions, just as it had finally sunk in that he would probably never see Packard again, were badly timed. Until Packard, losses had been nameless faces from a briefing room or mess; this was, in effect, Broussard's first experience with a combat casualty.

Jim sulked as he thought about Lieutenant Johnson's obvious interest in Pritchard. But how could she not be intrigued? Few women wouldn't be. The son of a bitch was not only great looking but a fine pilot as well. And it would probably also turn out that he danced like Fred Astaire and was rich as hell. He moped some more as he thought about the situation, then brightened as he remembered that she had said she would visit after dinner. He began to grow bored and restless with the sterile routine. Medical staff wandered in and out of his room in a fairly constant pattern. Most spoke in numbers and Latin and did odd but brisk evaluations of his vital signs and well-being. These procedures probably went on in any hospital, but Jim had nothing to compare them to since he had never before been a patient.

Eventually, the dinner trays arrived. He was not pleased to see that the hospital featured the same mystery meat as did the club. The Thais, who handled most of the cooking, had strange ideas about American food. It was not unlikely to find ice cream deposited on top of meat, or pudding and string beans mixed together into a stewlike gunk.

The wound in his leg was beginning to ache, and after the trays were removed he was tempted to call a nurse for a painkiller. It wasn't really pain—just an annoyance. But he also felt hyper and wide awake, although he'd been up since 0330, and he felt sure he'd get no sleep that night. That was his last conscious thought.

Some time later, Jim was awakened by Donkey arguing with one of the staff doctors. They stood in the hallway debating whether Donkey should be allowed to wake Jim.

"Hell, Doc, it's visiting hours, isn't it?" Donkey said, very loudly.

"Yes, Major. But that in itself does not give you the privilege of entering a patient's room and disturbing him."

"Shit! He's not a real patient anyway. He's a member of my flight. And I'll bet he's awake. Are you awake, Jimbo?" This was delivered at the top of his lungs, ensuring that not only everyone in the hospital but probably the entire base had their eyes open.

"Yeah, Donkey, I'm awake. Come on in," Jim called.

Pritchard trailed Donkey into the room, followed by a hulking lieutenant colonel whom Jim had not met but who had been pointed out as their squadron commander. Lieutenant Colonel Smithers did not appear to be completely sober, but then neither did Donkey. The staff doctor stared from the doorway in prim disapproval, his lips pursed as if he were about to stamp his foot. Abruptly, he turned and left, perhaps to find a gun or a security guard.

Lieutenant Colonel Smithers peered at Jim groggily, trying it first with one eye shut, then the other as he tried to get

him into focus. He scowled, as if it were Jim's fault that he
was having vision problems, then sank heavily into the one
straight-back chair in the room.

"You doing OK, boy?" the colonel asked, punctuating
his question with a mighty belch.

"Yes, sir. I'm doing just fine. They said they'd let me
out of here in the morning."

"Well, you just let me know if they don't treat you right."
He rose and swayed, then tottered toward the door, his duty
to the sick and maimed fulfilled and his desire obvious to
get back to the bar before he missed any more drinking
time. At the doorway he stopped and looked once more
at the prone figure. "What did you say your name was
again?"

Actually, Jim hadn't mentioned it and hadn't been asked
for it. "Captain James Broussard, sir."

"Broussard? That's some kind of frog name, isn't it?"
With that he tacked out of the room, perhaps to search
for more exotically named squadron members in need of
cheering.

Donkey grinned at Jim. "Smithers. That's some kind of
asshole name, isn't it?" He stepped to the door and scanned
the hallway theatrically, then, miming exaggerated caution,
pulled two cans of beer from the leg pocket of his flying
suit. He popped the tops, passed one can to Jim, then sat
down in the chair vacated by the squadron commander,
propping both booted feet on the bed.

"So, how's it going, Jimbo? Got everything you need?"

"Yeah. After all, they're going to release me in the
morning so I guess there aren't too many things I can't
do without for one night. Listen, Donkey, I didn't get a
chance to tell you before, but I'm really sorry about what
happened to Bobby. I didn't get to know him that well but
he seemed like a pretty nice guy to me."

"Yeah, a nice guy," Donkey repeated. "Well, forget it,
because it happens. You do everything you're told to and
you try to do it right and sometimes it still happens. Shit!
That raid ended up costing this wing and the 503d five
frigging airplanes and three pilots today. There's nothing
on the ground in the whole country worth that. But those
kinds of thoughts aren't what they pay us for. Isn't that
right, Andy?"

Pritchard, who had yet to say a word, leaned against the wall and finally spoke: "That's about the size of it, Donkey." He didn't look toward the bed.

"Who are we getting as a replacement?" Jim asked Donkey.

"Well, nobody for a few days until your leg is ready to fly again. The CO decided that with you laying around on your butt and Bobby Packard probably trying to chew through the wall of the Hanoi Hilton right about now, it might be a good time for old Andrew and me to take a few days off. Maybe head to Bangkok or try to set an all-time beer-drinking record. How about that, Andy? What d'ya say?"

Pritchard shrugged and smiled. Somehow Jim couldn't picture him in a drinking contest. He cautiously sipped on the can Donkey had sneaked to him. He didn't really want it but appreciated the effort that had been made to get it to him. Donkey took a healthy draught on his own can and faced Jim, suddenly serious.

"Listen, Jimbo. You did OK today, except for getting shot in the ass. The thing you gotta remember when you're working low to the ground is that you don't want to give the gunners time to track you. What you have to do is keep the bird in a turn, even a small one, right up until it's time to shoot. Every ground attack pilot in the world knows the odds are against him when he attacks a fixed gun site or even interlocking 12.7s. The public, and even the grunts on the ground if you're doing close air support, see this big bastard of an airplane you're driving around at five hundred knots and think those poor little dinks don't have a chance against you. Well, that ain't real life. He's stabilized in a position and you've got to move your whole damned airplane just to change your firing angle.

"This isn't like it is down in South Vietnam, where unless things get real hairy, you can pick your headings and fly right down the tube the way you did it in gunnery school. Try that shit up here and you'll get a new asshole stitched for yourself. There are just too damned many guns up here. Ain't that right?" He turned to Pritchard as if what he had said needed to be verified. It didn't, at least for Jim.

Pritchard answered seriously, as if explaining a problem to a particularly obtuse student. "Absolutely. Even a small turn tremendously complicates the tracking pattern for the gunner. Theoretically, your wings should never be level until that instant before you squeeze the trigger, just as Donkey said, then you have to immediately start jinking out of the gunner's cone of fire. A lot of pilots seem to think that it has to be a hard turn, but actually what you need are quick, erratic banks with the nose of the aircraft always in a turning moment. That way you don't lose the benefit of the speed you've built up during the dive. With a long turn you only give the gunner that much more time to solve his tracking problem.

"There's always an exception, of course. If the target is heavily defended," Pritchard continued, "for instance, in the Hanoi area, all the nonradar-controlled guns are given sectors of the sky to fire into. Even old papa-san with his SKS rifle is told where to point and blast away. In an area like that any jinking you do might as easily bring you into the zone of fire as away from it. Psychologically, though, it helps to be doing something other than just sitting there and watching all that crap fly by."

"Listen to the man," said Donkey without his usual smile. "Andy was with a group of Voodoo recce birds that they brought up here in '65 or so to fly back and forth across the countryside, just the way they used to do it down in South Vietnam. The system worked so well down there, they just assumed you could do the same thing up here. Only they forgot a few small things—like, for instance, the North Vietnamese have between six and seven thousand antiaircraft guns shooting at us, backed up by almost two thousand radars. Unless we stay real low, they can pick us up just about as soon as we launch on a raid. Tell him what happened to your squadron of RF-101s, Andy."

"They brought twelve of us up here to fly out of Thailand, and in six days they had shot down eight. At least five of the pilots were killed and the others are still missing, presumed captured but maybe dead."

Donkey looked at Jim and was immediately concerned by what he saw in his face. "Hey! I said to think about it, not take it to bed with you. You gotta remember, kid, that no matter what those assholes at headquarters say about the grand design for this war, it all boils down to random chance. Just like life. You can plan and plan, but if you draw the black bean, it still all goes down the crapper anyway. Or you can stay loosey-goosey and things will probably work out just as well in the end. Don't worry about it. You'll do just fine when you get a few more notches on you."

"There just seems to be so much to learn and not much time to learn it."

"My philosophy exactly!" Donkey agreed enthusiastically. "So much to drink and so little time given to each of us to drink it." With that, he tilted the can and was knocking off a large swallow when Lieutenant Johnson walked into the room without knocking. Jim had been hoping that his flight mates would depart before she returned, wanting her all to himself. In particular, he was concerned about Pritchard, with his dark good looks. If that guy turned on the charm, Jim knew his own chances would be nil. But, he thought philosophically, maybe life is just a series of random events, as Donkey said.

"My God," she cried in mock consternation, hands on her hips, "I leave you alone for a couple of hours and find that you've started a regular bacchanal in the base hospital." She stared at the beer can tilted over Donkey's face and the one that Jim was trying unsuccessfully to hide beneath the sheets. "Are the Thai boom-boom girls scheduled in next?" She shook her head sadly. "And you looked like such a nice young man. Tell me, did this obviously dirty old man have anything to do with this?" She stared sternly at Donkey, whose beer can had stopped just beneath his half-opened mouth, as if he'd been turned to stone. Jim couldn't blame him. She was pretty breathtaking.

Lieutenant Johnson wore khaki shorts and white sneakers with a red sleeveless blouse tied into a knot across her tight stomach. Long brown legs seemed to go on endlessly. Her breasts completely filled the pocket made by tying the blouse ends, and they seemed to be pointing at targets to her eleven and one o'clock positions. The red and brown offset her tan perfectly and made the short auburn hair look almost black. Tiny laugh lines at the corners of her large brown eyes crinkled with amusement as she took in the three pilots.

"What's with him?" she asked casually, tossing her head at Donkey. His eyes were almost bulging, and he was making choking noises as though he'd swallowed a peach pit. "If he's trying to get mouth-to-mouth resuscitation, it's not the smoothest approach I've ever seen."

"My God, if I thought you'd do that I'd give you my firstborn and my American Express card," Donkey said, finally finding his voice. "I'd try to swallow this beer can if I thought there was the slightest chance of you trying to revive me."

Jim couldn't figure any way not to introduce them, since they showed absolutely no interest whatsoever in leaving. Rather sullenly, he said, "Major Donkey Sheehan and Captain Andrew Pritchard, may I present Lieutenant Johnson," following the military formality that always had the junior presented to the senior, regardless of gender. "And in case you've forgotten, I'm Jim Broussard."

"Yeah," she said with an evil grin, "and I know what your middle name is, too, and I'll bet they don't. Call me Kate." She turned away from Jim and stared at Donkey for a moment. "I'm almost afraid to ask why they call you Donkey."

"Perhaps when we're better acquainted."

"I'm afraid we may never get *that* well acquainted," she said with a grin and extended a strong-looking browned hand to him. He looked as though he was prepared to swallow it.

Kate turned slightly, and more slowly offered the hand to Pritchard, taking time to study him, smiling, the grin put away for the moment. They looked at each other much longer than Jim thought was absolutely necessary before Pritchard reluctantly released her hand. She seemed to be in no great hurry to withdraw it either. Well, thought Jim, there goes the fucking ball game. Unless he could sneak up on Andy some night and bash his head in with a rock. Or maybe capture a krait and slip it into his bed. He was startled when Kate whirled on him.

"Just what do you think you're doing with that beer?" she asked. Donkey sprang to his feet in afterthought and offered her the only chair in the room. "You know," she continued, "I'd be honor-bound as an officer to take this directly to the staff OD if I had the slightest idea that you were sitting around guzzling alcohol with a bunch of your flying cronies." She rose from the chair and stretched across Jim to take the can from his hands. Her loose breasts in the tiny bound shirt just brushed his chest. Jim almost choked on his tongue and had to raise his knees under the sheet.

Kate put the can to her lips and the three men watched in awed silence as she drank, then patted her flat browned belly. She looked curiously at each of them in turn when she felt their eyes on her.

"What's with you guys? Have I said something wrong?" she said, completely misunderstanding the nature of the silence. "I told Jim earlier that I'd be along after dinner to chat with him. He was nice enough to tell me a little bit about the kind of flying you do. If I'm interrupting anything I can come back later."

The three men hastily assured her that she was not interrupting a thing and that they would feel terrible if she left. "Besides," Pritchard told her, "I'm sure that Captain Broussard can tell you all about combat flying. After all, he's had so much experience." Jim's flushed face could have lighted the hospital.

"No," she said coolly looking at him with a level gaze while pretending not to see Broussard's flushed face, "he only mentioned a few things that a lot of us should have known about all along. In fact, he was very complimentary toward you two. He seems to think highly of both of you as pilots and men."

Jim had said no such thing, but he was grateful to her for getting him off the hook. Pritchard looked uncomfortable.

"As a matter of fact, he told me he was almost a beginner and had done only six missions but that you were the *real* fighter pilot," she teased, batting her long eyelashes at Donkey.

"Well, he sure as hell got that much right, at least," agreed Donkey. "I find it amazing how perceptive this young man can be at times. Tell me, Kate Johnson, what do you do for fun when you're not playing Nancy Nurse?"

"Oh, I try to get a little sun every day at the pool, have a few drinks and a meal at the club, seduce the commanding officer of the Seventh Air Force—you know, the usual sorts of things."

"You mean that hideout the medics call a club? Hell, girl, why don't you come over to the official club and have a drink with the menfolk?"

"Well," she answered with a smile, "I've heard about that club. In fact, I've been warned about it. What we hear is that you guys do everything but burn Christians over there."

"Untrue," Donkey stoutly contested. "That's just a rumor we've started to keep out the riffraff, like doctors and lawyers. You let people like that begin coming into your club, and before long they'll start trying to talk to you, and no telling where that could lead. Before you know it, they're standing at the bar, drinking and carrying on like they were real people."

"I'll cut you a deal," she said like a Texas horse trader, "you guys come over and have dinner with me at our place, then I'll let you take me to yours. What could be fairer? That way, we'll get to look over each other's spread. How about tomorrow night if you aren't busy?" She looked at Pritchard and Jim. "All of you guys."

Jim glanced at Pritchard, hoping he would be busy bombing the Pathet Lao or something. He wasn't, of course. "As Donkey said, only if we can return the favor," he said graciously.

"Just as long as she doesn't bring any of those wimpy doctors," Donkey broke in. "What time tomorrow?"

"Oh, they start serving dinner at 1600—I mean 1700. Crap! At six o'clock. Come a little earlier than that and I'll let you buy me a drink and maybe tell me why they call you Donkey."

"Deal! We'll all see you at 1800 then."

"At 1800?" she mused. "OK, 1800 it is." She handed Jim the now-empty beer can, smiled and patted him on the shoulder, and strode from the room. The view she presented going out was as good as the one coming in.

The men sat silently in pleasant thought for a few moments before Donkey spoke. "Well, I'm sure going to feel rotten about writing my girlfriend and telling her we're through, but it's obviously got to be done, because Kate is crazy about me."

Pritchard continued to sit silently, a small, pleased smile on his face, as if he knew he were in the catbird seat with the good-looking Nurse Johnson. Jim was afraid of that as well. He remembered the long look they had given each other. Suddenly, he wanted both men to leave so that he could have a good sulk. After a little more small talk, mostly concerning Kate, they did exactly that.

"Well," Donkey announced, "I'll tell you sports fans one thing. It surely was lucky that old Jimbo decided to get shot in the ass today, otherwise that gal might never have met me. I think we're going to make a real darlin' couple. Come on, Andy, let's leave this suffering bastard alone for the night. He's got to get his rest if we're going to be up to some major partying with the medics tomorrow night."

He slapped Jim on the shoulder; Pritchard nodded, and they slipped through the doorway, leaving Jim to dispose of the two empty beer cans and sniff the lingering fragrance of Kate's perfume. There was an empty feeling in his belly, as if he were coming down with something. He was afraid that something was Kate Johnson. He tried not to compare his attributes with Andrew Pritchard's, knowing how that would end up. Finally, he hid the beer cans in the leg pocket of his sweat-encrusted flight suit and called the floor nurse for a sleeping pill.

Still, sleep was hard to come by. His mind raced over the events of the day, his eyes flickering so rapidly beneath the lids that he had to forcibly hold them closed.

There were so many things that needed to be considered in detail. Getting hit, Bob's capture, the mission, and now Kate Johnson. Why couldn't things be spread out? Why did you have to have it all heaped up on you at once? Jim was trying to decide which item he should worry about first when the pill got him.

First Lieutenant
Katherine Elaine Johnson

The soft crooning of the popular singer was suitably subdued over the club's high-fidelity system as Kate entered
the cool, darkened room that was the bar and cocktail
lounge. She stood in the semidarkness waiting for her eyes
to adjust from the bright glare of the late afternoon sun.
The rumble of the air conditioner fought the singer for the
low notes. Finally, Kate was able to make out shapes, if
not faces, at the tables and bar. She glanced at the big,
round clock hanging behind the bar—1740. She mentally
began the maddening process of deciding whether to add
or subtract twelve hours to come up with the local time.
To hell with it. It had to be 5:40 P.M., for she had come
off shift at 4 P.M. and had gone for a swim, then showered
and changed. In her military training, the instructors had
tried to explain the reason for using the twenty-four-hour
system but not to her satisfaction. Then, they had brought
up "Z," or Zulu time—based on the Greenwich meridian
and used by the military—and her mind rebelled. When she
arrived in Thailand she found to her horror that the base also
used "H," or Hotel time. She decided she would tolerate
no more of this sidereal nonsense and would henceforth
stick with A.M. and P.M. and let the rest of the world
go hang. Shift changes were at 0800, 1600, and 0000.
Those were the only concessions she would make to military time.

She returned the greetings of several nurses as her eyes adjusted, and she walked toward the full bar, her skin feeling taut from the hour at the pool behind their club. She'd always loved the sun and, despite the red hair, her skin toasted to a deep golden brown. Her earliest memories were of building sand castles on the beaches of the Texas gulf coast as her mother read beneath an umbrella and her father surf-casted for redfish. Now that she thought about it, most of the fun things in her life had taken place in the sun, usually on a beach. She could become downright despondent on a gloomy day, and wondered if they would have to lock her up when the threatening and imminent monsoons began.

"Buy you a drink, Kate?"

Her eyes weren't fully adjusted to the dimness and she peered squint-eyed down the bar, eventually making out the stocky frame of Dr. Roger Everett. He was wearing a golfing shirt and white shorts, his sturdy legs squeezed into the knee-length white socks affected by most of the male medical staff as a compromise between comfort and dressing for dinner.

"Why, yes, Roger, that would be lovely. Gin and tonic, please."

Roger signaled to the Thai bartender for two drinks, then turned again to Kate. "So, have you found a way to cure your boredom yet?"

"Maybe so. Remember that pilot who came in with the leg wound yesterday? Well, I invited him and two members of his flight over for dinner tonight. They ought to be here in a few minutes. I wish you'd join us 'cause they look like they're fun to be around. The flight leader, Donkey Sheehan, is a real hoot, although they all seem like nice guys. Really, two of them are not much older than boys."

Roger looked slightly pained as he frowned. "You know, Kate, you've only been over here for a little while, and I'm not sure you understand that what you've done is not a particularly good idea. I mean, they've got their own club, you know, and this could be like . . . well, setting a precedent. We've all tried to more or less keep this place as our home away from home, if you know what I mean. We want it to be the kind of place where we can come when we're off duty and relax with people we know, in a comfortable atmosphere. We're all over here for a full year, whereas those pilots spend only long enough to fly their hundred missions or whatever it is. They're almost like transients and, nothing against them personally, but they do tend to act like members of a fraternal lodge away from home on their yearly convention."

"Roger's right, you know," another voice added. Kate turned and saw that another doctor she knew slightly from the hospital had joined them and overheard his statement. "A year is a long time to do over here and I, for one, would like to make it pass as painlessly as possible. This club . . . *our* club . . . is one of the few places on the base that doesn't cater to the fighter pilots. If given the opportunity, they'd probably overrun it as well. You do realize, I hope, that for having the privilege of this sanctuary, we pay double club dues. Theirs is the official officers' club and, although we may have to support it, we don't have to use it!"

Kate was both surprised and embarrassed by the vehemence of the barrage flung at her. She was also beginning to get a little angry. "Well," she said, staring at the men, "I guess there are at least three of them you won't have to worry about screwing up your club. I understand that's how many the wing lost yesterday." She decided she didn't like stocky doctors who wore shorts and long white socks.

Roger raised a placating hand and opened his mouth to speak when a raucous voice began bellowing a song outside the club entrance. The high fidelity sound system didn't have a chance; Donkey had clearly established air superiority:

Oh, there are no fighter pilots down in hell!
Oh, there are no fighter pilots down in hell!
Oh, the place is full of queers, navigators, bombardiers,
But, there are no fighter pilots down in hell!

Oh, there are no bomber pilots in the fight!
No, there are no bomber pilots in the fight!
They are back on native shores, making mothers
    out of whores!
But, there are no bomber pilots in the fight!

• • •

Both doctors looked at Kate as if their point had just been made, then deliberately turned their backs on the spectacle making its entrance into their club. Kate was feeling murderous. They could tell her what to do in the hospital, but this was way out of line. She was reaching to rap Roger on the back and regain his full attention for a few additional words on the subject when she heard Donkey's voice: "Well, lookie here." He swept her with his eyes, grin loose and a little sloppy. "Fetching! Mighty fetching!"

Kate pulled her attention away from the back view of the doctors and looked at the three figures standing before her. They still wore their baggy green flight suits, and she was glad they had. After the tiff with Roger and his friend she was beginning to identify with these men. Besides, Donkey had the same mannerisms as her father; he clearly liked people and was only really happy in a crowd. Impulsively, she gave him a hug, as if he were an old friend, and indeed he did seem so. When she unclasped Donkey she gave Broussard a wink and a pat on the shoulder, and extended a cool hand to Andy Pritchard. She linked arms with Donkey and marched with him to the small opening at the bar, the other pilots following them. Defiantly, she glared again at the broad back of Roger. He and his friend ignored them.

"Sorry about the singing," Pritchard told her, "but Donkey likes to make an entrance, and though you'd probably never guess it, he had a few before we got here."

"Good! Though I'd *never* have guessed it. Let's have more."

Donkey ignored the small talk, inspecting his new surroundings with great interest, as if preparing to make an offer on it. Kate noticed that although most of the medical men kept their eyes away from the newcomers, the nurses stared back boldly.

"Hi ya, Doc, or whatever," Donkey said, squirming until he had made a comfortably sized opening for his body next to Roger Everett. "Are you a specialist or a regular old chancre mechanic?" He settled contentedly into his newly acquired nest.

Roger looked at him as if he was a new stool specimen upon which he had to report. "I'm an internist, Major. Are you a regular old pilot or perhaps something of a specialist yourself?"

"Doc," Donkey said with a straight face, "you just happen to have the privilege of rubbing drinking arms with not only a special fighter pilot but the very best fucking fighter pilot in the world!"

"My, such modesty," said the other doctor, hardly looking up from his drink.

"Doc," Donkey bellowed, ensuring that he had the attention of everyone in the club and possibly on the base, "you ought to have looked up enough assholes in your life to know how common they are. Modesty ain't got a thing to do with it. Either you are or you ain't. And I am. If you ain't a fighter pilot, you ain't shit! And I'm the shit hottest one around." He beamed at the doctors as if he knew that they agreed with him. Then, he insisted upon shaking hands with everyone in the bar, including the Thai bartender and waitress, much to their amusement.

Broussard, Pritchard, and Kate ordered drinks and sipped as Donkey worked the room like a professional entertainer, going from one table to another, laughing and taking drinks offered by the nursing staff. In an amazingly short time, he had made himself thoroughly at home and had assumed the role of host. The doctors tried to ignore him, contenting themselves with hurling venomous looks at Kate for bringing this court jester into their midst. Yet there was something about the court jester that prevented them from provoking a direct confrontation. Donkey's foolishness covered a hard, tough core, much as a strong man's fat was a veneer for the muscles beneath. His looks suggested the type of man no one would want to meet in an alley fight, since you'd probably have to kill him to stop him.

Pritchard and Broussard tried to chat with Kate as they sipped their drinks, ignoring the fact that she spent more time glowering at a pair of men down the bar than paying attention to their conversation. The two pilots looked at each other, not knowing whether to be embarrassed or amused, as Donkey taught, then led, a quartet of nurses in several ribald songs. The words to the songs finally penetrated Kate's consciousness. She hastily had them order a last round, then drag the reluctant Donkey with them into the dining room. He walked backward as he left, continuing to sing and wave to the nurses.

"I don't know about you guys but I'm starved," she said as they sorted themselves out around the table. She was still hanging onto Donkey's arm and ignoring the stares directed toward the odd foursome. Donkey again insisted upon introducing himself to the waitresses and nearby diners. When he eventually returned to the table, Pritchard looked at him with a wry smile.

"Donkey, I'm not an expert on the social niceties, of course, but is a guest supposed to insult everyone in sight? I mean, you could have made less of a stir by squeezing off a two-second burst of cannon fire in there. Not that I'm complaining, mind you, but it might not be a good idea to alienate every doctor on the base. Who knows? We may need another one someday."

Pritchard turned to Kate, sitting between him and Broussard. "Actually, the Donk doesn't believe he's had a good time unless no one is left unoffended at the end of the evening. He's really on his best behavior now. At least, there's been no blood flowing."

"Yeah, but the night's still young," chortled Donkey. He was completely happy, like a mischievous child, pleased with the havoc he had wreaked in the bar. "Let's get some more drinks," he said, "and then we can decide what we want to eat. Naw, what you guys don't understand is that it doesn't make a damned bit of difference whether we piss them off or not. Pardon my language, Kate. But what the hell do they have to do with us or the war?"

"Well," said Broussard, "one of them did stitch up my leg yesterday. The one you just insulted, if I remember correctly. That ought to count for something."

"It doesn't count for crap. That's just one of the exceptions that prove the rule. How many guys do you know in this wing," Donkey asked Pritchard, "who have a Purple Heart? Damned few, except for junior, here," he pointed to Broussard, then swung back to Pritchard. "Yeah, I know you've got a couple, but you picked them up someplace else, flying something else. You didn't get them in Pack Six. Flying Thuds, the only people who get a Heart are those who eject outta the plane real close to home. They get 'em almost automatically, whether they're really hurt or not. But, usually Thud pilots don't need anybody to sew 'em up because they're either home OK or they're dead or captured. So what good are these guys to us? Let 'em pounce around in their little shorts and white socks and feel sorry for themselves because they aren't making big bucks back in the States. They're still making a hell of a lot more than either of you two. . . . Hey! Let's dance!" The Thai band began playing slow songs as Donkey pulled Kate from her chair and swept her toward the small dance floor.

"Order something for us," she called back over her shoulder. "Anything at all. And for this crazy man as well."

Donkey was surprisingly graceful even in his combat boots, twirling Kate to the slightly discordant strains of the music. "How am I doing?" he asked.

"Pretty darn good," she answered honestly. "I'd probably keep you around if I ever thought there would be a chance to housebreak you."

"Not a chance, lady!" They laughed together. "Now one of that pair sitting back there at the table, looking all forlorn because I'm holding you, just might fill the bill."

Kate leaned back in his arms to look him directly in the eyes. She noticed that he was about her height. "Well, smart guy, if you had to choose one for me, which one would it be?"

Donkey apparently was giving the matter serious thought, for he said nothing for several minutes, even during the break between songs as they stood together on the small floor rather than returning to the table. Finally, as though there had been no break in the conversation, he spoke. "You could do a lot worse than either one of them. Of course, I could say that about half the young bucks in the squadron. Andy's a career man, and if he lives through this tour I've got no doubt he'll end up as a general officer some day. He's sharp, smart, and a damned good fighter pilot. He's ambitious, but that's no crime if you go about it the right way, and he will. Any gal could do a lot worse than to side up with old Andy. He's a damned good man.

"Of course, I don't know Jimbo nearly as well, but you can learn a lot pretty quick when you live and fly together the way we do. He says he's getting out of the Air Force as soon as he gets back to the States, and that'll be a pity, 'cause he's the kind of young guy the service needs. But, knowing the Air Force, they'll find some way to drive him to the airlines for sure. Right now, he's not too confident, but he's a hell of a lot better pilot than he knows. Before long, he'll be flying rings around everybody in the squadron—except me, of course. And he's got the best kind of guts. The kind that make you do something when you'd rather be doing about anything else in the world.

"Now, Andy is braver than a bull, too. But he's that way simply because that's the way he is, if you know what I mean. He'll figure the odds and always do the right thing. That comes from his training and the confidence he has in himself. Jim'll agonize over problems, but I think they'd both come to about the same solution. Just a different way of getting to it. Did that answer your question?"

"You know damned well it didn't! According to you they're both perfect but in different ways. That's not fair."

"Well, they're both fighter pilots."

Kate danced with the other two pilots in turn, not surprised to find that Andy Pritchard was as smooth as silk on the dance floor. Jim Broussard, on the other hand, had to be blackmailed before he consented to join her.

"I don't know," he said, "my leg is still pretty stiff from those stitches. Besides, I'm not really that good at it."

Kate grabbed both his hands and pulled him to his feet. "No sweat, GI. I'm good enough for both of us. And besides, if you don't dance I'm going to announce to the world over the band's loudspeaker that your middle name is—"

"OK, OK," he said, jumping up quickly and letting her lead him among the swaying couples. She *was* good enough for both of them and she loved to dance. Despite his awkwardness, her graceful figure cleverly led him through the movements. The food had arrived by the time the song had ended.

After the last bowls of spicy Thai food had been cleared away, Kate again began eyeing the men for another trip to the dance floor. Donkey, eyes shining, had other ideas.

"Tell you what, I've got the preacher's jeep, so why don't we head on back to our club for an after-dinner drink?" The others looked dubious, especially Kate, remembering some of the tales other nurses had told her.

"Donkey, I'm not sure I'm dressed for it," she said, looking to the younger men for help. They both shrugged.

"Hell, you've got a dress and shoes on. What do you think you have to wear, a flight suit?"

The stolen jeep's wheels skidded sharply across the dusty ruts as Donkey cut them sharply to avoid the front porch of the sprawling clubhouse. From more than a hundred yards away Kate had been able to hear Beatles music spilling through the open doors and windows, overpowering the normal night sounds. Voices sang along with the high-fidelity music while other groups competed with different songs. Spirited conversation filled the pauses.

"Here we are," Donkey said and spryly helped Kate out of the jeep. She took a deep breath before clutching his arm firmly and stepping through the door of the club. Her eyes widened as she took in the sixty to seventy young men, dressed alike in baggy flight suits, only a sprinkling of short-sleeved khaki uniforms to be seen. Most of those were worn by older men. The young men were distinguishable from one another only by colorful scarves worn around their necks and tucked into the open throats of their flight suits.

Stanzas of songs, of the variety Donkey had sung, were being bellowed by members of different groups, all of whom clutched beer cans in their hands. The room seemed to be made of beer cans. Mountains of them dominated the tables, and in one corner an elaborate totem pole was under construction using empties from only one brand of beer. Solitary figures walked over and made their offering to it as they finished their drink, carefully arranging their can so as not to disturb the fragile figure.

The only men who seemed to be completely sober sat together in a small group, reading, talking, or simply drinking coffee and observing the show with amusement.

"They gotta fly tonight," Donkey pointed out to her, almost in apology. "That's why they can't have any fun."

Donkey half dragged Kate to a group of standing pilots and began introductions. Pritchard and Broussard were waylaid by another group who forced beers into their hands.

"Folks," Donkey began, "let me introduce Lieutenant Kate Johnson, one of the good guys at the hospital. Kate, this is Frank Killeen, One-Eyed Bennigan, David Sellers. . . ." The names became a blur and Kate retained only the impression of faces. They were much alike at a distance, but with proximity there were startling differences, primarily in the types and growth of the mustaches all seemed to favor. Most popular seemed to be the large, bushy, handlebar style. Up close, the men seemed to act quite normal, and Kate began to relax a bit. She was soon to realize that was a mistake. Still holding her hand, Donkey led her to the next group. Expecting more introductions, she let a light smile play on her face.

Donkey grinned at the group and said in a normal voice: "Anybody who doesn't know how to tap-dance is queer."

There was a momentary pause, then each man in the group began clogging up and down, back and forth, in his own personal interpretation of what constituted a tap dance. Heel and toe, heel and toe, they sawed back and forth in a mad frenzy. The movement was contagious and other green-suited figures joined in. Kate stared with disbelief as the madness reached the far corners of the large room, sucking in everyone. The club became devoid of conversation, only the taped music accompanying the sixty-odd pairs of clumping flight boots. The men's faces were drawn in concentration, as though they were auditioning for the Rockettes and this might be the lucky night when they would finally be chosen for the chorus line. With alarm she realized that Donkey no longer held her arm and that he and the other members of Cadillac Flight were bucking and reeling with the crowd.

"Dance you fool!" Donkey yelled at her. "Do you want all these guys to think you're queer?"

She opened and closed her mouth guppy fashion several times, and as if responding in a dream sequence she began to slowly dance along with the other inmates. Even the Thai bartender and waitresses tapped along in their nimble Asian fashion, their expressions plainly showing that if there were other jobs that paid equally well, they were ready to apply for them.

Kate continued to dance along with the crowd, beginning to enjoy the ridiculousness of the situation. She found herself improvising new little steps and turns. Looking around she found most of the faces turned her way, everyone grinning broadly as if she'd just been accepted into a cult after a bizarre ritual. Does it ever end, she wondered, or do we just continue this insanity until we drop? It was getting to be sort of fun, though. Individualism was apparently encouraged, and she finally turned herself loose to invent even more innovative steps.

Just when she felt she was getting the hang of it, Kate heard a strident voice from across the room: "Dead bug! Dead bug!" The cry was picked up by others and spread to the far reaches of the mass of undulating green larva. Her mind almost rebelled at the spectacle of waves of men flinging themselves to the floor on their backs, both hands and feet sticking aloft in an insane parody of a dead cockroach. Could grown men really be doing this?

Kate felt a hand grab hers and she drew back the other, clenched, to deliver a killing blow to whomever or whatever it was. Another unseen hand grabbed her cocked arm and the weight of the men on either side of her bore her backward to the littered floor. This is it, she thought grimly, gang raped by the entire fighter wing. Well, she decided, she wasn't going peacefully. She fought those holding her arms while wriggling her hips in a futile attempt to get her dress down enough to at least cover her panties. She raised her head from the floor to take in the scene: It looked as if some farmer from a nightmare had produced a fine crop of arms and legs. Except for the music, there was no other sound in the room. An unwary pilot appeared from the dining room, engrossed in a copy of *Stars and Stripes*, unaware of the events within. The unnatural silence alerted him, but too late. By then he was well into the room, and the only person not flat on his back.

He looked around sharply at the inverted smiles. "Aw, shit!" He continued to the bar and announced, "Caught is caught, I guess," then rang the small bell hanging there. The dead bugs rose, laughing, to get their free drink.

The men crowded around Kate, trying to help her to her feet. She was in no mood for their help, particularly when the hands began removing flattened cigarette butts and mopping beer stains from her linen dress. One hand in particular was giving more attention to the job than was required. It was lovingly caressing the right cheek of her bottom rather than brushing away debris. She looked

over her shoulder and saw that the culprit was a balding
lieutenant colonel with a red scarf around his neck, and he
didn't appear to be completely sober. He was engrossed in
his task, petting her butt as though it were a kitten.

Too much! This stops now, she thought. She recocked
her right arm and, before anyone could restrain her, she
smashed her small fist onto the lieutenant colonel's nose.
It made a satisfying splattering sound and she felt the carti-
lage give way beneath her knuckles. The force of the blow
knocked the man from his crouching position into the legs
of a full colonel, later to be identified as the deputy wing
commander. Together the pair fell backward into the crowd,
taking several pilots and a very confused Thai waitress with
them to the floor. Several of the noncombatants tried to
untangle the group, only to have the participants grab their
hands and jerk them into the heap, until the mass resembled
a pile of writhing maggots.

The crowd cheered Kate but remained well away from
her as she turned to face them with both fists cocked.
Donkey finally worked his way to her through the crowd
and placed one arm around her shoulders and held onto one
of the trembling fists.

"Gentlemen," he shouted above the noise from the group
still trying to get untangled at their feet, "I want all of you
to meet a very special friend of mine who will forevermore
be welcome into this club as my guest. Never let her pay
for a drink and let her always feel safe when she comes
here. She's one of the good ones. Now, everyone come
meet her."

There was a huge cheer and the pilots lined up as orderly
as cadets to shake her hand and give their names. Each
spoke a few words of welcome. She was astounded at
how gracious they could be. Their names eventually ran
together and she simply nodded and smiled at each, her
good humor again restored. Eventually, the lieutenant colonel who had fondled her ass stepped forward with his
hand outstretched. She eyed him warily for a few seconds,
then grinned and shook his hand. As he stepped away,
she motioned him back and whispered in his ear, "Was
it worth it?"

He wiped the blood from his nose and whispered back,
"Absolutely!"

She searched through the crowd, trying to find any of her original escorts. They seemed to have melted away. Then she saw Broussard standing between two pilots at the bar. Their hands were making flying motions through the air. They became quiet as they noticed her approach. One of the pilots she remembered. He was hard to forget since he had only half a mustache, growing on the left side of his face. He caught her disbelieving glance and smiled. "Lost a bet. I've got to wear it like this for another week yet."

Kate looked at Jim, her face solemn. "Can you take me home now? A girl can make only so many new friends and have so much fun in one night."

Major Delbert "Donkey" Sheehan

The squadron commander, Lt. Col. Bennie Smithers, beck-
oned Donkey into his office with the wave of a hand, then
resumed staring at the personnel roster on the wall. "Sit
down, Donkey," he growled without taking his eyes from
the chart. "We've got us a little problem."

"Where do you get this 'we' shit, white man?" Donkey
replied, slouching into one of the chairs in front of the
gray, air force–issue desk. He had known Smithers since
the Korean War, where he had given the new butter-bar, a
new second lieutenant, his initial combat checkout in Sabres
before becoming his flight leader. Donkey considered the
fact, not for the first time, that he had been a captain then,
two grades higher than the man on the other side of the
desk. Even more rankling was the ill-concealed truth that
Lieutenant Colonel Smithers was not considered, in the
Tactical Air Command, to be a barn-burning, fast-track,
overachiever himself. Just where, Donkey wondered, does
that place me? During the past decade the two men had
served together in two different fighter squadrons before
coming to Thailand.

Smithers ambled loosely back to his desk chair and sank
heavily into it, immediately putting a match to the stub
of a cigar retrieved from the ashtray. It looked much the
worse for wear. The smoke turned the room's air foul as
the commander made ineffectual efforts to disperse it by

idly waving his hand back and forth in front of his face.

"Jesus," Donkey swore, "there ought to be a statute of limitations on how long you can keep those damned things." Smithers smiled at the joke of long standing, which had begun in Korea.

"I don't know what the hell difference it could make to you, Donkey," the squadron commander replied, "since I know from personal experience that you've spent a good part of your adult life hanging out in smoke-filled bars that would make even this smell good. But, listen, I didn't call you over here just to hear you complain about air pollution. I said we've got us a problem and that means it's partly yours. At least you're going to be part of the solution."

Donkey decided he didn't like the sound of this.

"You know," the colonel continued, "that they're just about scraping the bottom of the pilot barrel back in the States and in Europe to keep our Table of Organization up to strength."

"And I'd like to add that I think they're doing a pretty piss-poor job of it," Donkey interrupted. "Me and every other flight leader ought to have at least six or seven pilots and we're trying to do the job with the minimum—four. That's crap and we both know it."

"Please hear me out, Donkey. What I was about to say was that it's just about time to get down to the nut-cutting back there if they expect us to continue this farce. And all of a sudden the boys who've got farts and darts on their cap bands are finding out that what they've got on paper and what they've got in real life are two different animals. It seems like just about every damned fighter pilot in TAC, including the old man himself, has made at least one tour over here or down south. Now, it turns out that all those nice little lists of pilot pools that some asshole brigadier is supposed to keep up to date in the Pentagon are filled with nothing but forty-five-year-old bird colonels who haven't been in any kind of a cockpit since the big one ended in '45, and they've never touched a jet fighter. And, besides, each one of them claims that he's much too valuable where he is, moving all those colored pins on a map; as much as they'd like to, they just don't have time to come play with us. Unless we happen to have a nice staff billet open and a base flight gooney bird so they can continue to draw their flight pay.

"Hell, they've even used up most of the instructor pilots from ATC and interceptor pilots from the Air Defense Command. Even out at Wright-Patterson field there's not a safe slot for any scientist with a pair of wings on his chest and a pair of balls in his jockey shorts. That leaves only one major source of pilots, and where do you think they are?"

Donkey was certain he didn't like what was coming. "Please, Colonel! Don't tell me what I think you're going to tell me. I'm asking you as an old friend and former flight mate who's saved your ass more often than I'd like to remind you. Don't do this."

"Sorry, Donkey, but I'm afraid that your new flight member is coming right out of Headquarters, USAF, and that his background is SAC, specifically, B-52s." Smithers had the grace to avoid Donkey's incredulous eyes and instead stared out of the window at the sultry day. It was just possible that his news might inspire Donkey to violence.

"Jesus Christ! You can't do that to me. I don't know which I hate worse, SAC or Headquarters, USAF. Not only that, I hate everybody who's ever served in 'em."

"For your information, Donkey, I happened to have a tour in the Pentagon."

"That's what I mean! Any multiengine pilot is a pain in the ass, but I can't imagine one that's been in SAC *and* swivel-hipping around Washington. The fucking SAMs, and flak, and MiGs will eat the poor bastard alive. Why, he'd have fifty sorties in, if he was lucky enough to last that long, and still be trying to figure out how to fly his airplane. I don't like multiengine drivers, but I've never hated one enough to do this to him. And why me, anyway? How come some other flight commander doesn't get the privilege of herding this headquarters weenie around long enough for him to win a DFC and take over a staff position? Jesus Christ!"

"Calm down, Donkey," his squadron commander urged. "You know that we've already had a couple of guys in from the heavies who transitioned into the Thud without any big problems and they're doing a pretty good job."

"Horseshit! Those guys were just kids for the most part, and they hadn't gotten into the 'gear up, flaps up, shut up' stage of being a many-motored copilot. And if you get right down to it, they ain't all that great, are they? They're just like kids right outta flight school who've finished the transition course. They may be able to bomb the target but they need someone to lead them every step of the way. They're adequate but there's a hell of a lot of difference between being adequate and really knowing what the hell you're doing. We both know that. What in hell are they going to do next? Send us helicopter pilots? And getting back to my problem, there's a hell of a lot of difference between a pilot only a year or two out of flight school who hasn't had long enough to get into the rut of multiengine flying and some ring knocker who grew up with it. And you never did answer—how come I'm getting stuck?"

"Everybody's getting stuck, as you call it. We're trying to get all the flights back up to at least five pilots so I don't have to fly every time one of 'em gets a cold. You know I hate that shit." Donkey had to grin in spite of himself, for he knew that the commander would rather be flying than drinking. Which said a lot. "A couple of flight leaders are getting two of the new pilot levy, so consider yourself lucky that you're getting just the one. I was trying to be fair, since you already had one new guy . . . what's his name? Something froggy sounding."

"It's Broussard," Donkey grinned, "and you damned well know it."

"Yeah, Broussard. How's he coming along anyway, other than getting shot in the ass all the time, I mean. He wasn't a TAC pilot either if I remember right."

"He's going to do OK, but remember, he didn't come to us outta one of them damned aluminum overcasts either. He'd been flying small jets for more than three years in ATC, so at least he knew how to fly formation—and they've never made the bomber or transport puke who can do that. They may get to the point where they can hang behind a tanker without killing anybody and everybody will think they're shit hot formation pilots. That's a bunch of crap and has about as much to do with a tight four-shipper as entering the captain of the *Queen Mary* in speedboat trials. Look, I don't mean to put them down, honestly. They do the jobs they're given and they do them well. But it just ain't the job that we do. Not even close. But I can see that I'm not going to change your mind. When do I get to see this new flying wonder?"

"That whole bunch of newbies the wing got in are finishing up their base orientation today and will be sent down to the squadrons tomorrow morning. We'll funnel 'em on to their flights in the afternoon. Here's his personnel folder," he shoved the multilayered brown folder across the desk, "so at least you'll have some idea of what you're getting. Actually, this one doesn't look that bad. But I'll be honest with you, Donkey, since we go back a long way. He's in your flight because there's not another flight commander who he doesn't outrank."

"You mean I'm getting another old passed-over geezer my age?" Donkey smiled.

"Not exactly." Smithers seemed uncomfortable and once again seemed to be avoiding Donkey's eyes. "He's been on every below-the-zone promotion list that came out since he graduated from the academy."

Christ, thought Donkey, they didn't even *have* an Air Force Academy when I got my commission. "Well, just how old is this whiz kid?"

"He just turned twenty-eight."

"Twenty-eight! Jesus Christ! How old was he when he came on active duty? Twelve? I've got underwear older than that."

"Actually, he's already got three years in grade as a major. He had one of those temporary 'spot' promotions that SAC gives out for not spilling your coffee in flight or having your boots shined *really* good for a whole month, or some silly shit like that. But it all counted as time in grade when he came up for the real rank and was selected for the Pentagon."

Donkey was silent, thinking. The flight would definitely have to be rearranged now. It wouldn't do to have—he glanced at the name on the folder he held—Major Richard Nelson Stark flying the wing of a lowly captain like Andy Pritchard. No, he'd have to put him into the number two slot on his own wing and move Broussard into number four position on Pritchard's wing. He didn't remember whether Pritchard outranked Broussard or not and he didn't care. There was an old military axiom stating that rank among company-grade officers was like virtue among whores—

nonexistent. Actually, it was usually said about second lieutenants, but Donkey figured it would do for captains as well.

He grinned as he thought about the move. If this didn't make Pritchard and Broussard play ball with each other, then nothing would. It was difficult to ignore the other person in a two-man element. The more he thought about it the more he liked the idea of moving him to Andy's wing. They were both smart and capable young officers, though Andy had the edge in combat experience. It could make a damned good combination while he dealt with Maj. Richard Nelson Stark.

He looked at Lieutenant Colonel Smithers. "Are we going to get a chance to train these new people properly down in the easier route packs or just take 'em straight Downtown, like we did with Broussard, and try to kill 'em off the first day?"

Smithers looked at him with unblinking eyes. "Donkey, we'll do whatever we have to do to get the job done that is fragged to us by Headquarters, Seventh Air Force. If we can, we'll try to get them ten missions down in the bottom part of the country or Laos, just like we used to do. But, I'm making you no promises. If we need 'em to make up the force that goes to Pack Six, then that's where they'll go. They're all big boys and I think they'd go wherever we asked."

"Oh, I know they'd go. I was just wondering if any of them would get back."

Donkey sat strapped in the cockpit of the Thunderchief, awaiting the "start engines" time, mentally reviewing the pertinent portions of the mission briefing. His stopwatch showed there were still several minutes before he would bring the huge Pratt & Whitney engine to life. He would wait until the last possible moment to conserve fuel. Other thoughts tried to worm their way into his head: the week of down time that Cadillac Flight had enjoyed, Bobby Packard's capture, the change in the flight's structure.

He shoved all the extraneous thoughts from his mind and concentrated on the major potential problem facing Cadillac Flight: Maj. Richard Stark. Donkey could just see Stark's airplane two revetments down, preparing for engine start.

It was Stark's first combat mission with Cadillac Flight. He had been given several local missions under the tutelage of one of the squadron instructor pilots to include tactics and several trips to the local makeshift bombing range. Donkey had not mentioned the results to the remainder of the flight, but the instructor pilot, an old friend, slipped the word to him on the sly. "The guy had a hard time even hitting the ground with his bombs," the instructor had reported, "and I don't know what formation we were flying, but it sure as hell wasn't anything I've ever seen. Now that I think about it, I don't know what the hell he did that was right. I want to tell you straight out that if you're expecting this guy to cover your ass, you're going to have a real problem."

Donkey thought hard about his problem. Now there were two new wingmen in the flight to be nurtured until they developed the necessary survival skills, although, except for a few minor mistakes, usually misunderstandings, Broussard had no problem flying his aircraft or his slot.

Stark was earnest enough. Probably too earnest. It was easy to see how he'd made the early promotions. The problem was that he beat a thing to death, wanting answers to the unanswerable. Wanting, almost demanding, details and a rigid set of rules that were impossible for a complex combat environment. Donkey could sense the man's apprehension and tried to ease it. Stark was having none of that. When he had flown as an aircraft commander in the B-52, he'd known precisely what to do at any given time. Flights were planned down to the last detail and each crew member knew what was expected of him. Donkey knew that Stark wanted the same from the F-105 and was very concerned when his flight leader could not provide it.

The apprehension made Stark appear stiff and cold and quite unlikable. His questions had become more brusque and his comments more abrupt as the time for his first combat mission came closer. He was almost pushy in his demands, much more so than the other new men in the squadron. And although humbleness had never been a trademark of the fighter pilot, normally anything claimed could be backed up by performance. Stark had shown no indication that he could back up anything in an F-105, although he pored over the aircraft flight manuals and after-action reports as though he was trying to find comfort in their printed words.

Donkey well remembered the day he'd about washed his hands of his new wingman. It was the day Stark read the classified report from one of the larger think tanks in which the analyst proved conclusively with his statistics that it was impossible for an F-105 pilot to complete a hundred-mission tour without being shot down by the Vietnamese.

"Have you read this?" Stark demanded.

Donkey had not and had no intention of doing so. "Don't sweat it," he advised the new man, "you know what they can do with statistics."

"How can they expect anyone to fly with odds like this?"

Donkey was losing his patience. "Look, I told you. Don't sweat what some asshole back in Washington has dreamed up to make sure he can keep drawing those big bucks. Plenty of guys finish a tour. Hell! Some of 'em are on their second tours!"

"Well," Stark grated, "I know what you think of SAC, but they wouldn't allow something like this to continue."

That was the wrong thing to say to Donkey. He glared at the major. "I'll tell you what, Dickie. As far as I know, nobody dragged your ass into Thuds. But since you're here you'll take your chances just like everybody else. So quit your whining and worrying about things you can't do a damned thing about and try to learn your job well enough to have a chance of living through your tour. And while we're talking about it, you might try to be a little more pleasant to Pritchard and Broussard. They're the ones who are going to have to cover your ass, you know. It wouldn't hurt you to have a beer with them every now and then. You always make a point of eating and spending your time with the wing staff people. Hell, you still have two captains in your own flight calling you Major Stark like you were at the Pentagon or something. Loosen up, man! You could get a lot of information out of Andy Pritchard."

"I don't see what's wrong with wing staff people," Stark retorted. "Some of them are old friends from the Pentagon. And I've never believed that subordinates had to like you to do their job correctly. I doubt if I'd have ever won a popularity contest on my bomber crew."

Donkey turned to leave, then faced Stark again. "This is not a bomber crew and the only thing subordinate about those guys is their rank. Either one of them could fly you into the ground. You're no longer somebody who sits in an airplane that's on autopilot and gives directions, Stark. You're going to have to suck it up and do it yourself."

Donkey shook his head to clear it and fumbled for the tube to the water bottle. He took a quick sip and stowed it, noting there were thirty seconds before start time. He nodded his head at the crew chief and glanced quickly around the cockpit to ensure all switches were set for the starting sequence. He double-checked them, thinking that if he kept thinking about Stark, he'd have to go back to using the written checklist opened on his kneeboard.

He watched the crew chief slip on the large earphones and microphone cup, which allowed him to talk to the pilot when the powerful engine had been started. The end of the wire from the headset plugged into a receptacle on the belly of the aircraft.

Donkey twirled his finger overhead in a circular motion, showing he was initiating the starting sequence, and received the ground crewman's nod in return. He hit the starter and immediately the air was filled, first with the odor then the smoke of the black powder cartridge that initially whirled the engine into its starting revolutions. The acrid odor of the smoke was so strong that he clipped on his oxygen mask and moved the regulator to one hundred percent.

The RPMs and tail-pipe temperature increased, then settled into the idle range. The other instruments were in the green. He signaled for the external power cart to be removed, then busied himself for a few moments rechecking the map coordinates he had earlier inserted into the Doppler navigational system. During the next five minutes, he and the crew chief went through dozens of checks to ensure that the aircraft was indeed ready for flight. He squared his helmet once more and checked the stopwatch. It was taxi time. Simultaneously advancing the throttle and pushing the transmit button on the throttle handle, Donkey called check-ins. The response was characteristically crisp, even with a new flight member.

"Two."

"Three."

"Four."

A spare should have checked in with the flight at this point, but no spares had been available for several weeks. If one aircraft aborted, then his wingman was briefed to come back as well.

Donkey began to taxi before the last check-in call was complete: "Ground Control, this is Cadillac Lead with a flight of four Thuds. Taxi and takeoff."

"Cadillac Lead, this is Ground Control. Roger, taxi to runway three five. Wind is three zero zero at zero five. Altimeter is two niner niner eight."

"Rog. Two niner niner eight on the meter."

Donkey carefully watched the sergeant crew chief marshal him onto the taxiway and render his usual stiff salute, one that would have made a Coldstream Guardsman proud. He returned it as crisply as possible, being hampered by the parachute and shoulder harness. The two men would have been embarrassed to put it into words, but the salute had great meaning to them both. The sergeant's salute meant that he had done his very best to put up an airplane that would get the pilot to his target; the pilot's gesture relayed to the sergeant, the real "owner" of the airplane, that he was proud to fly this particular machine and that he would do his utmost to bring it home unscathed.

Donkey strained in the cockpit to watch Stark, now the second element, pull in behind him. All together, Cadillac Flight began its elephant march to the arming area. There, the familiar ritual would begin—rechecking switches, arming weapons, and checking the aircraft. He looked to the right toward Stark, as the flight taxied into the arming area. Donkey raised both gloved hands so they would be in view of the arming crew. He let his eyes drift back to Stark while the armorers knelt below the bombs hanging from each wing. His wingman's head moved around while he nervously scanned his instruments. This guy could be a real problem, Donkey thought. He switched his gaze to the other element. Broussard and Pritchard sat in the cockpit as though they were boneless, slumped against the constraining straps. If they were anxious it didn't show. Both of them are good boys, he thought fondly. He was determined to do his damnedest to see they finished their tour in one piece.

Captain James Evelyn Broussard

Jim Broussard was also watching Major Stark's head bobbing up and down in the cockpit. Nervous as hell, he thought. First combat mission and, if the reports were correct, not that good a pilot. He also had all the makings of a real pain in the ass. That didn't particularly bother Jim. There were many royal pains in the ass in the squadron. Considering fighter pilot egos it was almost a fact of life that many would be obnoxious. Almost forty guys and each convinced that he's the best pilot not only in the squadron but possibly the world. And almost all of them *were* good.

But Stark was not like the other pilots. One of the senior men in the squadron at twenty-eight, he'd made it clear that he was not afraid to use his rank. He expected the two captains to defer to him. A worm of worry came to Jim. What would happen if Stark took over after Donkey left? Cadillac Flight could be in for a world of hurt if that happened. But perhaps Jim was worried about nothing. Maybe by the time Donkey rotated stateside, Stark would have come around. Frankly, Jim doubted that this new guy would be able to pick up the necessary combat and flying skills to lead a flight and keep it out of trouble. Andy was the logical man to claim the vacated flight leader's position after Donkey left. He had the experience and was confident of his abilities.

Broussard smiled as he thought of the look on Donkey's face when Stark had asked, in all seriousness, whether he should plan on assuming command of the flight should anything happen to its leader. Donkey had stared at him as if he were insane, then pointed out dryly, and with obvious self-control, that perhaps they should follow the time-honored policy of the last fifty years amongst fighter pilots and allow the second element lead to take over in the very unlikely occurrence of the flight leader's demise.

How about emergency procedures? Stark had persisted, his nervousness over the mission becoming apparent in his search for answers. Well as for emergencies, Donkey had said, did Dickie want to talk about those found in the aircraft flight manuals or maybe about one of the thousand or so that could happen when they pissed off the natives by dropping bombs on them? For instance, if an ejection were necessary in Laos, procedures didn't really mean much, since the Pathet Lao had a habit of severing the pilot's head from his body as soon as they captured him. Some of the North Vietnamese were apt to do the same. There were many more potential emergencies, Donkey explained patiently, but he didn't expect Dickie to concern himself with them immediately. Stark had turned a rosy hue, his mouth tightened into a straight line. Jim felt pity for the man. He was out of his element, his experience limited to missions in the peacetime bomber force, which could be planned with the utmost precision. Stark wasn't accustomed to being thrust into a knife fight. Come to think of it, neither was he.

Jim turned his gaze from Major Stark and looked at the aircraft to his immediate right, momentarily shocked at seeing Pritchard staring back at him in his unaccustomed position. He quickly moved his head and broke the eye lock. Looking straight ahead, Jim wondered how all this was going to work out. Neither he nor Pritchard had made any overt sign when Donkey announced the position changes within the flight. He knew Pritchard was glad that it was him in his element now and not Stark. Andy probably couldn't stand either of them but at least he knew Jim could hang onto his wing.

Cadillac Flight was fortunate in that today would be almost a training sortie into Route Package One, just north of and adjacent to the DMZ. Their target, a section of the country's north-south rail line, should be relatively safe as long as all the pilots were attentive to their business. Safe, that was, as any place in that gun-loaded country could be considered safe, for there were flak sites paralleling the tracks. Intelligence had no indications of SAMs, and the MiGs wouldn't normally work that far south. However, they could expect to see guns of up to 100mm protecting the switching yard.

"Cadillac Flight, go tower," Donkey ordered as he pulled away from the arming area. The pilots hurriedly switched radio frequencies and followed the lead ship toward the runway. The second hand of the stopwatch swept through the briefed takeoff time and Jim watched Donkey's aircraft begin to slowly trundle down the runway, then accelerate sharply as he stroked the afterburner for additional thrust. Black smoke from the water injection system blurred the aircraft's receding image.

The pale light of the false dawn was just giving way to the direct sun rays as the wheels of Jim's aircraft lifted from the concrete, more than a mile from his starting point. The four aircraft were still strung out chasing the lead ship when Donkey called the frequency change to the radar controller for their initial vector toward their tanker. Jim picked up the black smoke from Pritchard's laboring engine in a reversing turn back to the east and increased his intercept angle to cut him off. Stark was not in position and appeared to be having problems catching the leader. Jim increased his bank angle and slid beneath Stark and into his slot on Cadillac Three's right wing. Before he moved in tight, he glanced to his left to find Stark. He was not in sight. Jim then looked back to his element leader and moved in gently until his left wing almost overlapped Andy's right wing. Stark couldn't find the handle and was still not in position. Jim thought about calling Donkey and telling him he was shy a wingman but decided to hell with it. Let Stark call if he wanted help. He did.

"Cadillac Lead, this is Two. Give me one."

Stark's request was that the lead ship power back by one percent RPM to assist him in the overtake. Such a request normally came only in a straightaway chase, not with the lead flying a lazy turn to allow the flight an easy intercept.

Donkey's head snapped to his left for the first time since the takeoff roll, searching for his wingman. At the moment his job as lead consisted of navigating the flight to the tanker and the target and then putting the flight into a position to bomb and escape. It was not to play screw-around with a wingman having problems with basic formation flying. The thought had never occurred to Donkey that a fighter pilot would not be in position by the time the lead ship had completed the long takeoff leg. Already, Donkey carried less than full climb power to give his wingman an edge in catching him. He had little choice but to honor the request for a further power reduction, but he was not happy about it.

"Cadillac Two, this is Lead. I hope we'll be able to dispense with this kind of shit in the future." Stark did not answer.

From his number four slot, Jim could see only the back of Donkey's helmet, which meant he was keeping his head turned toward Stark—a definite departure from his normal manner. Jim grimaced at Stark's gyrations as he attempted to get into and stay in position. The number two aircraft bobbed up and down and slid forward and aft as he wrestled with the controls. Christ, Jim thought, this guy looks like some of my old students just learning to fly formation, not an experienced pilot. How did he ever get through the F-105 transition course? But Jim knew there was always a way, particularly if you had an academy friend for an instructor pilot, or if some general or colonel expressed an interest in your progress. That was usually enough to alert the instructor or his commander that the student had a sponsor who probably wouldn't be pleased if someone washed out his protégé. Jim's grimace turned to a smile as he thought what Donkey would have to say if they came in for a landing with a formation like this, knowing that every fighter pilot on the base was watching. It would be a complete humiliation for him.

Contact was quickly established with the tanker and the descent to refueling altitude begun, Stark still weaving in and out like a drunk driving a car. The rest of the flight looked as though they were tied together with a rope, moving as one aircraft instead of three. Watching Stark's struggles, Jim realized that he no longer thought about flying the aircraft; he simply did it. It was as though his thoughts were linked directly to the controls and were enough to activate them correctly. He wondered what it would be like to fly a B-52 bomber, as Stark had done. Straight and level for hours at a stretch, five more crew members to watch and care for, no flying on the edge. He decided immediately that he couldn't do it. Where was the fun? Why would anyone want to do that? Maybe flying straight and level all the time introduced a degree of caution that was unknown to fighter pilots. It must be the way a race car driver would look at a bread van driver. It was as if the term *pilot* shouldn't apply to both groups. Jim shuddered at the thought that it was theoretically possible for him to be reassigned to a SAC unit when his combat tour was completed. Just as suddenly, he remembered that if he survived this tour he planned to apply to a major airline to earn his living. Was that so different from flying bombers in SAC? And was this all that much fun? He decided not to think about it anymore.

Donkey contacted the tanker once more and gave the refueling order, beginning with Stark in Cadillac Two slot. He reminded all aircraft of the need to cycle off—to replenish their tanks the second time before the flight departed for the target.

"No sweat, Lead," the tanker replied. "Green Four has beaucoup fuel and we've got a solid contact on you. We're leaving orbit and turning down track at this time. Steer ten degrees left for rendezvous."

Broussard was embarrassed that there were witnesses, albeit necessary ones, who watched Stark's attempt to replenish his fuel tanks. Time and again he positioned his heavily laden aircraft beneath the tanker and the boom would be inserted into the refueling receptacle, only to get an automatic disconnect as he exceeded the boom's lateral or fore-and-aft limits. Each attempt succeeded only in gaining him a few hundred pounds of fuel. He was barely staying even with the fuel being burned.

The tanker's boom operator, despite the normal radio silence during air refuelings, realized that a potential problem was developing. He began to coax the recalcitrant fighter into position long enough to sustain contact and deliver the scheduled off-load. "Cadillac Two, forward four, up two," the boomer pleaded with the rattled pilot. "Go easy, Two. You can do it. Forward one, up two. Contact. Fuel is flowing." Then, finally, "Disconnect."

Cadillac Two, tanks filled at last, pulled back from the KC-135. Jim realized that they were much farther up the track than scheduled, which increased their distance to the target. They were also far behind on their times. The others in the flight smoothly and quickly took their scheduled off-loads. Donkey, he knew, must be seething, though he had not said a word during the fuel transfer.

The raw, overpowering odor of jet fuel filled the cockpit as Jim moved back under the tanker to top his tanks for the second time. By the time the flight pulled away from the tanker, they had traveled even farther up the track.

Donkey was not pleased. "Cadillac Flight, this is Lead. Let's see if we can't make up some of the time we lost screwin' around back there," he growled over the radio. "There's no way we can make our TOT, but we're going to do our damnedest to make up every second we can."

Only one other flight, Apple, from a sister Thud wing, would be working their target area, supposedly following Cadillac in by five minutes. Jim knew there was little chance of making up that much lost time, though Donkey was leading them with the throttle cobbed full forward. He glanced quickly at the ground-speed indicator. Nearly 600 knots. They were much too far from the target to be making that kind of speed and still have a safe margin of fuel to tank coming out, especially since they'd flown fifteen minutes longer on the refueling track than planned. At full throttle, the large jet engine really slugged it down.

Over Laos, the Plain of Jars flowed beneath their wings, an almost treeless expanse where some ancient culture had implanted huge earthen jars. At 20,000 feet some were visible. Why did they do it? To bury their dead? Store their rice? Catch water during the wet season? What the hell— maybe they just enjoyed digging big holes and burying jars in them.

Jim banked automatically to follow the formation's turn to the south, then on a signal from Pritchard moved into a right spread formation. Jim noticed that Pritchard automatically quartered the sky, moving his head back and forth, though they were well south of the MiGs' normal hunting grounds.

Through the haze he began to pick up the blurred outline of the mountain range that formed the spine of Southeast Asia. The visibility was terrible, as usual. The smog was worse than any he'd seen, even in Los Angeles. It was a combination of smoke from thousands of charcoal kilns, open fires, and farmers burning off new plots of land to plant their crops—all of the pollution held within a few thousand feet of the earth's surface by a tremendous inversion layer of warmer air. It would take the coming monsoon to eventually clear the air of pollution, only to fill it with huge thunderstorms, which would prowl Southeast Asia for months.

Broussard glanced at his Doppler navigational system indicator and noted that they were only a few miles from their last turn point. The final leg would take them directly across the panhandle of North Vietnam to the target.

Stark continued to have problems formatting on the lead ship. It was apparent that he was working too hard at it. His ship would start to close rapidly with Cadillac Lead, and he would react by reducing the power, so much so that his ship would drop rapidly out of the correct position. The Thuds were at their maximum gross weight, which didn't help. How had the man ever gotten through a fighter transition school? The guy *must* have had a sponsor, someone looking after his career. Jim wasn't sure that Major Stark's guardian angel had done him any favors, for unless the man's flying skills improved dramatically, there was every chance he wouldn't live to see the end of his tour.

"Let's clean 'em up and green 'em up," Donkey transmitted as they began their turn to the east. "Let's go strike frequency."

Jim switched his UHF radio to the preset strike frequency, then checked and set the myriad switches that would properly release the bombs. The weapons were normally unarmed until they crossed the enemy's border; that way, if an aircraft had to jettison the load, they'd be in the safe configuration. Laos, over which they had been flying, was fragmented between Communist Pathet Lao forces and those of the Royalists and Neutralists. Most of the time, no one knew for sure whose troops occupied what pieces of ground, so bombs were always jettisoned safe unless they had a specific target assigned. Laos was a very confusing country. Jim decided he agreed with the French writer Bernard Fall, who once said Laos was a political idea and expediency rather than a real country.

Donkey made contact with Apple Flight, already over the target and none too happy with the situation. Scheduled to follow Cadillac Flight, they found themselves orbiting the area all alone, trying to look like clouds. The Viet gunners were not fooled and were ranging the flight with antiaircraft fire.

"Apple Lead, this is Cadillac Lead. We're inbound at this time, about zero five out. What's your position?"

"Right over the damned target, Cadillac Lead, where we've already made two orbits waiting for you. Did we get the wrong word at the briefing, or weren't you supposed to lead this gaggle in?"

"Negative, you're correct, Apple Lead. We got hung up on refueling, so why don't you go ahead and go to work on your assigned targets. We'll follow you when you're through."

"Might as well. There's no sense hanging around here getting our asses shot off. A couple of those guns are getting our altitude. OK, Apple Flight, this is Lead. Let's do it, then get out of here."

Donkey would be seething at the rebuke by Apple Lead, Jim knew. Bursts of North Vietnamese antiaircraft fire could indeed be seen on the horizon, identifying the location of Apple Flight as though they were towing a banner with their name on it.

One certainty existed. The Viet gunners now knew what section of the track was going to be attacked. After Apple Flight's orbits and attack, they would be waiting. Rail lines were like bridges in that there was really only one method to successfully strike them. The bombs had to be released in train, one after another, rather than all together, and the attacking aircraft had to angle across the track, since a near miss did nothing but produce a crater and a great deal of loose material for the repair crews. Properly accomplished, the bombs would walk across the rail line and at least one of them would demolish a section of track. No one had any illusions about how long this was going to hold up the

North Vietnamese supply trains. Probably by nightfall, the beginning of their normal operating hours, they would be headed south on repaired rails.

The bomb explosions from Apple Flight could be seen through the haze as Cadillac reached the IP, as yet unbothered by the flak guns concentrating on the other flight. Jim tried to find their IP—a small patch of woodland with the crossroads that disappeared within its darkness. The aircraft began to buffet as their speed increased in the descent to roll-in altitude. He glanced quickly to his left to check Stark's position. Stark seemed to be falling behind as the flight continued to accelerate. Small, angry, gray puffs of flak began to appear to their front, still out of range but closing rapidly with the speed of the approaching flight.

The rail line and switching yard were clearly in sight, outlined by the rising smoke from the earlier bombs. Jim caught the glint of the sun off the wings of one of the elements of Apple Flight as it jinked off the target. The flak caught up with Cadillac Flight but remained about a thousand feet below as the gunners ranged them, perhaps confused by the thick haze. They adjusted quickly, and in moments the bursts were almost at their altitude.

The aural tone of the radar warning device had been warbling gently in Jim's helmet for several moments, almost unnoticed. Suddenly, it took on a new, strident tone as the gun-laying radars acquired them and began to track their progress to the roll-in point.

Broussard quickly rechecked the nine switches necessary to release his bombs armed on the enemy, then returned his wide-eyed stare to his element leader and the lead ship. Come on, Donkey! He kept his eyes glued to Pritchard and Donkey for a clue, for he knew from past experiences that Cadillac Lead did not feel it necessary to give warnings to his wingmen before he began the attack. He expected all of his flight to be watching him carefully.

Strings of bright orange balls reached out for them as they came within range of the 37- and 57mm guns. These were often more dangerous than the larger-caliber weapons, because they were fed with clips of six and the gunners could repeat the bursts with amazing quickness. A detonation rocked Jim's aircraft, then, in quick sequence, another. He saw Pritchard glance quickly at him to see that he was still in position. He was still there, flying through the metal-filled sky Pritchard had just negotiated.

Come on, Donkey! Let's do it and get our asses out of here! Even as he thought it, Jim knew his flight leader would never roll in early on the target because of heavy flak. Donkey clung stubbornly to his simple creed: "You get paid to put the fucking bombs on the target."

The radar warning was now wailing like a soul in hell, and Apple Flight could be heard clearing the strike frequency. As if that were his cue, Donkey suddenly rolled his aircraft inverted and hurtled toward the ground in a sixty-degree dive. Jim saw Pritchard delay, waiting for Stark to follow so that he could take Broussard into their own attack and get the hell out of the area. The flak was getting thicker and closer. It was distracting as hell. Seconds passed as Pritchard waited. They were getting far out of position to make a proper attack. They couldn't wait much longer.

"Take it down, Cadillac Two! Take it down!" Jim heard Pritchard call.

Stark immediately rolled his aircraft into a dive and plummeted toward the earth as if he had been awaiting a command to do so. Pritchard was close behind him, pausing only briefly before he rolled the heavy Thud inverted and used forward stick pressure to keep the nose of the aircraft in level flight. Jim followed him. They were well past the planned roll-in point, and as the blood rushed to Jim's head he searched the ground for their briefed target. He saw it immediately, as Donkey's bombs marched across the multiple tracks in the yard. Only then did he release the stick pressure holding his aircraft inverted and allow the nose to slice toward the ground in an almost vertical dive.

Another quick look at his element leader showed Broussard that he was holding tight to his position despite the unplanned attack sequence and the negative-g flight time. He concentrated on bringing his sight pipper onto the target.

Stark's bombs exploded in a line well west of the switching yard. The lighted sight in Jim's own windscreen settled just to the left of the primary rail line as the large fighter stabilized in its dive, still bucking and shuddering as the airflow warped around the bombs beneath its wings.

Jim squeezed in a little right aileron and rudder to correct the sight picture. The aircraft shook violently as an antiaircraft shell exploded nearby. Probably a 100mm gun, he thought absently to himself as he steered the plunging fighter back to the proper course from which it had been flung by the near miss. Wonder why they don't call it a near hit, the uninvolved part of his brain mused. Better get your mind back on the business at hand, he scolded.

Looking quickly at the altimeter, Jim saw the tape unwinding rapidly through 8,000 feet. Another 1,500 feet to go before release. More flak shook the aircraft, and he was momentarily dazzled as more orange balls darted across his windscreen. This was much worse than planned. Finally, 6,500 feet! Pickle and pull! He felt the bombs kicking from the diving fighter, one after the other, each leaving the aircraft lighter and more responsive. He counted the last bomb off. Pull! He tried to get the stick back into his belly.

His speed was so great now that the aircraft seemed to act in slow motion as it fought through the centrifugal force. Finally, the nose began to slowly rise as the ground rushed at him. He felt the g suit begin to inflate and clamp tightly to his thighs and belly. His eyes sought the accelerometer. Almost seven g's. Seven times the weight of his own body pressed him back into the seat to the extent that he couldn't force his hand to move the throttle outboard to engage the afterburner. The tight-fitting oxygen mask sagged far down on his face. The flesh of his jaws and lips pulled downward as the gravity forces made him into a parody of a drooling idiot. His vision field narrowed and turned a dark gray as the blood lost the fight to enter his brain, straining against the g forces. For a moment, he thought he would black out altogether. The inflatable bladders of the g suit helped, as did the adrenaline coursing through his bloodstream and the fear-constricted blood vessels, which pushed his blood pressure to the extreme. He eased some of the back pressure on the stick when it became apparent he was not going to plow into the ground. His vision began to return to normal.

"Where the fuck is everybody?" Donkey asked over the radio.

"This is Three," he heard Pritchard mumble against the g's into the built-in microphone in his mask. "Just coming off."

Jim followed as Andy began to jink his aircraft, slamming it into left and right turns. He fought to hang on in the hard turns.

"Where's Two?" Donkey asked.

"This is Cadillac Two. I've lost you, Lead, but I'm about five miles west of the tracks on a heading of two seven zero degrees," Stark answered. His voice was high and tense.

"What the hell are you doing out there? You're supposed to be on my wing, which is where I thought you were until I just happened to look out there and found nobody home and that I'd made the run all by myself. Rejoin the flight immediately."

"Lead, this is Two. I'd be glad to rejoin if you'd just tell me where you are."

There was a lengthy pause before Donkey answered. "Two, we're going to circle about ten miles north of the target, right over the tracks at twenty thousand feet. Now, get on over here and get joined up so we can hit the tankers before we all run out of fuel."

Stark intercepted them at altitude; except for a few wild bursts of flak fired from well out of range, the guns had grown silent. Smoke and dust from the bomb blasts were clearing, and gaping holes could be seen in the switching yard and along the main track leading into the yard. One, maybe two nights' work and it'll be operational again, Jim thought. Then we'll come back and blow some more holes in it so they can start rebuilding it again. Hell of a way to make a living. He looked closely at his fuel quantity, knowing it was going to be very tight making the tanker, particularly if Stark had trouble again. He deliberately kept his eyes from returning to the indicator.

The flight entered Laotian airspace and pointed toward their refueling rendezvous in eastern Thailand. All aircraft were throttled back to the best endurance power settings, almost hanging in the air from the reduced airspeed. It was going to be very, very close.

Donkey switched the flight to refueling frequency, though he delayed joining them there while he talked to the orbiting command post aircraft, trying to expedite the refueling. He refused to call the situation an emergency, which perhaps would have provided more prompt action, because a Mayday had the possibility of diverting the tanker from someone more in need than Cadillac Flight. Personally, Jim didn't see how anyone could be in worse need of refueling. His eyes crept unbidden to his rapidly vanishing supply.

"Crown has a tanker barrel-assing toward us, so keep alert. He'll be up this freq in a minute or two," said Donkey.

Broussard noticed that he didn't bother asking their fuel state, but only gave them their refueling sequence.

"Two, you'll be first; then Four; then Three. Two, you're going to have to back off after you grab a couple of thousand pounds. Same for you, Jimbo. Grab a couple of thousand and Andy and me'll do the same. We may have to keep cycling off that way for quite a while, so let's everybody be sharp."

It was obviously Donkey's plan to have each aircraft take only enough fuel to keep it in the air for a few more minutes while the other thirsty birds refueled. It was the only way it could be done and not have the last two aircraft run their tanks completely dry before they had the opportunity to hook up.

"Cadillac Lead, this is White Anchor Three Four," a new voice cut in. "How do you read?"

"I've got you five by five, Three Four. Refueling order will be Two, Four, Three, and Lead. We're all hurting, so just give each aircraft a couple of thousand, then we'll cycle off until we can get this thing together again."

He had said the magic words "we're all hurting." The tanker crew knew that when the fighter pilots admitted to such a situation, it meant that they were only moments away from a flameout.

"Rog, Cadillac Lead. Come right five degrees. We've got a strong return on you and we're starting up track at this time. On roll-out, you should have us at your one o'clock at about five miles. We'll be expecting recycles and we'll also notify Crown of the situation."

"Thank you, Three Four. OK, Cadillac has you visually just as advertised. Two, get on in there and get on the boom. Boomer, don't forget that we want a disconnect after two grand has been transferred to each receiver."

Stark edged his aircraft slowly forward, following the line of the boom beckoning him with seductive little up and down motions before it retracted out of the way, lurking to one side to stab him when he was in position.

It was not smooth or pretty, but Major Stark took his two thousand pounds with only one inadvertent disconnect when he exceeded the boom's limits. The boom operator retracted the metal tube and swung it to one side away from the fighter.

Broussard was immediately into position beneath the tanker, knowing that the other two who waited would be unable to keep their eyes from their fuel gauges. He had no disconnects, but each second of waiting for him to finish had to be agonizing for the others.

"I'm really hurting, Lead," Jim heard Pritchard radio quietly. "Down to zip." He knew how much that had cost Andy to say, knowing that Donkey had no more fuel than he did and was still two aircraft away from getting any. Jim knew his element leader had felt obliged to make his situation known, however. Both the flight leader and the element leader could be only a minute or so from flame-out. Broussard immediately initiated a disconnect from the tanker. "I've got more than a thousand pounds now. Come on in." A thousand pounds wasn't much, only a few more minutes' flying time, but it was more than Pritchard or Donkey had.

Pritchard was ready and moved quickly into position. The boomer knew that he had the makings of a major catastrophe on his hands and he was not about to lose time by trying to make a gentle connection. He was slamming it home like a rapist.

As Jim watched with rounded eyes, Donkey slid under the tanker beside Pritchard, trying to save a few seconds. The stubby wings of their aircraft almost overlapped. "On your right, Andy," the leader called, alerting Pritchard to his position should he not have seen him move in. After Andy had his shot of fuel he would have to move only slightly left and back away while Donkey slipped a few feet into position. Donkey had to be in very bad shape to try such a thing, for it put both of them as well as the tanker in a very dangerous situation should someone make a bobble. Pritchard responded with two clicks of his mike switch, the accepted aviation acknowledgment of a message when the pilot was in no position to respond verbally.

Pritchard initiated his own disconnect when the boomer called that a thousand pounds had been transferred. He immediately slid aft and left, vacating the space for Donkey, who was already nuzzling up to the boom like an eager calf trying to suckle.

"Flameout," Donkey reported calmly before a contact could be made. "Three Four, how about slowing and starting downhill and maybe we can still pull this thing off. Boomer, you're probably going to get only one shot at me."

"That'll be enough, Cadillac Lead. I can thread a needle with this thing."

"Just my luck," Donkey responded as the tanker began an immediate descent. "Of all the boom operators in the world, I've got to get one who practices sewing rather than refueling."

The remaining three Thuds pulled their throttles to idle and followed their leader. No matter what happened to Donkey, they had to be next to the tanker or they would all soon be out of fuel. They watched as he maneuvered his powerless aircraft beneath the descending tanker. They knew that without power the large, stubby-winged fighter had the glide characteristics of a falling brick. Donkey was making it look easy, though.

"Contact!" the boomer called. "And you're getting fuel!"

"Yeah, and I've also got a relight. Put as much pressure on that thing as you think it'll stand, because the rest of the flight is probably just about dry again. Come on in, Cadillac Two. I've been on long enough. Good work, Boomer."

On and off the flight cycled, never able to break the vicious chain that had been established. Each aircraft would take only the minimum fuel needed to sustain flight for another few minutes before backing away and letting another at the nozzle. Each pound became precious, for none of the pilots was able to get away from the danger of almost immediate fuel exhaustion.

"Donkey," Broussard called from his number four position as Pritchard took his turn, "we're going to look awfully silly entering the traffic pattern this way."

"Ain't that the truth. It's really going to be embarrassing."

"Cadillac Flight," the tanker pilot called, "you'll be pleased to hear that Crown has finally decided to send us another tanker to get us out of this mess. He'll be joining us in a few minutes."

"Rog," answered Donkey. "Lead will take the first element to the new tanker when he gets here, and the second element will stay here with old Three Four until everybody gets topped."

The arrival of the fresh tanker took the flight out of danger. Long after they had replenished their own tanks, Pritchard and Broussard flew behind the first element, watching Stark resume his fight with the tanker. The task was now made more difficult by the increased weight of his aircraft. There was little reason for him to have completely filled tanks, because they were nearing their home base. Jim suspected the reason Donkey insisted upon it was revenge.

Practice had not made perfect, but eventually the refueling was completed. The flight rejoined for the relatively short trip to Takhli. Donkey was so pissed that he made no comment on the ragged formation as they approached the airfield.

Broussard pulled himself wearily from the cockpit and, accompanied by the crew chief, walked around the aircraft, inspecting it for battle damage. He couldn't remember how many times they'd cycled off the tankers, realizing that if he were exhausted by it, Stark must be almost comatose. He gathered his gear and walked to the taxiway to await the arrival of the van to take them to debriefing. Pritchard trudged toward him, helmet and map bag swinging from his hands.

They stood together, unspeaking for several moments, trying to ignore the scene taking place across the ramp, where Donkey was debriefing Stark in his own fashion, forefinger continually jabbing at Stark's face and chest. Stark stood stone-faced, like a plebe on parade—eyes straight ahead, body rigid.

Broussard felt a wave of compassion for the man. He hadn't, after all, screwed up on purpose, and it was as much a fault of the system as his own. How could headquarters allow a pilot with so little aptitude for this type of flying to be sent to a wartime operational unit? The wing simply didn't have the time or resources to train him to an acceptable state of competence. Didn't they realize they were almost surely signing his death warrant? Didn't anyone back there know that Hanoi was ringed with three times the antiaircraft defenses that Berlin had in World War II? Perhaps they were so out of touch that they really didn't know what was happening. Or perhaps they just didn't care.

"It's crap like this," Jim said, turning to Pritchard, "that can ruin your whole day."

Pritchard looked at him, misunderstanding. "I don't know. I feel kinda' sorry for the guy. I know how he must feel."

Rather than explain that he had been referring to the entire mission, not just Stark's part in it, Jim let the comment pass and watched the two majors approach. Donkey was obviously cooling off after his explosion at his wingman. Stark walked stiffly but seemed under control. His face had more color than might be expected from the Thailand sun.

"I don't know about you young pukes," Donkey announced, "but I'm ready to get outside some beer."

Captain Nguyen Thi Minh

Minh sat in the cockpit of his fighter, helmet off, listening to the sound of the air raid siren compete with the noise of the APU providing external power to his aircraft. He held the helmet upside down in the crook of his arm resting on the canopy rail so he'd be able to hear the controller should they decide to launch him today. At least, he'd hear some of it the first time—enough to know to put on his helmet, then catch the rest on the inevitable repeat. He knew the instructions by heart now, and they never varied. He figured the odds of his launching today at no better than two to one.

He glanced down at the new captain's insignia, just visible beneath the parachute strap, awarded only the day before on the occasion of his fourth victory. It had been simple, he told his friends as they tried to empty his wallet after he'd promised to buy the beer for the evening. He'd broken out of the clouds and the ground controller had positioned him perfectly for a rocket attack. He had punched off two air-to-air missiles, and the first one looked as if it had flown up the tail pipe of an F-105.

He'd even made a joke about the way the controller managed to just get him back into the clouds and hidden away before a flight of U.S. Navy F-8s cut off his escape route. Even so, one of their rockets had exploded close enough to shred the top of his stabilizer, and he'd been lucky to get the aircraft to the home field. The ground crew had been up throughout the night trying to repair the damage for today's launch, but even with their efforts his aircraft was not ready in time. Minh had thanked them and distributed cheap Polish cigarette lighters in appreciation for all their work and as a way to say thanks for the part they had played in his promotion.

He looked around the cockpit of his borrowed aircraft. All the instruments and switches were the same, yet it felt strange. He rubbed his gloved hand around the handle of the control stick and knew it wasn't the same as the one in his aircraft, although they were identical in outward appearance. He smiled to himself, thinking that what was strange was probably the pilot, and not the aircraft. Probably all pilots, presumably even the Americans. He tried to imagine himself as a Yankee fighter-bomber pilot attacking Vietnam—taking a large fighter down behind the limestone karst hill they called Thud Ridge and increasing the airspeed until the aircraft shivered and bucked with its heavy bomb load, knowing that enemy defenses were waiting. It must be a harrowing way to live.

As a boy he had seen for the first time the American P-40s and P-51s blast entire formations of Japanese aircraft from the sky, almost over Hanoi. Those American pilots had been his heroes then and had instilled in him the desire to fly. He wondered if some of those same pilots he'd seen in 1945 might be over Vietnam today in attacking aircraft. He added it up. If the pilots had been, oh, twenty-one during the earlier war, then it was possible that they could still be flying as senior pilots at the age of forty-two. In a way, he hoped that they were not. There were already enough disillusions in the world.

A dull ache behind his eyes reminded him of the previous night. Often, he thought wryly, it became quite a chore to live up to the image of a fighter pilot. He wanted a cigarette, having taken up the habit only within the last few months. No, what he really wanted was a Salem cigarette. There was something downright exotic and decadent about the mentholated smoke as it filled his lungs. A company mate had introduced them to him, during the celebration of his third victory two weeks earlier. He had purchased them on the flourishing black market, probably smuggled in by one of the truck drivers returning from the south.

Given his residual hangover, Minh rather hoped that if
he did launch, it would be one of the more simple missions.
A few vectors and a quick shot, then home again. He wasn't
sure that he felt up to dueling air to air with an F-4 or
F-105.

As soon as that thought entered his consciousness, he
knew it was crap. He'd leave Mai Lin in midstroke to
have a one-to-one shot at an American. He grinned at the
thought. If it did happen it might be best if the Yankee won,
for surely Mai Lin would be waiting for his return with a
butcher knife.

He'd had only one opportunity to try his aerial skills
directly against an American. Several weeks earlier he'd
cut off an F-105 coming off the target whose wingman
had been either separated or shot down. He positioned
himself between the American and his flight in a head-on
pass, ignoring the screaming voice of the controller. Both
aircraft had blazed away at each other with their guns,
neither scoring a telling blow; then they were past and
Minh had racked into a hard-g turn to give chase. He was
surprised to find that his opponent, rather than attempting to
rejoin his formation, was also in a turn back toward him. In
moments, they were in a nose-to-tail circle, each trying for
the turning advantage and a quick gunshot. It was a game
that Minh figured the American couldn't win; the MiG-21
was simply a more maneuverable aircraft.

Soon Minh was creeping into a position that he thought
would allow him the winning burst of fire. His aircraft was
shaking as he pulled it tighter and tighter, just avoiding the
stall. The g forces were dragging his mask from his face and
his vision was tunneling, the first indication of a blackout.
But he knew he'd win. The F-105 with its stubby little
wings just could not pull tight enough against him.

But Minh didn't win. The Thunderchief suddenly broke
from the death circle and dived for the ground and the
protection of Thud Ridge, his afterburner clearly visible
to the pursuing Minh. It had been a hopeless chase. There
was not an operational aircraft in the world that could catch
the F-105 when it unloaded, as the Americans called it, in
straightaway flight. The maneuver, Minh had learned, was
accomplished by putting a slight negative g force on the

aircraft and going into burner. This one had easily outdistanced Minh, jinking so hard that he could not get a clean missile shot. He'd scarcely had fuel for a safe recovery at home base.

The aggressiveness of the American pilot had surprised Minh. Obviously, the F-105 pilot had to have known he was in an inferior ship for that sort of tactics compared to the MiG-21. Nevertheless he had tried to take the fight to Minh. On reflection, Minh decided he would have done the same in the American's situation. The policy of his own air force was to avoid such confrontations; instead, they used the air defense tactics proven most effective in the air battle—radar vectors to a firing position on the attacking formations, one shot, and vectors away from the danger. Minh understood the reasoning: a lack of trained pilots, too few aircraft, the need to keep the MiGs clear of the tremendous antiaircraft fire placed in each sector of the sky. Nevertheless, just once he'd like to meet the incoming formations with one of his own. In truth, Minh admitted only to himself, the Americans were better pilots, for the most part, than the Vietnamese. But he was convinced that the only way to change that situation was to actively engage in aerial combat with the attackers. There would be heavy losses initially, but with experience and the weeding out of the weak pilots—which combat accomplished so well—the People's Air Force would in time be second to none in its capability.

The antiaircraft guns began to pound and Minh slipped his helmet onto his head. If they were going to launch, the message would be coming soon. He shifted the helmet to a more comfortable position, which the ground crew took as a signal to scamper to their positions for engine start. He shook his head at them and waved them back to the safety of the revetment walls. His hand was still outside the cockpit when a flight of four F-105s crossed directly over the airfield at 200 meters. They had appeared and disappeared into the mist before Minh's brain could grasp the reality of their presence. They must have been lost in the low-lying clouds blanketing the entire Red River valley, for they normally avoided the airfields by a wide margin. That was another source of wonderment for the company pilots: Why were the Americans forbidden to even approach the North Vietnamese airfields? Just another American eccentricity.

Minh knew that, should they decide to bomb the airfields, the result would be catastrophic; the majority of the Vietnamese interceptors would be destroyed on the ground within minutes. The survivors would have to be moved north to China, where their limited range would make them all but ineffective against air attacks in the Hanoi-Haiphong area and farther south. Thus far, however, not a bullet or bomb had impacted on a single one of the airfields. This was proof enough for Minh that although their leaders had strange ideas in some areas, their knowledge of the Americans was accurate.

The radio remained silent. He thought of his friend Trach, with whom he had trained and flown his first sortie. As Minh had secretly predicted, his friend had not been good enough to fight the MiG-21 against the Yankees. He'd been a competent pilot who would probably have had a long and enjoyable career if he had chosen to fly transport aircraft or helicopters. Unfortunately, as a fighter pilot he had the misfortune to be spotted by a U.S. Navy F-4, which had dispatched him so easily that Minh had been embarrassed for his friend even in death. Poor Trach. His beer-drinking friend had always been able to find them girls whose socialistic morality didn't extend to fighter pilots. He missed him very much.

Minh wondered what American pilot training was like. Did they have an elimination rate as high as the Vietnamese group had suffered in the Soviet Union? Probably so. He suspected that it was much the same in all countries, or at least those in which relations and connections didn't determine position. Maybe after the war he'd get a chance to talk to some of the F-105 pilots, perhaps drink some beer and talk airplanes. If there was one thing he knew for certain, it was that they would have a common ground. Even their Soviet instructor pilots were serious with them when someone began talking airplanes and flying. Those not flying fighters could never realize how consumed the fighter pilot was with his job—indeed, his calling.

He'd heard that the Americans were convinced their political system was the best for the world. He knew that the Soviets felt the same. The truth, he suspected, as in most things, was somewhere in between. Maybe Vietnam would be the first to find the perfect system. Minh didn't really care, just so long as they continued to let him fly fighters.

"Dragon One Zero, this is Control. Start engines and prepare for takeoff! Start engines and prepare for takeoff!"

"Dragon One Zero understands. Start engines and prepare for take off." He was motioning for the engine start to the ground crew as he spoke. He would have no wingman today.

He watched the instruments peak and motioned for the wheel chocks to be removed as he shoved the throttle forward. Control acknowledged his taxi call and gave him immediate clearance for takeoff as well as handoff instructions to Hanoi Sector for the ground-controlled intercept.

He was doing more than thirty knots as he made the turn onto the runway, pushing the throttle forward into the afterburner range and making his final checks on the roll. He felt the agile little aircraft quickly gain speed, and in a very short time he was able to rotate the nose gear off the ground, followed quickly by the mains. He sucked them up immediately while the aircraft was still only a few feet above the concrete runway. Then he let the aircraft accelerate into a 350-knot climb before switching radio frequencies as he entered the overcast. Minh still didn't care for instrument flying, though he'd had ample experience at it now.

"Hanoi Control, this is Dragon One Zero. Airborne through one thousand meters, heading three four zero degrees."

"Understand, Dragon One Zero, this is Hanoi Control. Turn hard left to two eight zero degrees. Increase speed to five hundred knots and climb to eight thousand meters."

They were sending him higher than usual today. Either the clouds had considerable vertical buildup or the Americans were making higher approaches. He followed the controller's instructions and armed his weapons for a missile attack. He was given another turn farther south.

Suddenly, his aircraft popped out of the dense cloud into a blindingly beautiful blue sky. He savored it for a moment before reporting to the controller, who immediately took him down a thousand meters back into the murk for concealment. He fine-tuned his radar and waited for the final attack vector.

"Dragon One Zero, turn farther right to one seven zero degrees and prepare for engagement. Hostile flight of four will be at your one o'clock, approximately four miles. Climb back to eight thousand meters after the attack to confirm results, then recover on a heading of three four zero, five thousand meters. Acknowledge."

Minh watched the enemy flight appear on his radar screen and saw that the interception angle was good. Just another minute or so. He waited patiently, knowing that the F-105 radar warning devices would be screaming at the pilots, but there was nothing they could do since he was hidden by the clouds. Another moment, his thumb caressing the missile firing button, then he jabbed it firmly, waited five seconds, then jabbed it again. The flare of the burning missile motors almost blinded him in the dark cloud. As soon as his vision returned he pulled back on the stick to take the aircraft above the cloud layer.

The impact of the missile came as he popped free of the clouds. It landed square against the tail cone of the lead ship of the second element of F-105s. He knew that the aircraft was dead as soon as he saw the explosion. The other missile had either missed or misfired, not an uncommon occurrence. He glanced quickly around the sky and was not surprised to see a pair of swept-wing F-4s maneuvering toward an intercept. Quickly he turned into them and jammed the stick forward, diving once more into the cloud cover, following the ground controller's instructions. The Phantoms had airborne radar, which would pick him up regardless of the clouds. He moved the throttle into the afterburner range and headed north, secure in the knowledge that they would have little chance for an interception. Even if they followed, he could rely on the controller for assistance. There was no radio message, so he assumed he was clear of the danger of attack. He sat out the remainder of the raid in an orbit, well north of the city. The shootdown had been almost anticlimactic. Too easy for him to accept.

Victory number five! He knew that had to put him in the top echelons of Vietnamese interceptor pilots. Only Colonel Toon and Major Thich had more, unless someone had an exceptional score today. He realized he should be happy to share the honor with the ground controllers who had placed him in such a beautiful position today, but he was in no mood to feel magnanimous. To hell with them. They risked nothing more dangerous than falling off their stools as they sat before their radar sets in the darkened underground bunkers.

News of his fifth victory had already been flashed to the airfield by the controllers before he landed, which made Minh feel a bit ashamed at his earlier attitude. He accepted the congratulations of the ground crew as he walked around the aircraft, inspecting it for battle damage. Behind the right wing root he found three small holes that could only have been made by an AK-47 or another small weapon. It must have been fired by some clod in the People's Defense Force, unless the Yankees had begun to carry assault rifles in their cockpits. The stupid fucking farmers would kill him yet!

He walked slowly toward the revetment where his own aircraft was being repaired. His regular ground crew was delighted with his success but unhappy that he had not done it in their aircraft. And they had a surprise for him. They proudly drew back the canvas concealing the vertical stabilizer of his MiG-21. They had not only repaired it but had painted it bright scarlet, enscribed with a small golden dragon. The metal glowed from the coats of paint and wax they had rubbed into it.

Well, Minh thought, at least the Americans would now know who was dropping some of their aircraft. He didn't want to tell the ground crew that their bright paint job just might make him a marked man among the enemy pilots. But what the hell! That's what flying fighters was all about!

First Lieutenant
Katherine Elaine Johnson

Kate could feel the beads of sweat trickling down between her breasts, which were mashed flat against the plastic pool chair. She estimated the time to be almost 2 P.M.; the sun was getting too hot even for someone with her tan. Still, she hesitated, sensing without seeing the flabby German salesman who refused to be rebuffed. If she gave any indication of being awake she knew his moves would start again, and unless she wanted to leave the pool she'd have to come down hard on him if she were to have any peace for the remainder of the afternoon.

She had arrived in Bangkok on an early morning shuttle flight from Takhli to the city's Don Muang airport, then came directly by taxi to the President Hotel. It was her first trip away from the air base, and considering the price of the hotel room she didn't fancy having her weekend ruined by some fat kraut who wouldn't take no for an answer.

The German wasn't the only one. During the two hours she had been at the pool, Kate had parried pickup attempts by two American GIs on R and R from Vietnam, their pores still clogged with red highland mud; a husband and wife team on vacation from Saint Louis; the entire crew of a B-52 bomber stationed on Okinawa but in town with a broken airplane, which they were in no hurry to have repaired; and, of course, the German.

"Would you like another Singha beer?"

Jesus, she thought, he must have been watching me like a hawk. She had wanted to turn onto her back for quite a while but had no desire to expose the front part of her body to his gaze. She raised her head from where it had been pillowed by her folded arm to squint at him, determined to salvage her day even if it meant ruining his. Without the beach shirt his waist was thick and paste-colored. His thin blond hair was turning gray.

"No, thank you. As I said before, I really don't care for another beer. And I really do insist on being left alone."

Kate was saved by the Thai bellboy, who walked by holding aloft a small black slate with her name printed on it. At intervals he rang a small bicycle bell to attract attention to his message. Kate twisted away from the German and waved her hand to the bellboy. His teeth showed white against his dark face in a wide grin as he hurried toward her. "Telephone, Miss."

"Where can I take it?"

"At the bar, please." The small Thai was almost at a canter as he tried to keep up with her long-legged stride. She was almost five feet nine inches, perhaps half a foot taller than the bellboy. He didn't seem to mind as he cast admiring glances at the sway of her buttocks.

"This is Lieutenant Kate Johnson," she spoke into the telephone, afraid of what might be coming. Probably her weekend canceled, at the very least. Or bad news from home. Instead, a familiar voice answered her.

"Is this the incredibly good-looking red-headed nurse from Texas?" asked Jim Broussard.

"No, you idiot, this is the short, fat one from Arkansas. What in the world are you calling me for? Where are you? What's wrong? Has someone been hurt? What—"

"Hold on, hold on," Jim laughed. "Nothing's wrong. Believe it or not, I'm in Bangkok."

"In Bangkok? But, how? I just saw you night before last and you didn't say anything about it."

"I didn't know anything about it then. This just came up this morning. Donkey and Stark had to fill in as the lead element for another flight going south. It's mostly a training mission with real new guys in it, and they had this pair of Thuds down here to be ferried back. They took one pilot from Cadillac Flight and one from Ford Flight. Donkey had

me and Pritchard toss for it and I won. So here I am. They
let us have the night here and we fly out first thing in the
morning."

"Well, where are you for God's sake?"

"They've put us up at the Transient Officers' Quarters,
but me and Mad Monk are free until 0800 tomorrow morning. I just thought that maybe we could get together for
dinner, unless you're already booked up, of course." His
voice trailed off as though this was a possibility he hadn't
considered.

"You bet I'm booked up. With you, Doofus. And Mad
Monk as well, whatever that is."

"Great!" his enthusiasm returning. "It'll be about three
or four hours before we get all the paperwork done and
are able to get cleaned up and into town. Mad Monk is
the other pilot I mentioned to you. How about we meet at
the bar in the President at 1800. We'll decide what we'll
do over some drinks."

"Sounds great. Now if I can only figure out what 1800
is, I'll be there."

His laughter filled her ear. "That's six o'clock to you
civilians at heart."

Kate walked back to the pool, pleasantly tingling with
both the sun and the anticipation that she would soon be
with Jim Broussard. She saw the fat German staring at the
bounce of her breasts in the tiny cups of her bikini. She
glanced at her watch and saw that she could either spend a
couple of hours shopping or get a little more sun and shop
tomorrow.

She opted for the latter. Behind the darkened lenses of her
glasses, her eyes watched the German raking her from stem
to stern. She bent over her chair and straightened the towel
covering the plastic, then carefully arranged herself on her
back, front turned to the sun. She tugged her bra down
until it just covered the tips of her breasts, then arranged
the bottom of her swimsuit to catch the maximum amount
of rays. Suddenly, she no longer cared whether the German
was watching her or not. Eat your heart out, Adolph, she
thought as the sun lulled her to sleep.

Kate arrived early at the hotel lounge, hoping to find
a quiet corner where she and Jim would be able to talk

without the competition from the small Thai jazz band. She knew she looked good in her haltered sundress. The jade-colored silk and matching sandals set off the coppery tone of her skin and made it look polished. Her only makeup was a light lip gloss and a hint of eye shadow. Small brown toes with nails painted bronze peeked from her flat sandals. The silk swirled around her long legs as she walked, briefly outlining her slender thighs and hips.

The lounge was packed. Every table seemed to be occupied by several young Caucasian males. Many turned to stare as she entered the room. She stopped in indecision when she could find no place to sit. Two young men standing at the bar motioned her toward their seats. Neither could have been twenty, and their hair was cut so close to their head that they appeared bald. Both had advanced cases of acne, their faces covered with unsightly pimples. She noted that their arms were covered with open sores and the backs of their hands looked as if they had been lashed with a whip. Both wore polyester trousers and gaudy short-sleeved shirts. It took no outstanding deductive reasoning to know that these were bush soldiers from the killing fields of South Vietnam. Both seemed ill at ease as she approached.

"Here, ma'am," the shorter one said as she came closer, "you can sit here. We're about ready to pull outta this place and find a bar where they don't soak you half a month's pay for a drink."

"Thank you," Kate replied with a smile. "I had no idea the place would be this crowded. Have you two been in town long?"

"Nah," said the other one. Kate saw that he had a long scar down the side of his neck. "Just pulled in from Danang today. We're marines, on R and R. Six more days and there's no way we're going to make it at these prices. Come on, Kelly. Drink up and let's blow this joint. Most of these assholes look like officers, anyway. Begging your pardon, ma'am."

Kate smiled at him. The taller man tilted his beer bottle and drained it. They both grinned broadly and swaggered from the bar, their contempt for its patrons apparent. Kate watched them leave, then turned to survey the crowded lounge. Closer inspection showed a few Thai men and women sitting together, sipping their drinks and listening to the band. There were a few Thai women with Caucasian men. Most, however, were young Americans in for R and R.

Not all of them were American. One of the exceptions slid onto the vacant bar stool next to her. She was irritated but not surprised to find it was the German electronics salesman from the pool. His raw silk sport jacket was cut to conceal his paunch. A tiny piece of matching handkerchief peeked from the lapel pocket. He was still perspiring heavily in the chilled air of the bar. Kate made eye contact, then with a curl of her lip deliberately turned her back to him. She could feel his eyes on her bare back and shoulders. The Thai bartender approached with a toothy smile.

"Your pleasure, Miss?"

"I'll have a gin and tonic with lots of lime," Kate answered.

"Make it two, and put it on my tab," said the inevitable voice behind her.

Kate looked the bartender squarely in the eyes. "I will have *one* gin and tonic and it will be on my ticket. Do you understand?"

The bartender flicked a glance at the German and nodded. He moved away to prepare the drinks.

"I think you misunderstand me, Miss," he began. "We are both alone and in a foreign country. What could be more natural than to share a drink and perhaps some dinner. I assure you that I shall make no unwelcomed advances. In fact—"

"Hey, Kate!" a familiar voice rang above the noise of the band, now seemingly confused as to whether they were attempting jazz or rock and roll.

"Jim!" Kate felt a genuine rush of pleasure as she turned and saw his lanky frame coming toward her. Broussard came close enough to take both of her hands in his, then stood back at arm's length to survey her, a look of admiration on his face.

"Kate, you are one beautiful sight. You look great!"

"You'd look pretty good yourself, if it weren't for that shirt," she laughed, feeling a little breathless.

Jim looked down at his chest as if noticing the shirt for the first time. "You mean you don't like this? I bought it this afternoon, specifically to impress you." The object in question was navy blue with a sheen like crushed velvet. Back and front were painted with huge, gaudy parrots sitting amid varicolored jungle foliage. Kate couldn't stop giggling.

"It's you, it's really you." As she spoke she became aware of another presence behind Jim—one that was hard to ignore. Being just three inches short of six feet tall herself, Kate was visually conditioned to the normal height range of the American male. This one exceeded the norm by some inches. She guessed he was at least six feet five inches and 250 pounds. He dwarfed Jim's six foot two frame, not so much by his height but his bulk. Kate knew he was exceedingly large by fighter pilot standards, which ran more to the short, stocky man. Still, it was his presence that commanded attention. His hair was long and curly, much longer than the regulation haircut. The nose started out to port, then leaned to starboard. Slightly protruding ears seemed mismatched, one being larger and sticking out more than the other. But it was the eyes that commanded the full attention of the viewer. They were the eyes of a madman, or one slipping into madness. Beneath shaggy black brows they burned with a chilling intensity. These were not eyes that wandered around idly in search of something interesting to observe. They locked onto an object. This had to be the Mad Monk.

"I was just about to buy the young lady a drink. May I get you one as well?" Kate had forgotten about the German salesman in the pleasure of seeing Jim.

Jim looked at him, then turned with a quizzical look to Kate. She frowned and shook her head slightly. Jim got the message and turned with a harder look at her bar mate.

"You can buy me a drink," a soft voice said. Kate was surprised to hear it coming from Jim's large companion. It had a lilting, musical quality that was totally incongruous with his hulking appearance. "You can buy me lots of drinks," he continued, stepping around Broussard to lay a log-sized arm around the German's shoulder. He stared dreamily into the salesman's face while his large hand crept up from the shoulder to gently massage the neck. The German's eyes widened in alarm and he made as if to stand. The weight of the arm kept him in his seat. The thick fingers found the earlobe beneath the razor-cut hair and began to tug it gently. "I like scotch and water," the monster said, almost whispering to his captive on the bar stool.

"Of course." The accent was losing some of its polish and becoming more guttural. "Bartender, please bring this gentleman a scotch and water and whatever anyone else wants."

"I want lots of scotch and water."

"Of course, of course. Bartender, please bring this gentleman anything he wants and charge it to my room. As long as he wants it. Now, you must excuse me, please, I have a very important appointment."

The loglike arm lifted from his shoulders and permitted him to stand. "Do you really have to go?" the soft voice murmured, disappointed. "I feel as if I was just getting to know you."

"No, no. I really must go. A pleasure. Good night, everyone." The salesman almost ran for the door.

Kate watched, mouth partially open, as the bulky figure disappeared from the lounge. She turned toward Jim, finding him staring at his companion with a broad grin on his face. He turned back to Kate.

"Kate, may I present Mad Monk Morrison, the Shame of Atlanta. Monk, Kate Johnson."

Monk held out a massive paw, which engulfed Kate's hand. The grip was gentle and the deep-set eyes were twinkling with glee, making him look like a huge naughty child who had just pulled a good one on an adult. "How do you do, Kate." The voice was still gentle but no longer had any sinister quality to it.

"My God, you're scary!" she blurted out, without thought.

The Shame of Atlanta seemed to take it as a compliment. "Thank you very much. I appreciate that."

The bartender sat drinks before them and nodded at Mad Monk's directive that they were to be added to the bill of their departed host.

"Monk hopes to go on to a career in professional wrestling. His drama teacher told him that he seemed to have a flair for it," Jim said with a straight face.

Kate looked from one to the other, not sure whether she was being kidded. "Is that true?" she asked Monk.

"Not really," he smiled benignly at her. "What I really want to do is be the host on a kiddie show." His voice took on the eerie, deadly quality it had earlier: "Like a piece of candy, little girl?" He smiled at her again. "How was I?"

"That's the most frightening thing I've ever heard in my life," she told him honestly.

"Shoot!" He looked disappointed. "Guess I'll just have to work on my stage presence." He drained his drink and grinned at them. "Well, I'm off. Nice meeting you, Kate. See you at 0800 tomorrow, Jim." He lapsed again into his sinister voice: "Have a good time, you two. And don't worry about a thing. Someone will be watching you." The hooded, crazed eyes flashed at them, then he was gone from the bar, walking directly to the door, scattering patrons who scurried from his path.

Kate stared at the departing back for a moment before turning to Broussard. "Is he for real? I mean, is he really an actor or something? Is he actually going into wrestling?"

"Naw, the Shame of Atlanta is a computer engineer who's married to an ex–Miss Georgia. He told me that they've got three little girls. He's going to do some shopping for them."

"God, he can be frightening."

"Well, at least he was able to get rid of your new boyfriend." Kate gave him a scowl. "Sorry," he continued quickly, seeing it was a sensitive subject, "let's finish these drinks and decide where to go for dinner. I'm hungry enough to eat a boiled owl."

In fact, they had several more drinks before they decided on Nick's Number One Cafe, at the bartender's suggestion. Neither of them knew Bangkok, so they had him write the address in Thai before leaving the hotel in search of a taxi. Several little Japanese automobiles were queued in front of the hotel as they strolled out. Kate felt light on her feet, as though she could float should she really put her mind to it. She held onto Jim's arm, leaning against him as they waited for the cab to pull up to the embarkation zone. The doorman explained to the driver where they wished to go, though he seemed to speak adequate English as he touted shops en route.

It was just after nine when they arrived at the restaurant. The streets were as crowded as they had been at midday.

Clumps of Occidental faces stood out above the crowd of bustling Thais. The smells of the city were exotic to Kate, reminding her of the Mexican cities she had known from childhood. The natives seemed good-natured and happy.

Even the food reminded Kate of Mexico—hot, spicy, and aromatic. though rice replaced the corn and legumes to which she was accustomed. Jim continued to wolf down his food long after she had been sated. They ordered another bottle of wine, which she sipped as he waded through an impossibly sticky dessert. She watched him as he ate. Though she had known him less than a month, he had changed considerably from the awkward-appearing young man she'd first seen in the hospital.

For one thing he'd lost weight. Never heavy to begin with, he was now almost gaunt. His cheekbones protruded as if any excess fat had been burned from them. His eyes seemed to be more recessed and no longer shifted away from her as he spoke, but looked directly into hers. Most apparent was the new look of maturity, as though he knew he could control any situation. Still, as he bent over his plate, the same errant lock of hair fell over his forehead, making him look younger than he was. He certainly didn't have a poker face; his emotions would always be mirrored there for all to see. But it was a good face, she decided, one that could grow on you.

She contrasted it to Andy Pritchard's. Now there was a face to write home about. He looked like the movie star John Derek. Or rather the way he used to look. Just short of being beautiful, yet masculine. Kate was no fool; she knew that Andy Pritchard cared for her very much and she admitted to herself that there was a sexual attraction between them. She also realized that there was no real spark within her for the man. He seemed to have it all: looks, personality, intelligence. But, in the end, she knew they'd never last as a couple. Somehow it just wasn't enough. She'd never feel completely comfortable with Andy.

She looked more critically at Jim Broussard as he finished the last of his dessert and tried to get some of the sugared sauce off his ridiculous shirt, scrubbing away intently with his napkin. She wasn't sure just what love was, certainly not the Hollywood version. She liked the way this man looked, and felt comfortable with him. She didn't

have to watch what she said around him and he made
her laugh without being completely zany. He was bright
without being overbearing, and still modest. Maybe love
was just adding up all the little things you liked about a
person. She knew that she would miss him terribly should
he not return one day. The prospect was so gloomy that she
pushed it from her mind and helped him clean his shirt.

They walked arm in arm down Pat Pong Road, stopping
often to look at the goods displayed in the lighted windows.
Bangkok never seemed to sleep, and shop owners were in
attendance, beckoning them within. They passed on, neither
of them really anxious to shop at eleven o'clock in the
evening. As they passed a clothing store, Kate suddenly
stopped and pulled Jim inside. A chubby Thai woman
beamed at them.

"We need a bathing suit for him," she said to the pro-
prietress, trying in vain to keep a straight face, "one that
matches his shirt, if possible."

The woman continued to beam, obviously not understanding a word of what she was hearing, and tried to
pull them to a display of batiks. Kate was determined. She
attempted to sketch the idea of bathing trunks on her own
body, with no visible results except for a good-humored
chuckle from the woman. Broussard entered into the spirit
of the play, making swimming motions.

The woman clapped her hands with glee as she finally
caught onto the charade, and directed them to a rack at the
rear of the shop. There they found a large tier of women's
swim wear, and the game began once more to determine if
there was also a stock of men's clothing.

"These look like they ought to do," Jim called from a
corner, holding up a pair of midthigh walking shorts. Kate
joined him and found what she felt was just the right pair—
bright orange with tiny red stripes superimposed over an
impressively green palm tree.

"Yup," she said solemnly, "these are just right to go with
your shirt. No doubt you'll be the hit of Takhli Air Base
when they see these."

"I'm sure you're right, but why do I need them tonight?"

"Because, dear boy, we're going back to the President
and hit the pool so you can work off some of those calories
you put away tonight. What do you think?"

"Sounds OK, I guess," he replied, a little dubious. "Let's grab a cab and do it."

Kate could feel her muscles pulled pleasantly taut as she completed her last lap in the pool. The water felt slick and heavy on her skin. The night was still sultry but refreshingly cool after the day's heat. She hoisted herself to the side of the pool and watched Jim floundering away at the far end. He seemed to be able to swim. Just. At first she'd been astonished, as only one who had grown up in the water could be, that he wasn't a good swimmer. It was almost beyond her comprehension that a function that was for her as natural an act as walking could be done so poorly. Then, she became amused at the gaudily clad figure thrashing away at the water as if he were trying to beat it into submission.

She glanced around the pool deck. There were at least two dozen other people either in the water or sitting in the lounge chairs. She was relieved that she didn't see the German salesman. She slipped into the tepid water and eased toward Broussard, now thrashing blindly for the far wall. Ten yards behind him she lowered herself beneath the surface to complete her approach. She almost swallowed a mouthful as she choked back a laugh when she saw his orange-covered bottom wallowing from side to side, legs kicking in uncoordinated movements.

Just before he reached the wall she grasped one foot and hauled down on it. It was as if he'd been torpedoed. His thrashing took on a new note of desperation, as if he was convinced a great white had him in its maw. Kate released his foot as she began to become concerned. He flung himself on his back, head beneath the water, arms flailing wildly. In his attempt to right himself his head began pointing downward toward the vertical. Thoroughly alarmed now, Kate grabbed the back of the orange trunks and hauled upward. As her head popped clear, she felt the buttons on his trunks rip free. She was treated to the sight of the globes of his milk-white buttocks undulating frantically as swirls of bubbles rushed toward the surface. She took a deep breath to go for him just as his brain seemed to sense the proper direction and he surged upward, propelled by wildly pumping legs.

His head popped free not more than two yards from the wall. He lunged toward it and clung to its rough surface, taking large draughts of air. She hurriedly swam to his side and put one arm around his waist in support, the other clinging to the wall. "Oh, God! Are you all right? I'm so sorry!"

He stared at her for a moment as if he didn't recognize her, eyes still large with fright. "Jesus! What the hell happened?"

At that moment, Kate looked down and saw the orange walking shorts shimmering beneath twelve feet of water and she began to giggle. She shifted her arm from around his waist and on impulse let her hand drift down to tweak his bare bottom. Then her laughter really began. Deep from her belly the guffaws came, one after another. She laughed until there was a stitch in her side and she thought she would lose her grasp on the wall of the pool.

Jim stared at her in consternation until he realized that he was naked. Then he, too, began to smile, finally joining her in raucous peals of laughter. The pool's other patrons stared at them as if they were insane.

Finally Kate was in control enough to dive to the bottom for the errant shorts. As Jim slipped into the buttonless garment, she turned her back, giving way to another bout of giggling.

"Come on," she said, leading him to a darkened area of the pool deck, "let's see if we can't get you out of here and up to the room before you get arrested. Walk real close behind me and we won't stop for anything. Just don't try waving your hands around." She began laughing again.

They lockstepped to the elevator, manned by a young Thai who had long since given up making sense of Americans. Unfortunately, before the elevator door could close two middle-aged couples boarded. Jim turned his back to them and faced the wall as Kate smothered her laughter in her hand. Their floor was below that of the other occupants, and Jim scuttled around the wall, keeping his back to them, as he made his way into the hall.

"Why the hell didn't we take towels with us?" he grumbled as he walked quickly toward Kate's room.

"Just think what we'd have missed," she said with a smile as she took her room key from the small strap around her wrist. There was no room for it in her tiny bathing suit.

"Here," she said once they were inside the room, "wrap yourself in that while I wash off the chlorine." She tossed him the terry cloth robe furnished by the hotel. "Open us a nightcap of that brandy in the liquor cabinet. It's the least I can do before I send you on your way."

In the bathroom Kate peeled away the bikini and started the warm water running in the shower. It felt delicious on her skin. She realized that her heart was pounding as she stepped from the tub and began to dry herself with the large, soft towel. She combed her hair straight back and applied a moisturizing cream before she slipped into her robe. She took a deep breath and opened the door. Jim was sitting in the easy chair with his bare feet propped on the coffee table, sipping from a small brandy glass.

"Will you stay with me tonight?" she asked softly.

She watched his eyes open wider, then she stepped to the bed and folded back the coverlet before going to the door and locking the dead bolt. She turned to him and flipped off the light switch. The outdoor light spilled through the undraped balcony door and made dusky shadows across the room.

Slowly, almost lazily, Jim rose from his chair and walked toward her in the half shadows. He opened his arms and she stepped into them without hesitation. His fingers smoothed her wet hair. She could smell the chlorine on his skin as she kissed the hollow of his neck. His lips brushed hers gently before moving to trace the length of her throat to the opening at the top of her robe. Kate gently tugged his head with both hands to bring his lips back to hers. Fiercer, now, she felt his tongue and dueled it with her own.

Kate disengaged and stepped back with a smile, grasping his hand to lead him to the bed. Dropping her hands, she released the tie of her robe, and as it swung open she shrugged it from her shoulders to the floor. She stood motionless, feeling rather than seeing his eyes roam over her body. The firm, rounded breasts, the slim waist above the gently sloping hips, the soft curve of her thighs. He reached toward her with one hand and placed it on her waist. She shivered beneath the touch and untied his robe. It fell to his feet. Kate looked at the lean, hard body and shivered once again, though the night air coming through the open balcony door was warm and heavy. She sat on the edge of the bed and reached for his turgid sex, tugging him toward her.

She lay with her head on his chest, listening to his heart rate return to normal. Probably about sixty-five per minute, she thought professionally. A good recovery time, too. She recalled a line from an old movie and leaned on one elbow to stare into Jim's half-closed eyes. "When you speak of this in years to come, and you will, please be kind."

His eyes opened and he stared at her without comprehension, then as he remembered the Deborah Kerr scene he began to chuckle. "Maybe I ought to say the same thing to you. How do you think I'll feel when you start telling tawdry stories about me in the nurses' dressing room. My reputation could be shot."

Kate smiled and placed her head on his chest again. She felt pleasantly fatigued and satisfied. "You didn't have a chance," she murmured, "not after I saw those cute little buns flashing in the pool. I knew I'd have my way with you . . . What time is it?"

Broussard peered at his wristwatch. "Almost 0230. I guess I ought to get in gear and go on out to the field." He made no move to rise.

"You probably should." Kate didn't move either. She felt the hand that had been caressing her shoulder slip down to cup her breast and capture the nipple. It rose to greet him. She turned to straddle his body. "Are you sure you can't stay a little while longer?"

She could see his teeth flash in the darkness. "I probably couldn't get a cab now, anyway," he said as he pulled her to him.

The sun was streaming through the open balcony door when she awoke. She stared groggily at her new Seiko watch. God, already ten o'clock. Where was Jim? A rumpled pillow next to her was the only reminder of his presence the night before. An insistent knock on the door was probably what had awakened her. Struggling with her robe, she walked sleepily toward the pounding, opened the door, and peered into the hall. A Thai bellman stood beaming, holding an immense bouquet of tropical flowers.

"For you please, Miss."

"Who are they from?" knowing the source even as she spoke.

"I dunno. Shop just say to bring to you."

Kate bade him wait while she fumbled through her purse for a handful of baht, not bothering to count it. It must have been a substantial tip, for the bellboy looked extremely pleased. She set the vase on the small table and picked the card from among the flowers. It read:

> You looked so beautiful when I left. I'll see you back at Takhli and I won't talk if you won't!
> P.S. Did you know you sleep with your mouth open?
> Love, Jim

Captain James Evelyn Broussard

Jim wondered what sort of target in Laos could possibly be important enough to send out aircraft in weather like this. Cadillac Flight had briefed to take off in pairs, since the chances of finding one another in the storm at night might prove to be impossible. The fighters simply didn't go alone, for they needed someone to cover their backsides or at least to start the rescue operation should someone get unlucky.

Pritchard led the second element of Cadillac Flight as they roared down the pitch-black runway. Jim tried to maintain his wing position, sometimes by guesswork, as they hydroplaned through puddles of water. At best, he'd been able to see only the vague outline of the other ship just a few feet away. When water spray from the lead ship covered his canopy, it obliterated his view. He held his breath and hoped like hell that Pritchard's aircraft would reappear before he had to give up and move his eyes to the runway in order to stay on concrete and not end up in a rice paddy. The lights of the lead ship became visible once again just as he thought the runway was ending.

The two aircraft broke ground together and Jim sucked up the gear, moving in as close to Pritchard as he dared. In less than a minute the lead ship would be on instruments as they entered the low-lying cloud deck; Jim had to maintain visual contact or they would both be in extreme jeopardy as they groped blindly through the clouds. He felt as though both planes' small wings were almost overlapping as they turned together toward the tanker rendezvous point.

Pritchard was flying a good lead, doing everything as smoothly as he could. Nevertheless, the aircraft bumped and ground through the turbulent air as they entered the cloud base. The formation flying became even more difficult as they were flung about by the fury of the squalls.

Jim tried not to stare at any particular light on the lead ship but concentrated on shifting his gaze from point to point while he maintained station. Staring at a single point would make him more susceptible to vertigo, a phenomenon that caused many bad-weather crashes among the unwary. Vertigo starts when the eyes, which are accustomed to a visual horizon to orient the brain to a level position, can't find the real horizon. The brain insists on having a horizon as reference, in order to send its position signals to its receptors. Denied a real horizon, the brain creates one of its own. The sensation is much like staring over your own shoulder at the instrument panel. The only cure for vertigo is to lock onto the flight instruments and believe them rather than relying on sensations the brain is feeding to the body. Unfortunately, a wingman cannot use his flight instruments, because he must hang onto his leader, despite the fact that his brain is screaming that he is doing everything all wrong.

So Jim hung on, but he wasn't enjoying the flight a great deal. Pritchard's aircraft was occasionally outlined by the diffused lightning as the clouds spit and grumbled. The radar controller vainly tried to vector the element around the larger buildups, but his radar was not designed for weather avoidance, and to be able to pick up the aircraft on his screen, he had to eliminate most of the depicted weather. In the end, it boiled down to sucking it up and doing it.

Jim was only vaguely conscious of Donkey swearing on the radio someplace in the clouds ahead of them. Jim had enough problems of his own just trying to stay with Pritchard. As the words seeped into his brain, Jim realized that Donkey was complaining loudly about losing Stark, either on takeoff or climb-out. He was not happy. The radar controller was attempting a rejoin, an extremely hazardous procedure should they remain in the clouds.

"Cadillac Lead," Donkey called shortly, "is on top at thirty grand. Looks like we'll be in and out of the stuff for quite a while. Two, bust your ass and get on up here and get rejoined before we're into the glop again."

"Lead, this is Cadillac Two," Stark replied. "I'm approaching thirty thousand feet and still on solid instruments. Radar control has me only one-half mile from your position and I still can't see you. I'm aborting at this time and returning to field."

Donkey was silent for a long moment. Jim knew that if Stark aborted, then Donkey should as well. However, his next transmission was not totally unexpected. "Understand, Two. You're returning to field. Takhli Radar, gimme a vector for join on Cadillac Three and Four."

Pritchard and Jim popped free of the clouds just below 30,000 feet. Jim moved out from his element leader and breathed a heavy sigh of relief. That was hairy, and he wasn't sure he blamed Major Stark for not trying it. He could have easily crashed into Donkey. Jim knew that Donkey wouldn't buy that, but no one except Stark would ever actually *know* whether he could have made a successful join-up.

Pritchard spotted the lead ship first. "Cadillac Lead, this is Three. I've got a tallyho on you at our one o'clock, about five or six out."

"Rog, Three, this is Lead. I've got you now." It sounded as if Donkey was talking as he strained to look over his shoulder. "I'll make a quick three-sixty and join up on you. Just hold your present heading to the rendezvous point."

Jim slid his aircraft a little farther from Pritchard so he could divert his attention long enough to watch the join-up. He'd never seen Donkey fly except as lead, but as he should have known, he slammed the heavy Thud into position on Pritchard's left wing as if it had taken root there.

Broussard shrugged his shoulders and rolled his head, trying to loosen the tension. Actually, he was glad that Stark had aborted. There seemed to be so many ways to get killed over here that he didn't feel the need for anyone to invent new ones. He watched the bulges of the thunderheads in front of them, continuously outlined by lightning, and realized he wasn't contemptuous of Stark. He envied him. Stark would not have to try to hang onto an elusive refueling boom tonight. And no one would be shooting at him. On the other hand, although there'd be no overt criticism of his decision, he'd still have to endure the raised eyebrows at debriefing and at the club as he tried to explain what happened. That, Jim decided, would probably not bother that son of a bitch in the least.

The three aircraft just skimmed through the tops of the showers; most of the lightning came from below. Donkey allowed Pritchard to keep the lead until the refueling, so they followed him back down into the murk to find the tanker. They would refuel in order.

The steer from the tanker, Red Three One, placed them almost on course to the rendezvous point. It was getting very rough again as they approached their refueling altitude of 20,000 feet. Clouds were layered now, which gave them some space to relax in before they entered the real turbulence once more.

"OK, Cadillac Flight, this is Red Three One. We've got you at one mile. Do you have us in sight?"

"Are you kidding?" answered Donkey. "This is like looking up a baboon's asshole."

"OK, Cadillac Lead, just keep that heading and increase your speed by ten knots. We've got on the rotating beacons and our pilot director's lights on the belly. You ought to grab us pretty quick."

The flight inched forward. Pritchard called, "Tally on you Red Three One, 'bout a quarter of a mile dead ahead."

"Rog. This is Three One Boomer. I think I've got you spotted, too. Keep her comin' straight ahead and slow, 'cause we're bouncing all over hell tonight." The boom operator's voice was punctuated by a bolt of lightning darting horizontally ahead of them. A storm on the other side answered in kind.

The flight stabilized just aft of the tanker and Pritchard began his cautious approach, wary of the strong convective currents that could hurl his aircraft into the bottom of the tanker. Twice, his aircraft had automatic disconnects as it was flung beyond the limits of the boom nozzle. But, finally, he had his off-load and backed away.

Jim had never worked harder at keeping his position beneath a tanker. As the turbulence would appear to diminish, the tail of the tanker would suddenly rise from some errant gust of air, and his aircraft, sitting only yards aft, would be shoved in the opposite direction. The boom operator made no attempt to correct their position by voice or lights, knowing it was futile. Maybe Stark had the right idea, Jim thought. You can't screw around with Mother Nature all the time and expect to emerge a winner. When he had his scheduled off-load he felt as if he'd been wrestling alligators. Despite the cool air coming from the air conditioner, he was drenched with sweat.

Donkey's bout with the tanker was conducted like everything else about flying that he touched—with as little sweat as possible. Even he, however, was slung from the boom while taking on fuel. There was also the opportunity for the big replay as they all cycled off again to top their tanks. Thank God that Stark isn't along, Jim thought, or none of us would have received enough fuel to make it to the target, much less home. The major's air refueling technique had improved with practice, but it still would have been viewed as laughable by most TAC pilots.

Donkey reclaimed the lead as they trudged back up through the storms, seeking smoother air. On top, the flight checked in with Hillsboro, the C-130 command post, who in turn passed them on to the FAC (forward air controller). He would direct their attacks against any targets he'd found that night along the Ho Chi Minh trail. The FAC was flying an OV-10, a twin-engine turboprop, with an observer using a night scope in the rear cockpit.

The weather improved as they flew south into Laos until they could see the ground in places between the broken clouds. It could have been the jungle, ocean, or Gobi Desert so far as Jim could determine, for he couldn't see a single light.

Donkey checked the flight in with the FAC. "Nail Two One, this is Cadillac Lead. A Flight of three Thuds, wall to wall with Mark-82s and twenty mike mike. We can give you about twenty minutes on station."

"That's what I like about you Thud drivers," a querulous voice answered. "My poor, dragging ass has been hanging out here for four hours with two fifty-seven mike mikes trying to stitch me a new navel, and you've got the nerve to tell me you're gonna give me only twenty minutes of your precious time? What is it? You boys got a party you're missing?"

Donkey chuckled. "If I ever hear a happy FAC I think I'll just turn and head the other way, 'cause I'll know for sure that something has got to be wrong."

"Well," the voice sighed, "I guess we might as well plan on going to work. Elevation around here runs from about a thousand feet to well over three thousand. Many hills and mountains, so try not to get too fancy on your delivery and pullouts. The best bailout area is going to be as far as you can get to the west, 'cause the land is flatter there than it is around here. As I said, I've had a couple of guns working me. Either thirty-seven or fifty-seven mike mikes. I think they were just trying to scare me off, so there may be more that haven't fired. Probably are, in fact. Watch yourselves on pullout, because we've got a Spectre gunship coming on station after we leave. He might be early and won't be showing any lights. There are negative friendlies around. Y'all got any questions?"

"What's the target?"

"Shoot, man! We're after trucks. What else? They're moving down there right now without lights. What I'm going to do is put in a ground marker for a reference point; we'll also dump flares as long as I've got 'em, and mark with Willie Pete rockets. Even after I put out a flare you probably won't be able to see the vehicles, so just put your bombs, one at a time, where I smoke. OK, Hillsboro has got you about six north of my location so I'm going to put my lights on, real brieflike, so's we can get an ID. After you see me they're going right off. You folks can do what you like with yours, but I'd suggest you do the same. After I clear you in, then you can choose the direction of the pass and pull-off. Just let the rest of us know. I'll be sitting right over the target at five thousand so I shouldn't be a bother to you. Here we go."

The FAC's lights stood out like a beacon as they descended toward their bombing altitude. Donkey called Nail in sight and the lights on the small aircraft immediately went dark. The aircraft fell into trail formation at Lead's command and began to take their interval. During the bombing pattern they would keep their top formation lights on until they were ready to turn toward the target.

A flare lit the countryside, and Jim got a glimpse of a red dirt road cutting through the scrub jungle. A white blossom of smoke exploded on the ground as the FAC fired his first smoke rocket. Jim couldn't see him but assumed he had taken his place right over the target, probably the safest place to be with three unlighted fighters screaming toward the ground. They should pass well under him after bomb release unless someone screwed up. Jim knew the small FAC aircraft didn't carry many flares and it would be necessary to go right to work.

"Let's arm 'em up, nose and tail; select singles," Donkey called, already on his downwind run.

Jim had always enjoyed night flying. Night bombing, however, was hell. Particularly since there were large mountains and hills to fly into and large trees that stretched skyward and unseen. And also because angry people were shooting red and orange strings of glowing balls through which you had to fly.

The FAC was right. There were more than the two guns alongside the road; several more in fact. There were also many light automatic weapons spitting their thin green line of tracers, barely visible to the speeding jets but nonetheless deadly. Jim felt his body begin to draw in on itself, trying to become a smaller target. His shoulders were hunched against the constraining straps as though he was trying to get into the crash helmet. Relax, he told himself. You know there's not nearly as much ground fire down there as there was on the Hanoi strike. Screw you, his brain replied. Just look at all that shit. At least, he told his brain, there are only soldiers down there. No civilians, just combatants. Who cares, his brain jeered, whether it's a soldier or a civilian with a gun if he kills you.

The ground fire didn't increase, since every gun on the ground was firing flat out from the first pass, but Jim did grow more aware of it with each attack. He caught himself using body English leaning away from the strings of orange balls that came in groups of six with only a short pause as the gunner inserted a new clip, then another six. He was hyperventilating and knew it but was powerless to slow down. The FAC occasionally placed a new marker and, in the same laconic voice, gave them further directions. Jim had seen at least two secondary explosions showing up bright orange against the dark backdrop of the forest.

Broussard rolled into his last pass and turned out all of his exterior lights. The cockpit lights were already reduced to the point that he could hardly see his instrument panel, which helped his outside vision. He aligned the aircraft in its dive toward the new target and nudged the dimly lit pipper just to the west of the new smoke ball, compensating for the easterly wind. He had the bombing parameters nailed and made sure he had neither hand nor foot pressure unconsciously cranked in. He punched the pickle button and pulled the stick hard back toward his lap.

"Good bomb, Four," he heard the FAC call as he fought against the g forces and announced that he was off the target to the south. More orange balls glowed briefly across the nose, then all was darkness again and he looked for his flight.

"OK, Nail," Donkey transmitted, "that does it with the bombs. Do you want guns?"

"Yeah, Cadillac Lead. I believe I do. We've still got some movers down there as well as some that are parked under the trees waiting out the strike. What I'm going to do is toss out a couple of flares and put in a string of three marking rockets and let you folks shoot right down the line. One pass, OK?"

The flares appeared and for the first time Jim saw the small twin-engine spotter aircraft as it dove beneath them. Flak from several guns converged directly in front of the aircraft and Jim held his breath, waiting to see the aircraft blown apart. It plowed through them, apparently unscathed, and three rockets flashed toward the dark earth. He glanced at the ground and there were three new blossoms of white smoke about fifty yards apart. Donkey was in like a cat on a mouse, his M-61 Vulcan cannon pouring a stream of 20-mm high-explosive slugs toward the road. There was a large explosion in the trees.

Jim followed Pritchard in for the strafe, triggering the cannon into action along the same line. The bright glare from Jim's cannon fire forced him to close his eyes to avoid night blindness. His vision was blurred in any event as he pulled from the target, hunting Pritchard again. As he leveled he heard the FAC already giving the bomb damage assessment to Donkey.

"Cadillac Lead, I'm giving you one hundred percent of your flight's ordnance in the area. Can't tell at this time how many trucks we got but I counted at least five secondary

explosions. I'm going to clear you from the area, because
Spectre is already on station and I imagine he'll want to go
right to work. You folks did a right smart job of bombing
and I hope we can work together another day. Take it easy
now. Good night. Nail, out."

Rejoining the formation, Jim looked over his shoulder at
the target area, now easily visible with the burning trucks.
The Spectre gunship, a modified C-130 transport with side-
firing cannons, night movement detectors, and infrared
gadgets, was already beginning to work. Streams of cannon
fire, so closely packed that it appeared to be incandescent
water squirted from a huge hose, poured toward the ground.
Spectre would be working the trail for the remainder of
the night and was, though no fighter pilot would admit it,
more effective at busting trucks than any other aircraft.

Cadillac Flight steered west northwest out of the target
area toward the tanker rendezvous point, easily identifiable
by the large thunderstorms sitting in the area. With the
planes cleaned of their ordnance, the refueling proved to
be anticlimactic. Only Jim was flung from the boom by the
turbulence as the tanker, their old friend Red Three One,
circumnavigated the largest of the monster cells. Red Three
One was also much lighter, having given away most of his
fuel to hungry fighters prowling the skies of North Vietnam
and Laos, and was able to adjust the refueling altitude so
that eventually they could top the monsoonal clouds. At
the higher altitude the refueling went smoothly, and there
was no need to cycle off the tanker after they had taken
their off-loads. There was no need, but they did it anyway
at Donkey's insistence: He thought they needed the night
refueling practice. He reiterated one of his quotes for them:
"The only time you can have too much fuel is when your
aircraft is on fire."

It was just after 0100 when Cadillac Flight switched
radio frequencies to the GCA (ground-controlled approach)
at Takhli airfield for radar vectors to the runway. Some of
the larger storms had moved away from the area, but there
was still hard rain and the ceiling was down to 400 feet
with only three-quarters of a mile visibility. Close, but not
too close.

One by one they were vectored onto the final approach
course for landing. There, the final controller took over the

delicate job of interpreting the scope quickly and accurately enough to land the fast-moving jets.

"Cadillac Four," he called after he had safely recovered the first two aircraft of the flight, "turn left five degrees to zero two zero. You're one mile from descent point. Recheck gear down and locked."

The voice was casual but authoritarian, as though he had done this thousands of times. Indeed, some of the older sergeants on the radarscope probably had. The controller kept his mike button depressed continuously as he issued a steady stream of instructions. Occasionally, he would break for five seconds, in the event the pilot had anything he wanted to say. Short of an emergency situation, the pilot never did.

"Cadillac Four, you're approaching glide path; begin descent. Nice entry; you are on the glide path drifting slightly right of centerline. Correct two degrees left. On centerline; on glide path. Going slightly high on the glide path; increase rate of descent slightly. Back on glide path but drifting right of centerline. Correct two degrees left. Glide path looks good. Back on centerline. You are two miles from touchdown. Now, drifting left of centerline. Turn right one degree; fly right one degree. Glide path is good. You are one mile from end of runway, on glide path and on centerline. You should have the runway lights in sight. If so, take over and land visual if not, turn left to two seven zero degrees and climb to two thousand feet. GCA listening, out."

Jim's eyes had been glued to the instrument panel, flicking constantly from one instrument to another in the practiced cross-check so necessary for a successful instrument pilot. At the final controller's last words, he glanced up through the windscreen and saw, as advertised, the lights of the runway. At first, they were barely visible, then much brighter as the aircraft moved toward the runway threshold.

"Thanks, GCA," he transmitted as he flared the aircraft for landing. "That was a real good one and I do appreciate it."

"You're welcome, Cadillac Four. Anytime. GCA, out."

Leaving the de-arm area, Jim followed the other two aircraft back to the squadron. The rain was falling in a steady downpour and he had to leave the canopy closed. It fogged over despite the cool air blowing from the air-conditioner vent. The cockpit became a sauna before he could be marshaled into the hardstand.

The pilots of Cadillac Flight huddled in the back of the van, wet, hot, and miserable for the short ride back to ops. Jim felt himself sweating even as the rain pelted down on him. They deposited their wet gear in PE and dashed through the rain to the debriefing room in the ops building.

Stark waited for them inside, sitting and talking to one of the wing intelligence officers. He stood as they approached. Donkey didn't spare him a glance but sat at one of the tables and immediately began the debrief. There wasn't much any of the pilots could say about the mission except to pass on the reports the FAC had given them.

"Were there any refueling problems due to the weather?" the intelligence officer asked innocently.

"None," Donkey answered, turning to look directly at Stark. "The three of us who completed the flight had no problem whatsoever."

Stark's face flushed and he turned abruptly and walked from the room. The rest of the flight gathered their personal items and followed Donkey in Stark's wake until he abruptly held up his hand and stopped them. "There's going to be a meeting of the field-grade officers of this flight and we don't need any company-grade pukes like you two around. So, go powder your noses or whatever it is young captains do and I'll see you tomorrow. You both did real good tonight. That first goddamned refueling was really something, wasn't it?"

Donkey turned and left the room, leaving the two captains standing in their own puddles. A wing staff sergeant looked at them with disapproval, and a major asked them to take their dripping bodies elsewhere. Hunched against the rain, they walked wordlessly back toward their quarters. They muttered "good night" and went their separate ways. Jim felt a vague disappointment that Pritchard had said nothing and hadn't invited him in for a drink, since he was really beginning to feel as if he was becoming a productive member of the team. But then, maybe "good night" was better than the usual sarcasm or stony silence he got from the man. More important right now was a shower and eight hours of sleep.

Major Delbert "Donkey" Sheehan

The soft padding sound of the hootch girl walking bare-footed across the darkened room woke Donkey. She was gathering his dirty clothing that had been piled carelessly in the corner. He seldom slept straight through the night anymore unless he had put away a prodigious amount of beer. The night flight into Laos and his "conference" with Richard Stark had kept him from the bar.

The hootch girl shut the door and he sat up in bed feeling the soothing chill of the air conditioner. One good thing about having a flying job was that you had air-conditioned quarters rather than having to sweat most of the night away. Higher ranks, lieutenant colonels and above, also lived in air-conditioned quarters. Donkey knew that the pilots would still be living in the most primitive quarters were it not for their need for day sleeping so they could fly at night. Nevertheless, he was extremely grateful for the air conditioner and even for its whining noises, since they helped block the outside sounds of an active air force base.

He pulled himself upright with a groan, walked to the tiny bathroom he shared with another major, and relieved himself. He scratched his hairy belly and glanced with disgust at the reflection in the mirror. His paunch sagged down over the top of the green GI boxer shorts, and his body and limbs were pale caricatures of what they had once been. Too much booze and too little exercise. Maybe he ought to start working out a little.

He curled his arms downward, clasped his fingers in a parody of a bodybuilder pose, and tightened his muscles. It succeeded only in making him look constipated. Ah, well. The baggy flight suit, his only apparel since his arrival in Thailand, concealed his figure, and since flight physical examinations had been waived for aviators in the combat zone, he figured he still had awhile before someone jumped his ass about physical conditioning. Undoubtedly the flight doc would give him hell when he checked into his new stateside base, but he'd worry about that later. For now, he had more pressing problems.

Somehow, some way, he was going to have to get rid of Stark before the man did something that got one of them killed. The session last night had left him with a bad taste in his mouth. They had talked for more than an hour and he'd been unable to make a dent in the man. Even when accused blatantly of wriggling out of the night strike, Stark's facade had remained intact. He had been adamant that he'd never made visual contact with Donkey's aircraft after he'd lost him on the takeoff roll. There was no way Donkey or anyone else could prove that Stark was lying even though the other ships had managed to get together.

"Look," Donkey had said, "this is just between us girls and it won't leave this room. But, I've got to tell you that you ain't hacking it. I've never threatened anybody with a bad fitness report in my life and I sure as hell don't want to start now. But, let's face it, this just isn't your cup of tea. You've got no business in a fighter cockpit. You're going to end up getting somebody hurt. What the hell ever made you volunteer for Thuds anyway? With all the connections you're supposed to have, you could have had any slot in Southeast Asia. You could be living it up in Saigon right now with your own villa and hot and cold running baby-sans. Or you could have been a big cheese with the B-52s at U-Tapao or Okie or Guam. Those would have been logical assignments for somebody with your background, not screwing around out here trying to play fighter pilot."

Stark had looked at him mutely for a long moment, no expression on his face, before he answered. "Major, you may not think I'm a good fighter pilot, but I assure you that I will be, with enough experience. I've never failed at

anything in my life and I don't intend to start now. As far
as volunteering for fighter training, if it were any of your
business, which it isn't, there was a perfectly valid reason
for it. I know that I could have picked my slot over here.
But then I still would have had a one-faceted background,
with no operational experience except in heavies. I need
a completed combat tour in the most macho kind of flying there is. And that means Thuds. You may not have
noticed, but general officers are selected partially due to
the wide variety of experiences in their background. Oh,
you can make bird colonel easily enough specializing, but
the crunch comes with flag rank. And I assure you, one day
I expect to wear stars. Does that answer your question?"

"Yeah," Donkey had said. "That answers the fucking
question. You intend to get those stars if you have to
crawl over a stack of dead bodies to do it, 'cause that's
more than likely what will happen if you continue to screw
up. You sent us out last night one plane short because you
didn't happen to like the flying conditions. It makes me
wonder what'll happen if we get into another bind that
you just don't happen to like. Are you going to leave us
then, too?"

"Major," Stark had answered with a stony face, "if there
was a screwup last night you were the one who made it. I
may not have been here long, but I know that if an aircraft
aborts for whatever reason, the other ship in the element is
supposed to go home with him. And I don't remember you
doing that."

Donkey had stared at the man's audacity. "Dickie," he
said softly, "let's me and you get one thing straight. This
is my flight and I make the rules. The entire flight lives or
dies by them. If you think I'm going to let some shit from
headquarters threaten my command of this flight, you've
made a bad mistake. If you want to press a charge, we'll
wake up the old man right now. Otherwise you'd better
keep your fucking mouth shut. In fact, I think it might
be a good idea if you asked for a transfer to some other
flight."

"Believe me, I've already tried it. The squadron commander said he wouldn't do it," Stark had replied. "If you think I
want to be in this flight led by a drunken old has-been, then
you're even more mistaken than you think I am. And don't

ever threaten me with a bad effectiveness report again. For your information, I do have some connections. I can get any report you've written purged from my files. For that matter I have a few friends back in Washington who can have you sitting out the rest of your career on the polar ice cap. So be very wary of making threats to me, Major. You might just find they jump up and bite you back."

Donkey had risen from his chair, thinking seriously of kicking Stark in the balls. "Let's us remember one thing, Dickie. You don't fly worth a shit, and it's going to take everything an old, worn-out fighter pilot can do to keep you from getting your ass blown away. And something else, Mister Major-Would-be-General Stark, before takeoff last night I talked to the old man, and the picnic is over. The wing is going back Downtown, and you can bet your ass that Cadillac Flight is going to be part of it. If you think you've seen shit in these last few sorties, then you're about to find that going after those damned bridges around Hanoi is un-fucking-believable. I have to take your word that you couldn't join our little party last night because I can't prove otherwise, but when we go into Pack Six, everybody goes, including the old man. And it's gonna look real suspicious if you just 'happen' not to find us again or have engine trouble or any of that shit. Nobody turns back on these even if they've got a legitimate gripe with the airplane. They know that every swinging dick who makes the trip will think they're chicken shit.

"I've tried to give you every chance to pull it together on some of these easy missions, but you haven't done it. I'm telling you that from now on if you don't stick to my ass when we roll in, or if you have trouble taking fuel, you're going to find yourself single ship in an area that has more air defense weapons than any other place in the world. I'm not going to have time to wipe your bottom, because I'm going to be busy trying to keep the rest of my flight alive. Do you understand what I'm telling you?"

Stark had nodded slowly, eyelids blinking quickly. "I can hack it, if you can."

"Well, I guess if you want those stars bad enough, you'll learn in a hurry."

Donkey had returned to his room too keyed up to sleep. Only the pilots on the early strikes would be up now and no one felt like socializing before a mission. He brought out his private bottle of scotch and poured a waterglass full. He held it to the light and admired the color before sipping it. Say what you would about the war, they made sure you got to drink cheaply. He'd paid only about three dollars for the bottle of premium double malt.

What a screwed-up mess, he thought. Four pilots in a flight that should have double that number; two of them want to be a general and the other one can't get out of the service quickly enough, led by a crotchety old fart who'd been passed over so many times that he'd have been released from the service had it not been for the insatiable need for experienced fighter pilots. Pritchard and Broussard were good boys, though. Both were already excellent pilots and would become good tactical fighter pilots with seasoning. Stark was going to have to be mighty lucky to survive a hundred missions over North Vietnam without getting himself dinged. Or more likely somebody else, Donkey thought darkly. He might indeed have been a shit-hot bomber pilot, but that didn't mean crap when it was time to fight the air defenses in Pack Six. Donkey knew that he had just been blowing wind when he threatened to leave Stark alone if he screwed up. Donkey had never left a wingman alone in a fight in the air or on the ground. He wasn't about to start with this officious asshole. He tossed off the rest of his drink and headed for the shower before the early rush. Already many of the pilots who were to fly that day were being awakened by a swearing duty officer.

Freshly shaven and in a clean flight suit, Donkey ambled out of the field-grade quarters toward the club. The midmorning sun promised another scorching day. The monsoon clouds were developing early. As he strolled he noted a half-dozen joggers spread out along the well-worn track surrounding the Thai soccer field. He stopped in the sparse shade of an old flame tree near the edge of the field and scrutinized the runners. Two looked familiar. Yeah, there was Broussard on the near side of the field coming toward him, grinning like the village idiot. It was infectious. Donkey squinted and made out Pritchard running on the far side. They couldn't have gotten any farther away from each other and still stayed on the same track. Ain't we the happy family, he thought.

"Hey, Donkey!" Broussard yelled. "Did you come out to run?"

"In a pig's ass!" he replied as the younger man slowed to a walk, joining him under the tree. Donkey leaned back against the trunk as Broussard walked in a short circle, trying to regain his breath. "Rumor has it that you met Kate in Bangkok. Anything to it?"

Broussard's face got redder. "Yeah, I saw her down there. Me and the Shame of Atlanta had a drink with her."

"Don't get all worked up," Donkey said with a grin. "You're both grown-ups. I just don't want it to cause any more trouble between you two," gesturing with his head toward Pritchard, now laboring around the near turn of the track.

"Look," Broussard said between deep breaths, "I don't need any more trouble either. I don't even know what started it between Andy and me, but nobody wants it patched up anymore than I do. I've got to fly the guy's wing, remember? Besides, I figure we might have something more important to worry about than that—don't we?"

"Could be," Donkey admitted, not surprised by the young man's grasp of the situation.

Pritchard gasped to the group and stood panting, a slight smile on his face. Their bodies were drenched with sweat. Christ, thought Donkey, it's got to be more than ninety-five degrees with even higher humidity. How do they do it? Through squinted eyes he mentally compared their physiques with the one he had inspected earlier in the mirror. It depressed him. Neither appeared to have an excess ounce on his body. Well, he thought philosophically, I have to pay somehow for a lifetime of debauchery. As far as he was concerned it had been worth it.

"What's up?" asked Pritchard as he got his breathing under control.

"Not much. Just wondered if you youngsters wanted to grab a sandwich and a beer at the club, since we're off all day."

"Sorry," Broussard said immediately with a guilty look at Pritchard, "I'm meeting Kate in about half an hour over at their club. She's going to give me a swimming lesson."

Donkey glanced at Pritchard, who kept a wooden face. "A swimming lesson? Jesus Christ! Are you serious?"

Broussard looked down. "Yeah, I can stay afloat but that's about all. She said to invite you guys as well."

"Sorry, I've got some things to do," said Pritchard, and turned away.

"Why not," said Donkey. "I might, if I don't have to swim or talk to any of those pussy doctors. Sure, I'll join you for a little while. Is Kate off today, too?"

"Naw, she has the midnight to eights this week."

They walked toward Broussard's building while Pritchard pushed himself back onto the track for more running. Sweat was beginning to drench Donkey's fresh flight suit. In Broussard's room he sprawled on the neatly made-up bunk and idly thumbed through an old *Time* magazine while Jim showered and changed into swim trunks. Jim returned and smiled as he looked at Donkey resting the magazine on his rounded stomach.

"Major, sir. You are, without a doubt the type of field-grade officer young captains like myself try to emulate. You look the very embodiment of a warrior. That clean-cut, pristine military figure, that commanding presence, that—"

"Oh, blow it out your ass! Hard bodies don't fly airplanes good; hard minds do. You're obviously a little younger than me and maybe in just a tiny bit better condition, but you'll never fly like me and you know it. Not if you live to be sixty, which is pretty doubtful if you don't start doing a better job than you're doing now, asshole. As some of us age gracefully we acquire what I like to think of as a mature male figure. It sets us apart from callow youth and is the secret of our success with the ladies, knowing as they do that it is virtually impossible to drive a nail with a tack hammer."

Donkey stood with a sigh and glanced through the opened closet door. "Where in hell did you get a pair of orange shorts like that?" He was intrigued as Broussard began to blush. "Well, come on. I want a beer and I'm so hungry I could eat the asshole out of a mule. Come to think of it, that's probably what we've been getting."

Kate wasn't at the pool when they arrived, though there seemed to be acres of other Occidental flesh slowly burning in the hot Thai sun. Donkey headed immediately to a

vacated table shaded by an umbrella. Several women lay
on towels around the pool, bra straps undone to achieve a
uniform tan. Most wore bikini swimsuits. Some of the men
did as well.

Donkey unabashedly surveyed the feminine forms, nod-
ding often in appreciation and showing open disgust at
the men in their abbreviated costumes. The Thai waitress
took their sandwich and drink orders. Donkey noted with
satisfaction that some of the medics didn't appear to be in
much better shape than he was. He shuddered at the thought
of what a couple of hours of noonday sun would do to his
own pallid body.

"Hey guys. What's happening?" Kate walked up quietly
behind them, speaking in an exaggerated Texas drawl. She
wore a short terry-cloth robe, which came to mid thigh.
Long brown legs seemed to extend forever from beneath
its hem. She leaned forward to kiss Donkey's cheek, then
palmed Jim Broussard's shoulder, squeezing it before drap-
ing a proprietary arm over it. To Donkey it was apparent that a relationship of some sort had been established
between them. Jim couldn't take his eyes from her and
seemed slightly dazzled. Good on both of you, Donkey
thought. The waitress brought their order and Kate immediately commandeered Donkey's beer can for a swallow.
"Want to take a few laps with us?" she inquired of Donkey,
untying the belt of her robe.

"Don't be ridiculous," he snorted.

She pulled Broussard to his feet before he could bite
into his sandwich and shoved him toward the water. He
moved forward reluctantly. Donkey admired the firm orbs
of Kate's bottom as she trotted behind the younger man, the
edges of each cheek just protruding from beneath the black
one-piece suit. In the water she was sleek as a dolphin.
Broussard had obviously not exaggerated his swimming
prowess. He thrashed like an injured whale as Kate tried to
improve his technique. Several of the medics were frowning
at the couple. Screw them, Donkey thought as he squirmed
himself into a comfortable position in the lounge chair and
shut his eyes.

As he perspired heavily even in the shade of the umbrella,
Donkey found his mind wandering into an area he seldom
let it go. He'd have to face up to it before much longer,

though. He was fast approaching the magic one hundred mission mark and his time for rotation back stateside. What in hell did the air force plan on doing with him back there? He'd accepted that any chance of further promotion was a fantasy. He hadn't made it yet and now he never would. No sense fooling himself about that anymore. What kind of dead-end job could they possibly send him to now? There certainly wouldn't be any pilot slots available with all the surplus of young pilots just back from combat.

Maybe an ops officer's job in some squadron. Not likely, since that was the track to squadron commander and he had no illusions about that. There'd be only eleven months after his return before his mandatory retirement. That was a scary thought! It was also one that he'd been successfully ignoring for the last year or so. At first, when he had seen what combat's loss rate was, it didn't seem worth worrying about. Now, it looked as if he was really going to make it. OK, say he lucked out and finished up the tour. Then what? Flying fighters was really all he knew, and there sure as hell wasn't much need for that in civilian life. Or was there? Maybe not in the States but perhaps someplace in Africa or South America. Hell, he'd spent more time outside the U.S. than in it for the last twenty years. He pictured himself climbing into a thirty-year-old Sabre jet wearing a Pancho Villa–style hat and crossed bandoliers on his chest under his parachute. He thought it suited him. For sure, he wasn't going to hang around the club like some of the retired geezers and bore the pants off everybody.

The sun was slipping beneath the horizon when he woke, not sure where he was until he heard the soft murmurs of the young couple. Broussard was telling her about growing up in Santa Fe.

"It wasn't much of a tourist attraction then. Now, you can hardly walk around the main plaza without tromping on somebody from New Jersey. There are artists from all over the world living there now and there's even talk of starting an opera. One thing they don't have a lot of is water, which is why I'm not much of a swimmer. But the winter snow skiing is great and so is the hunting and fishing. My only problem is that if I hook up with an airline after I get out, it'd be a hell of a commute to get there from wherever I'm stationed."

"Did you ever think of staying in?" asked Kate softly.

"Not much chance of that," he replied. "Just look what they do to people like Donkey there. He gives 'em his whole life and then they boot him out after he's done their dirty work. Now they say he doesn't have the right credentials to stay aboard or be promoted. Who needs that?"

Donkey was hearing more than he wanted, so he snorted a few times, then yawned and stretched mightily to get their attention. There were only a few stragglers by the pool.

"I was just about ready to have Kate check your pulse," said Jim, "except the sound of your snoring assured us that you were still alive."

"I do not snore," Donkey said, "and there are hundreds of women around the world who can attest to that. Have you young pukes eaten yet or just made fools of yourselves by drinking all afternoon?"

"We thought we'd just grab a salad out here, if that's OK with you. That way we don't have to go back to our rooms to change. Of course, you can eat inside with all the doctors, if you like," Kate added innocently. "I'm sure there must be a few of them you haven't insulted."

Donkey snorted. "I might be forced to whip all their asses just on principle. You two go on and eat here. I'm heading back to the club. Just remember to get him in early."

"What's up?" asked Broussard, hearing something out of the ordinary in his voice.

Donkey peered at him in the gloom. "Don't spread it around, but the little truce we've had with the dinks is over. We're going back Downtown tomorrow."

Captain James Evelyn Broussard

At the crew chief's signal, Jim eased the Thud to a stop and began to numbly go through the shutdown procedures. The engine and the gyros spooled down and he tugged almost frantically at the helmet strap, obsessed with getting the heavy helmet from his head and feeling the breeze. He held the helmet in his lap and forced himself to take deep, measured breaths to try to keep from hyperventilating.

The young crew chief placed the ladder next to the F-105 and scampered up to help the pilot from the cockpit, only to find him staring straight ahead, giving no indication that he was prepared to leave. The sergeant suddenly understood, and he twisted to look at the other aircraft pulling into their parking slots. One was missing, number 689, but he hadn't noticed who had been flying it that morning. The ground crew members of the missing bird were going through the typical reaction: wandering aimlessly around the revetment, not looking at one another. One hunkered down and began to idly toss small stones at the revetment wall.

The crew chief brought inquiring eyes back to Captain Broussard, who still sat sagging in the ejection seat as though he didn't have a bone in his body. The sergeant wanted to ask about the missing plane but hesitated. Some pilots had become almost violent when pressed with questions before they'd had time to absorb the loss of a friend. He decided to take no chances although he knew Broussard well.

"Hey, Snuffy," an unseen voice called from beneath the aircraft, "we've found a hole just forward of the speed brakes. Looks like it's probably a small arms round. Tell Captain Broussard that—"

"Shut up, fool!" Sgt. Sandifer "Snuffy" Smith muttered quietly but loud enough to be heard by his assistant beneath the belly of the aircraft. He turned his shiny black face back to the cockpit to see that the captain was finally stirring. Snuffy leaned into the cockpit to take the map bag and helmet from the pilot. He noticed there was a tic under the pilot's right eye.

Jim Broussard finally turned, making eye contact with the crew chief, and rose from the ejection seat. He saw the unasked questions there. He knew he would have to say it, although he could barely force it from his mouth. He could scarcely think about it. "Donkey," he said quietly, "Major Donkey Sheehan. They nailed him coming off target."

"Christ!" said Snuffy and turned once again to gaze overly long at the empty revetment. One forlorn figure had his arms around another, shoulders shaking with unheard sobs. "I never thought they'd get the Donkey." Both men stood quietly as they thought about it. "Did he get a good chute?" asked Snuffy.

"Nobody saw one but we were separated from him. We did see that he was a flamer," Broussard told the man in a flat voice.

Snuffy helped the sweating pilot from the cockpit and aided him onto the stairs. His muscles were obviously cramped from the long flight, apparent as he climbed clumsily down the ladder. Snuffy asked no more questions, knowing that the line chief would be by after the pilot debriefing with the full story. He watched Captain Broussard gather his gear and walk a slow, old-man walk toward the waiting truck.

As he clambered into the rear of the vehicle, Broussard avoided eye contact with the other two pilots. Both looked equally exhausted and depressed. The truck stopped to pick up the pilots from another flight, who immediately braked their happy after-mission chatter as they saw the survivors of Cadillac Flight. All were quiet until the truck commenced its run toward PE and ops debriefing. Finally, the Ford Flight leader looked at Andy Pritchard and asked: "Donkey?"

Andy nodded his affirmative.

"Shit!" the other man said. "Good chute?"

Andy shrugged his shoulders. "Went into the clouds and we couldn't see, but the bird was on fire."

"Shit!" the pilot repeated and stared at the floorboards.

Jim was staring at the cumulus that was building toward an afternoon crescendo along the distant horizon. Major Stark had his eyes fixed dead ahead. You asshole, thought Broussard, the final scene forcing itself unbidden into his mind. He pushed it away, still unable to come to grips with the reality of it. He surveyed the passing scene, seeing it with fresh eyes. He'd stopped registering the ugliness, his mind acclimating itself to the bleakness of the landscape: the absence of trees, long since devoured in the local charcoal kilns; the nutrient-poor, laterite soil showing a dull red in the erosion scars cutting through the woods and elephant grass. If Donkey couldn't make it, then no one had even a reasonable expectation of doing so. Christ! This day had been a nightmare.

The Thai driver stopped the blue air force truck in front of the PE section and the pilots climbed stiffly and silently from the rear. Stark led them through the door. Inside, Jim wearily shrugged out of his parachute and survival vest, hanging them on the pegs below his name. He removed the baby bottles and emptied them of water, then placed them back into the leg pockets of the g suit, which he hung on another peg. He walked to the counter and removed the .38 Special revolver from its shoulder holster, pointed it into the clearing barrel, and removed the shells from the cylinder. He turned the weapon over to the clerk behind the desk, who inspected the serial number and returned his gun card. Finally, Jim removed the packet containing the blood chit and gold coins with seal intact to another clerk, and headed out the door, not noticing whether either of the other two flight members were with him or not. They were.

They straggled the short distance to the ops building for debriefing, hunched against the light rain that had begun to fall, which preceded the squall lines of thunderstorms. Jim felt drained, completely washed out.

Inside the ops building the debriefing room was crowded. The entire wing had been on the strike, nearly thirty aircraft. Jim leaned against the wall, waiting for a debriefing table to open, and looked at the hyperactive pilots filling the room. Most were talking too much and too fast; others looked drawn and listless. The wing commander, a stocky bird colonel with a large handlebar mustache and a sweat-stained flight suit, moved from group to group, engaging each in animated snatches of conversation before slapping the nearest shoulder and moving on.

A debriefing table came free and the intelligence lieutenant waved Cadillac Flight toward it. Jim followed Stark and Pritchard and sat down at the table. The lieutenant got his forms ready and filled out the flight name at the top.

"Gentlemen," he began softly, "we've had a couple of reports from flights debriefed earlier that your flight lost an aircraft. I'm really sorry to hear that. Could you tell me who it was, please?"

No one answered, so Broussard spoke up. "It was Major Sheehan, the flight lead."

"I understand. I'm truly sorry to hear that, for I've always admired the major. Did he have a good chute?"

Broussard held his hands up to indicate he didn't know and turned to Andy. Andy only shrugged.

The lieutenant glanced from one to the other, then directed his next question to Major Stark. "Are you the other element leader, sir?"

"No," replied Stark.

"Was Major Sheehan in your element?" Jesus, thought the lieutenant, this is like pulling teeth.

"He was my element leader," replied Stark.

"Could you please explain what happened to him?"

"I didn't really have a chance to see what happened."

OK, thought the lieutenant, I'm going to get to the bottom of this if the fucking debrief takes the rest of the afternoon. Something happened, and I'm going to find out what it is even if it pisses off every one of them. "Gentlemen," he said with an exaggerated show of patience, "let's start from the top. Would someone mind telling me who's the second element leader?"

"Me," replied Pritchard.

"Then, please, sir, would you tell me what you can about the loss of Major Sheehan?"

"They began picking us up as we came in off Thud Ridge," he began. "The flak was pretty heavy."

Pretty heavy! thought Jim, sitting motionless in the chair. That's like saying an elephant is a good-sized animal. As Pritchard spoke in a flat voice, devoid of emotion or adjectives, Jim's thoughts flashed to the scene: Cadillac Flight storming down the ridge. They were part of a twelve-ship formation of Thuds escorted by outriders of F-4s above them for MiGCAP and a mix of F-105s and F-100s as flak suppressors. Two teams of Wild Weasels preceded the strike formation, trolling for SAMs somewhere ahead of them in the murk.

By the time the flight left the ridge, the weather had deteriorated and communications discipline was already shot to hell, as almost sixty aircraft from three different wings tried to coordinate their individual attacks on the Thanh Hoa bridge. The briefing had described the different roll-in headings for the individual flights of attack aircraft, emphasizing the critical timing necessary to get one group of aircraft on and off while another prepared for attack.

But then came the SAMs spurting up through the low-lying cloud deck, giving no more than seconds for the heavily loaded aircraft to respond to the threat. The North Vietnamese had made good use of the bombing halt to install and hide hundreds of new missile and gun sites.

The weather was briefed to be broken to overcast at 2,000 feet but actually hugged the deck in spots where the aircraft force penetrated. Donkey brought Cadillac in at less than 500 feet, weaving his way around storms and showers, getting them to the target but losing time in the process, as they all did. The briefed split-second timing in which individual flights attacked every thirty seconds had degenerated into a first-come, first-served brawl, with flight leaders trying to make on-the-spot coordination calls with preceding and trailing flights. Then the losses began, with screaming emergency beepers blotting out vital radio transmissions. The confusion had rattled Jim.

The mission commander eventually realized the hopelessness of the plan and announced that flight leaders should switch to their flight discrete frequencies and continue the mission. On their own frequency and aurally isolated from the remainder of the strike force except for the emergency frequency, Cadillac Flight had continued toward the IP.

The flak suppressors had already detached from the main body of the flight and surged ahead to engage the guns around the bridge. Theirs was not an enviable task. The Wild Weasels had their own problems, as evidenced by the continuing calls of SAM launches over Guard channel. Later they would find that the Viet missileers had, during the bombing halt, refined their launch techniques. Before, the tracking radar had remained active after the missile launch until either the SA-2 destroyed its target or went ballistic. This often allowed the lead Weasel ship, with the EWO (electronic warfare officer) in the rear cockpit, to find the signal and launch antiradiation missiles to track it to its source. The remaining F-105 Weasels could then attack the site after it was marked.

But the puzzled EWOs in the rear cockpit of the tandem-seated F-105Fs had found that the SAM radar was being turned off after the missile launch, reappearing only in short interludes to redirect the lethal weapon to its target. These brief snatches of signal were seldom enough to permit the airborne antiradiation missile to find its target. Sweeping the frequencies with their black boxes, the Weasel crew members had found that the wily Vietnamese were also directing some of the SAMs from remote radar sites or switching active control between two or more sites.

Cadillac Flight had plunged in and out of the low-lying clouds, groping their way toward the IP; strained voices calling "SAMs airborne" filled the ether. Broussard saw Pritchard briefly looking over his right shoulder to check that Jim was still with him. The momentary glance often lost them sight of the first element in the clouds as Donkey made a small heading correction. They always reappeared just as Jim began to think they were lost for good.

Through the murk, the small arms fire made for an insane parody of a fireworks display. Balls of lethal cloud from 37- and 57mm antiaircraft guns melded with the cumulus clouds, invisible until detonation. The 85- and 100mm bursts were easier to see, exposed by their fiery orange centers framed against the backdrop of the sullen clouds.

The voices of the controllers in the airborne command post orbiting somewhere over Thailand added to the general confusion as they transmitted the useless information that more missiles were airborne. Their messages were received minutes too late to be of more than academic interest to the aircraft under attack.

"MiGs airborne! MiGs airborne!" a radar controller called excitedly over Guard channel.

"Goddamnit! Where?" an unknown voice responded. The controller didn't reply.

"Break left! Break left!" an excited pilot cried, also on Guard.

"Ah," an unknown laconic voice responded. "You probably just got every flight over North Vietnam to break left. Now if you could be just a little more specific, it might be more help to us."

Broussard glanced at the airspeed tape before gluing his eyes once again to his element leader. They were at attack speed. He would have known without looking at the indicator because of the buffet. They had to be nearing the IP, though he didn't know how Donkey could have found it in this crap, Doppler or not. More heavy bursts of flak rocked the formation as Donkey started his climb to bombing altitude. Pritchard and Broussard in the second element followed the steep climb and half roll at 14,000 feet as Donkey hung momentarily inverted, peering downward to search for the river.

The old boy knows what he's doing, thought Broussard, for though the bridge was still invisible beneath the cloud deck, Donkey had found the river and was prepared to follow it to the target. He made a final transmission before the attack.

"We'll have to go in damned low," Donkey drawled, seemingly not excited about the situation. "Two, stick close to me. Second element, you're going to have to do a three-hundred-sixty-degree turn to separate yourselves enough to avoid the blasts. We'll rendezvous over this bend in the river when we come off, then head straight back to the ridge. Let's do it right."

The two aircraft of the first element hurtled downward toward the river, and Jim followed Pritchard in a hard turn to the left, trying to keep the river bend in sight. The time

for the turn should give them blast clearance from the
bombs of the first element, but Jim wondered how many
of the other attack aircraft were boring in toward the same
target at just this moment. He pushed the thought from his
mind. He'd rather not know.

The bend came into view and Andy rolled his heavy aircraft inverted, starting a sixty-degree dive toward the river.
Jim, slightly disoriented by the maneuvering around and
through the clouds, followed. Sparkling ground fire covered
the countryside on either side of the water. Bright streams
of tracers filled the air to their front, joining the glowing
balls of cannon fire as they drew closer to the ground.
Jim's aircraft bucked as it flew into and out of a cloud
of exploding flak. He tried to ignore it. He could not.

Andy pulled the element level only 500 feet over the
water, and any doubts as to the bridge's location were
quickly dispelled. Several miles ahead through the mist,
enormous explosions roiled the air. More came from the
opposite bank. Jim couldn't tell if the explosions were from
Donkey's bombs or from another flight. Then, the bridge
was in view as another set of near misses left the spans
unscathed. Still several miles out, Jim followed Andy as
he corrected the angle and headed for the south bank so
the attack could be made at a slight angle to the spans.

Quickly they were in attack position and the element
started a climb to the very base of the cloud deck. The flak
increased as they came into view of the gun sites situated
around the bridge. Broussard quickly rechecked the armament panel and nudged the aircraft a little away from his
leader. Pritchard rolled into the dive and Jim followed, trying to place the pipper so that the bombs would walk across
the bridge. The bombs began to fall in train well before they
reached the bridge. He could feel the shudder as each fell
away. Both aircraft accelerated into afterburner and began
a hard left turn, staying as far as possible from the bridge's
defense. As they hung together in the misty sky, Jim turned
briefly to glance back at the bridge through g-induced tunnel vision. He saw that both bomb loads had been close
but all spans of the bridge remained intact. Its huge steel
pilings sat unperturbed in the fast-moving muddy waters.
He wanted to turn off Guard channel with its screeching
and wailing of emergency beepers but knew he could not.

The bend of the river that was to be their rendezvous point slid into view just as Donkey's voice came over his earphones. "OK, Cadillac Three. I've got your element at my two o'clock going to three. Come outta burner and I'll pull in front and take the lead. There's a little maneuvering room at about eight grand between cloud decks. We'll head for that when we're joined. Wonder what genius decided to go ahead in this weather, huh? Come on, Two," he said, shifting his conversation to Stark, "pull it in. What the hell are you doing way out there, anyway?"

"I've got you, Lead," said Andy.

Jim watched the two aircraft cutting in front of him and Andy, the rear ship far out of position. The second element took the angle to join as Donkey began a rapid climb through the cloud deck, still in a steep bank.

"SAM airborne! SAM airborne!" a frightened voice leapt at them out of the ether.

Automatically both Pritchard and Broussard lowered first one wing, then the other to scan the ground for any missiles headed upward. Guns winking but . . . Jim's heart felt as if it was going to explode: Through a break in the undercast he momentarily saw the distinctive doughnut of smoke and debris from a SAM booster ignition and the streaming white trail of kerosene and nitric acid of the second stage. The rocket engine was a pinpoint of light against the cloud-darkened backdrop of the earth.

"Cadillac Flight, SAM airborne beneath us. Coming this way! Two o'clock, low!" Jim called.

"I've got it," Donkey's measured voice came back. "Get ready to evade, Cadillac Flight, if it's locked onto us."

Donkey was turning them toward the onrushing missile. The only true test of whether the missile was indeed after Cadillac Flight was to play a game of chicken with it. The pilots had to wait until its relative motion was apparent, either away from the aircraft or steady, head on.

"Relative movement is stable, sure enough. Looks like it's us," the flight leader announced calmly. "Three, you take your element to the right and we'll go to the left."

Jim felt as though the thudding of his heart was shaking the aircraft.

"Cadillac Flight. Break, now!" called Donkey.

Pritchard put his aircraft into a ninety-degree bank to the right with Broussard following. After almost forty-five degrees of a five-g turn, the second element leader began a barrel roll to the left, hoping the stubby wings of the missile, really more guide vanes than wings, would be unable to compensate for the high-g forces. Inverted, Jim caught a brief glimpse of the first element doing the same maneuver in the opposite direction. The SAM, still accelerating, tried to bend its flight path toward the first element, but it had been beaten and quickly passed from sight through the upper cloud deck behind Donkey and in front of Pritchard.

Another missile broke through the lower clouds, frighteningly close. Jim was conscious of Donkey's shout over the radio in the background but neither Pritchard nor he had time to answer. The elongated telephone pole–sized shape pointed directly at their element.

"Break!" was all that Jim heard from Pritchard before the aircraft in front of him slammed into a hard left turn. Jim had the stick sucked back into his belly until he felt the first shuddering of a high-speed stall. His vision grayed as the g suit inflated and pressed his legs and thorax. He held his breath waiting for the impact, body tense in its fight against the g force and in anticipation of the explosion.

"It missed," Donkey said conversationally.

Jim released back pressure on the stick and, as his vision cleared with the free flow of blood to his brain, looked for his element leader. He picked him up and rejoined, sticking to him like a leach. His body sagged with relief. The first element wasn't in sight.

"We're at your three o'clock, heading zero five zero degrees," Donkey said, anticipating the call.

Jim wouldn't have been able to pick them up if Stark hadn't been trailing out of position, far behind. They stroked into burner for the join-up. On the ground was the familiar twinkle of small arms fire. Jim realized there had been no flak from the larger weapons for a few minutes, perhaps because they were so low that only the 37- and 57mm guns could engage. The planes had been in and out of the clouds, so maybe the guns were having problems locking onto the flight. A more chilling thought hit him. Maybe the reason they weren't seeing anything except light weapons was that

MiGs were being vectored for an attack.

With relief, Broussard made out the first swellings of limestone karst hills marking the start of Thud Ridge. The hills disappeared as more densely packed clouds obscured them. Donkey climbed steadily for a few minutes. Jim noted they were passing 15,000 feet.

"Two, this is Lead. What the hell is your problem?"

Andy and Jim were on the far side of a sweep crossing over the tail of the flight as Donkey spoke. Jim glanced over and saw that Stark was at least a half mile behind the lead ship.

"Lead, this is Two," Stark replied in a shaky voice. "I don't think I'm going to have enough fuel to get to the tankers."

"What's your state?" to which Stark replied with the numbers. "Hell," Donkey told him, "you've got enough fuel to damned near get home. Goose it on up."

Stark continued to lag. "Cadillac Lead, this is Two. I've lost you!" The voice sounded close to panic.

"Three, this is Lead," Donkey said, sounding disgusted. "I'm going to make a three-hundred-sixty-degree turn and latch onto Two and stay with him. Take your element on toward the tanker and we'll be right behind you." He switched his call to Stark. "Two, this is Lead. You'll pop outta the clouds in just a minute. I'm turning back to hold your hand, killer."

Jim looked at the lead ship as it began a hard right turn, its belly blind to the north. At that moment the silver MiG-21 popped up through the overcast and launched two Atoll air-to-air missiles. Both were probably intended for Stark. It was an unfortunate accident that Donkey had placed his aircraft between them and their intended target. The first missile went wide, but the second impacted squarely on the tail pipe of Cadillac Lead. The F-105 pitched nose high and quickly rolled inverted, nose pointing almost vertically toward the hills below. A sheet of flame swept over the fuselage.

"He was in sight for less than ten seconds," Andy told the debriefer, "then he went into the lower clouds. Right after the shot, the MiG made a hard left diving turn back down into the cloud deck. We turned back to the southeast until we were pretty sure that we were away from the hills, then tried to come back into the area beneath the clouds. No use, though. The crap was right down into the valleys. Everybody was well beyond bingo fuel, so we called Hillsboro with the coordinates and went hunting a tanker.

"After we refueled we went back into the area but by that time they'd called off the search attempt. Then we came on home. There was no fucking reason for it to have happened."

The intelligence lieutenant sneaked a look at Major Stark. He sat, stony-faced, staring at the wall. Broussard squirmed in his chair, feeling that he'd rather be almost anywhere than at this table.

"Well," the lieutenant said, "I think that about covers it. Thank you for your time. I'm really sorry about Donkey. He was one of the good ones."

Neither Pritchard nor Broussard answered but rose immediately and started to shamble from the room. Jim stopped and turned back to the lieutenant: "The MiG that got Donkey had a red tail."

"You mean," the lieutenant said, "the entire tail section was red and the rest of the aircraft was the traditional silver?"

Jim thought about it. "No, just the vertical stabilizer. The rest was silver." He turned and followed Andy out the door.

"I think," Major Stark said, finally looking directly at the debriefer, "the record needs to be accurate before it's forwarded."

The IO turned and looked at him in surprise. He hadn't realized that Stark had remained seated at the end of the table.

"Essentially, what Captain Pritchard said was correct except that he was not in position to observe my actions or to understand my intentions. I think that needs to be clarified.

"I was flying a somewhat looser position than normal because I'd used excessive fuel during the strike, possibly due to an engine malfunction. I figured that by flying with as little power as possible I could conserve quite a few pounds. I knew that the other element led by Captain

Pritchard would be extremely tight on fuel due to the additional maneuvering they'd had dodging the second SAM, and I wanted to be ready in the event they were unable to reach the tanker in time and had to eject. I just wanted to set the record straight."

"I understand, sir," said the lieutenant. "I'll be sure to include that in the report."

I understand perfectly well, you asshole, the lieutenant thought to himself, and I'll make sure that the rest of your flight knows about your record-straightening as well. He watched with contempt as the tall, straight figure marched to the door, then waved another flight toward the table.

Jim peered at his watch in the darkened room. Almost 1800. He flopped back onto the bunk on which he had been wallowing for the past three hours, trying to catch up on much-needed sleep. They had been alerted for flight at 0330 that morning and he'd been unable to sleep much before that. The anticipation and, yes, the fear had kept him wide-eyed until shortly before the duty officer had begun to awaken the swearing pilots. He knuckled his eyes, still unable to believe Donkey was gone. It was as if he'd lost his rabbit's foot. With Donkey leading the flight, somehow he'd really felt that he could make it through the tour, despite what had happened to Bob Packard.

He closed his eyes again, willing himself to stillness in hopes of catching sleep unaware. His eyes flickered wildly beneath the closed lids and when he tried to hold them steady he could not. He knew he was breathing much faster than normal and consciously tried to slow the rate. Shit! He sat up, turned on the nightstand light, and swung his feet to the floor. He stared at his naked toes, then wiggled them experimentally. Dissatisfied with their performance, he diverted his eyes in search of something more entertaining.

He looked at the reflection in the wall mirror across the room and tried staring it down but lost the match. Then he began to scrutinize the shadowed outline critically. Not much noticeable change except for dark smudges around the eyes. He stuck out his tongue and waggled it at the man in the mirror, trying to provoke him. The figure returned the scowl and gave as good as he got with his tongue.

I've got to be realistic, he thought. The wing lost five birds today but it's all a matter of chance, a huge crapshoot. It was Donkey but it could have been anyone. Yeah, that's what worried him. No matter how good you were, chance could still jump up and bite you on the ass. And if Donkey hadn't turned back, the MiG's Atoll missile would have taken out Stark. Would he have felt any better about that? Jim decided he would have. The man was such a shit!

Trying to divert his thoughts he reached into the nightstand drawer and pulled out his secret logbook. Secret only because their presence in Thailand was supposedly classified, although everyone in the civilized world knew they were here. There was little attempt to hide it in any way except officially. That gave the Thai government an opportunity to pretend that the American pilots didn't exist. All incoming personnel were therefore warned against keeping personal diaries or logs. Everyone ignored the directive.

He counted the missions he'd flown and noted the targets he'd struck. There weren't many of them when compared to the hundred in North Vietnam he needed in order to complete his combat tour. Ironic, they could blow your ass away in Laos as easily as over North Vietnam, but those weren't "counters." At this rate, it would be at least five more months, maybe more, before he would hit the magic figure. Now even more depressed, he tossed the little spiral-ringed notebook back into the drawer and closed it. He was restless.

He glanced at his watch, noting with little satisfaction that less than two minutes had passed since his last look. He might as well get dressed and head over to the club. It would probably be a morgue tonight after the heavy losses, but it had to be better than sitting around his cubicle. He really wanted to be with Kate. Let her help take away some of the hurt. But she had duty until 2400, and in any event she'd been devastated by the news of Donkey's loss. There'd be precious little comfort from her tonight. He'd been a little surprised at the depth of affection she'd felt for the crusty major. She'd taken the news hard. Maybe he could see her tomorrow.

Clad in a clean flight suit, Jim walked quickly toward the club. He stopped by the soccer field, puzzled. The noise from the tin-roofed building that was the USAF Officers'

Club rolled over him like the shock wave from a Mark-82 bomb. The din was deafening. Strains of "Shagging O'Reilly's Daughter" overwhelmed the sounds of the Thai night. A loud crash, as though furniture was being smashed, punctuated the last stanza. Jim hurried toward the fracas.

At the open, swinging doors, he paused long enough to survey the scene. It was not a contemplative crowd. Someone had constructed toilet paper letters to spell out the names of the pilots lost that day. Donkey's name led the list, which was ordered not by rank but by the numbers of missions completed. The highest, Donkey, had ninety-three; the lowest name on the list had twelve. Not depicted were the names of the three pilots shot down that day but successfully recovered.

A captain had formed a group of lieutenants into a parody of the Vienna Boys Choir. They forced high notes as they went from one ribald song directly into another. Jim noted that one choir member wore a bloody bandage around his neck and seemed to be missing at least half an ear. They were accompanied on the piano by an almost bald lieutenant colonel, chewing an unlit cigar and playing the melody from a completely different song. Neither choir nor pianist seemed to be aware of the difference. A flight-suited full colonel unknown to Jim was pouring beer into the piano's top to "lubricate it," he announced loudly to an admiring bystander. He had obviously been at it for some time, for the piano's tone was sending lugubrious warnings and threatening to expire completely. It sounded as though the notes were coming from a fish bowl.

The colonel was scornful: "Can you imagine," he said to the operator, still blissfully pounding away at another favorite, unaware that his performance sounded like a xylophone being played underwater, "they built this fucker without any redundant systems. One hit could put it completely out of action. Give me a baby grand anytime. It can take it and still get you home!"

Jim drifted toward the bar, which had been wetted down and made into a "bowling alley." Beer cans were stacked at one end; at the opposite end were the "bowlers." These lunatics would run down a measured takeoff distance, fling themselves onto the bar belly down with arms stretched out in front, then slide down the bar in an attempt to knock down the cans. Unfortunately, those with sufficient velocity to take out the cans usually went off the end of the bar onto the grimy floor. Thai bar-backs assisted the players to their feet and provided first aid or beer, whichever was deemed appropriate. They giggled and grinned, dark eyes bright with amusement at the antics of the American pilots.

Jim did a double take. His peripheral vision caught a movement of what appeared to be a wall hanging. Closer inspection proved that the object was indeed moving. Racing actually. A bootless captain and a major were in a contest to negotiate the circumference of the room without touching the floor. They'd been stymied momentarily by an uncurtained section of the race course. The major had backtracked to gain access to a curtain on which he evidently planned to swing across the void to the next firm handhold. Noting the move, his opponent, in desperation, tried to heave his body from its precarious perch on a light fixture to the next windowsill, but he suffered a high-speed stall and crashed nearly eight feet to the floor. He landed inverted on the referee, whose job was to ensure that the participants' feet did not touch the floor. Neither appeared to be seriously injured, although the cigarette of the lieutenant colonel officiating had apparently set him afire when the falling body struck him.

Jim saw Andy Pritchard talking with the Mad Monk, the Shame of Atlanta. Both sat on the back of a bedraggled wicker sofa, their feet on its seat cushions. Another pilot was with them. Jim started to turn away, then decided, what the hell, and moved toward them. "Andy, Shame," he greeted them.

Pritchard nodded and the Shame of Atlanta raised his beer can in salute. The other flight-suited figure was young and wore on his shoulder the new camouflage-patterned silver bar of a first lieutenant, black with just the silver outline showing. It looked quite new. The pilot looked bright-eyed and excited.

Pritchard spoke in a level voice, almost indecipherable against the noisy background. "Meet Mike Patowski. Just before the squadron commander passed out, he told me that Mike's the newest member of Cadillac Flight. He's going to be in the number two slot." Pritchard had a small, sardonic grin on his face.

Jim was puzzled. He shook hands with the newcomer and tried to work it out. If Mike Patowski was going to be in number two slot, that must mean Stark was moving somewhere else, since Stark was new and not worth a shit in general. That had to mean Pritchard was taking the flight and he, Jim, was being moved up to element leader. A flash of panic started forming a greasy seed of nausea in his belly. Jesus, he didn't know enough to lead an element. He'd get everyone killed!

Pritchard seemed to follow his thoughts, for his grin grew even more distorted. "Don't sweat it," he said, holding Jim's eyes, "you're not moving anywhere. Our new flight leader has decided to take young Mike here under his wing, so to speak. You and I will remain the second element."

"New flight leader?" Jim looked from Pritchard to the Shame of Atlanta in confusion. They must have really changed things around. The Shame looked away, compassion in those dreadful eyes. "Who's the new flight leader? You mean it's not you?"

"Oh no. Somebody evidently decided I didn't have the experience or whatever for the job. No, our new leader is none other than that old, hardened combat veteran, Major Richard Stark."

Jim was stunned. There had to be a mistake. That man couldn't lead a flight. Hell, he could barely fly the airplane. This was ludicrous! He stared at Pritchard, hoping it was a joke. It wasn't, judging by the expression on his face. His mind whirled. Jesus! His chances of survival just went down to about five percent. He began to feel sick to his stomach. "Are you sure?" he asked, knowing that Pritchard was not joking. No one could be that cruel.

"Oh, yes. I'm sure. I've just had quite a lengthy discussion with the CO about it. He was sympathetic but said there just wasn't a damned thing he could do. Seems there is someone higher up in his chain that is most interested in our Major Stark getting all the experience he can. He wouldn't talk about it much except to buy me a free drink and tell me to watch my ass. A big help."

"I know," said the Shame, "let's break Stark's legs. We could get a baseball bat and sneak up on him at night when he couldn't identify us, and I'll hold him while you guys break both his fucking legs."

"Shame," Jim smiled at the big man, "you could be identified at midnight at the bottom of a coal mine."

Mike Patowski, the newest member of Cadillac Flight, was quickly losing his excited look as he listened to the other pilots. In fact, he was definitely beginning to seem concerned. "Look," he said, "is there something I should know about Major Stark? I've only met him the one time today and he seemed a little hard-nosed but OK to me. What the hell's going on, anyway?"

Broussard and Pritchard looked at each other. Pritchard answered after a moment. "Well, it's just that the major hasn't had a great deal of combat experience. Fighter experience, either, come to think of it."

"How many missions does he have?" asked Mike Patowski, looking as if he'd rather not know the answer.

"Oh, about seven or eight," answered Andy breezily. "Though, of course, he's had only one into Route Package Six. That's the area around Hanoi."

"Any idea of how much fighter time he's got?" asked the lieutenant casually, trying to make it appear that it didn't much matter.

"At least sixty to seventy hours. However much he got in that transition school you just came from and about another twenty or so over here."

"I see. Well," said Mike, desperately trying to find something good in what he was hearing, "I guess he's a pretty good pilot and all, huh?"

"Can't fly for sour owl shit," said Jim with a grin.

"You're dead meat," the Shame said sorrowfully to the lieutenant, and wandered to the bar in search of more beer.

"Speaking of the devil, there's the birthday boy himself," said Pritchard, looking toward the door.

Jim turned to see Major Stark marching directly toward them. He stopped in front of the small group and stared pointedly at Pritchard's feet on the seat of the sofa. "Why don't you get your feet off the furniture, Captain?"

"Why don't you get fucked?" Pritchard answered casually.

Stark smiled grimly. "You may have the misapprehension, Captain Pritchard, that since you have more combat experience than I do, I'll allow you more liberties than I would another junior officer. I assure you that won't happen. It's not my way. I know you've been informed by the commander that I've taken over the flight. I can understand your disappointment, but if I were you I wouldn't let that interfere with the job I had to do. Some say that you expect to stay in the Air Force. If you give me any more of your shit you'll be lucky if they let you finish out your tour, with the effectiveness report I'll hang on you." His eyes bored into the other two pilots of his flight before he turned them on Pritchard once more. "I repeat, Captain, get your feet off the furniture. I expect all of you to act like officers from now on."

"And I repeat," said Pritchard, "why don't you get fucked? If you want to take it up with the old man, I think he's lying in his own puke beneath the sofa."

Stark glared for a long moment before turning on his heel and striding purposefully from the room.

Jim peered fuzzily at his watch, noting that it was almost 2200. The noise in the barroom continued unabated, though there were fewer athletic contests going on, since most players had given up and settled into serious drinking. The bell over the bar chimed as the wing director of operations slammed the lanyard back and forth to gain everyone's attention. The wing commander, the bird colonel with a handlebar mustache, made several attempts to clamber onto the bar before he was able to actually make it. One end of his mustache was singed where someone had tried to light it.

"Gentlemen," he managed, "before I declare these festivities closed, I'd like to propose a final toast to our departed brethren. We sincerely hope that they've joined some of our other friends in the jug up north. But, if they haven't, fuck it! Here's to them anyway. Damned good men and damned good fighter pilots!"

He drained his glass, as did the remainder of the pilots, all now on their feet. The colonel lowered his glass and wiped both sides of his mustache. A startled look came over his face as his hand felt the damaged half. He looked for a likely target for his glass. There was however, little need in Thailand for fireplaces, the normal repository for the glasses after a toast. Baffled, he turned in a complete circle before his eyes settled on the far wall. His glass crashed against it, followed by nearly fifty others. A cheer rose from the group. Their dead were buried.

Jim saw that the young lieutenant with the bloody bandage around his neck had tears leaking from his eyes, much to the disgust of his companions.

"Jesus Christ!" one of them shouted at him. "You're acting like a goddamned MAC pilot. What the hell's wrong with you? These ain't the first or the last ones this wing's gonna lose, so stop your damned sniveling!"

"It's not that," he sobbed, "it's just that my ears don't match anymore." He fingered his left ear, the bottom half of which had evidently been blown away during the strike. "I was so damned *pretty* before. What's my girl going to think when she tries to grab 'em when I'm rooting around. She'll feel this nub and get disgusted!"

The crowd roared and began to pour beer over him. Jim wandered through the debris to the bar and grabbed a full scotch bottle, turning so the dazed Thai bartender could see his name tag and make the necessary charge.

His head was spinning as he stumbled down the steps of the club, wandering vaguely back toward his quarters. He realized that his guidance system was malfunctioning when he nearly ran into a strange obstruction. He'd tacked across the soccer field and was staring nonplussed at the bleachers before he realized his navigational error. No matter, he needed to sit and think for a while anyway. This was as good a spot as any. Better, in fact, than his room, where anyone could pop in at any moment.

He slouched onto the bleacher seats and broke the seal on the bottle. He was already drunk, and he really didn't want anymore. He wasn't that good a drinker. Nevertheless, he tilted the bottle and let the amber liquid pour down his throat, knowing he was going to regret his actions in the morning. Yet he didn't care. He coughed and spluttered and almost lost the bottle, as well as the contents of his stomach, as the drink hit home. No sweat, that was just a practice drink; he'd improve with experience. He really did prefer beer, though. But, with beer, he knew he'd just fill up and go to sleep. Somehow he owed this to Donkey, wherever he was.

Back to business. He tilted the bottle again. True enough, it did seem to stay down a little easier that time. His mind felt out of gear, thoughts irrational and difficult to process and hold onto. On impulse, he unlaced his flight boots and pulled them and the cotton socks from his feet. Leaning back, he wiggled his naked toes in the warm night air. What about snakes? asked a tiny, sober voice in his head. Fuck 'em; let 'em get their own bottle, he thought belligerently. I don't have time to screw around with reptiles who can't pay their own way.

Jim admired the lightning display on the horizon, happy to be able to do so from a distance. The moist, heavy air promised that the rain was not far away. He listened to the gecko lizards screeching their defiance at intruders; the sound was much like a human obscenity. In the distance he saw a solitary figure tumble down the steps of the officers' club and then scrub around in the dust for a few moments before righting himself and launching in the general direction of the bleachers. Jim watched him and hummed a little childhood song to himself, feeling contented and happy: "Jesus loves me, this I know; 'cause the Bible tells me so."

He wasn't aware that he was singing aloud until the approaching figure stopped and peered through the gloom toward him. He couldn't remember the rest of the song.

"Who is it?" the shadowy figure demanded, trying to stand erect but swaying in synchronous movement with the flame tree branches now restless with the proximity of the approaching storm line.

"I am Captain Midnight," Jim replied, sitting erect, "defender of truth, scourge of criminins and bad mens!"

"Criminins? What the hell is a criminins?" the dark figure asked scornfully.

"I meant to say criminins," Jim replied with dignity.

"There! You said it again!" the figure shouted.

"Did not!"

"Did too!"

That seemed to settle the matter. Jim leaned back against the wooden seats again, refocusing on the lightning display and only vaguely aware that the other man had taken a seat a couple of yards away from him. He too was watching the thunderbolts. Jim turned his head to speak to the man and forgot what he was going to say. A huge lightning flash briefly lit the darkness and Jim recognized the man as Andrew Pritchard. "Hello, Andy," he said. "It's me."

"Who?" asked Pritchard, startled, apparently forgetting that someone else was sitting there.

"It's me, I, whoever. James Evelyn Broussard."

"Oh, it's you."

"That's what I said," Jim explained patiently.

A lengthy period of silence followed as both men lost interest or forgot what had been said. They watched the approaching storms loom larger on the horizon as they neared the base. In the lightning flashes, Jim noticed that Pritchard was staring at his feet. "You don't have your boots on," Pritchard accused.

"I know."

"Why not?"

"Why not what?"

"Why, why don't you have your boots on?" Pritchard stammered.

"Because, because of the snakes," replied Jim, laughing to himself at his unusually clever mimicry.

The answer seemed to satisfy Pritchard's curiosity, for he nodded and rested his chin on his folded arms, continuing to watch the storm develop.

"Why don't you like me?" Jim asked impulsively.

Andy thought about it before answering. "I guess because you always seem like so much of an asshole amateur. And not only that but somebody who's proud to be an asshole amateur."

"I don't understand," Jim said honestly.

"I don't know how to explain it, but you guys who're planning on leaving the Air Force can't wait to tell any-body who'll listen what chumps we career people are. How do you think that makes guys like Donkey feel? Per-per-personally, I don't give a damn what you think. But, you gab away at it to somebody who's given his whole frigging life to it and you can't keep from letting him know what a sucker he is for staying in and fighting his shitty little wars and having to get out on a major's half pay, while Mister Shit-hot like you is going to screw 'em at their own game. You're going to take all their millions of dollars worth of training and shove it up their butts. You're going to be Captain James Broussard of Pan American Airlines, and people like the Donk can take care of the other little chores. . . . Gimme a drink outta that bottle."

Jim passed the bottle and listened to the gurgling as he thought about what Pritchard had said. He reclaimed the scotch and had a drink to help the process. Maybe he had been insensitive to the situation of Donkey and others like him, but then so had many others in the wing. "I don't understand," he said. "Maybe you're right, but I'm not the only one. How about Bobby Packard or lots of others? They feel the same way."

Pritchard reached for the bottle again and studied its contents against the lightning flashes. "Yeah, they do the same, I guess, but the reason you piss me off is that you're good enough for the whole enchilada, good enough to go the whole way, if you wanted to."

The enormity of the statement took a few moments to sink into his whiskey-soddened brain. He turned on the bleacher seats to stare at Pritchard.

"Yeah," Pritchard said conversationally. "You've got everything you need to go right to the top. For your experience level, you're probably one of the best pilots I've ever flown with, already almost as good as Donkey, and better than me. You've got the education, the ability to get along with people, and you're bright. Now you'll have a combat tour behind you. I don't see how you can miss. Only you don't want it and I do. I want it so bad that sometimes I could scream. You don't have any idea of what I've done trying to get augmented into the regular Air Force. Je-Je-Jesus! Do you think I fucking like flying combat? And here I am on my second tour. Two Purple Hearts and so damned shook-up after each mission that it takes both hands to get a drink to my mouth. And tonight did it. If Stark doesn't get us both killed, he'll make sure I never get a regular commission. Shit!"

Light rain had begun to fall on them. The old flame tree threw its limbs about in an ecstasy of movement. Jim grabbed the bottle for another drink, then passed it back to Andy. "But, but, but . . . ," he began until his tongue tied itself into a knot and refused to continue.

Pritchard began to laugh. "You got everything including that horrible fucking middle name of yours. How did you piss off your parents enough to make them do that to you?" His laughter grew as he thought about it.

Jim retrieved the bottle again, noticeably lighter than it had been. "I want you to know," he said with as much dignity as he could muster under the conditions, "that Evelyn is an old family name that . . ." His voice was lost in a clap of thunder. Pritchard continued to laugh as Jim tried to collect his thoughts, which seemed to have been misplaced by the noise.

"Does flying into Pack Six really scare you?" Jim asked Pritchard. In a lightning flash he could see the other man staring at him as if he were insane.

"Of course it does. Are you crazy?"

Jim thought about it. "No, I don't think so. Just wondered, 'cause it scares the crap out of me. I didn't know if it bothered everybody or not. Do you think it scared old Donkey?"

"Hell, no! Nothing scared the Donk!"

"Why do you think he never got promoted? I've never seen a better pilot."

Pritchard laughed scornfully. "Because Donkey was too good a major to be promoted to light colonel. 'Cause he never played their little game. Our leaders always insist rank is made on merit. You, you hafta be pretty damned naive to believe *that* shit. Look, anybody comes outta one of the academies is guaranteed to make chicken colonel. And if you're an academy man *and* you got some general watching over your career like ole Major Stark has, then you got a lock on flag rank. The average slob from Iowa or the University of Texas can expect to retire as a light colonel, tops. 'Course, the system has gotta allow a few worker bees to advance to prove it can be done or everybody'd just quit and go home, like you're gonna do." He laughed. "Who'd be left to do all the fightin' for them? Jesus! You can't be a big-time leader with nobody to lead."

Jim tried squinting at Andy with one eye. That didn't improve the focus so he closed it and tried the other. "What's all that got to do with Donkey's not getting promoted? So, he's a worker bee. He at least ought to have made lieutenant colonel."

"Naw. People like the Donk scare them, 'cause they see through all the bullshit and laugh at 'em. Our fearless leaders know that guys like Donkey can eat their lunch any day of the week when it comes to combat flying. One reason is, that's all Donkey's ever done. He never took a buncha' years out to get the right ticket punched and be seen at the right party in Washington. So what happens is that they try to make the shit *they* do seem more important than what the worker bees do. Anybody with half a brain can see that it isn't so. What the hell could be a more important job in the Air Force than flying combat airplanes? My God! That's really what we're supposed to be all about! Everybody else in the entire Air Force is supposed to support us! And those people would like you to believe that logistics, or some bullshit field like that, is where it's at. Crap!"

"Why do you want to stay in the Air Force if it's like that?"

Pritchard thought a minute. "I love the Air Force. I like flying. I think I could have made a good senior officer. Maybe not as good as you would have been, but pretty damned good. I wanted to be one of those worker bees that made it. Maybe I couldn't have changed anything, but I could have tried. Not that it makes any difference anymore, not with the effectiveness report Stark'll give me. I work my butt off to try to get ahead. I even fly their second shitty combat tour, and that bassard's going to wipe it out in one lousy little instant. But the golden boys like you just float through without anything bad ever happening to 'em. Jesus! You even get a cheap Purple Heart! When I got my first one I was in the critical ward for damned near a month. You get an overnight stay and meet the most wonderful woman in the world! Man, it just isn't fair!"

"Let's be gentlemen and leave my girlfriend out of this conversation," Jim said with dignity. He thought about it for a moment. "Kate is the most wonnerful girl in the world, but I'm a little surprised you think so. You never came around with us, even when Donkey did. I didn't think you cared for her or anything. You always acted kinda, kinda cold, I guess you could say, when you were around Kate. Or was it just me?"

"That just proves my poin' as to what a jerk you are. I mean, you're unconscious. I fell for that girl the first time I ever set eyes on her. So what happens? She looks right through me and falls for Mister Unconscious. What else? She won't even give me a look, except as a friend. You don't even try and she's all over you. You just float right through, adding another charm to your bracelet like an unthinking, brainless, brainless . . ." Andy couldn't think of the word he wanted.

"Twit?" Jim supplied helpfully. Andy shook his head. "Swine? Ass? Bounder? Oaf? Parvenu?" Andy looked at him queerly. "I once thought I wanted to be an English major," Jim commented with a shrug.

"Doesn't matter anyway," Andy said with the sagacity of the very drunk. "If we live through this tour, it looks like *both* of us will be trying to go with the airlines."

The two men were quiet for a time, staring at the storms almost upon them. "God! I'm going to miss Donkey," Jim said suddenly, startled since he hadn't even been thinking of him.

"Yeah," Pritchard said. "Me too."

"What are we going to do? I mean, how are we going to make it with Sctark, Sctork, Stark, leading the flight? That bassard's going to kill us all."

"Probably. Probably."

The rain was upon them. The sky opened and an almost solid sheet of water hit the already sodden earth. Both men sat, brooding and passing the bottle back and forth.

"Do you think Donkey's really dead?" asked Broussard.

"I guess so. Don't see how anybody could have gotten out of that."

"Look, Andy," Broussard stammered, "I'm sorry about what Stark says he's going to do. Maybe things'll work out. I'll do anything I can to help."

"Thanks, but it probbly dun' matter anyway. The way things are going we'll both be dead meat before he gets a chance to write an ER on us."

"Yeah," answered James Broussard solemnly. "Well, I guess we oughta get out of the rain and back to the hootch."

"Guess so."

Neither man moved except to pass the nearly empty bottle of scotch.

Kate found them a little after midnight. She used her flashlight to identify one of the bodies on the bleacher as

Jim Broussard. Another unidentified lump was curled in the fetal position in the mud in front of the lower seats, an empty liquor bottle beside him. The rain had slackened to a drizzle as the squall line receded into the distance, but isolated cells still rumbled in every quadrant.

She pushed the hood back on her rain gear and shined the light into Jim's face. He groaned and tried to cover his face with his hands. Kate shook his shoulder gently, then more firmly until he gave evidence of coming to life. "Jim! For God's sake, wake up. We've got to get you out of the rain. And who the hell is that on the ground?" Kate was quickly losing her patience.

"That is my old friend and element leader, Captain Andrew Pritchard," Jim slurred. "We decided to take a little nap before we went back to the quarters. Confidentially, I think ole Andy has had just a drop too much to drink."

"Yeah, I'm certainly glad you were around to look after him. You fool, I've been looking for you for half an hour." She pulled him into a sitting position and dug his boots out of the mud, but quickly gave up trying to get him erect. She checked Pritchard, then stood, arms akimbo, staring at the pair. Threatening Broussard with physical harm should he move, she trudged back to the club, where she recruited a small group of pilots to help her.

The men entered into the spirit of the adventure and accompanied her back to the bleachers. The rain began to fall heavily once more. Kate explained that if they would take Pritchard to his room, she'd be able to manage Broussard. Laughing, the pilots grabbed Andy's limp extremities and bore the fallen warrior toward the company-grade quarters. Jim still sat erect, although weaving badly. Kate sat beside him to gather her strength.

"Kate," he said, sounding very sober, "I really miss Donkey. Without him I don't think I'm going to make it. I don't think any of us are going to make it."

The anger left her and the tears came, streaming down her face and mixing with the raindrops. She wrapped her arms around his soaked body and buried her face in his neck. "I know. I know." She didn't know if she was crying for Donkey, Jim, or herself.

Major Delbert "Donkey" Sheehan

Goddamnit, that hurts! Donkey's eyes focused slowly on the green wall around him. Water dripped steadily from a liana onto his face and sought a way into his helmet. He moved his head slightly and felt the accumulated drops puddled inside, almost covering one ear. His head hurt and he found himself drifting back into the nice warm cocoon of unconsciousness. He shook his head more vigorously and some of the cotton floated away. Something sharp was digging for his spleen and he tried to shift his body away from it. He forced himself to lie silently and tried to rid his brain of its numbness.

Donkey took a deep breath and tried to order his thoughts. OK, he was on the ground somewhere, so that meant they had nailed him. With what? SAM? Never mind. That didn't matter anymore. With frightening clarity he suddenly remembered the explosion and groping for the ejection handle, only to have the g forces tear his hand away from it. The Thud had felt as if it were tumbling, slamming him from one side of the cockpit to the other in a matter of seconds.

Suddenly he did remember grabbing the ejection handle during one of the less violent movements of the stricken aircraft, but there he lost it. A complete blank. Perhaps he'd died. He rolled his eyes and studied his environment as well as he could. Probably not. This didn't look like heaven or hell. A bright verdant lizard sat on a small rock outcropping within his field of vision and stared at him. He tried to remember how far they were along the withdrawal route before whatever it was had gotten him. He had just turned back to get Stark, and they had been over the limestone karsts of Thud Ridge. That had to be it. But if he was on the ridge, why didn't he hear aircraft overhead capping him for the rescue birds? How long had he been on the ground? He tried to look at his watch, but his wrist had disappeared somewhere behind his back. He couldn't feel it at all.

He sighed resignedly. Might as well get it over with, he thought. Time to find out just how badly I'm screwed up. He raised his head in an attempt to get oriented and was surprised to find his feet above him. One was caught between two limbs of a bushy plant; the other was bent at the knee and resting on a rock ledge. His parachute hung from a sturdy limb of a large tree. He seemed to be flat on his back but headfirst in a hole. He drew his free foot into the hole and used it to gain purchase against the muddy wall. He made some headway, then the foot slipped on the muddy bank and he fell backward into the hole once more.

Shit! He lay there and contemplated the tree canopy. Water was now dripping into his face from many sources. Probably raining topside. He eyed the parachute canopy. There, that's what he should have done the first time. It was still attached to his harness, and he ran a critical eye over the point where it was snagged on the tree limb. Secure enough. Didn't look like you could blast it off that perch. He gave an experimental tug and it indeed held firm.

Grunting with effort, he pulled himself hand over hand up the side of the hole, digging in with the toes of his boots for additional purchase. He rolled himself over the top and sat up, panting with the exertion. After his breathing slowed somewhat he looked around. It was not encouraging. Flying over the hills and escarpments that formed Thud Ridge had made them look like minor irregularities in an otherwise flat surface. These were fucking mountains!

God! He'd like to have a drink right now. Or an ice-cold beer. He realized that his tongue was sticking to the roof of his mouth, and he began to search for one of the three baby bottles of water he normally carried in his g-suit leg pocket. His relief was enormous as he felt their bulges. He dug one from the zippered pocket, slugged it down in a single draught, and immediately felt better.

Where the hell was everybody? It wasn't like Thud drivers to leave one of their own unprotected after he was down. Unless, he choked on the thought, they had capped him while he was unconscious and believed he was dead. Or the weather was too low to get beneath it. That would have to be mighty low, he knew. Maybe they were sitting on top of the cloud deck just waiting for a call.

Excited now, he hurriedly pulled the small emergency radio from its pouch in his survival vest and pulled out the antenna. He turned on the radio and while waiting for it to warm up he checked his other assets. The vest held a small flashlight; a whistle; fishhooks; spare ammo for his .38 Special, still secure in its shoulder holster; a couple of cans of water; pencil flares; a signaling mirror; and several packets of freeze-dried food.

The sight of the pistol and ammunition suddenly made him wary and he stopped his inventory. What if the dinks were around while he'd been sitting here like a Boy Scout getting ready to go to Jamboree. He drew the revolver and crouched low, peering through the dense foliage. Nothing moved. He slid off his sodden helmet and cocked his head to listen . . . for what? Damned if he knew. Dinks, water buffalo, tanks, the Beatles? Feeling foolish, he returned the revolver to its holster and began peering into other pockets of the survival vest. Tree-lowering device, really a long piece of heavy-duty strap and a pulley; another knife; a first-aid packet. That made him think. Was he hurt? He hadn't given it much thought since climbing out of the hole, which he was slightly embarrassed to see was only some four feet deep. It had seemed much more cavernous from the other end.

Methodically, he checked his limbs and torso. Damn! He wanted a drink. He came across his escape and evasion kit in the leg pocket of his flying suit and was briefly distracted from his investigation by the thought that there were gold coins in the kit. He entertained the idea of walking into a North Vietnamese bar and ordering a double scotch and drinks for the house. He continued his investigation. His butt was sore. So was his left wrist, as if there was a slight sprain. The left leg of his g suit was split down the side, revealing a long but shallow furrow in the pale white skin beneath it. Probably caught on a branch of a tree coming down. Black holes, some smaller than others, covered his flight suit and survival vest. He was aware of a tenderness beneath them. The bird had to have been on fire to account for those. For the life of him he couldn't remember anything after grabbing the handle.

Nothing seemed to be seriously wrong with his body, he decided as he completed his survey. He pulled the survival map from the E and E packet and squinted into the quickening gloom until he could make out the elevation contours of Thud Ridge. Using his fingers he roughly figured the distance to the Thailand border. Only 250 to 300 miles. He glanced up at his surroundings. Ought to be able to make about half a mile a day unless he had to stop and hide. Say about two years, give or take six months. He snorted and refolded the map and returned it to his pocket.

The tropical night was falling fast as he struggled to his feet, swaying with shock, fatigue, and indecision. First he had to get through the night, and he was already beginning to feel woozy. He took the signaling mirror from one of the vest pockets and stared at his face in the growing darkness. Superficial scratches covered it, indicating he must have lost his mask on the way down. A deeper cut ran from beneath the outer corner of his right eye to a point almost at his chin. Whatever it was that did it had probably been responsible for taking the mask. Dried blood caked the gash and he could tell it was full of dirt. He'd need to get that cleaned and patched before he holed up. An infection was the last thing he needed just now.

With his neck scarf and sparing use of another baby bottle, he got most of the dirt from the wound and disinfecting salve on it before complete darkness. A hissing sound got his immediate attention. Slowly, he looked around until he traced the source of the noise to the little survival radio. He had forgotten about it. There'd be nobody up there to talk to now anyway, and even if there were, they'd have a hell of a time locating him at night. He'd wait for first light. After turning off the radio to conserve batteries, he crawled back into his hole and leaned against the muddy wall. He could hear the rain now, dripping steadily through the multiple canopies of leaves. He pulled on his helmet. The soggy earphones were cold on his ears. God! He wished he had a drink.

The first light of a greasy dawn seeped beneath the canopy of the rain forest as Donkey woke from an uneasy half sleep. He had dozed fitfully, more like passing out than real slumber. He lay on his side shivering, hands clasped between his legs. It was the first time he could remember being cold in Southeast Asia. The wet flight suit, clinging to his shaking body, was now almost completely covered with red mud from wallowing in the hole.

Groaning, he pulled himself first to his knees, then erect to peer woozily into the foliage. Dense fog cut his vision to only a few yards and filled the air with moisture. The cut on his face felt hot as he scrubbed his hands across his bearded cheeks. He grabbed the parachute shroud lines, which still dangled into the hole and were attached to the discarded harness, and began trying to hoist his aching body out of the depression. His sprained wrist made the task more difficult than it had been the day before. He rolled over the lip of the hole and glared at his wrist. He wiggled his fingers experimentally; all seemed to be functioning, though it was painful to double his hand into a fist. Jesus! What he'd give for just one cup of hot coffee.

Donkey dug the survival radio from its pocket, extended the antenna, and turned it on. He realized with drooping spirits that if the rest of the Red River valley was socked in with low clouds and fog the attack aircraft would be diverted southward to more open targets or cancelled altogether. There was the outside chance that they might have a few weather recce birds up to check out conditions over the Hanoi area, but they'd have to come mighty close for him to be able to reach them with his little radio. He sat and considered his gloomy prospects as the radio warmed up. Bullshit! He had to try.

"Any aircraft. Any aircraft. This is Cadillac Lead. Mayday! Mayday! Does anyone read?" he croaked.

His voice sounded strange, hoarse, and distorted by the fog. It reminded him of the way the soft but heavy snowfalls in South Boston could mute sounds. God! That had been a

long time ago. Getting up on Sunday mornings and bund-
ling up to stroll with his father through the neighborhood,
which had been turned into a fairyland by the fresh white
covering. His mother would have a hot breakfast waiting
for them when they returned with the Sunday papers. He
tried to remember the details of the breakfasts but could not.
Only their essence remained in his memory. Too bad old
Mom wasn't here now, he thought wryly, since she always
had an answer for everything. How about it, Mom? Got
any ideas for your little boy, now? Maybe she should check
with Father Michael, that ultimate source of authority and
one who was always sure to back her. Maybe you, Father
Michael? You have any advice for a downed Thud pilot?
You used to have plenty on every other subject. Maybe you
could ask for a little divine intervention. Donkey quickly
crossed himself, a holdover habit from the Catholic schools
but one he restrained from using in public. This was no
time to be thinking sacrilegious thoughts and maybe piss
off God.

"Any aircraft. Any aircraft. This is Cadillac Lead.
Mayday! Mayday! Does any aircraft read Cadillac Lead?"

The only response from the radio was a warm, sizzling
sound, as though a small elf within was cooking himself a
few rashers of bacon. The thought of warm bacon made
Donkey start to salivate. He began digging into the survival
vest again in search of edibles.

A freeze-dried packet promised that it contained chicken
stew. Maybe not what he'd have chosen for breakfast at the
club, but it didn't sound that bad either. He unsealed the
package and, following the directions, poured in some water
from his next-to-last baby bottle, then carefully refolded the
top and mashed the contents around. Damn! That wrist hurt.
Maybe the sucker was broken.

When the chicken stew felt as if it was mixed properly, he
reopened the package and peered in suspiciously. It resembled baby vomit, or at least what he thought baby vomit
should look like, never having encountered any personally.
A tentative sniff was not unpleasant, however. He searched
through the vest's pocket for something he could use as a
spoon, but whoever had stocked it had overlooked the silver
and napkin. He solved the problem by upending the package
over his gaping mouth until chicken stew overflowed onto

his cheeks. He sat and chewed, his feet dangling into the hole, until the package was emptied.

Donkey topped off his meal with a mighty belch, then looked around guiltily to see if Ho Chi Minh or his henchmen had appeared, guided to him by the noise. No red hordes had shown up and he relaxed once again, reminding himself that though he'd heard no one, that did not ensure his isolation from enemy forces.

He wanted a cigarette badly, which was strange since he'd never smoked. Nevertheless, he had a real desire to light up and sit back against one of the large trees. If—*when*—he got back, he was positively going to take up smoking. There were lots of things he was going to do when he got back, and foremost among them was to kick Dickie Stark's ass all the way to the Gulf of Thailand. That miserable fucker! Donkey thought it through and realized he must have been nailed as he turned back to get Stark. It could have been a SAM or a rocket or just a lucky shot up through the clouds. No matter, Stark had to go, even if Donkey had to talk to the wing CO himself and call in a few markers from times past. It didn't matter who they gave him as a replacement, he'd have to be better than that asshole. OK. One more try on the old radio before he'd put it away and save the batteries.

"Any aircraft. Any aircraft. This is Cadillac Lead. Do you read me?"

The radio sizzled at him until he turned it off, retracted the antenna, and returned it to its vest pocket. A rumbling in his belly announced that it was time for his morning purging. He searched through the vest pockets for some sort of tissue and found none. He considered the leaves around him but rejected them for their dampness. Finally, he took out his wallet and extracted the smallest denomination Thai bill.

With his flight suit down around his ankles, he balanced his bottom across a small log, the bark painfully scratching the tender backs of his thighs. As he waited for his bowels to complete their job, he critically inspected his lair. Donkey was a man born and bred to the city. He'd always hated the thought of nature and had indeed successfully avoided it his entire life, except for mandatory attendance at aircrew survival schools. Even there he had taken pains to avoid as much of its unpleasantness as possible by secreting small bottles of scotch and Hershey bars about his person. He cheerfully lied when asked if he had contraband goods. He figured a good lie was a successful part of his survival technique, even if it was frowned upon in the officers' code.

Even to Donkey's inexperienced eye it was apparent that a successful rescue from his present location would be difficult, if not impossible. He estimated that the mountainside had a gradient of nearly twenty degrees, and the tops of the trees were tall enough to be lost in the fog. The rescue choppers would have a hell of a time even locating him here, much less conducting a successful rescue. Obviously, he was going to have to move to a more suitable location, but which way should he walk? He considered his options while zipping up his flight suit. He thought about his meager resources. There were one and a half baby bottles of water in addition to the two eight-ounce cans in the vest. There were four more food packets, but he knew that food was not a real problem. He'd either be found before he starved or it wouldn't matter anyway. He'd be either captive or dead.

No, water was going to be the problem. Already he was sweating and the sun wasn't even visible through the fog. The early-morning chill had vanished rapidly. He'd need to find a source of water soon, as well as a suitable pickup zone. Donkey's grasp of physics was slight, but he was reasonably certain that water didn't flow over the tops of mountains; therefore, the best chance of finding it would be to head downhill. Besides, it would be easier going.

He shuffled back to the hole and looked into its red maw, really noticing for the first time the roots of the large tree that had once occupied it. They seemed to be very short roots for a tree of such dimensions. The tree itself already looked as if it were decomposing, although the scar on the ground where its roots had pulled free of the clinging mud showed little erosive activity. The rain forest was trying to reclaim it quickly; already the leaves had been absorbed into the poor laterite soil.

He stared at the discarded chute harness in the hole and wondered if he would need it. Probably not, and it would just be something else to drag around. Donkey picked up the emptied food packet and tossed it on top of the harness, deciding to hide any evidence of his existence. But what the hell could he do about that stupid parachute? He stared up into the fog and saw it snagged securely far above his head. He pulled his air force switchblade knife from its pouch on the inside thigh of his g suit and severed the shroud lines as far up as he could reach. The ends dangled just above his head like dead white worms. Perplexed, Donkey pondered the problem. The damned thing stood out like a beacon and, anyway, it would be nice to have the chute canopy to wrap around himself in the chill of the night. He reached for the severed shroud lines and gave them a tentative tug. A high-pitched voice yelled on the mountainside below him, which solved the immediate problem of the parachute.

Donkey froze, the hair prickling on the back of his neck. A voice replied to the first, much closer but still out of sight in the dense fog and foliage. He backed slowly away from the hole until he hit the roots of the downed tree. He squatted there and held his breath, ears straining for noises in the sound-deadening fog. Suddenly, he heard the crackling of limbs being thrust aside. Whoever it was made no efforts at stealth. Idiot, he thought. But why should they? No one's hunting them. He tried to slow his racing heart and think logically. Perhaps they were not hunting for him. Maybe they were just woodcutters or something like that. Unlikely. Even if they were, he'd probably be worse off if they caught him rather than army men. The civilians had a habit of killing downed pilots and turning the bodies over to the military. Anyway, if they were civilians they'd probably know these mountains better than soldiers.

The thrashing sounded closer, coming up the hill. There was no other way: He was going to have to leave immediately, and uphill at that. Donkey rose from his crouch, checked his survival vest and meager belongings, then began to move cautiously up the hill. The humus of the jungle floor sucked at his boots and the undergrowth tore at his clothing. His movements sounded very loud to Donkey, even through the pulse pounding in his ears. Another shout from below spurred him into an undisciplined gallop, ramming the bushes and small trees aside. He was close to panic. Within twenty yards his sprint slowed, his breath coming in ragged gasps and pains shooting through his legs as they rebelled against the unaccustomed activity.

Deliberately, he made himself stop and control his breathing as the shouting continued in the fog below. He stood quietly and looked at the trail he had made through the undergrowth. It looked like a hippo had charged through. He was surprised to find he still had the severed shroud lines in his hand. He started to fling them away, then reconsidered and slipped them into a pocket of his flight suit. His empty hands reminded him of his pistol. He withdrew it from the shoulder holster and faced downhill, crouching behind a bush and feeling more foolish than heroic.

The searchers, if indeed that was what they were, made almost as much noise as Donkey. OK, he thought, let's see if I can't work myself out of this. Moving carefully, he took a long stride away from his newly created trail, taking pains to conceal his boot print. No one shot or yelled. He felt just a tiny bit more confident. He repeated the movement and gained himself another yard away from the disfigured vegetation. The thrashings continued below, still concealed by the blanket of fog. Donkey found a rhythm: one step and a minute of listening for pursuit. He checked the ground after each movement, determined to leave no marks. If his boot skidded on the wet floor he hastily covered the telltale scar with a handful of leaves scooped up during one of his waiting periods.

A huge jungle emergent became his target, though his progress toward it was painfully slow. Fewer than ten yards from the tree he smelled a cigarette. Donkey sagged gently to his knees, then prone onto his belly. He stared until tears began to seep from the corners of his eyes. Then he saw the smoke hanging heavily in the still air until another plume stirred it. Slowly, Donkey rolled under a low canopy of big-leaved plants, keeping his eyes toward the searcher who was still identified only by an occasional eruption of new smoke. Some of the hunters didn't seem to be taking the search too seriously.

Donkey rolled another complete revolution and came to rest belly down in the fetid mat on the jungle floor. He buried his face in it, aware of the pungent odor of rotting matter. Slowly, he moved his hand beneath the carpet of decaying leaves, seeking and finding the dark mud beneath and bringing it back to smear onto his flaming red face. It felt cool on his overheated brow. He peered closely at the smoke erupting from behind the bole of the jungle emergent. It sagged in the breathless air, almost invisible against the foggy background.

A slight movement on the ground near his eye level caught his attention. Carefully, he turned his head toward it. Donkey swallowed hard and squeezed his eyes shut so tightly that it actually hurt. They popped open again in horror. Less than two yards separated him from a vigorous little snake gracefully serpentining its way directly toward his face. In another environment perhaps Donkey could have admired its compact, brightly banded body, only a foot long. He knew, however, that he was about to have his first introduction to the krait, a normally nocturnal little beast reputed to be highly venomous. It was the legendary "two-stepper," so-called for the number of steps the average person might expect to make after the little devil had struck.

Donkey squeezed his eyes shut again; they popped open like one of those stupid dolls he remembered his sister playing with. If that little fucker even *touches* me, I'm going to die, he thought, close to panic, the smoke blower momentarily forgotten. The krait appeared to have taken a bead on Donkey's nose, now only a yard or so away. He blew vigorously at the small snake, which stopped in the new breeze, scenting the air before resuming its path. Holy shit! The krait was so close that Donkey had to cross his eyes slightly to focus on it.

He eased forward the .38 Special as the snake hesitated momentarily, just becoming aware that something large and alive was stirring in front of it. A sharp voice sounded beyond the smoker, then again. A mumbled reply from the smoker was audible. At the sound of the first voice Donkey jerked in surprise, then froze, torn between moving his eyes toward the tree and keeping them on the krait, now taking a defensive stance as Donkey jerked. It peered myopically into his face less than a yard from his muddy nose. Sweet Jesus! How far could one of those things strike? He wiggled the pistol barrel at the snake, hoping it would be astute enough to realize he had the drop on it. The krait eased forward and tentatively thrust out its tongue toward the barrel of Donkey's service revolver.

As though perceiving the possibilities of the front blade sight on the barrel, the snake began rubbing the underside of its head back and forth over it in reptilian rapture.

Hand trembling, Donkey tried to withdraw the snake's newly found love object but, slavishly, it followed the moving revolver, moving ever closer to his face. Sinuously, it rubbed against the front sight on the revolver barrel like an affectionate kitten. Donkey shut his eyes and swallowed hard. Perhaps he should just stick the gun barrel in his mouth and pull the trigger. Swallowing a bullet could hardly be worse than the possibilities he now faced. A tirade in Vietnamese forced his eyes open. Another small movement in his peripheral vision made him take his eyes from the krait, still making amorous moves against the gun barrel, to another small clump of green several yards away. A small mouselike creature, perhaps disturbed by the human voices, crouched and twitched. Sensing a meal, the krait immediately disengaged from the pistol barrel and began to glide toward the small creature. Both hunter and hunted disappeared beneath the low foliage and small thrashings could soon be heard.

A final sharp burst of Vietnamese and Donkey could hear, then finally see, the smoker. His small pith helmet just showed above the low growth as he moved away from the huge tree. There had apparently been an ass-chewing by his superior. His face was plainly visible as he looked about the forest before moving steadily into the fog and vanishing. He carried an AK-47 assault rifle and was clearly military. Donkey heard other sounds as the North Vietnamese soldiers swept up the hill. They were hunting someone and Donkey was sure who that was. Someone must have seen his aircraft crash or his ejection.

Carefully, he scanned the area for the snake, then crooked his arm and rested his face on it. Long, deep breaths eventually slowed his heart to a reasonable rate. He began shaking as he thought of what had almost happened. He'd been prepared to blow the snake away regardless of the consequences. If he had fired, there was no doubt he'd never have been taken prisoner. They would have blasted away until they were certain the perceived threat was dead.

He lay on the jungle floor looking as if he, too, were awaiting decay. He was distinguishable from the other detritus only by his quivering shoulders. He hardly heard the enemy soldiers moving away.

Captain Nguyen Thi Minh

"Drink up, Minh," the colonel told him. "At this rate the rest of the squadron is going to have my pockets emptied before you finish that."

Minh flashed a smile at his new commander and accepted another liter bottle of beer. Colonel Toon patted him on the shoulder and wandered away to join a group of young pilots newly arrived from their flight training in the Soviet Union. Had he not known who they were, Minh still would have been able to tell the newcomers from the veterans. They sat stiffly, smiles fixed on their faces, looking completely out of place at their table in the cafe. They had hardly touched their beer, provided tonight by Colonel Toon in celebration of his ninth aerial victory. With any luck, half of them would still be alive next month.

Minh loosened the tie of his uniform shirt and slumped wearily into a chair. He tallied in his head and realized that he'd launched more than forty times in the two weeks since the Americans had again begun attacking in the Hanoi area. The hours of cockpit alert on the hot pad were in many ways more tiring than the actual flights. Waiting always seemed harder than actual combat, particularly if you happened to have an active imagination.

He glanced at the table where the new pilots sat and saw that Colonel Toon was pulling his magic again, almost as if his aura embraced everyone around him. And the man flew like a dream. Minh knew, for he had been his wingman on several occasions, though there were too many new pilots to allow experienced flight leaders the luxury of an old-timer covering his six o'clock. He watched Vietnam's leading ace simulating an attack with both hands, laughing with good humor but getting his point across nonetheless. The squadron was lucky to have him, Minh knew, for there had been a rapid turnover in commanders since he had joined the squadron fresh from training. The Yankees had blown three of them from the air before Colonel Toon arrived to take charge of the Hanoi sector fighter defense. Now they used the techniques the colonel brought with him, and there had been a definite reduction in their loss rate, with a corresponding increase in kills. The colonel's gentle demeanor covered an aggressive spirit that had little use for the timid methods employed in the past.

True enough, the colonel's approach to aerial combat was a little hard on the inexperienced, for although it used the traditional ground-controlled radar attack, it did so with modifications. No more single ships; they now flew in pairs. And after the radar approach and attack, they no longer dived for the clouds to slink away; instead they used the quick-turning abilities of their aircraft for another slashing visual thrust before their quarry could escape. Minh himself had been hard-pressed to hang onto Colonel Toon's gut-wrenching reentry into the fight after his rockets had broken up the Yankee formation. The younger pilots were often lost in the hard turns or subsequent maneuvering. Questioned by some who thought their losses were unnecessarily high, the colonel had smiled his gentle smile and said only: "Our job is to fly fighters and to destroy enemy aircraft. We can't do that sitting on our asses in an orbit, away from the attacking bombers. The good pilots will survive and learn. The others should have been in another line of work anyway."

Minh's hand shook slightly as he raised his glass of beer. Consciously, he steadied it. The past two weeks had been rough. He looked around the cafe at his flying mates— drinking, laughing, and singing. Half of them he no longer knew. Many of the veterans had been shot down and ejected at least once. He smiled and waved at Thranh, who toasted him from across the room with a glass of beer. Thranh was an average pilot who had shown extraordinary skills at survival. He had been deplaned by the Americans on three separate occasions—twice by American naval pilots in F-4s and once by an American air force fighter of the same type. He joked about having heard that the U.S. Marines were looking for him as well and he sincerely hoped the Yankee coast guard did not fly Phantoms.

Minh knew he had been lucky. Even a skilled fighter pilot, which he knew he was, had to have luck on his side if he was to remain alive in this business. His last kill had proven that. He had released his air-to-air missiles and popped through the clouds just in time to see the missiles impact on the lead aircraft of an F-105 formation. Minh had followed the common practice of aiming at the last ship, in this case one that must have had battle damage since it was lagging far behind the others. The flight leader, always the more experienced pilot, was in the process of turning, obviously to help his damaged wingman, when Minh's missile had torn into the aft section of his exposed belly. It had been bad luck for the flight leader, who had taken the missile meant for the other aircraft.

When was his own luck going to run out? He knew that it was virtually impossible to continue launching three or four times a day for combat and remain unscathed forever. He gloomily considered the prospects as he drank more beer. Already, his head was feeling weightless from a combination of the heavy beer and exhaustion. He really should be sleeping, but it would have been discourteous not to accept Colonel Toon's invitation to his victory celebration. He suspected the colonel did it more for the morale of the pilots than for himself. He didn't appear to need adulation from anyone.

Minh drank and brooded. That damned red tail had come to be a fixation with him. He very much wanted the anonymity of a silver aircraft but had been ashamed to tell his ground crew to remove the paint. Colonel Toon had been amused when he saw it and had gently asked if perhaps Minh was not marking himself for the Yankees. Hell, of course he was! But he didn't know how to get out of it without shaming himself. Every time he looked at that ghastly appendage he shuddered inwardly, imagining squadrons of Americans briefing to be sure to take out the idiot in the MiG with the red tail.

"Well, fearless fighter, why so quiet tonight?" asked a voice behind him.

He turned and saw Lieutenant Thieu, a member of his flight class in the Soviet Union, and Thranh, the survivor. Both held glasses and bottles of beer. He nodded his head toward the empty chairs and looked at them from beneath lowered lids as they slid bonelessly into them. Neither appeared to be completely sober. Thranh was giggling in his high-pitched manner. Thieu's handsome face had the fixed smile of the inebriated.

"I can't believe it," Thranh started and momentarily lost his speech in another burst of laughter. When it subsided, he tried again: "Did you hear what this idiot did today?" Again, he lost control and hooted with laughter.

"I suppose not," answered Minh. "At least, I don't remember anything that amusing the entire day." He swallowed more beer, hoping to kill the dull pain starting behind his eyes.

"Well," snickered Thranh, "if you remember I was flying his wing on the last scramble of the day. They vectored us for a radar pass but we never got close enough to do any damage. We broke out of the clouds while they were setting us up for another attack, and below us, right on the deck, was this flight of F-105s. They were so low that they hadn't even been picked up on radar. I mean, they were having to lift up to miss houses! So, down we went, completely ignoring the radar controller's orders, because we were sure of at least one kill. Wouldn't you know it? Just before we got within attack range they went back into the clouds and we lost them completely.

"Not only that. I lost my glorious flight leader as well when he attempted to pull the wings off both our aircraft trying to chase them. Well, the ground controller was trying to get us back together when Thieu ran into clear weather southeast of the city while I was still groping around trying to get back on top. Unfortunately, he found himself flying a rather close formation with a flight of four Phantoms. They took a look at each other and tried to pounce, but old Thieu dove right into the middle of them, knowing he was dead if he tried to outrun them. So, there they were, in a gigantic daisy chain. First two Phantoms, then Thieu, then the other two Phantoms in this huge circle, none of them able to get a shot at him, but he wasn't able to get away either.

"Do you know what he did then? He called Hanoi Sector Control and told them that he had four American Phantoms surrounded and would they please send assistance so he could take them prisoners! Control was laughing so hard you could barely understand them."

"What happened then?" asked Minh, smiling in spite of himself at Thieu sitting in the chair, waving gently as if a wind were pushing him about. The same set smile was on his face.

"It became obvious to me," Thieu answered for himself, "that the Yankees did not want to become my prisoners. So, I broke hard left out of the circle—"

"That's sure death!" Minh interrupted.

" . . . and that's what I counted on. That they wouldn't be able to believe their eyes. After I broke, I counted to five very slowly—and I'd like to say that was the longest five seconds of my life—then broke hard back into them and shoved the nose over and headed for the deck. I was afraid to look back. But, it worked because I got away from them in the clouds."

Minh shook his head slowly in wonder. The American fighters didn't make that sort of mistake very often. Thieu had been a lucky man.

Thranh's laughter had stopped. He'd been watching Minh as Thieu related the last of his story. "How goes it with you, old friend?" asked Thranh. "You look as if you could use a few days away from the war. Can't you wrangle a few days' leave? Maybe take that pretty girlfriend of yours someplace nice and quiet and think of nothing but anti-socialist debauchery for a while?"

"Where would you suggest?" asked Minh, still smiling. "There's nothing quite so disquieting to a night of debauchery, as you call it, as the air raid sirens blaring at the critical moment and then having to hobble down to one of those spider-hole shelters. Lovemaking loses some of its spice if that happens too often."

"Nevertheless, you look as if you could do with a few days away from the cockpit."

"We all do," he answered. "I doubt if Colonel Toon's taken a day off in the last year."

"I know," Thranh said soberly, "and unfortunately he's no more invulnerable than the rest of us. He's good; no, very good. The best—present company excluded, of course. But, it takes only one little mistake and he's with the ancestors just like us." He and Thieu rose to leave. "You know, Minh, you fly more sorties than the rest of us and, believe me, there'd be no hard feelings from anyone if you were to take a small break." He clapped Minh on the shoulder. "Think about it. Meanwhile, I'm going to see if there's any free beer left."

Minh sat in the cockpit and drummed his fingers on the canopy rail. Cockpit alert had to be the most boring human endeavor ever devised. He considered the low clouds. The Americans wouldn't come today if they had any sense at all. The radio antenna was only half visible in the clouds. Still, if someone had to sit in the mist, it was his turn after the weekend pass.

It had been embarrassingly easy. He'd barely had to mumble a few words to Colonel Toon about having a couple of free days, perhaps during a period of forecast bad weather, before the smiling man had enthusiastically agreed and immediately had the papers drawn. He had further embarrassed Minh by insisting that he take a full rucksack of rice and foodstuffs from their local commissary stores. When Minh had returned to pick up the packed rucksack, he found that a huge bottle of Japanese rice wine had been included, with a note from the colonel stating that it was his duty as a socialist soldier to enjoy his furlough to the utmost.

He and Mai Lin had bicycled toward Ap Duc Co, a tiny village where his uncle and his family lived, some twenty kilometers southeast of the Hanoi suburbs. Both had felt self-conscious as he had explained to her parents that she would be under the watchful eyes of his uncle and aunt. Her father had scowled, but there had been a tiny smile on her mother's lips. She knew, he suspected, that the relationship between him and their daughter had grown beyond the platonic.

It had been months since Minh had been outside the city and he was astounded at the changes. Along the roadway, small concrete bomb shelters had been set into the ground a few meters apart. Large enough for a single person, the rough circles poked above the ground like so many small cisterns. Many had woven bamboo tops for either concealment or protection from the elements. Every hamlet had communal shelters connected to the huts by trenches, some more than six feet deep. Few farmers were to be seen. Most, one told them, ventured into the fields only for a few short hours at dusk or dawn for fear of the American aircraft. Nearly all had rifles or automatic weapons either strapped to their backs as they worked or stacked so as to be easily accessible. Many of the peasants cheered him as they recognized his uniform and emblem identifying him as a pilot. It made him proud and sad as he thought of their hardships and determination to fight the Americans.

Posters proclaiming the inevitability of the socialist victory were stuck on every tree, and signs with patriotic slogans were stretched above the roadway before each village. Everywhere people could be seen digging more shelters and trench lines as if they expected the American forces to land at any moment.

Minh and Mai Lin had stopped at a small hamlet and asked for water to quench their thirst. An old man insisted that they accompany him to view the wreckage of a Yankee air pirate's aircraft, which the village defenders had shot from the sky a month before. Before the short walk had taken them more than a few yards toward the wreckage, they had been joined by almost every member of the village.

The wrecked F-105 sat in the middle of a rice paddy, the front part of the fuselage crushed beyond recognition. The village elders proudly described the fight in which they had destroyed the aircraft by the combined volume of their gunfire. Minh nodded in admiration and praised their marksmanship while noting the gaping hole of either a large-caliber antiaircraft shell or an air-to-air missile just at the rear of the tail pipe. It was obvious to him what had actually downed the aircraft. These villagers could have been the ones that kept shooting holes in his own aircraft. He continued to smile, however, and he and Mai Lin shared a glass of beer with the group before they left.

It had been late afternoon by the time they reached the village of his uncle. It was larger than the others they had biked through and had a lookout tower at each end, presumably to watch for enemy aircraft or possibly enemy pilots who had been shot down and not yet captured. Minh looked at the people scurrying around the countryside, hurriedly completing chores before sunset or getting ready to join road repair teams. He thought it would be difficult indeed for a Caucasian pilot to go undetected in this country.

The introductions were rather strained and formal between his uncle's family and Mai Lin. Neither his aunt nor uncle approved of their unescorted trip together. Feelings thawed quickly, however, as he opened the rucksack containing the food brought from the air base. His uncle caressed the large wine bottle.

That night, he and Mai Lin had made love on the sleeping mats inside the hut while his aunt and uncle slept soundly in their underground bomb shelter, helped by the bottle of wine. Few words passed between the lovers. They were not necessary. Minh knew he couldn't let the relationship ripen, not in his line of work. He could live only for the moment. Mai Lin was safely tucked away in the corner of the bomb shelter when his aunt and uncle awakened the next morning.

The bicycle ride back to Hanoi had been tiresome, made even more so by the wretched conditions of the roadways, churned into a muddy froth by the passing truck convoys during the night. For them to venture onto the roadways during the daylight hours was suicidal, even in periods of rain and fog. Some of the American attack aircraft obviously had terrain-avoidance radars as well as sensors for picking up the heat generated by the engines of the trucks. No one was sure how accurate these devices were, but enough attacks had occurred during periods of reduced visibility to make those directing the convoys nervous about any daytime travel.

Minh dropped Mai Lin at the building in which she lived with her cousin, both students at the university. She studied foreign languages, specializing in, of all things, English. Minh found the entire idea slightly contradictory even after she explained the need for it.

"After the war, the country will have a great need for English speakers," she had told him. "Even after we evict the Americans, they are much too powerful and rich to be ignored. If we're to take our place with other nations, we'll have to do business with them eventually."

"Why can't they just as easily learn Vietnamese?" he had asked, tongue in cheek. "After all, it will have been the Vietnamese who won the war and kicked them out."

"For the same reasons that French is almost a second language with us and we kicked them out." She had said it with a smile, knowing she was being teased.

"Well, it seems to me that we have enough American speakers by now, anyway. Almost everyone in Saigon and the south seems to have picked up the language, from what I hear."

"Actually, you pilots are the worst," she said, teasing him in turn. "Almost half the phrases you use are English. How about 'afterburner,' or 'roger.' All of you do your best to emulate the American pilots in everything, and you know it."

"Maybe so," he grinned, "or maybe it's just that all pilots think alike, no matter what their nationality." He became serious. "Do you think you could teach me English?"

"I don't suppose you'd be too dense to learn, but why?"

"I don't know. Perhaps something to keep me occupied when I'm standing alert. Just sitting in that cockpit can become terribly boring."

"If you're serious I'd be glad to help you. It'll do me some good getting the practice, too. When do you want to start?"

"Tonight, if you think you can keep your hands off me."

She smiled tenderly at him. "Not much chance of that, I'm afraid."

Colonel Toon had been in the headquarters building when Minh had reported back for duty. He looked even more tired and wan than normal. "Ah, Minh, glad to see you're back. Did you have a nice weekend?"

"Yes, I did, Colonel Toon. I really appreciate what you've done for me. And now, I'm ready to go back to work. How have things been?"

"Not too good, I'm afraid. The Americans have been hitting us around the clock. The F-105s and F-4s during the day and the Navy A-6s at night. We've been hard-pressed to get enough aircraft or pilots to meet them."

"I apologize, sir," Minh had said, feeling as if he'd been caught slacking off from his duties. "I should never have requested that leave."

"Nonsense, Captain, nonsense! If you hadn't asked for it, I would have sent you off anyway. Remember, this is going to be a long war, and an exhausted pilot gets careless." The colonel put a hand on Minh's shoulder before he continued. "I am afraid I do have some bad news for you, though. Your friend, Lieutenant Thranh, was killed yesterday. I'm very sorry to have to tell you."

Minh felt as if he'd been hit in the chest. Thranh! The survivor. Three safe ejections. "Does anyone know what happened?" he asked the colonel.

"Pretty much so, I think. He was scrambled early on Thieu's wing and they made the standard GCI attack against a flight of F-105s. They weren't successful and they were trying to position themselves for another run when they were jumped south of the city. Thieu said that a missile flew right up Thranh's tail pipe. The aircraft exploded instantly and no chute was seen."

"Did Thieu know what sort of aircraft got him?"

"Oh, an F-4, of course. I think that was Thranh's fate all along."

The mist turned to rain and Minh signaled the ground crew that he was going to close the canopy. They nodded and watched, then took cover under a makeshift shelter in the corner of the revetment. In moments the canopy had fogged over, until he felt as though he were isolated by a cotton shroud. Only the sizzling radio reminded him of his link to the world outside the cockpit.

Poor Thranh. No more beer parties or girls chasing after you, old friend. He tried to remember all of his classmates from the Soviet Union. He was surprised that he'd already forgotten many of their names. At least half of them were gone now, either shot down or having crashed because of pilot error or mechanical failure. It had turned into a war of attrition, and the Americans seemed to have an endless supply of aircraft.

Minh saw that his hand trembled slightly as it rested on the control stick, and he smiled ruefully. Big, bold fighter pilot indeed! He clenched the hand firmly around the stick head to stop the tremor, glad that the fogged canopy concealed him from the ground crew. It wouldn't do for them to see one of their top aces acting like a frightened new man. Safe behind the opaque canopy he furtively wiped the sudden sheen of sweat from his brow.

"Dragon One One and Dragon One Four. Stand by!" The urgent voice from the radio startled him.

Quickly, he slipped the helmet over his head and waited. Surely the raiders were not coming in this weather. He opened the canopy to clear the fog and stared into the sky. The ceiling seemed to be lower than before. The ground crew saw the canopy open and dashed into position.

"Dragon One One and Dragon One Four, this is Control. Scramble! Scramble! Cleared to the active runway and cleared for takeoff. Contact Hanoi Sector Control when airborne."

"Dragon One One. Understand. Scramble and cleared for takeoff."

As he spoke, Minh punched the start switch and watched the engine spool up to idle revolutions. After a quick check of the instruments, he gave the signal for the chocks to be removed. Over the noisy engine he could hear the base siren begin to wail, announcing the approaching raid. He moved the throttle steadily forward and released the brakes, giving a thumbs-up and a grin to the ground crew.

He noted that his hand had lost its tremor.

Captain James Evelyn Broussard

The leader of Ford Flight, a lanky, florid-faced major, was on his feet facing the ops officer standing at the podium. Jim could see that the flight leader barely had his temper in check, for there was a ring of white around his compressed lips. His stance was rigid and angry.

"Let me just make sure I've got this right," he said, staring at the ops officer unblinkingly. "The wing is going to launch a maximum effort against Slaughter Alley, but each aircraft is going to carry only *two* 500-pounders?"

"Essentially, that's correct," the ops officer said, looking everywhere in the briefing room but at the assembled pilots. "Except for the Wild Weasel flights. They'll be taking the normal load."

"Could anyone enlighten us," the major's voice dripped sarcasm, "just why in hell we're sending more than twenty aircraft into that fucking killing ground with only two bombs apiece? It seems to me that common sense should tell even headquarters that it's completely senseless to risk that many aircraft when the same tonnage could be taken by one-fourth the number and reduce the risk by three-quarters."

The ops officer, a newly arrived bird colonel, shook his head. "I suggest you hold your questions for a few minutes, because the wing commander is on his way over here. I think he wants to say a few words to all of you, which may clear it up. So, just hold your water for a minute."

Mike Patowski turned to Jim as the pilots of the strike group sat and waited. "What's Slaughter Alley? I don't like the sound of that."

Jim leaned forward and pointed to the map opened on the table. "Here," he said, indicating with a pencil, "is the restricted area around Hanoi in which we aren't allowed to bomb. And here," he moved the pencil, "is the thirty-mile restricted area along the Chinese border. Now, if you look between the Hanoi restricted area and the Chinese border restricted area, you see there's about a twenty-five-mile stretch of railroad track that falls between the two of them. The railroad goes from Hanoi into China. You don't have to be too bright to figure that if this is the only section of the tracks we can hit, then it's the best place to put guns and missiles. I've been there only once, but it seems that the sites damn near overlap. Then, when you consider that the only sure way to get a cut across the rail line is to come in and fly almost right down the line before you drop . . . well, it can get to be an interesting few minutes."

Mike looked at him with big eyes bright with excitement. This was to be his first mission into the heavily defended Route Package Six. He was like a kid ready to go to camp for the first time. Excited and apprehensive but not frightened. Jim glanced at Andy Pritchard, who, noticing it, gave him a quick grin, then turned his attention back to studying his map. Things had certainly been better along *that* front, Jim thought with relief. There had been a gradual thawing in the relationship between him and Pritchard since the loss of Donkey, and Stark's taking command of the flight.

Stark sat at the end of the table, his face cast in its habitual frozen expression. Jim's contempt for the man grew daily, though he tried not to let Mike Patowski, Stark's new wingman, become aware of it. Aside from being a first-class jerk, the man was just plain incompetent. He still had difficulty getting his fuel from the tanker, and his bombing was atrocious. Somehow he was always able to find a plausible excuse as to why Cadillac Flight arrived late, or didn't hit the target, or missed the refueling time. Jim thought he must have an already-prepared list to choose from.

Unfortunately, the reputation of the flight was beginning to suffer under his leadership. There had been a few too many jokes in the club about Cadillac's inability to make a TOT or even a takeoff time. The bantering didn't seem to bother Andy Pritchard, but then he had already completed one combat tour and was more than three-quarters of the way through this one. He could afford to be nonchalant about the sarcasm. If it bothered Stark, it was not apparent.

"Gentlemen, the commander," the ops officer intoned. The pilots rose to their feet as the short, pugnacious bird colonel strode to the podium. He reminded Jim of James Cagney doing his tough man impression. The colonel had a few quiet words with the ops officer before whirling to look at the pilots. Glaring, he kept them standing for a few seconds before motioning them to their seats.

"What's this shit about some of you not liking the weapon load?" he said immediately.

The Ford Flight leader shot to his feet, not put off by the colonel's manner. He reminded Jim a little of Donkey. "Just an explanation, Colonel, on why we're risking twenty-four aircraft when we could do the same job with a hell of a lot less."

The wing commander stared at the major for a long moment before audibly expelling his breath, appearing to deflate. "I could just tell you to follow orders and do your damned job, but I think I owe you all more than that." He motioned the flight leader back to his seat. "The truth of the matter is that we're just about plumb outta bombs. We've run low before but there was always a bombing halt to let us restock. Right now, there ain't anywhere to restock *from*. They're out of them back in the States, too. A friend of mine in the Pentagon let me know this unofficially; seems they're scouring the world trying to buy iron bombs back from our allies. Even some that have been considered junk sales have been repurchased.

"Between the B-52 raids and all the fighters dropping weapons over here and down south, we seem to have completely used up the inventory. Remember, one of those big fuckers drops more than a hundred 500-pounders in one raid. My source tells me that they've stripped all the stateside and European air force and naval depots of conventional weapons. We're just going to have to wait until the munition makers get cranked up big time back home."

Another flight leader stood. "That explains about the bomb shortage, but why are we sending out all these aircraft to do the job when a few of them could do it just as well? It doesn't make sense to any of us. Hell, I'm not trying to get out of flying it. I'll take the other flight leaders in here and make up our own flight to hit the tracks and leave these young pukes at home if you want to do it that way."

"Well, Ralph," the wing commander responded, "you see, that's not the problem. I know we could do the job with a lot fewer aircraft. But that ain't what Seventh Air Force down in Saigon wants. And it's not what PACAF wants. Those folks want us to keep our sortie rate up so we don't fall behind the Navy in flying time or sorties."

"You mean we're playing 'count the sorties' with everybody's lives?" The flight leader stared at the commander incredulously.

"Well, I wouldn't exactly put it that way, but there it is."

The briefing room became very quiet.

Cadillac Flight was late again. Jim checked their position as they crossed south of Dien Bien Phu heading eastward toward their target on the border of Route Package Six Alpha. To get there they would have to traverse the defenses at Yen Bai, where a particularly virulent group of gunners seemed to be mad at the world. A few bursts of flak grew off their left wing far below them and well out of range. They were fortunate that missiles had yet to be emplaced in this part of the country. The Black River meandered to their front, appearing only occasionally beneath the almost solid cloud deck. A month of monsoonal rains had made the rain forest appear greenish black.

"Arm 'em up, Cadillac Flight," said Stark, the new Cadillac Flight leader. Mike Patowski held his position well on Lead's wing. The aircraft looked odd with only two 500-pound bombs, one hung from beneath each wing. The aircraft did handle much more easily with the reduced weight. Jim had been astounded at the reduction of his takeoff roll. The Thud had literally leapt into the air.

"Cadillac Three, this is Lead. My Doppler's out. Move forward and take the lead and my element will follow you in," Stark called to Pritchard.

"Rog, Lead. Moving up," said Andy after several moments' hesitation.

Jim grinned sardonically under his mask. Yeah, just about on schedule, he thought. On at least half of the last several missions since Stark had assumed the lead position, he had some sort of mechanical difficulty that kept him out of the lead slot. Donkey would have simply called for the other element leader to give him directions and kept the lead. Twice now, Stark had taken his wingman and returned to base due to mechanical problems, leaving Jim and Andy to proceed to the target on their own. The aircraft problems, though legitimate, would have been ignored by any other pilot in the wing; at worst, the lead would have opted to change to a wingman's position. It had become apparent to everyone that Major Stark, though coveting the lead position, had little faith in his ability to fly under adverse conditions. If there's much more shooting, Jim thought, Stark will start aborting on the ground.

The early warning radars crackled more forcefully in his headset as Jim followed Pritchard into the forward element position. "Cadillac Flight, let's go button two," said Andy, directing a change to strike radio frequency.

The flight checked in and Jim listened to the sound of the battle already commencing almost 150 miles in front of them. At 10 miles a minute they'd be in attack position in fifteen minutes. Say, another five to six minutes for the run-in and recovery, then another five minutes of climb would mean that they'd be all through with it in about twenty-five minutes. Then, barring the unforeseen, nothing to worry about until tomorrow. A hell of a life!

Jim added throttle to keep his position on the lead ship. Andy was already starting down toward the undercast. He flew a good lead. Everything smooth and precise, much like Donkey had flown. Jim smiled as he thought of their drinking bout the night of Donkey's loss. God! That had been terrible. It had been almost noon the next day before he could even sit up. And Kate had been so mad she didn't speak to him for two days. Poor old Donkey. Jim suddenly forced himself to clear away the daydreams. He would be

joining Donkey and a lot of others down there if he didn't
get his mind back where it belonged.

Nghia Lo pinpointed itself by unleashing a barrage of 85-
and 100mm flak at the attacking aircraft. The larger-caliber
weapons had the range to reach the flight's altitude but had
little chance to bracket them before they were past. The
stick began a mild buffet in Jim's gloved hand. Just over
600 knots. Andy was obviously trying to make up some of
the delay they'd had during the refueling. Stark continued
to have difficulties taking on the required fuel. On the other
hand, Mike Patowski, his green wingman, seldom had an
inadvertent disconnect, acting and flying his aircraft as if
it were the most natural thing in the world to be connected
by a metal tube to another aircraft.

Andy steered Cadillac Flight fifteen degrees to the right,
angling slightly away from Yen Bai on their nose, to a
course that would place them between those bristling gun
fortifications and those at Phu Tho. The clouds beneath
them looked solid, although it must be workable below the
stratus deck, for the sounds of battle could already be heard
as the flak suppressors began their deadly job of attacking
the gun sites. If things went properly, there should be about
three minutes between each attacking flight of Thuds. From
his limited experience in Pack Six, Jim knew that things
seldom went right.

"This is Cherry Lead! Cherry Lead! Valid launch! Valid
launch!" Jim felt his gut tighten as the first of the calls
came through the air, warning the strike pilots that SAMs
had been fired. He didn't recognize the call sign but hoped
it was another flight well away from their target. Hardly
likely though, since it came over their strike frequency.

"Tucker Lead, this is Scooter Lead." The F-4 MiGCAP
wanted to talk with the F-105 airborne commander.

"Go, Scooter Lead, this is Tucker." The answering voice
was tight and unwelcoming. Tucker Lead wasn't in the
mood to chitchat with the fighter cover flying far overhead.
Jim checked the stopwatch on the instrument panel. Little
wonder that Tucker Lead wasn't being hospitable. He was
due to commence his attack within two to three minutes.

"Rog, Tucker. Just wanted you to know that we've got
eight bent wings up here."

"Understand eight. Out."

The MiGCAP flight commander was understandably concerned that the Thuds coming off target be aware that there were eight swept-wing American fighters over them and that they shouldn't confuse them with any other swept-wing aircraft, that is, any MiGs. The Thud pilots were nervous and had a tendency to shoot first, then question the type of aircraft.

The clouds began to break as they neared their area of assigned tracks. Dirty gray puffs of flak immediately began to seek their altitude. Jim knew without looking that they had to be abeam Phu Tho, the western boundary of their hard times. Cadillac Flight entered the tops of the ragged clouds at 10,000 feet, safe for the moment from all but the radar-controlled guns and the SAMs. If the surface-to-air missiles were directed against an aircraft in the clouds, there was little the pilot could do in his defense.

Fortunately, the cloud deck was less than 3,000 feet thick and Cadillac Flight was quickly beneath it and approaching their base altitude of 13,000 feet. The ground fire was now visible to any who cared to look at it. Jim did not, preferring to focus his eyes on briefed checkpoints. The unbidden thought crept into his mind that for every visible 37- or 57mm gun flash there were probably a hundred that could not be seen. Determined not to look down until necessary, he fixed his eyes on the lead ship, then guiltily remembered that he too should be looking for SAMs and fighters and should not rely too heavily on Pritchard to see them.

The flight was rocked apart by two well-directed bursts. Jim thought he could feel the metal fragments hit home, but a quick scan of the instrument panel showed nothing amiss. He turned his head to glance at the other element and was shocked not to see them. He brought his head around to peer in the other direction. "Cadillac Lead, this is Two." He had automatically reverted to his Cadillac Two call sign when Pritchard took the lead from Stark. "I don't see the second element."

He saw Pritchard's head snap around and study the sky behind them. His ship didn't bobble.

"They're there, Two," Pritchard answered, "they're just so far back that they're hard to see. Cadillac Three and Four, would you like to join us in this or do you prefer to bomb alone, because we're not turning back or slowing up for you."

"Roger, we're moving up," Stark replied, ignoring Pritchard's sarcasm.

Jim checked his Doppler and saw that they were less than a minute from the IP, then glanced quickly at the lagging element. There was no way they could be in position in time for the descent to low level and pop-up for the bombing. Pritchard showed no indication that he was prepared to wait for them.

"This is Royal, this is Royal. MiGs airborne! MiGs airborne!"

"This is Scooter Lead, Royal. Where are they?" The fighter CAP wanted directions.

"Damnit it, everyone this is Tucker Lead. Clear this frequency!" The bombing commander was getting pissed at the unnecessary chatter on his primary radio frequency.

The radar warning device began to rattle rapidly in Jim's earphones. He had mentally tuned out the routine search radar warnings, but the lock-on of the Fansong missile tracking radar brought him to full alert. "Cadillac Lead . . . ," he began, wanting to alert Pritchard to the danger.

"I heard it," he responded. "It's time to start down anyway."

"SAM! SAM!" It sounded like Mike on Stark's wing.

Jim rocked his aircraft onto a wing and at once saw the white doughnut of the launching missile, followed by a blast of ground debris blown by the booster rocket. He twisted his head to watch the telephone-pole sized missile begin to accelerate and pass behind them. It seemed to split the space between Cadillac Three and Four. Neither aircraft tried to turn away from it as it sped from sight into the overcast.

"Sometimes it's better to be lucky than good," Andy said, also an obvious observer of the missile's track.

"Goddamnit, this is Tucker Lead. Clear this frequency unless there's an emergency!"

Cadillac Lead began the left turn from over the IP and let the airspeed build for his element. Jim was only vaguely aware of the white flak bursts until they appeared directly in front of them. Pritchard made no move to evade them. Then they were through. Jim picked up the rail line snaking northeast toward China and rechecked his arming switches.

They were down to 500 feet with throttles full forward. The ground raced by, buildings disappearing in a flash, when suddenly Pritchard was leading them into a twisting pop-up to bombing altitude. The g forces tugged at Jim's mask and he felt the pneumatic bladders of the suit inflating around his legs and belly.

There were several moments of weightlessness as they floated to their bombing altitude, then inverted and dived back down at a sixty-degree angle toward the rail line. They were running almost parallel to the tracks, only slightly offset to provide a good angle for a cut. Jim fed in right stick and rudder to get the sight where he wanted it, then glanced once again at Pritchard in time to see the two bombs kicked from the ejector racks by the small explosive charges. He thumbed his own pickle switch on the control stick head and felt his own two 500-pounders ripple off.

Both sides of the rail line were alive with the tiny sparkles of small arms fire, interspersed with the larger blossoms of flak. Jim felt a definite "thunk" on his aircraft as he pulled hard on the stick, trying to keep Pritchard in sight through his graying vision. He stroked the throttle outboard and the afterburner cut in.

He followed Pritchard westward at 500 feet, sagging down to 300 as they flashed across a small town. He hoped sincerely that their sonic boom blew out every window in the town. The lead ship began to turn back to the east. Was he crazy? Those people were trying to kill them back there! Then Jim realized that Stark and Patowski weren't with them. Jesus! Was this going to be a repeat of how they lost Donkey?

"Cadillac Three, this is Lead. Where are you?"

"We're just coming off target," Stark said shakily. "Turning to the west at this time."

That meant they had a closure speed of well over 1,200 knots even though the first element had come out of burner. Pritchard started his 180-degree turn back to the west, climbing so he would be able to pick out the lagging element. Jim's disgust almost overrode his fear. Why the hell was Andy turning back for that guy? Then he remembered that Stark had said his Doppler navigational system was inoperative. Jim had assumed that was just excuse number twelve. But what if it was actually malfunctioning? No flight leader would leave a member of his formation in such a predicament. Christ! Why didn't Stark ask his wingman for guidance? Guiltily, he realized Mike's newness.

"Tallyho, Cadillac Three. I've got you at our ten o'clock, about two miles out," Pritchard called. Jim swiveled his head to the left, searching for the second element, then picked them up low on the ground to their front. Strings of flak followed the two aircraft as they made their way west. "Take it about fifteen degrees to the right," Andy continued. "We need to get north of Phu Tho."

Stark didn't answer but led his element obediently into the turn. Mike was sticking to him like a jockey on a horse. Jim could imagine what the young lieutenant was feeling about now after experiencing the guns and missiles of Route Package Six for the first time. As Jim thought about it, however, he realized that it didn't get any better with experience. Heavy flak from their left again pinpointed the town of Phu Tho. Just a little bit farther, he thought, and we'll be out of the worst of it. The Red River flashed beneath the flight. Just a few more miles.

A blinding light flared between Jim's aircraft and the lead ship. It took his brain a moment to react. Jesus! That was a missile, but it had come *down* at them. He was the only one who could have seen it, since Stark and his wingman were still in front of them and it was behind Andy's ship. The light dawned.

"Cadillac Flight! Break left! Break left!" he cried.

There was no indecision on Andy's part. Immediately, he threw his Thud into a gut-wrenching, steep diving turn to the left. Jim was hard-pressed to stay with him, sliding far outside his radius. Two more missiles flashed by between the two aircraft. Jim's vision grayed until he slacked off the back pull on the stick. He tried to force his head around to look over his shoulder at their still-unseen assailant. He could see only sky and clouds. He'd even lost sight of the lead ship.

Then he saw Andy, burner alight in an attempt to gain altitude. The MiG-21 was several thousand feet above him, turning hard to put himself in position for another firing pass. Unconsciously, Jim admired the sleek little aircraft's turning performance. It was much like the T-38 in which he had instructed for more than four years. He tried to bend his heavy aircraft around to help Andy meet the threat but found he was being forced farther outside the fight. Damn these stubby little wings!

Jim armed the internal cannon of his aircraft and pulled the aircraft up until it was almost at the vertical before allowing it to roll back nose down toward the fight, sacrificing speed for altitude. It quickly became obvious that Andy had a real problem unless he could get some help, for although the Thud was faster than the sporty little Russian-built aircraft, it definitely lacked the MiG's turning capability. The MiG was nibbling away at the distance and angle needed for a killing shot. Where the hell was Stark? They needed help.

Once again Jim pulled the nose of the aircraft up and began a high-g barrel roll, stopping the aircraft in the inverted position, then, completing the roll with his nose pointed just behind the MiG. He could never hit it, but he had to try to divert its attention long enough for Andy to disengage. If they could do that, there was not an aircraft in the theater that could stay with them as they unloaded and let the Thud have its head. The range had to be more than 1,500 yards, well outside the lethal spray of the aircraft's cannon, but he squeezed the trigger anyway and felt the rapid vibration and buzzing of the Gatling gun.

As he anticipated, the deadly stream of fire fell well behind the enemy aircraft. The MiG didn't go for the feint but continued the pursuit of its target. Jim pulled into a vertical scissor, designed to cut the distance between his aircraft and those locked in the duel.

There wasn't enough time. The MiG had achieved a firing position and unleashed another pair of Atoll air-to-air missiles. The first one missed by a scant few yards; the second flew up the tail pipe of Andy's aircraft.

One moment there had been a twenty-five-ton aircraft flying over the countryside; the next there was a rapidly decelerating formation of junk metal. The explosion was complete. The wreckage tumbled toward the earth looking little like an aircraft. There was no chute or emergency beeper.

Savagely, Jim pulled the nose of his aircraft skyward, completely losing his vision, then rolled inverted once more, searching for the MiG. He picked it up as it climbed vertically toward him. They passed, canopy to canopy, going in opposite directions. The vertical tail of the Vietnamese aircraft was painted completely red. Quickly, he pulled hard to his right. A burst of tracers flew by his wing from an unseen aircraft. He continued the hard turn, only to see another MiG-21 maneuvering toward the saddle position. His original foe was now abeam and angling back toward him, trying to pincer the Thud between the two aircraft.

Jim had no choice. He stopped the turn on a westerly heading and eased the stick forward until he had zero g's on the accelerometer, then lit the burner and headed for the treetops. As he passed Mach 1, he banked his aircraft enough so that he could see behind it. Both MiGs had apparently given up the chase, knowing the futility of a race with the F-105.

He glanced at his fuel totalizer and realized that making it to a tanker would be very close. He switched to the refueling frequency as he wondered what had happened to the other two aircraft of Cadillac Flight. He'd heard voices over the radio but had been too occupied to absorb their meaning. His mind still refused to accept the enormity of what had occurred. Almost dispassionately, he watched the flak blossom around his aircraft but made no attempt at evasion. An hour ago his heart would have been racing with concern. Now, he watched the explosions almost without interest.

"Blue Anchor, Blue Anchor, this is Cadillac Two."

The response was immediate. "Cadillac Two, this is Blue Anchor Four Four. Go ahead."

"Roger, Blue Four Four. Cadillac Two is a single ship estimating RP in two zero minutes. Fuel state is critical. I'm coming out on the high route."

"Cadillac Two, this is Four Four. Rog. We've got the other element of your flight with us at this time. As soon as they're finished, we'll head back your way."

"Then you might as well forget it, because I'll be dry long before that."

There was a slight pause before the tanker pilot answered. "Understand Cadillac Two. We're turning your way at this time. We'll also extend our orbit past the RP if that'll help you out."

"Yeah, that'll be great," Jim responded flatly.

Jim's body was operating on autopilot, hands and feet doing the things they were trained to do, but his mind was still in the sharp, violent dogfight that had killed Andy Pritchard. He realized that they had not exchanged a word after they were jumped by the MiGs. He was overcome by an incredible weariness. And Andy Pritchard was dead. The man who wanted to be a general was dead. And Donkey Sheehan was dead. And Bobby Packard was hopefully a prisoner but he might be dead as well. The horror of it welled in his brain. Andy and Donkey were gone because of Stark, who was as responsible for their deaths as the Vietnamese pilot flying that red-tailed MiG. All gone. He clawed at his mask, barely releasing it before he vomited on the deck of the aircraft.

Jim slumped in the folding chair at the debriefing table and listened as Stark talked to the intelligence officer. "When the MiGs jumped the other element," he was saying, "our fuel status was so critical that I felt it was prudent to egress the area. I assumed Captain Pritchard would evade them and follow us, particularly since my Doppler was out. There was no indication that he had decided to engage them."

"He didn't engage them," Jim cut in, "they fucking well engaged us."

Stark stared at him with unblinking eyes, then turned back to the debriefer and continued. "Had I known that he was in trouble I would have turned to help, but neither aircraft made any sort of radio call."

"Listen, I—" Jim felt the hand of the squadron commander rest on his shoulder. He had been standing behind him during the after-mission session, listening to the debrief of Cadillac Flight.

"I think that's enough for this flight, Lieutenant," the CO said, his hand still on Jim's shoulder. The pressure of it kept him in the chair. Stark rose and left immediately, followed slowly by Mike Patowski, who looked more than a little worried. The large lieutenant colonel sat at the table beside Jim after the others had left. A glance sent the intelligence officer scurrying away. "Jimbo," the commander began, "this was a tough one, especially after losing Donkey and Bob Packard."

"Colonel," Jim said bitterly, "there was no reason to lose either one of them. It happened both times because they turned back to help Stark. The man's a complete incompetent and he's chicken shit to boot. Everybody knows it but nobody does anything about it."

The CO slowly nodded his head as if he'd known it all along. His large hands toyed with a pencil on the table. His brow was furrowed. He turned bloodshot eyes to Jim. "Well," he said, "all I can say is 'welcome to the real world.' We don't always get to pick and choose who we want to fight with or against. I couldn't move him out if I wanted to, and I do. Always have. He's got friends who can block anything anyone tries to do.

"I kinda' hate to be the one who showers any more bad news on you, but I might as well tell you before somebody else does. We've just got a twix of the lieutenant colonel's promotion list and Stark's on it." The pencil snapped between his fingers. "Yep. The son of a bitch made lieutenant colonel below the zone."

The big man rose wearily from his chair and patted Jim clumsily on the back. He smiled at the look of incredulity on Jim's face. "It's a funny old world, ain't it?" the commander said. He lumbered from the room, leaving behind a dumbfounded Captain Broussard.

Jim's knees trembled as he walked slowly from the debriefing room. He felt sick to his stomach. Stark was waiting just outside the door.

"Listen, Captain, I need to talk to you. I'm making you the second element leader and I want to make sure you understand my procedures."

Jim continued to walk, head down and not looking at the man. He didn't answer.

"Captain Broussard! I'm talking to you!"

Jim continued to trudge forward until Stark grabbed his arm. Jim snatched it away and whirled to face the major, eyes ablaze. "Touch me again, Dickie, and I'll rip your face off!"

Stark stepped back. "I thought we'd be able to come to an understanding, but it appears I was wrong. So be it. But get one thing straight, Captain Broussard. This is my flight now and it'll run the way I want it to run. You'll do what I tell you to do, when I tell you to do it. Do you read me loud and clear?"

"Oh, yes, Dickie," Jim answered quietly. "I hear what you're saying. Now, let me ask you something. How's it going to feel to be leading *your* flight knowing that I'm sitting there at your six o'clock with a loaded Vulcan cannon every time we take off?"

Jim turned and walked away.

Major Delbert "Donkey" Sheehan

Donkey thrust his bearded face through a small hole in the thick foliage and peered suspiciously at the banks of the fast-moving jungle stream. The tumbling waters overflowed onto the forest floor as the stream made a sharp turn down the mountainside. The bedraggled figure crept to the swollen streambed and quickly filled the baby bottles, then scuttled back into the undergrowth. Wary as a hunted animal, he paused by the bole of a large jungle emergent and listened for the sound of pursuit. Satisfied that he had not been seen, he sank wearily to the ground and leaned back against the huge trunk.

He emptied one of the bottles down his throat and used another to dampen a filthy handkerchief and gently clean the festering cut on his face. The wound was hot to the touch and ached painfully. Ablutions satisfied for the moment, he stared in disgust at his swollen left wrist, now almost completely black under the layer of mud. Well, he thought, that fucker's broken for sure. No doubt the damned cut on his face was infected as well. He continued the inventory of his deteriorating body: a sprained ankle from yesterday's fall down the ravine, deep cuts on his uninjured hand from elephant grass and brambles, face and exposed neck almost completely covered with angry red lumps from the mosquito attacks, and several small festering sores on his chest and arms where hot metal fragments from his burning aircraft had pierced his flying suit and survival vest.

I need to look on the bright side, he thought. At least I don't have a tipped uterus, or gout from a lot of rich food. He unzipped the front of the flight suit and stared malevolently at the sluglike body hanging near his navel, growing fat on his blood. He pulled his sheath knife and delicately raised the rear end of the creature. It slid from the knife blade, giving no indication that it was bothered at all. To hell with it. In one swift move Donkey scraped the leech from his skin and flung it aside. The head was said to remain within the skin and fester if they were removed like that, but he figured that another sore, more or less, didn't make a hell of a lot of difference. Through a rent in the leg of his flight suit he saw another of the slimy creatures inching toward his crotch. It joined the other on the jungle floor.

What had it been—seven, eight days? Maybe more. He tried to remember when the food had run out, but at the thought his rumbling belly began to ache. Add that to the list—one good bellyache. Well, he wasn't room temperature yet, although it was getting closer. He massaged his aching gut, noticing that his potbelly had disappeared, leaving a depression where it had once been.

If this stupid weather didn't lift soon he'd never be able to contact an aircraft before the dinks ran him down or he starved to death. The gray pall had covered the earth like a close-fitting blanket since the day he ejected, effectively keeping American aircraft away from his location. They had to be working, however, for he had felt the concussions of distant exploding bombs. He'd used the small compass from the survival vest to shoot their azimuth, and figured they must be hitting north of Hanoi, probably the rail tracks leading into China. If that was the case, then there would be no reason for them to overfly his area. He'd just have to suck it up and try to remain free until they returned.

It wasn't going to be easy. Apart from the first brush he'd had with the North Vietnamese troops, he'd almost been caught on two other occasions. Once, he had tried to fill his water bottles at a small stream, and he'd just managed to make the cover of heavy brush before a three-man patrol ghosted by on the opposite bank. Only a small splash had given away their arrival. Another time he'd been lying on his belly watching and listening for pursuers when two of them walked by less than ten yards away. If he'd heard them in time he would have probably tried to move, and undoubtedly his motion would have been noted. Instead, they walked past with eyes focused to the front.

Other times he'd heard voices in Vietnamese talking or calling to one another as they moved about the mountainsides. Always, he'd been able to find a hiding place. He suspected that when the weather cleared, the hiding holes would become more precarious, as the light filtering beneath the trees would help illuminate the earth and low bushes.

When Donkey's watch had stopped, he had lost all concept of time in his gray and green world. When the darkness settled beneath the triple canopy of trees he would seek a secure place for the night. At first light he was moving cautiously, seeking water and shelter for the day. Somewhere he had lost his fear of his surroundings; they became his friend rather than a frightening unknown. The rain forest was, after all, the sole reason the dinks hadn't caught him— that and the thick fog that enveloped the mountaintops in which he hid. The leeches were still repugnant, and he remained cautious of the snakes, although he found that if he moved slowly enough, the deadly little kraits would clear his path. Moving slowly was one thing Donkey had learned to do very well.

The muted birdcalls caused Donkey to prick his ears. Another bit of woodlore he'd learned in the rain forest was that birds when disturbed sounded different from when they were just squawking around. And these birds sounded pissed. Quickly, he eased his water bottles back into the pockets of his flight suit and got on his hands and knees. He looked as if he were ready to play horsey. Slowly he backed into the thick undergrowth and stretched full length on the wet jungle floor. He drew the pistol from its shoulder holster and tried to calm his heartbeat. He still felt faintly ridiculous whenever he drew the weapon.

He heard them before he saw them—a four-man patrol easing along the stream, assault rifles at the ready, eyes flickering from the ground along the bank to the undergrowth around them. Searching. Donkey shut his eyes momentarily, but they popped open immediately. He stared at a leech standing on its tail section, its forebody weaving about as if testing the wind for the smell of blood. It seemed undecided whether to head in his direction or toward the Vietnamese.

The patrol stopped by the stream and knelt out of Donkey's sight, but he knew with a sinking heart that they were looking at the spot where he'd filled his water bottles. They'd seen some sort of mark he'd left, despite his care. Peeking at them from behind the broad leaves, he saw them in a quiet but animated discussion. One soldier, obviously the leader, silently indicated by hand gestures which way they were to split and go.

Donkey watched the smooth-faced young man creep cautiously in his direction. He tried to move the pistol slowly and unobtrusively, yet keep it centered on the man's chest. He moved his eyes and watched the remaining Vietnamese vanish into the fog in other directions. His searcher moved more slowly, studying the ground and foliage with great care. As he moved closer, Donkey realized that the man was older than he had first thought. Probably closer to forty.

The soldier stopped by the bole of a giant tree less than ten yards from Donkey's hiding place and looked carefully around before leaning his assault rifle against the tree. Slowly, his eyes searched the undergrowth. Donkey's heart pounded. But, the soldier's eyes flicked past him without pause. Satisfied that he was alone, the Vietnamese unbuckled his belt and lowered his trousers to squat in a tiny clearing.

Donkey could hear the man softly humming a song as he waited for his bowels to recognize the occasion. He squatted facing Donkey, head moving slowly back and forth as he enjoyed the early-morning freshness of the rain forest. Here it comes, Donkey thought, the inevitability of the situation was apparent. Please! Just do your business, pull up your pants, and go away! It couldn't happen.

Donkey watched the brown eyes wander over his inert form, then come quickly back again. He watched the eyes widen with recognition and disbelief at what they were seeing. They opened to an unbelievable dimension. The men stared at each other for a long moment before Donkey shot the soldier in the face, blasting him backward into his own droppings.

Donkey was up, running and stumbling blindly through the forest. His injured ankle banged painfully into a tree snag, ripping the top of his jungle boot. Breath came in long, painful gasps until the ache in his side became unbearable and he had to stop for a long moment to bend and retch. Then, he ran again. There was no thought in his mind except to get away from the immediate area. Finally, he could go no more and sank to the earth, his face flush with the muddy leaves. Long, shuddering gasps were inadequate to fill his lungs. He quivered to stillness, though his mind continued to replay the nightmare long after his breathing had returned to normal.

Finally, Donkey was able to pull himself to a sitting position. He tried to shove from his mind the picture of brain tissue being blown from the soldier's head. He shuddered violently and retched again; only clearish liquid came forth. In two wars, that was the first time he'd been close enough to one of his victims to see the actual trauma of violent death.

Distant shouts brought him back to reality. He wearily pulled himself to his feet and began a drunken, stumbling run once more. His legs were rubbery, and only the knowledge of sure death kept him on his feet. There would be no mercy from his pursuers now that he had killed one of them.

The forest floor was mushy, the leaves like wet sponges. And then it was gone and Donkey found himself flailing through emptiness as he free-fell toward the bottom of a hidden ravine. The landing made him cry aloud as the sprained ankle twisted violently to one side. He lay beneath the brambles and limbs, his exhausted muscles twitching. This was the big one. There was no way he could go on. He heard the pursuit getting closer before he lost consciousness.

Rain dripping from the leaves awakened Donkey in the darkness. He was flat on his back, legs spread, good arm cradling the injured one to his chest. Nocturnal noises became apparent as hunter and prey battled for life in the stygian darkness. Even with the cooling rain washing his face, he felt flushed and feverish. The hunters had somehow missed him again. Right now, he didn't give a shit one way or the other. The thought of a dry cell didn't seem all that bad. But even as he thought it, he knew it was not to be. No, he'd leave this place either in a U.S. helicopter or with his carcass slung between two poles, if the dinks even bothered to drag him out at all.

Perhaps it wouldn't even be that bad; certainly a dark nothingness with no pain or aches or despair was preferable to the existence he was now leading. Stop, damnit! he told himself angrily. Not now, not after everything he'd gone through just to avoid that ultimate penalty. No, by God! He'd do it just the way those talky drunks did it. One day at a time. And if he had to walk all the way to the Thailand border . . . well, he'd walk all the way to the Thailand border. He lay his head on the muddy earth and, oblivious to the swarming mosquitoes, slept.

The noise of jets woke Donkey from his almost comatose sleep. He struggled to sit upright, confused by the noise and his surroundings. Small shafts of sunlight stabbed the gloom beneath the trees, tiny motes shuttling back and forth in them. He took a small drink of water and tried to clear his brain. His ankle hurt like hell and there was a large lump on his head from his fall to the bottom of the ravine.

Another roar blasted into his depression before quickly fading from earshot. Jesus! Those were Thuds! There wasn't another aircraft in the world that sounded like that. Clumsy in his haste, he unzipped the survival vest pocket containing his radio and with shaking fingers turned it on and extended the antenna. He was reassured by the sizzling sound as the circuits came to life. Be cool, he thought. The dinks may be ten yards away, sitting and waiting for me to make a noise. He turned the volume to its minimum setting and listened carefully for foreign sounds. All he could hear was a cacophony of birdcalls, as if they too celebrated the coming of the sun.

Donkey forced himself to wait for anxious moments, then turned up the volume and inserted the earplug. He knew that none of the aircraft would be talking on Guard channel unless there was an emergency in progress and that his small antenna wouldn't pick up transmissions at any great distance. Still, he was disappointed when the radio was silent. OK, he'd wait until another flight came within earshot and he'd try again. If the Thuds were going into Hanoi, they'd almost surely use the normal route, letting Thud Ridge mask their approach as long as possible. Well, he was sitting right on top of the ridge!

Tensely, he waited for the sound of approaching jet engines. Somewhere not far to the east he heard the regularly spaced percussions of antiaircraft fire. There would be six equally spaced shots, then a pause, then six more. Must be a clip-fed 37mm, he thought. More guns joined the attack until the individual shots were no longer distinguishable.

Almost before it registered on his brain, the approaching flight was over him and on the way to the target. He had to try. "Any aircraft. Any aircraft. This is Cadillac Lead on Guard channel." There was no sound except the crackling of the circuits.

"Any aircraft. Any aircraft. This is Cadillac Lead on Guard channel. Please respond."

"Cadillac Lead, this is Robin Lead, up Guard. What's the prob—"

Donkey's heart leapt! But the transmission had been weak at best before it drifted into an unreadable din of competing tones. So tantalizingly near, then lost.

"Robin Lead, Robin Lead. This is Cadillac Lead. How do you hear?" With a sinking heart Donkey continued to transmit his pleas. No one answered. It's gotta be this fucking ditch I'm sitting in, he thought. It's gonna soak up all the transmissions unless I can get the antenna out into the clear. Frantically, he grasped an overhanging bough and pulled himself erect, only to collapse in pain as he tried to stand on the injured ankle.

OK, so we don't try it that way again. He rubbed what was left of a sleeve across his forehead. So, OK. How do we get out of this damned ditch? Laboriously, he again pulled himself erect, taking pains to keep his weight on his good leg. Good leg! There's a joke, he thought. His good leg felt as if it were boneless, barely able to support him. He leaned against the side of the ravine and caught his breath. Now, for my next act . . .

He surveyed the tangled world over his head. It didn't look promising. He couldn't see the lip of the ravine, and he might be a hundred feet down for all he could tell. He chose the side with the least gradient, hobbled to a likely looking spot, and drew his knife. He slashed at the weathered laterite slope, making irregular hand- and footholds. He made good progress until he had to cut well over his head. He tried to mount his jury-rigged stairs but was immediately stymied. How could he crawl up the steps with one bad leg? He cut more handholds into the mucky soil and hopped onto the first step. So far, so good.

He made a new handhold in the manner of a mountaineer and dug his fingers in tightly, then brought his bad leg up to the new indentation. He tried to get it to support his weight as he shifted his good leg upward. The leg collapsed and Donkey rolled back to the bottom of the ravine. Shit! Another flight of Thuds roared overhead just slightly south of his position. Donkey's mind raced wildly.

He looked at the piece of parachute shroud line hanging from his pocket, from which it had been dislodged in his tumble down the ravine wall. Maybe, just maybe. He forced himself to work slowly and thoroughly, tying several pieces of line together, carefully testing each new knot before moving to another. With his knife he cut a two-inch-thick branch from one of the trees, hacking at it until he had a piece almost two feet in length. Again, he painfully levered himself upright and studied the trees overhead.

He tied the shroud line to the middle of the stick and held firmly to the end of the line, then flung the stick upward with all of his strength. It immediately fell back into the ravine. He tried again and the stick disappeared into the tree growth, only to fall back toward him at the slightest tug.

Again and again he threw the stick upward with rapidly diminishing strength. Often it would catch, only to tumble back to him as he tried to put his weight on it. Then, it caught and held. Donkey was nearly too exhausted to care. He leaned against the wall of his prison and panted. It's gotta be now, he told himself, or I'll never get out of here.

Slowly, shroud line wrapped around his waist and gripped in his good hand, he mounted the footholds again. He ascended almost six feet before he reached the last of them. He hugged the wall and forced his injured hand and wrist to grip the line while he clumsily hacked a new hole, then transferred the knife back to his holster for the one step upward.

It was painfully slow but eventually the lip was in sight. He grasped a dangling tree branch, rolled over the top of the lip, and lay on his back panting like a blown horse. It has to be today, he thought. I can't make it another day. A sip of water from his last bottle helped loosen his tongue until he thought he might be able to talk.

He pulled out the radio, turned it on once more, and extended the antenna. His hand was shaking so badly that he had trouble getting the earplug in place. He crossed himself and muttered a half-forgotten boyhood prayer before he picked up the radio. "Any aircraft. Any aircraft. This is Cadillac Lead. Do you read me on Guard?" His whispered voice had taken on a raspy quality he hadn't noted before.

"Any aircraft. Any aircraft. This is Cadillac Lead. Mayday! Mayday! This is Cadillac Lead on Guard."

"Cadillac Lead, this is Lincoln Lead on Guard. Go ahead."

Donkey felt his eyes brimming over and for a moment he was unable to speak. They not only heard him but it was a flight from his own wing. Lincoln Flight. The contact with another of his own was overwhelming.

"Cadillac Lead, this is Lincoln Lead up Guard. Say again your problem. How do you hear Lincoln Lead?"

"Lincoln Lead, this is Cadillac Lead. I'm on the ground somewhere on the ridge—"

The Lincoln Flight leader broke in on the transmission, unable to contain himself with the realization that he was talking to an ex-ghost. "Jesus Christ! Is that you, Donkey?"

"Yeah, Jake. It's me," he whispered.

"Where the hell are you down there? We're just coming out of the target area, heading toward the ridge."

"Well, that's where I am, I think. Probably on the southeast extension, if my memory is right."

"OK, we must be heading right at you, because your signals are getting stronger all the time. We're going to aim right square down the ridge and you listen for us."

"OK, Jake, but watch your asses. They're starting to shoot pretty good just east of me." Donkey became suddenly aware that radio contact did not necessarily mean a rescue.

Lincoln Lead chuckled. "Yeah, it's probably us they're shooting at, cause we're two to three minutes from the ridge."

Donkey could hear the antiaircraft guns quicken their firing pace just as he heard the first sounds of the jet engines flashing by him, well to the south. "You just passed by me. A few miles to the south, from the way it sounded."

"OK, Donk! If that's us we'll be in a right-hand turn coming back toward you from the northwest. There's a whole shit pot of guns down there, and if you say you're west of them I think I've got an idea where you may be. We're alerting Crown to get the SAR cranked up. We're going to make this pass for you to identify us and then hold out west, away from the guns. Let me know if you hear us. Oughta be over your location in about two."

The flight of heavy jets swept past him to the north, heading east. The guns began yammering again.

"I had a flight go by a couple of miles north of me just now," Donkey whispered.

"That's us, Pard. We got your area marked and passed to Crown. We're going on to the west and I'm sending one element for a tanker while my element orbits about twenty west. When they get tanked we'll trade places. The only problem is that you're awful close to those guns for the choppers to make a pickup. It looks like there's some stunted trees up north of you a klick or two. Are you able to move in that direction? It'd sure make the pickup easier if you could."

"Uhh, yeah, I guess I can start heading that way, but it's gonna be awful slow going."

"Just get as far north of your location as you can," urged the Lincoln Flight leader. "It'll sure help in the pickup."

"OK, I'll be switching off and moving out now," advised Donkey.

"Rog. Check in again in half an hour at the max. OK?"

"I don't have a watch," Donkey said, realizing that his air force–issue watch had not only stopped but was no longer around his wrist.

"No problem. When you hear us come across again, just stop and switch on."

Donkey searched until he found the longest stick that had not yet been claimed by rot to use as a cane. He emptied his last baby bottle of water down his throat and started to throw the bottle aside, then reconsidered and placed it back into the flight suit leg pocket. The guns had become silent

as he took a last look around and began to hump northward.
He tried to make his movements as silent as possible, but he
found that he was lurching and swaying from side to side
and ramming through the undergrowth rather than moving
around it. He felt dizzy and light-headed and had difficulty
focusing his eyes properly.

Doggedly, he blundered northward, often forced from
his chosen path by huge rock outcrops. Another flight of
Thuds flashed overhead. Surely it hadn't been half an hour
already. He stopped and leaned on his stick. No, those had
been going the wrong way and sounded as if they were at
maximum power. Just another flight of fighter pilots trying
to clear the area and get home again. He resumed his march,
head down and limping badly.

Finally, he could walk no more and sank to his bottom
on the muddy forest floor, gasping for breath. His good
arm quivered as he held onto the upright stick for support.
Groaning, he rolled over until he was on one hand and both
knees, his bad arm still clutched to his chest. He let go of
the stick and began to crawl. A piece of cake, he muttered
aloud. Nothing to it. You just put out a hand and then a
knee and move forward. Actually, it's much easier than
walking, he decided. This way you don't get all those tree
branches in your face. His mouth hung open and he could
hear someone panting like an animal.

Donkey's hand slid in the mud and he fell full length
on his belly, the survival radio digging into his ribs. He
lay in the mud with his eyes closed, the wet earth cool
on his fevered face. He knew there was no way he could
go farther. He rolled onto his back, wincing with pain,
and gasped. With his good hand, he wiped some of the
mud from his eyes and blinked them open. A tiny beam
of sunlight struck him in the face.

The roar of the jets seemed to come out of nowhere.
There had been only silence, then the world was filled
with shrieking J-75 engines as two F-105s streaked almost
directly overhead. A flock of unseen birds disturbed by the
noise burst from a nearby tree and fled above the lower
canopy.

Doggedly, he unzipped the survival vest compartment
that held his radio. His fingers were not responding well
to the messages his brain was sending them. But then, the

radio was out and turned on, the little antenna extended toward the sky. "Lincoln Lead, this is Cadillac Lead," he croaked.

The return transmission was immediate. "Got you loud and clear, Donkey. Sorry it took us a little longer than expected, but we're back, full of fuel and a full load of cannon on board. The second element is holding high and directing the Sandies toward us. ETA in about ten. Can you give me the poop on the situation?"

Donkey tried to work up a little saliva in his mouth and unstick his tongue. "Rog, Lincoln. It looks a little thinner where I am now. Don't think I was able to get too far north of my first location. Sounds like the dink guns are mostly to the east, 'cause it's pretty rough country west of here. Hopefully, they can get a jungle penetrator down through these treetops."

"Understand, Cadillac Lead. Let me know if you have any pencil flares, and tell me your physical condition."

Donkey checked another pocket in the survival vest and found the flares. "Roger, Lincoln. I've got four pencil flares and I'm in good enough shape to get on the penetrator if they'll get it down to me."

"No sweat, Donkey. We'll get it down to you. Now, just hold fast for about another five until the Sandies get on station, then we'll haul your sorry ass outta there."

"I ain't goin' nowhere," Donkey mumbled. He sat and prepared the first flare, fitting it into the small black launcher and pulling back the cocking button. Then he waited. In the distance he could hear the whine of the jet engines of Lincoln Flight as they orbited. He jerked as a new voice jumped into his ear from the small earpiece.

"Cadillac Lead, this is Sandy One. How do you read me?"

"Roger, Sandy One, this is Cadillac Lead. I got you loud and clear."

"OK, Cadillac Lead, this is Sandy One. You're weak but readable. You want to hold for a steer?"

"Rog, Cadillac holding for a steer." He depressed the switch and counted a slow ten to himself. "Cadillac Lead, out."

"Good, Cadillac. We got a good one on you and I'll be asking you for another one in two to three minutes, but first, think you could answer a couple of questions for me?"

Donkey had forgotten completely about the authenticated questions each combat pilot had to prepare. They were filed away in the rescue headquarters in the event an airborne RESCAP had to make sure they weren't being lured into a flak trap by the Vietnamese. They were questions that only the individual pilot could answer. Christ! He couldn't even remember what he'd put down. "I can try," he said, "go ahead."

"OK, Cadillac Lead. What was the make and color of your first car?"

An easy one. "It was a black '50 Chevy."

"Bingo, Cadillac. You're a hundred percent so far. Now then, what did you call your grandmother on your father's side of the family?"

"That would be Maw-Maw."

The A-1 pilot chuckled. "Yeah, I guess it would. Now, for the Big Casino. What was the name of your first dog?"

Donkey's mind raced. What the hell was the name of that mutt? Sam? No, that was the one he'd had when he was in high school. He could picture the small brown and white animal but no name would come. "I can't remember," he said miserably.

"What the hell," Sandy One said after a few moments of silence. "Two outta three ain't bad. Hold down for another steer and tell me again where these guns are around you."

Donkey again explained what he could of the antiaircraft gun locations. Before he could finish he heard the deep, throaty roar of the R-3350 radial engines of the Sandy aircraft. The A-1 Skyraider had been designed back in the forties as a close-air-support aircraft for the Navy and had assumed new life in the rescue role for both Air Force and Navy. Its 3,000-horsepower engine could drag aloft the weight of the aircraft in ordnance, and its slowness and durability made it an ideal RESCAP aircraft.

"You damned near flew over me," Donkey blurted over the radio, forgetting to keep his voice down as he heard the huge engines surge overhead.

"Rog, Cadillac, I want you to fire one flare up through the trees. Try to aim it at a spot where it's likely to break through, then get out your compass in case we need your help in spotting the flak guns."

Donkey gazed wildly above him. It all seemed solid. He held the flare at arm's length and thumbed the firing button. A sharp jolt shoved his hand downward as a simultaneous crack echoed through the jungle.

"We've got your flare, Cadillac! Hold fast while we set up an orbit."

The ground fire began immediately. Donkey thought he could hear at least three guns shooting at the circling aircraft. He raised his compass to eye level and directed it toward the source of the firing, then glanced down through the sight while trying to hold it steady. He read the reciprocal heading toward the guns. "Sandy One, this is Cadillac. If you have my position, then the guns sound like they're just about zero seven five degrees from me. I'd guess less than a mile."

"Roger, Cadillac. Stand by and we'll see if we can't get them suppressed. Lincoln Lead, are you up this freq?"

"You bet, Sandy One, this is Lincoln Lead."

"OK, we may need you fast movers to sow a little destruction down here. Cadillac has pointed out some sites that look like they're either 37- or 57mm. Can you hose 'em down for us?"

"We're on the way. Can you mark?"

"Rog, Sandy One is in for the mark now."

There was a clearly audible swoosh, followed by two sharp explosions, then Donkey heard the straining of the radial engine attack plane pulling off target.

"Lincoln, this is Sandy. I put a couple of rockets real close to one of the sites. There are two others just north of there. Make your runs north and south and there shouldn't be any problem with old Cadillac down there on the ground."

"Rog, we've got your rocket smoke in sight and we'll be in on it in about half a minute. Arm the guns, Lincoln Flight."

Before Donkey could hear the sound of the jet engines, he heard the rasping of the Gatling gun of the lead fighter. The rest of Lincoln Flight followed their leader into the attack on the gun positions.

"Sandy One, this is Lincoln Lead. That ought to take care of 'em. We saved enough beebees for another pass if you need us. We'll be holding high and dry just over you at twelve thou."

"Thank you, friends. Cadillac Lead, this is Sandy. I'd like for you to give us another flare now, and me and my friends are going to do a little workout around you in case old Charles has some of his folks down there. In all modesty, we can thread needles with our ordnance, but just to be on the safe side maybe you ought to find something to get under. Let us know when you're ready."

Donkey pulled his aching body into a small depression and thumbed the transmit button on the radio. "I'm as good as I'm going to get. Let her go."

Almost immediately, the A-1s commenced their attack. During lulls in their assault, Donkey could hear small arms fire being directed at the aircraft. As the rockets impacted around him in all directions, he realized that they were giving him 360-degree coverage. An odd, vibrating sound could be heard when the firing slacked. Whomp, whomp, whomp. A helicopter! It had to be the rescue bird. He thought of raising his head to look for it just as shrapnel from an exploding antipersonnel bomb, dropped more than 200 yards away, cut through the foliage overhead. He buried his face back into the soft, slippery mud.

"OK, Cadillac," the lead Sandy pilot was yelling into his radio, "give us one more flare and prepare to direct the chopper in."

Donkey fumbled the fresh flare into the launcher and cocked it with his thumb. Again, aiming toward the least dense foliage, he held the launcher at arm's length and fired it. It was through the treetops before he could open his eyes. "Flare's away," he announced over the radio.

"Cadillac, this is Jolly Green Lead. We've got your flare in sight. How do you read?" The new voice was the pilot of the large rescue helicopter, popularly nicknamed the Jolly Green Giant for its color and size.

"Loud and clear, Jolly Green. Loud and clear," replied Donkey.

"OK, if you can aim your compass at my engine noise and call directional headings, it'll make this thing go a whole lot smoother. We're seven to eight hundred yards out at this time and starting to pick up a little ground fire from the south. Let me know your physical status before the engine noise gets so bad we can't hear you."

"I'm in not too bad a shape," said Donkey as he fumbled for the compass, "but I've got a bum arm and leg."

"In that case, we'd better send a jumper down on the jungle penetrator to help you. Do exactly what he says and don't argue with him. OK, we're about three hundred yards out from you. How does our course sound?"

Donkey aimed the compass at the sound of the approaching helicopter and looked down for the reading. "Your course ought to be about zero eight zero," he transmitted.

The helicopter pilot acknowledged. "Cadillac, we're about a hundred yards from your location and slowing down now. We want you to direct us by the sound, if you can't see us, until we're as nearly overhead as possible. Do you understand?"

"Roger." Donkey listened intently to the building crescendo of the helicopter's engines. "Sounds like you need to correct about five degrees to the right."

He watched in fascination as the huge jungle boughs began to sway as though a squall was approaching. The movement crept toward him. "You're dead on course, about fifty yards away," he shouted into the radio, not knowing whether the helicopter pilot could understand him or not. The noise was such that he could no longer hear the other pilot's transmissions. Suddenly, he could see parts of the huge green shape as it blew the tree limbs into a frenzy of movement.

"Come right about twenty yards and stop," he yelled into his radio. The huge machine obeyed his instructions. "Stop! Stop right there! You're almost exactly over me!"

The noise was deafening as the bulky helicopter hovered over him. He was unable to look up at it, for masses of jungle debris were being blown in all directions. It looked as though an apparition from another world was descending slowly through the tree branches. Donkey didn't realize that the figure was a man until he thrust out a foot to avoid a huge limb. His arms were wrapped around the jungle penetrator and a rifle was strapped over his back. He wore a green crash helmet.

Still some twenty feet in the air, the jumper spotted Donkey and began making "come here" motions. Clumsy as a new colt, Donkey rose unsteadily and began a lurching movement toward the dangling figure. I probably look like Boris Karloff playing the mummy, he thought grumpily. The figure hit the ground well before Donkey was in position. He was surprisingly young, Donkey noted as the man unstrapped his rifle and swept the surrounding jungle with his eyes. Really just a kid.

The jumper turned as Donkey at last arrived at the cable. Noise from the hovering helicopter made conversation impossible. The young man smiled briefly, then grabbed him by the good arm and urged him quickly onto the penetrator. It was shaped like a metal bullet, with small hinged seats pulled down from its sides, and was attached to the cable dangling from a pulley in the helicopter above them. Awkwardly, Donkey climbed onto one of the metal leaves and wrapped an arm around the body of the device. He waited for the other man to climb on, but that would mean he'd have to sit with his legs over Donkey's. Taking a quick look at Donkey's injured leg, the pararescue man decided it shouldn't have his weight on top of it. He looked up and jerked a thumb skyward.

Immediately, the tension on the cable tightened and Donkey started to ascend. He watched the young man on the ground crouch and peer outward with his M-16 extended, growing smaller until he was blocked from sight by the first canopy of leaves. Donkey hunkered over the penetrator and hugged it tightly, trying to keep his head tucked in and avoid being bashed against a tree limb.

The noise grew louder and Donkey suddenly popped free of the highest tree canopy and was in open air. He saw an almost cloudless sky for the first time in days. As the cable pulled him toward the vast open door, another crew member grabbed his shoulders and deftly spun him about until he was facing outboard from the helicopter and away from the door. Simultaneously, the man grabbed him and jerked him unceremoniously backward into the aircraft.

Donkey sprawled and scrabbled on the metal floor as the man untwined him from the penetrator, which he immediately lowered again. Long moments passed as the man stared downward, communicating with the pilot on his intercom system until finally he threw the switch that started the cable upward again. Donkey's rescuer appeared at the doorway, clinging to the penetrator, rifle restrung over his shoulder. More agile than Donkey, he scampered like a monkey into the helicopter.

The pilot immediately made a tight turn and headed west, both crewmen in the rear compartment stationed at the doorways behind machine guns. Both began firing, hot brass spilling overboard. Donkey clung to a seat, still sprawled on the floor, as the gunners fired. He could feel the helicopter accelerating, and as it banked to the right he saw an A-1 Sandy pulling out of a run with smoking guns.

It took twenty minutes before the helicopter pilot felt he had sufficient altitude, speed, and distance to avoid the major threats. Only then did one of the sergeants leave his gun and turn to Donkey with a grin. In one hand he held a large plastic water blivet, which he offered. Donkey worked on it with gusto, and even after his belly felt swollen from liquid, he continued to take occasional sips, just to make sure it was still there.

His leg and arm ached, his head was cut, and there was scarcely a place on his body that had not been bitten, lacerated, or scratched. There were jungle sores the size of silver dollars interspersed among the cuts, and he hadn't eaten in four or five days and had had damned little to drink. But, I'm alive, he thought. I beat the bastards.

Captain James Evelyn Broussard

Donkey lay on the hospital bed glaring, eyes like open wounds. Kate stood beside his head trying to retain her grip on his hand. Jim leaned against a far wall. The squadron commander had left after taking a full blast from Donkey. "How the hell can they do that?" Donkey had demanded. "That idiot couldn't lead a flight of fighters to the men's room."

Both Jim and Kate had decided it was a rhetorical question and remained silent. Donkey hadn't noticed.

"I don't care if he is a damned lieutenant colonel now, he didn't get to be a better pilot all of a sudden, did he?"

Jim shook his head wearily. It had been painful enough to be there when the CO had told Donkey he was to leave for the States the next day and would not be allowed to complete the two missions he needed for a full combat tour. To Jim fell the job of explaining the circumstances of Andy Pritchard's death and the new makeup of Cadillac Flight. He looked to Kate for help and saw only compassion in her eyes for Donkey. She clasped his hand between both of her own.

Donkey continued: "Hell, the man was never even an element leader and now they're saying he's suddenly capable of fighting a flight through to Hanoi? Ha!"

Jim could see that Kate was very concerned. Even the near miraculous return of Donkey had done little to assuage her fears after Andy Pritchard's death. Her eyes told him that she now realized the statistical probability that he would never live to see the completion of his tour. He watched as she forced a smile onto her face and leaned to hug Donkey.

"I'll see you later, hotshot," she said, a hand soothing the swollen jaw. "I'm due for the duty now." She looked to Jim. "Want to walk me to the ER? You can come back later and tell lies with this reprobate."

Jim made a waving motion toward Donkey and followed her into the corridor. They walked slowly toward the ER, occasionally touching arms or hips. Outside the door to the emergency room Kate stopped and leaned against the wall.

"Where does it all end, Jim? We get one of them back but lose another. Just where the hell does it all end?"

"Well," he said uncomfortably, "I'm getting on up there. I've got sixty-one in now. Just fourteen more and I'll be three-quarters of the way through." It was asinine and he knew it as soon as the words were out of his mouth. During the period of flying those sixty-one missions, three of the original pilots of Cadillac Flight had been shot from the sky. "Look at it this way. The odds have to be in my favor now. And heck, there are some flights where most of the aircraft haven't even taken hits."

Kate sighed heavily and slowly shook her head. "Did I tell you that I've watched your flight take off a few times? I know you didn't want me to, but I felt I had to know. So I asked that nice lieutenant colonel, you know, the one I hit in the nose the first night I was at your club?" She gave him a brief smile. "He drove me out to the end of the runway a couple of times when Cadillac Flight was flying. I thought I'd be caught up in the drama of all you young heroes flying off to do battle. But, you know what?" She barked a harsh little laugh. "All I could think of was that the entire drama was being underplayed. It was just a bunch of noisy fighters trundling out and flying away like it was an everyday sort of thing. No bands, no flags, no nothing. You all just taxied out and flew away. Not a hell of a lot of memories to leave a girl." She began to cry quietly.

Jim put his arm around her shoulders, acutely conscious of the looks they were getting from the passing hospital staff. Awkwardly, he patted her arm.

Kate suddenly clutched him fiercely. "By God, Jim Broussard, if you get yourself shot down you're going to be in real trouble. Not from those childish Vietnamese but from me! I don't take lightly what happened between us in that Bangkok hotel."

"Neither do I, Kate Johnson. Neither do I." He held her trembling body for a long moment before he gently extracted himself from her clutching arms. "I want to get back and talk to Donkey before briefing. It'll probably be the last chance I have before his flight early in the morning. I'll see you tomorrow, and that's a promise."

She held his head between the palms of her hands and looked directly into his eyes, then kissed him fiercely. "You're not going to get away from me, you know. There's no way."

He smiled at her before he turned and walked down the hall.

"How was it Donkey, really?" Jim sat in the solitary straight-backed chair next to the head of the bed.

There had been eighteen hours of drug-induced sleep, but the eyes in the gaunt face were still red rimmed. Jim watched as Donkey tried to move his casted wrist into a more comfortable position, wincing with pain. Another cast covered a foot and a leg. The toes sticking out were swollen and looked almost black. Salve covered his face and arms where the blotches and lumps from mosquito bites almost overlapped. He'd dropped at least thirty pounds. Even his hair looked thinner.

Donkey sighed. "Jimbo, it was god-awful. It was the worst thing I've ever experienced in my entire life. If I knew I had to go through it again, I'd probably just blow my brains out right at the start. I can't tell you how many times I gave up, and if the gomers had been around at those times I'd have just walked right up to them and surrendered." He shook his head wearily. "I know the Hanoi Hilton is awful but it's got to be better than that.

"Look," he continued, "I'm outta here on the early medevac flight and I know you've got a mission briefing pretty soon, but we've got to talk. Tell me again about Andy."

Jim did, leaving out no detail.

"And you're sure there's no way Andy could have gotten out?"

Jim shook his head. "Absolutely not. I was watching the wreckage all the way to the ground. No one got out," he concluded bleakly.

"That shit." Jim knew that Donkey was referring to Stark. "And you saw that the MiG had a red tail? Just like the one you say nailed me?"

"Absolutely. Saw it myself. There've also been other reports of red-tailed MiG-21s that have taken out some other Thuds. They don't know if it's a new squadron or what. There's been some speculation that they're being flown by foreigners. Either East Germans or Russians."

Donkey snorted. "Bullshit. Everybody seems to forget that those little people have been getting a hell of a lot of practice at air combat during the past year and a half. And they've got a damned fine airplane for it. But every time some twinkie who hasn't done a loop or an Immelmann turn in five years manages to get himself waxed by a MiG, everybody assumes it had to have been done by a foreigner. Can't stand the idea that the dinks might have a few good sticks themselves. But that's not what I wanted to talk about." He motioned Broussard closer.

"Listen," he said, "that guy Stark is poison. I should have let him get himself killed right away and spared everybody the pain of his existence. But I didn't. Here's what I want you to think about, Jimbo. That asshole has been responsible for getting two people in Cadillac nailed. I don't want there to be a third. I want you to promise me that if he gets himself into trouble again, and I've no doubt he will, you let him get himself out."

He held up a hand to silence Jim before continuing. "I know what I've preached: that a flight looks after each other. Well, I was wrong on this one. You do that with this guy and he's going to get you killed. And I think too much of that red-headed gal to let that happen. You listen to your old flight leader. You're an element lead now and it's your responsibility to take care of the new Cadillac Four. But, let it end there. Dickie Stark is just going to have to live with any mistakes he makes. Don't let him take you out, too. Promise?"

Jim nodded and forced a smile. "It's just not going to be the same war without you, Donkey."

"Ain't that the truth! Tell me, what's in store for you and that Texas gal? I feel like I've got a right to know, what with me being the gracious one and giving her up to you. Obviously, it was me that she first took a shine to."

"I'm just hoping that one of these fighter pilots doesn't take her away from me after I'm gone. She'll still have more than six months to do when I finish up."

"Fat chance of that! You've got a keeper there, son. I just hope you've got the sense to know it."

"I do." Jim shook his head savagely. "Damnit! It just doesn't seem fair. You're going home on a stretcher after all you've done and Stark is sitting back here getting his ticket punched and on his way to wearing stars."

"Jim, let me tell you something. That's one of the most dangerous men you'll ever meet. He's hungry *and* incompetent. That's a deadly combination. Treat him like you'd treat a wounded snake. He'll do whatever it takes to survive and move on. And if he goes down he's liable to burn everybody in the immediate vicinity as well. Always give yourself a way out when you fly with him. Fair? Naw, it's not fair, but it's the way things are."

The other pilots of the strike force had left the briefing room to suit up for the mission, but Cadillac Flight remained in their seats for an additional briefing by Lieutenant Colonel Stark. It had become a new routine for them—their flight leader going over the mission they'd just briefed. Jim was bored with it and made no effort to conceal that fact from Stark. The man insisted on drilling each pilot on all procedures, even asking surprise emergency procedures. It was a finely detailed brief. And it never worked. The combat environment was so fluid that only the most general items were considered unchangeable: tankers, targets, attack headings, and the like. The intangibles—weather, emergencies, aircraft losses, TOTs—had to be taken in stride. Lieutenant Colonel Stark seemed to think that these existed only to screw up his detailed plans.

Jim looked at his new wingman, Dave Bayer, a recent graduate of the USAF pilot training program who was still trying to find his way around in the cockpit of a Thud. He was in the middle of a recitation about a hydraulic system failure for the F-105 and appeared to have forgotten one of the procedural steps. Small wonder, considering their target. Stark waited impatiently for him to continue. Red faced, Lieutenant Bayer looked toward Jim, as if seeking assistance. Jim could stand it no longer.

"For Christ's sake, Stark! What are we screwing around with this for? Didn't you hear where the man said we were going? To the Paul Doumer bridge! You've never been there, but I'm going to tell you that everybody who gets there and back home today is going to be a hell of a lot more experienced than he was before." Even now, the thought of the bridge made Jim's stomach knot. "We'd better stop worrying about having utility hydraulic failure and start being concerned with getting in and out of that damned place."

"Captain Broussard, I think you'd better remember who you're talking to. If you don't think you can cut it, I'll call for the spare pilot right now. And if you call me by my last name another time without my permission, you'll make me very unhappy. I'll not tolerate another lapse in military courtesy by you or anyone else. If you don't like it, see the squadron commander and ask for reassignment. Until that occurs, you'll have to realize that you're nothing special simply because you have a few more missions than the other flight members. Do I make myself clear?"

Jim bit his lip in an effort to remain silent. He repeated Donkey's words to himself. Hungry and incompetent equals deadly. He had to remember that. He looked away as Dave Bayer began his struggle to remember all the steps in the hydraulic emergency checklist. The young man obviously had his attention on the coming flight rather than the technical order. Jim made his mind focus on the target, blotting out the foolishness going on at the table.

The bridge on Hanoi's outskirts handled all the supplies moving south from China and Haiphong; its nineteen steel spans across the Red River made it the longest in North Vietnam, almost a mile in length and nearly forty feet wide. Viaducts of almost 3,000 feet added to its length. The spans and rail junctures at either end were supported by eighteen massive concrete piers. Flak batteries, mostly 85mm, covered both approaches in nearly

overlapping circular patterns. The attack force would have
to run the gauntlet of more than three hundred antiaircraft
guns and twenty-four missile sites, each containing up to
six missiles. It was going to be an interesting day for
everyone.

Thirty-six strike aircraft were targeted against the bridge,
supported by two flights of F-105 Wild Weasel SAM hunters, two flights of South Vietnam–based F-100 flak suppressors, and two flights of F-4 Phantoms in the MiGCAP.
Pre- and poststrike photography would be done by RF-101
Voodoos. Three RB-66s out of Udorn, Thailand, would
lend ECM support. Tankers and airborne command post
birds would launch from other bases. All in all, the skies
near Hanoi were going to be pretty crowded.

A wing staff colonel walked over to Stark and spoke to
him quietly. The flight leader glanced quickly at his watch.
Jim did the same and saw that they would have to hustle to
make their takeoff times.

"All right," Stark told the pilots, "let's break it off and
get over to PE. We're running a little late."

Jim gave him a sardonic grin as he rose and ambled
toward the door, getting the satisfaction of watching Stark's
face redden. The other two pilots were almost jogging
toward the equipment room. They'd both be OK with some
experience. He smiled to himself. Probably someone had
been saying the same thing about him a few short months
ago. He'd have to keep a close eye on Dave, however, for
this was his first trip into Pack Six.

The pilots hurried into flight gear and filled their baby
bottles, stowing them carefully in their g-suit pockets. Jim
turned to follow the two newer men out of the deserted
equipment room as Stark spoke to him.

"Hold on a moment, Captain Broussard. There's something I want to say to you."

Jim stopped and turned to face his flight leader. Dave
and Mike had stopped as well and turned back toward
them. Stark waved them toward the truck, waiting until
they were aboard before he motioned Jim back out of sight
of everyone.

"We'd better get one thing straight, Broussard." Stark's
face had lost the set, stony look. It was contorted in a
barely controlled rage. "You may think you're impressing

someone with your constant sniping at my orders, but you aren't. All you're doing is getting yourself into deeper shit than you'll ever know. You've already screwed up any effectiveness report that I'll write on you and you seem to be bucking for a court-martial as well. Shape up, mister, or you're going to find yourself in front of the wing commander trying to explain away your insubordination."

Jim looked at him for a long moment, resisting the urge to smash his fist into his mouth. "Stark, I'm going to say this to you one time. I don't give a shit about any report you write on me. And if you want to take it up with the old man, then that's OK, too. You wouldn't make a pimple on a flight leader's ass and you know it. You've got to be the worst pilot in the wing, and as far as I'm concerned you were directly responsible for getting two members of Cadillac Flight dinged. You screw around with me and I'll take you out myself. And, Dickie, you know I can do it."

Broussard turned and started for the door when he felt Stark grab him by the parachute, trying to force him around. He lunged backward, knocking the other man into a metal locker before whirling to face him. "You touch me again and I'll break your damned neck," Jim snarled.

Stark sprawled inside the opened locker and stared at him. Jim turned and walked stiffly to the waiting truck and the two worried pilots. Both had heard the crash. Jim smiled shakily at them and looked away as a silent Stark crawled aboard. He stared from the rear of the truck for the short ride to the flight line.

Jim paid particular attention to the two massive 3,000-pound bombs hanging beneath his aircraft. They were huge in comparison to the normal 500- or 750-pounders normally carried. The wing's experience with the bridges of North Vietnam had shown that these monsters were necessary if they expected to drop the reinforced spans.

The aircraft took off at ten-second intervals, using more than a mile of runway before each heavy fighter deigned to fly. Jim and Dave Bayer joined smoothly on Stark's left wing. Mike Patowski was already in place on the right wing of the lead ship. A voice over the attack force common radio net complained that his aircraft had a problem with surging engine RPMs. His flight leader directed him to return to base and called for a spare. It would be rough to fill in with a strange flight, though right now he'd welcome any opportunity to get away from Stark.

The tankers orbited over Green Anchor route in northern Thailand awaiting the formation. Without waiting for Stark's signal, Jim instructed his wingman to depressurize his aircraft and go to one hundred percent oxygen. He was determined to take care of his element regardless of Stark.

The refueling went well, with even Stark and Dave Bayer staying in good position behind the tanker. During the lull between his refueling and the final top-off, Jim studied the cloud patterns below. A tiny itch was making the hairs on the back of his neck twitch. The Met briefing had told them to expect mid-layer broken clouds with decent visibility except for haze, but he could see fog lying in the valley pockets. Banks of stratus could be seen to their front. That had not been briefed.

The four aircraft of Cadillac Flight broke away from the tanker at the end of the refueling track and joined the larger formation. It turned east toward Laos and North Vietnam. The radio crackled to life as the flak suppressors and MiGCAP joined them and took position. Radio discipline had been amazingly good thus far. The Doppler showed that they were on time to make their 1552 TOT. The clouds almost completely obscured the ground beneath them. The Wild Weasels accelerated ahead to begin their search for the SAM sites, for the early warning radar signals were already beginning to warble softly in Jim's headset. The Vietnamese knew they were coming.

"Let's clean 'em up, green 'em up, and start your music." The attack force had entered enemy territory. Jim double-checked his arming switches and made sure his map bag was stowed, then flipped the switches for the ALQ-71 ECM pod. When the ECM was used in conjunction with those of a large strike force, it had an excellent chance of scrambling the enemy radars.

One hundred miles northwest of Hanoi the strike force crossed the Red River and aimed for Thud Ridge. Each flight spread and took varying altitudes and headings toward the target. The force was designed so that each flight would attack three minutes apart, and there would never be more than one within the lethal kill zone of the gunners at any time. The aircraft would also need the separation to protect themselves from the big blasts of the 3,000-pounders. Three minutes should give each flight a margin of error so they would not interfere with those following.

The strike force was well out of range of the nasty-tempered gunners at Yen Bai, but they began hurling shells anyway. The twitch on the back of Jim's neck now felt like mating caterpillars. The weather was really turning to crap.

"All aircraft, this is Zinc Lead. Let's get on down through this mess and see if it's workable," the airborne mission commander called.

"MiGs airborne! MiGs airborne! At 1525 hours," the orbiting command post transmitted. It was starting.

They descended through a cumulus of decaying flak blossoms and went into the wall of unbroken stratus. Jim tried to hold his position on the lead ship and to check his wingman at the same time. Dave was holding on. Then they were through the clouds, and the ground rushing to meet them looked impossibly green. Stark leveled the flight just below the cloud layer at 2,000 feet. The outcroppings of the ridge came clearly into view, only to vanish again as the clouds lowered.

"SAMs airborne! SAMs airborne southeast of Thud Ridge!" A flight ahead of them was already absorbing some of the missiles from the Red River valley sites. Smoke boiled ahead and to their left as the Weasels worked a site. Jim could just make out the aircraft as they wheeled and turned. They would leave the site as soon as the attack force was through the corridor, then push ahead for fresh hunting.

They flashed over the limestone karsts and Jim made a conscious effort to loosen himself in the seat. He adjusted his helmet and took several deep breaths. He could feel his heart thudding rapidly in his chest. He took a final look at his wingman and then concentrated on Stark's ship.

The flight cleared the ridge, and the openness of the valley lay before them. The gunners used the cloud base to range their bursts. The ground was alive with twinkling lights as the small arms fire and heavy guns threw up their protective shield. Five minutes to the target. Jim separated himself and his wingman from the lead element. Stark could stay there at the perfect altitude for the gunners if he wished, but Jim wasn't having any of it. He moved half a mile to the west of the track and led Dave Bayer toward the ground. They leveled at 500 feet and almost immediately he saw the river slowly twisting toward the sea in lazy swirls. He moved his eyes eastward along it until he could see the target. It was easy to pick out—a thin contrasting line spanning the muddy waters of the Red River. Even at this distance it looked huge. The clouds seemed to be lifting a little. Good. They'd need all the separation they could get from the weapon blasts. He glanced at Stark and saw he was still at altitude and attracting a growing formation of flak clouds.

Great billows of smoke from the initial explosions came as the first attack flights went in. At either end of the bridge there were individual duels between the flak suppressors and the gun sites. One of the aircraft burst into flames, and a tiny figure in an ejection seat shot from the aircraft just before it exploded.

"MiGs! We got MiGs southeast of the bridge on the egress route! Do you copy, Bimbo Flight?" A flight leader attempted to get protection from the MiGCAP.

"OK, we're heading that way. What kind and how many?"

"Two flights. Looks like one is MiG-17s and the other is MiG-21s. They're trying to cut us off."

"Rog," came the cool voice of the flight leader. "Just hold onto them for another couple of minutes if you can."

"Hold onto them? Jesus Christ! Are you nuts?"

"Would you clowns clear this frequency so the rest of us can go to work?" asked an unknown voice.

Jim checked his Doppler. They were within five miles of the pop-up point. He looked up at Stark and his wingman, still 2,000 feet above them. They passed the checkpoint.

"Pop, Cadillac Lead!" Jim called. The two high F-105s continued straight and level, flak rocking them from side to side with near misses. "Cadillac Lead, this is Cadillac Three. Pop now!" Either Stark didn't hear him or chose to ignore him. Screw it. He glanced at his wingman and pulled into a maximum rate climb. At 5,000 feet they went into the clouds, but he continued to the briefed 13,000 feet before allowing the nose of the aircraft to roll left and drop until they were inverted in a forty-five-degree dive.

Jim started a steady roll to bring them upright. He popped free of the clouds, with Dave hanging grimly on his wing. The bridge filled Jim's windscreen. He had no idea where Stark's element was.

His glance quickly took in the destroyed flak site on the south end of the bridge. Others were still working, however. The radar warnings were now screaming in his headset as the track radars found the element and locked onto them. Several well-placed rounds blossomed and Jim fought the controls as he pushed through the turbulence. An emergency beeper began its lonely wail on Guard channel.

He nudged the aircraft until it was crossing the bridge at a twenty-degree angle. The altimeter was unwinding in an alarming fashion. The dive should have taken no more than seven seconds. It seemed much longer than that: 8,000, then 7,000 feet. He hit the pickle switch and hauled back on the stick until his vision began to gray. He flashed over the bridge still heading south. Quickly, he rolled the aircraft, now considerably lighter, onto its left wing and shoved outboard on the throttle until the jar to his bottom let him know that the afterburner was engaged. The south bank of the river came up rapidly. It was lined with guns. He didn't want to show his belly to them, but they had briefed on an eastward egress. He tried to look over his shoulder to see if his wingman was still with him, but the g forces made it impossible until he rolled from the hard turn. Dave was still there, albeit pretty far out of position. The element was supersonic, and the suburbs and tightly packed villages flashed by in an instant.

"Cadillac Three, this is Cadillac Lead. Where are you?" Stark's voice was high-pitched and tense.

Jim listened to a flight following them call a damage assessment as they pulled off target. Only one span was down. Jim had no idea if he and Dave had hit anything or not.

"Cadillac Lead, this is Cadillac Three. Off target. Heading one one zero at angels six."

"Roger." Stark sounded as if he was about to lose it all. "We're into the clouds and can't find the target. We're aborting the run. Join on us southeast on the egress route."

Except for the squeal of the emergency beeper, the cacophony over the radio net vanished. Every pilot knew that the weather was workable beneath the clouds, and they were shocked to hear that one of them was leaving the target area with ordnance still hanging beneath his wings.

"Ah, Cadillac Lead, this is Zinc." The airborne mission commander in the lead ship would be hitting the ridge about now. "If it'll help I'll recycle my flight to assist you."

But Lieutenant Colonel Stark apparently had had enough for the day. "Negative, Zinc. Cadillac Lead and wingman are egressing. We don't want to screw up the timing for the Weasels."

"Your choice," Zinc answered. The contempt was apparent in his voice.

Jim turned his element toward the westerly egress heading. Both aircraft were out of burner to conserve fuel for the flight to the tankers.

"Where are you, Cadillac Three?" Stark's authoritative tone was returning as he left the hot area.

"Three and Four are running parallel to the river, about five miles south of it and just south of the city."

"Right, we're ten to twelve miles behind you. Suggest you slow until we can catch up and you can join on us."

In a pig's ass, thought Jim. He kept his element pointed toward Thud Ridge and at full military rated power.

"All aircraft! All aircraft! This is Hillsboro. Black Bandit, Black Bandit! Hillsboro, out."

According to the radar controllers on the orbiting command post, the first wave of MiGs launched from Phuc Yen were becoming short on fuel. However, others might have launched undetected. Jim scanned the area. How could there be sixty to seventy aircraft within this small space and he be unable to see anyone except his wingman?

"Heads up, Cadillac Three. Bandits at two o'clock, high." Jim spun his head at the call from his wingman. Good eyes, Dave! He searched the sky vainly until the sunlight reflected from the polished silver body of the MiG-21. Dave had moved about 2,000 yards to his right. There were at least two MiGs and they appeared to be turning toward them. Four, maybe five miles out.

"Cadillac Four, arm up the guns."

"Rog," said Dave, very cool. "But it doesn't look like they're heading for us. Looks like they're angling more toward the river."

"Yeah," Jim replied, his heart accelerating. "Cadillac Lead, it looks like they're coming for your element. Two MiG-21s that should be at about your one o'clock and your altitude."

There was no answer from Stark.

"Cadillac Four, this is Three. What's your fuel state?"

"Base minus two."

Crap! Dave had used up almost all of his fuel reserve trying to hang in position during the attack. They couldn't diddle around long before they had to find a tanker.

"They're shooting at us!" Jim recognized Stark's voice, though he'd used no call sign.

He thought of Donkey's words: hungry and incompetent equals deadly. Let the bastard get himself out of this. He pictured the hatred on Stark's face in their shoving match in the equipment room before the flight. And he thought of Donkey and Andy Pritchard who had turned back to aid the hapless bastard. To hell with him. Even as he thought it, he was turning his element toward the attacking MiGs, just as he knew Donkey would have done.

He watched the enemy aircraft as they maneuvered to achieve another attack position. Jim turned his element toward them, trying to give Cadillac Lead and his wingman an opportunity to escape the box they were in. Jim saw the two Thuds making for the ridge. Jesus! They were still carrying their ordnance: Both aircraft still retained the two 3,000-pound bombs beneath their wings.

"Cadillac Lead. Jettison your ordnance. Jettison your ordnance immediately!"

No wonder the MiGs were having no problem setting themselves up with a new attack solution. The bombs fell free from the aircraft. The MiGs broke north and climbed. At the apex of their climb they broke apart and turned toward the first element again. A small explosion blossomed just aft of his wingman's tail pipe. The aircraft bucked and almost went out of control before Dave righted it. Frantically, Jim swiveled his head from one side of the cockpit to the other. Out of the sun another MiG-21 raced past before it pulled into a vertical climb for another shot.

"Dave, you OK?"

"I think so," said a very worried Lieutenant Bayer. "It's

still flying, but every warning light I've got is lit."

"OK, head for the water back on the original heading. Fly one one zero degrees. They've got us cut off toward Thud Ridge. Cadillac Lead, Three has a problem. Can you handle things here? Somebody needs to escort Four to the coast."

There was no reply but both aircraft of the first element turned eastward. Sweet Jesus, what a screwup! What the hell was the matter with Stark? Was his radio out?

"Cadillac Lead, can you read Three?"

There was a long pause, and Jim maneuvered to place himself between the three retreating aircraft and the three MiGs. Finally, he was answered.

"This is Cadillac Lead. I'm going to escort Cadillac Four to the water."

Asshole. "Two, this is Three. What's your fuel state?" Jim wasn't sure he wanted to hear the answer.

"Cadillac Three, this is Two," answered Mike Patowski. "I'm down to base minus five. I'll be glad to stay with you."

Jim did some rapid calculations. Lugging those bombs all this way had cut down their reserve significantly. The first element would be lucky to find a tanker if they got over the beach. His own wingman was dinged. None of them would be of any help to him.

"Naw, Two. You three head for the water and I'll try to keep 'em off your tails. Best start calling for a tanker to meet you. It's going to be close."

"Cadillac Flight, this is Purple Lead. Can we be of assistance?" At last, some of the MiGCAP.

"Purple Lead, this is Cadillac Three. Rog. Three aircraft of the flight are heading for the water, just south of the Red and about fifteen south of the city. I've got three MiG-21s that I don't know what to do with. Everybody is short of fuel."

"Roger, we're going buster toward your location. Hang in there and we should be in your area in about seven or eight."

This situation would be resolved one way or another long before the F-4s arrived. Jim continued to watch the MiGs maneuver toward the retreating F-105s. He turned hard to place his aircraft between them and the wounded ship. In

one minute, maybe two, they'd be far enough away that
the MiGs wouldn't be able to catch them. Then, with a
little luck, he could turn eastward and unload. He glanced
anxiously at his fuel counter. It was going to be very close
if he had to go burner.

One of the MiGs broke into an unbelievably nimble turn
toward Jim and he saw the sparkle of the 23mm cannon.
He pulled hard right into a high-g barrel roll, stopped
inverted, then pulled through until the deflection was right
and squeezed the trigger. The M-61 Vulcan fired its load
of 20mm cannon shells at the rate of 6,000 per minute. He
quickly released the firing button as he saw his fire fall
behind the other aircraft. It broke away. He had to admire
its maneuverability.

He completed the roll and saw the MiG straining for
altitude in a vertical climb. Just a few minutes of turnin'
and burnin', everything nice and smooth and coordinated.
Just like they told us at school: It's not the jock who can
pull the most g's but the one who can get everything out
of his airplane. He pulled the Thud into the vertical and
brought in the burner. The first MiG pulled through the
horizon and fired a brief burst, which did no damage. The
first pair looked as if they were pulling out of the fight.
Maybe they were low on fuel also.

Jim scissored into the vertical, trying to keep the other
aircraft in sight. Damn! That airplane could turn. They passed, one going up into a vertical climb, the other descending, canopy to canopy. Neither was in position for a telling
shot. He rolled level and suddenly remembered he was still
carrying the multiple ejector racks. Cursing, he punched off
the protuberance and immediately the aircraft felt better.

The MiG was at his two o'clock, less than a mile out and
turning in toward him. Jim ignited the burner and went into
a nose low, high-g turn toward the other aircraft. Suddenly,
two missiles erupted from beneath the enemy aircraft and
flew toward the Thud. They passed well clear but puzzled
Jim. There'd been almost no chance of a hit by the missiles,
since his engine was turned well away from the MiG.

They were quickly by each other again and Jim went into
a hard right break, letting the nose sag below the horizon.
The g suit squeezed hard at his stomach and legs. After
reversing his direction he slackened the back pressure and

tried to refocus on the enemy aircraft. Surprisingly, it had not turned back toward him but had pitched down and was descending back toward Hanoi, away from the fight. Jim was at his seven o'clock and two miles distant.

Jim thought about the many design flaws in the F-105, but he knew that lack of straight and level speed was not one of them. There was not another operational fighter in the world that could stay with it. Jim reignited the burner and accelerated. Slowly, he crept forward. The MiG helped by making small jinking movements, which the American pilot used to his advantage. The MiG *had* to be low on fuel and unable to maneuver away from its flight path back to the airfield. On every turn Jim was able to cut the corner a bit until he was only five to six hundred feet behind the MiG. Almost casually, he placed the pipper just ahead of the aircraft and squeezed the trigger.

The Gatling gun almost cut the aircraft in half. Then it exploded, and the largest section of the fuselage began a lazy spiral toward the ground. Jim noted that the vertical stabilizer was painted a bright scarlet. Suddenly a chute appeared.

The antiaircraft guns had been silent during the fight but began once more in a fury. Jim glanced at his fuel counter and realized quite calmly that there was no way he could reach a tanker. At best, he had only a few minutes of the precious fluid remaining. He switched the UHF radio to Guard channel and tightened his chute harness until it was cutting into his groin.

"Mayday! Mayday! Mayday! This is Cadillac Three. Two minutes from dry tanks. Heading for 'feet wet.' Doesn't look like I'll be able to get that far."

"Where are you, Cadillac? This is Ringo Lead."

"About thirty southeast of the city at twenty-two grand."

"This is Ringo Lead. We're heading that way."

Jim slumped in the ejection seat, exhausted by the high-g forces of the fight. He watched with indifference as the angry flak clouds burst around him. Assholes! Why were they bothering? In a few moments he'd spare them the effort. Ahead, he could see the narrow ribbon of white sand of the coastal beach. It was bordered by the darker blue-green of the South China Sea. A glance confirmed what he already knew. The fuel indicator was showing empty. He wondered if the remainder of the flight had gotten away. He'd heard nothing on the radio.

Incredibly, the huge jet engine continued to run. A small germ of hope tried to push aside the presentiments of disaster. If he could just get to the water, then he had a good chance of a pickup. The flak bursting around him suddenly mattered again. It was a small chance, but it was a chance. Too bad that the F-105 had an engine-out glide ratio about the same as that of an anvil. If the damned airplane had real wings rather than those stubby guide vanes, why he could almost glide from here!

"Cadillac, are you a lone Thud?"

"Affirm."

"OK, we've got you at our two o'clock, 'bout five or six out. Can you make the beach?"

"I didn't think so but this thing is still running on empty."

"Well, if you can keep her airborne for another couple of minutes you'll be in pretty good shape for an ejection. We'll notify the Navy about your situation."

"Thanks. I appreciate the help."

Jim continued to slowly climb, trying for all the altitude he could get without bleeding off significant amounts of airspeed. Almost 26,000. The water was so close. The J-75 engine became suddenly indignant at being asked to perform without its customary diet and decided to quit. The quiet was uncanny.

"Cadillac Three has just flamed out."

"Understand, Cadillac. Navy's been notified. Try to stretch her as far as she'll go. You might just make it yet."

Jim trimmed for best glide speed, but the heavy aircraft seemed to eat up the altitude. Passing 15,000 feet he unclipped his mask and gulped the fresh air, then thought better of it and reclipped it into place. No telling how much longer his battery would last. He'd better get out a last transmission.

"This is Cadillac Three. I'm going to be unhooking everything now. Thanks for the assistance."

"Good luck, buddy."

Jim disconnected himself from the radio leads, oxygen, and g-suit plug-ins. He stowed everything that might become lethal during ejection and practiced his body placement, making sure his arms and legs were tucked in tightly.

The aircraft descended through 8,000. He could pick out the small fishing boats on the beach and in the water. It was going to be very close. At 3,000 he could see the automatic weapon sites on the beach with little figures turning their guns to fire at him. At a thousand feet he said to hell with it and pulled the ejection lever.

The opening shock of the parachute ripped the helmet from Jim's head, and he watched it spin into the sea below. He became aware of a painful pressure in his groin as the straps bit into the flesh, and he shifted in an attempt to relieve the pressure. Rational thought was slowly replacing the primal reactions. It seemed very quiet, and the air was cool as it licked his face.

The peace was destroyed by a loud noise. Jim twisted in the straps and watched the spectacular demise of his aircraft.

Something stung his shoulder and as he turned to grab it his eyes opened wide in fright. The sandy beach was only 200 yards away. Loud cracking noises floated to him as the people there knelt and banged away with their rifles. The throaty staccato of a machine gun joined the din. A parachute cord separated with a twang as a projectile cut it. Jim tried to draw up his feet so he would present less of a target, but his seat pack got in the way.

The seat pack! He had to drop the seat pack or it would take him under when he landed. Jim risked a quick glance at the water. It seemed very close. Frantically, his hand scrabbled for the release handle. Another part of his mind coolly observed that the groping hand was bloody from where it had clutched his stinging shoulder. There! He felt the seat pack fall free. He was connected to it only by a long nylon rope. The pack contained a one-man raft, which had inflated upon release and dangled below the pack. The pack also contained the survival equipment. He tried to remember what they'd told him in survival school. Hadn't they said that in a water bailout the pilot should unbuckle his straps so that he'd be free of the chute when he hit the water? He peeked down again. The water looked *very* close! Might as well do it before one of the shooters on the beach gets lucky. He hit the quick-release snaps to his chute.

In a more rational frame of mind, Jim would never have done that. He would have remembered that heights above the water can be deceptive. Additionally, he would have observed that the seat pack and raft dangling twenty feet below him had not yet struck the water. But this was not a time for careful consideration. Jim realized his error as he passed both objects in his fall, some thirty to forty feet to the water.

The momentum took him very deep into the surprisingly chilly waters of the Gulf of Tonkin. Completely disoriented and choking on the salty water, he did the only rational thing he'd done in quite awhile. He pulled both tabs on the underarm flotation packets. They billowed into large water wings, dragging him inexorably to the surface. He took great draughts of air before a wave smashed into his face, making him cough and retch as the water forced its way into his gaping mouth.

Riding the crest of a swell, he saw the orange raft bobbing in the next trough. It disappeared as the swell passed, but Jim knew where it was and struck out in that direction. He could hardly move his arms over the water wings, and was finally reduced to sticking his arms out to the side and making flapping motions with his hands. Then he remembered the cord attaching the raft to his chute harness and groped beneath him until he found it wedged under his bottom.

Hand over hand, he pulled the raft toward him until he was finally able to grasp its slick side. He clung to it weakly, after swallowing what seemed like most of another wave.

As Jim lay with his head and arms within the small raft, trying to regain his strength, he became aware that the people on the beach had not given up. Rifle and automatic weapon fire could be heard over the noise of the water slapping the side of his raft. A new discordant sound joined the others. It was a throbbing noise and seemed to be getting closer. As the next swell raised the raft, he stretched his neck up to peer at the beach. He felt sick. A small motorized junk had pulled away from the shore and was heading for him.

The shooters on the shore were becoming more accurate. The raft's international orange color, which made it highly visible to a rescue aircraft, also made it an ideal target.

A loud ripping noise froze him. Hair standing on the back of his neck, he peered toward the beach in time to see the junk disintegrate. The water around it was chewed into a froth, and pieces of the junk tumbled lazily into the cloudy sky. The lead F-105 pulled from its firing pass and stood on its tail to position for another run. The ripping sound came again and Jim watched the figures on the beach blown asunder like falling leaves by the second fighter.

Thrashing frantically, Jim headed for the open sea, trying to get away from the bright orange target. The raft followed. He fumbled in the special leg pocket on his g suit for the switchblade knife stored there. He pulled it out and quickly severed the cord connecting him to the raft, then replaced the knife and resumed what Kate had called "The Santa Fe Sand Crawl."

The distinctive sound of the M-61 Vulcan guns split the air again and Jim twisted around to watch the pair of Thuds work the beach. A film of sand and sod obscured the land as the 20mm cannon fire laid a swath of destruction. Jim turned his back to it and again began plowing for the empty horizon. He didn't know where he was going, but it was in the opposite direction from that deadly beach. A loud explosion fifty yards away jarred him and made him swallow more water. Jesus! What was that?

Another explosion came, muffled by the water, fifty yards to his front. A mortar! They were using a damned mortar! How could they even see him at that distance? Again he turned and found the orange raft slavishly following in his wake. He kicked his feet at it but it seemed to enjoy the game and tried to snuggle closer. He turned and paddled with all his strength. Another explosion landed only twenty yards behind him. They were closing the brackets.

New sounds joined the cacophony: whooshes and many different explosions. He let the swell turn him until he faced the beach. He saw the second F-4 as it began its roll-in, easily identifiable by the large black smoke trails. Two pods of 2.75-inch rockets flashed from the aircraft and darted toward the ground. After release the pilot leaned the Phantom over in a hard right bank, passing directly over Jim and his trailing raft. The backseater waved as the aircraft zipped overhead. Jim lifted a weary arm in return.

Something bumped his shoulder and Jim gave a gasp of horror. He imagined the gigantic maw of a shark; instead it was his friendly raft, nudging him like an affectionate kitten. He stared at it for a moment, then pulled his revolver from its shoulder holster and aimed right between where he thought the eyes should be. He pulled the trigger until the firing pin was clicking on the dead cylinders. Ears still ringing from the shots, he watched with satisfaction as the compressed air hissed through six holes. The persistent raft slid slowly beneath the surface. He could see it for several yards in the clear water before it disappeared from view.

Without the raft, he suddenly felt very alone and vulnerable. Watching it sink made him realize just how deep the water was. Never in his life had he been in water over ten feet deep, and the feeling made him uneasy. He looked around cautiously to make sure nothing was stealing up on him.

Killing the raft had gotten his adrenaline flowing again, and he used this spurt of energy to propel himself farther from the beach. He heard the F-4s return for another rocket run but didn't turn to watch, instead plowing determinedly toward Yankee Station.

Jim lost track of time, but it was probably only minutes before what seemed like an apparition appeared overhead. Possibly the ugliest aircraft he'd ever seen circled him at 400 to 500 feet. It was an amphib, and a crew member leaned into the slipstream from an open window in the fuselage. He waved and Jim waved back. Everyone was sure friendly today. He was disappointed when the lumbering SA-16 Albatross disappeared from sight. He resumed his paddling.

He was at the bottom of a trough when he was startled by a huge splash and the roar of radial engines. A giant plume of water shot into the air at his two o'clock. As the sea lifted him again, he saw that the ungainly beast had landed and was surging toward him. God! He hoped they had him in sight, for the aircraft was bearing down on him with reckless abandon. Jim saw the reason. Mortar shells were landing around the twin-engine amphibious rescue bird. Glancing back toward the beach, he saw that he'd made little progress. The beach was still only 300 or so yards away. The clouds were thicker, and in the gloom he could see the twinkle of small arms fire directed at them.

The aircraft was slowing and the mortars were ranging more accurately. Pieces of hot metal struck the ocean beside him, sizzling as they sank from sight, leaving tiny smoke trails. Jim sort of wished that the Albatross would just go away; it was attracting way too much fire for his liking. Then he took back his wish, for the aircraft appeared to be doing exactly that. Maybe they couldn't see him. He waved his arms excitedly above his head, but the aircraft kept steering at an angle away from him.

A crew member hung from an open hatch in the aft fuselage. As the big bird passed, he threw a coiled rope toward Jim, and as it dragged to his front, he was able to grasp it. The SA-16 never slowed, but turned toward the open sea, towing Jim like a capsized water-skier. A mortar round exploded almost under the wing of the aircraft, causing it to rock against the swell. The pilot goosed the engines and Jim hung on, wrapping the rope around an elbow. The strain was tremendous, and he endured it only because he couldn't stand the thought of being alone again.

Then the rope went slack. Jim's vision was blurred from saltwater being forced into his eyes, and he could no longer focus. Cautiously, he loosened his hold on the rope and rubbed his swollen eyes. He could make out activity by the rear door of the Albatross but couldn't determine what was happening. Something was approaching. He blinked his eyes some more.

Two sergeants paddled their raft next to him. One grasped his water wings and held onto him tightly as the other paddled back toward the waiting aircraft. Jim's vision had cleared by the time they reached the opened hatch. He could see that the beach was now several miles away. The sergeants were both grinning at him as he felt the aircraft begin to move again.

"Enjoy your swim, sir?" one asked as they pulled him onto the floor.

Jim opened his mouth and threw up saltwater on the man's boots.

Epilogue, 1986, Hanoi

The People's Banquet Hall in the Co Loa Citadel district was a balmy eighty-five degrees with the humidity hovering around one hundred percent. The Vietnamese were all smiles and teeth; the Americans, polyester and sweat. The general tried to pry his shirt from where it was sticking to his underarms without poking his hand directly under his military blouse. Discreet maneuvering was not doing the job. He looked at the dry faces of their hosts and felt sweat matting his short hair. Overhead, ancient paddle fans barely stirred the moist air, and smoke from the Vietnamese cigarettes clogged his sinuses. Nearly all of them smoked, he noted; none of the Americans did. Maybe that was the answer. We could simply outlive the little fuckers if we couldn't beat them.

He stared in distrust at the next dinner course that a waiter had placed in front of him. He suspected the Viets were having a good joke at their visitors' expense by serving foods they knew the Americans normally would not eat. Probably dog or monkey or some such. Damned if he would ask. Feigning gusto, he attacked the portion as though he were starving. The Vietnamese beamed. Probably goddamned rats.

An older Viet across the table spoke quietly to an interpreter, who then leaned toward him. "Ah, General. Mister Duc wishes to know if you are enjoying your visit to our city."

"Please tell Mister Duc that I'm certainly enjoying it more now than I did on my last visit twenty years ago."

The interpreter relayed the message and Mister Duc's eyes widened momentarily as he made the chronological connection. That's right, Mister Duc. I was a Yankee air pirate who bombed your country, he thought as he smiled serenely at the older man. That should give me a little respite from the small talk.

Mister Duc was not to be denied. Another message was breathed across the table in a cloud of *nuoc mam*, the pungent fish sauce the Vietnamese used on everything. "Mister Duc would like to know if the families in America who will receive the bones of their relatives will be happy."

"Please tell Mister Duc that they would be happier if they were not in a box at all. Of course, this is much better than never knowing their fate, as is so often the case." Might as well get a commercial in while I can, he thought.

"Mister Duc is sympathetic. The fate of many Vietnamese soldiers is also unknown."

"Yes, I can imagine. However, the Vietnamese government has the opportunity to search diligently for their missing young people, and unfortunately we do not. Then, too, many of our young pilots who were taken prisoner here have unaccountably disappeared, though they were reported to be in the custody of your government. These reports must have been mistaken, however, for no civilized people would deliberately harm unprotected prisoners. Such acts would be cowardly and disgraceful." *That* ought to take care of the small talk.

It did. Mister Duc looked away, but not before the general saw the anger in his eyes. He smiled innocently at the Vietnamese across the table. One, several seats down, he recognized from the receiving line at the airport—a short, stocky man in the uniform of the Vietnamese Air Forces. He'd watched them speak through the interpreter as though he understood both sides of the conversation.

The State Department foreign service officer sitting next to him leaned closer and murmured softly in his ear. "Take it easy, General. We're not over here to start another war. We're just getting out of the last one."

Cold blue eyes turned on him. "*We?* You look like you should have been about the right age. Where did *you* serve?"

"As a matter of fact, I had a student deferment until I was out of graduate school. By that time it was over." He looked uncomfortable.

"Yes, I can imagine," the general replied, and deliberately turned away from him. He noted that the stocky Viet was smiling as though he had understood this exchange as well.

A dull throb was starting in the general's frontal lobes as the dinner progressed to its inevitable conclusion. Too much heat and too much smoke. I've got to get out of here, he thought, before the interminable speeches pledging friendship and the other horseshit begin.

He excused himself and found the senior team member locked to the politburo delegate by an interpreter. He was not pleased by the general's early departure. The general didn't give a shit.

Jim Broussard stood by the window, blouseless and with tie removed, staring into the rain hammering the city streets. The day's light was fading rapidly and the few Vietnamese still outdoors hurried toward their destinations. From his window on the eighth floor of the old Metropole Hotel he could just see an ancient adversary—the Paul Doumer bridge. Now, they called it the Long Bien. In the dim light he could just make out the huge concrete pilings that had easily defied their early strikes. Some of the spans had been dropped by the 3,000-pounders, but little else of the massive structure had been shaken. Even now his heart quickened as he thought of his last attack against it.

There had been many highs and lows in his military career spanning nearly twenty-five years; however, everything paled in comparison to that day. But for the grace of God, or luck, and a damned efficient pair of F-105s, he'd never be looking at the bridge through this window. Vividly, he could still remember the opening shock of the parachute after he ejected with his Thud out of fuel, trying to reach the coast and safety. The absolute horror of watching the Viet soldiers train their weapons on him as he floated down toward the water, only yards from the beach. Without the quick actions of the Thuds and the flight of Phantoms, he would have had absolutely no chance. Their guns and rockets had allowed the rescue aircraft to pluck him from under the noses of the Communist gunners. Two days later he was leading Cadillac Flight into North Vietnam after Richard Stark had been transferred to the new B-52 provisional wing forming at U-Tapao, Thailand.

So long ago. But the memories remained clear and crisp though names had slipped away. Nameless fighter pilot ghosts still swaggered through his mind in their sweaty flight suits and parachutes, unzipped survival vests and accoutrements of their profession about them: leg-hugging g suits, knives and revolvers, helmets and map bags. They wore mustaches, bush hats, and scarves. And egos. Their egos fit them like a second skin. There was nothing they thought they couldn't do. Where could he have lost their names?

Not all of them, of course. Some would be with him forever. Donkey Sheehan, godfather of his oldest boy, who was now at the Air Force Academy. Donkey still lived on his sailboat in the Virgin Islands, flying the commuter run to Puerto Rico on the old airboats. He was a frequent visitor to the Broussard household.

Bobby Packard. Dead in a prison camp, or so the Vietnamese claimed, from injuries suffered during ejection. Strange that Bobby hadn't mentioned injuries in his last minutes of freedom. More than likely beaten to death for refusing to knuckle under to his captors.

Andy Pritchard. Aloof and handsome to the point of prettiness but all fighter pilot beneath his good looks. The one everybody expected to wear stars. Jim's eyes flickered to the uniform blouse thrown carelessly onto the hard bed. The two stars on each epaulet gleamed in the low-watt direct lighting the Vietnamese seemed to prefer. Don't forget James Broussard, he thought wryly. The man absolutely no one, including himself, expected to stay in the Air Force one day longer than absolutely necessary.

Major General Richard Nelson Stark. There was a name he'd never forget either. After his brief career as a Thud driver, it had been even odds as to whether he'd be court-martialed or shot down by his own flight. Neither had happened. His mission to the Paul Doumer bridge had been his last in a fighter. The wing commander didn't have the horsepower to overrule Stark's sponsor, a lieutenant general at PACAF headquarters, so a court-martial was out. But neither did that general pack the necessary gear to force the wing commander into giving Stark another combat mission in the F-105. He was, instead, given the most cruel punishment the wing CO could devise: nothing. Until his transfer was arranged he had no job and no friends, and was forced to spend each day sitting in the commander's waiting room. He had never left the bosom of the Strategic Air Command again.

Jim hoped that the "friendship banquet" was the final vexation of a bad day. The steady rain from a deepening tropical depression in the South China Sea had only added to the dreariness of the warehouse where he and two State people had seen the rough wooden boxes housing the remains of six American airmen. Inside, the light was poor and the heat stifling. Four of the boxes had rusty dog tags, the metal ID tags normally worn on a chain around the neck nailed to the box tops instead. The Vietnamese assured them that the dog tags matched the bones contained within. This would have to be verified by the Joint Casualty Resolution Center in Honolulu before they would be released to the next of kin.

Two of the ID tags had been for naval aviators. Another was so rusted and burned that Jim could hardly see the lettering. He pulled reading glasses from his shirt pocket and leaned close to make certain he was reading the lettering correctly. His hands began to tremble.

PRITCHARD   ANDREW R   FV3040294
            A POS   RC

Jim had straightened slowly, feeling slightly nauseous. He stared at the Vietnamese officer who accompanied the Americans. The short captain smiled cheerily. The two State Department officials had given only cursory glances to the boxes, then wandered to the open door seeking relief from the oppressive heat. Jim had felt dizzy and disoriented. His mind refused to accept that Andy Pritchard could fit into a wooden box that measured eighteen inches by eighteen inches by thirty inches. He placed both hands on the wooden box as if there was some way to communicate with its occupant.

"Are you about ready, General?" one of the young men had called.

Jim didn't answer. He continued to stare at the box.

"We're ready to go, General," the voice called again, more insistent. They knew it was only a formality. They had no way of knowing whose bones were in the boxes.

Jim had turned abruptly and headed for the door, walking with measured steps. He came abreast of the two men and without breaking stride stared into the face of the one who had called; "Fuck you," he said quite clearly, and continued to the waiting automobile.

He smiled as he thought of the expressions on the faces of the men. He knew he wasn't being completely fair, since both had probably been less than twelve when Andy was killed, but he didn't care. They were such prim and smug little assholes. Donkey would have eaten them alive.

The overhead fan stirred listlessly at the moist air of the hotel room, cooled only slightly by the rain. He tried to picture Cadillac Flight as they had been when he reported to the combat wing. Bob. Andy. Himself. They all seemed so young now to be doing such a job. Younger even than the men he'd shocked at the warehouse. Even Donkey had been several years younger than Jim's own forty-six. How could they get men to do such things? Reviled and spit upon in their own country. Poor pay. A better than even chance of being killed, captured, or wounded. Yet he knew that in his life before and after that time, he'd never been more alive than when he'd crawled into the cockpit of one of those huge, ugly, magnificent beasts. He'd never forget the sharp stench of his own fear mingled with the odor of jet fuel. The mixture of exaltation and weariness as you realized that you'd survived another trip Downtown. The camaraderie of the men and the certain knowledge that whatever tragedy occurred, as indeed it did daily, not a pilot would leave a mate until all chances of rescue had been exhausted.

The danger had been like a narcotic that heightened the perceptual powers until you needed it to exist. Afraid of it but unable to keep away. Some needed it so badly that it eventually consumed them. Perhaps other occupations

experienced the same exhilarations as combat flying in a
fighter aircraft, but he doubted it. Even Kate, as close to
him as it was possible to be with another human being,
didn't really understand.

A tentative tapping on his door broke his reverie. Who
the hell can that be? he thought grumpily. The rest of the
team members were still at the banquet, already sparring
with their hosts over the next load of bones and what the
United States would have to give in exchange.

He swung open the heavy wooden door and looked at the
short, stocky Vietnamese standing stolidly in the darkened
hallway. There was a newspaper-wrapped parcel under his
arm. In the poor light it took Jim a moment to recognize
the man as the air force colonel he had met yesterday in
the receiving line and who had sat across from him at the
banquet. What the hell was his name? Ming? No, Minh.

"Good evening, Colonel," Jim said. "Can I be of some
assistance?"

"Good evening, General," the shorter man said with a
slight bow. His English was heavily accented but good. "I
do apologize for intruding on your privacy, but they told
me at the banquet that you had been taken ill and, since I
wanted to have a small talk with you, I am presuming upon
your good nature to see if you need medical assistance or
merely relief from the wranglings of politicians."

Jim smiled in spite of himself. What *did* this guy want,
though? Could this be the initial feelers for a new deal of
some kind? Why would he bring it to me? Better bring him
inside and find out what the story is.

"The latter, to be frank," Jim answered the inquiry. "Won't
you come in and sit?"

"Thank you, if you're sure it's no bother."

The Vietnamese responded as though he had a straight
line to Jim's thoughts. "Believe me, there is nothing official
about my visit. I merely wanted a chance to sit and chat and
perhaps . . ." He held the package aloft, then unwrapped it
to reveal a liter bottle of what looked to be scotch whiskey.
"I didn't know if you indulged or not."

Jim laughed aloud. "Oh, I have the character flaws of most
fighter pilots. Yes, Colonel, I've been known to indulge."
He motioned Minh to a chair and turned to get glasses and
a pitcher of drinking water from the vanity. Minh opened

the bottle and poured each of them a stiff drink. He sat in one of the chairs and Jim sprawled his long frame on the other. Minh held up his glass to the light, peering at the amber liquid.

"Then you were a fighter pilot," he said. "Would it be indiscreet to ask what aircraft you flew?"

You really mean what aircraft I flew over Hanoi, thought Jim. "Oh, I've flown about every fighter type we've had in the inventory. Not for a long time, however. I'm well past the age where they'll let me take operational missions alone. At best, I have an instructor pilot looking over my shoulder to make sure I push all the right buttons." He held his glass aloft in salute. "Cheers."

"I apologize for the scotch," Minh said. "More properly it should be called Hungarian, since I believe that is its country of origin."

"You should have no trouble obtaining vodka, I suppose."

The irony was not lost on Minh. "No, that's one thing we're literally awash in. Unfortunately, I find it completely flavorless, and the only real reason to drink it is to become intoxicated in minimum time. Unlike our Russian friends, we Vietnamese need more subtlety in our drinking."

"Colonel, if you had seen the American pilots drinking after flying into your country twenty years ago, you'd have had the perfect example of drinking for intoxication."

Minh laughed. "Yes. It was much the same for us. Our largest problem was sometimes finding something to drink at all. Your F-105s blew up every major brewery in the country and we eventually resorted to making our own. Now I seldom touch it unless there is a special occasion, such as this." He raised his glass in toast.

"Incidentally, Colonel, I commend you on your excellent English. Where did you learn it?"

"Ah, from a young lady I knew quite well," Minh replied with a melancholy smile. "She was a student of languages at the university. We practiced almost every day for six years. She was also fluent in French and Mandarin."

"What happened to her?" Jim asked softly.

"She was killed in the B-52 bombings of December 1972. She'd been drafted into the defense forces and was assigned duty near my base. We were to have been married during the next Tet holiday."

"I'm very sorry."

"Yes, those were terrible times."

Jim made them fresh drinks. He was starting to feel loose. "Are you married now, Colonel Minh?"

"Oh, yes! I've been married to a wonderful woman for several years. We have three children—two boys and a girl. And you? Do you have a wife?"

"Yes, indeed. I married a nurse with whom I was stationed in Thailand in 1966. We have two boys and a girl, also. Our oldest son is at the Air Force Academy." He dug for the pictures in his wallet.

Minh set his drink on the low table and reached into his breast pocket for a pair of horn-rimmed glasses. He took the photos and peered at them closely. He smiled. "They all have hair of such an unbelievably red color."

"Yeah," laughed Jim, "they all took after their mother in that respect."

"I don't think you mentioned what aircraft you flew in our recent hostilities."

"No, I don't guess I did. It was the F-105 Thunderchief. And you? What did you fly?"

"What you in the West call the MiG-21. They still permit me to go aloft occasionally. Not too often, however; they fear I'm too old and have lost my reflexes. Perhaps they're right. Flying fighters is a young man's sport. Would you please answer one question for me, General?"

"Of course, if I can."

"Why did the Americans call your aircraft the Thud? It always seemed a strange name to us."

"I'm surprised you know its nickname," Jim answered with a smile. "I don't think anyone really knows where the name originated. I know it began as a term of derision by its pilots but changed to one of affection as they realized it could do one thing better than any other aircraft in the world: get them safely home with tremendous amounts of battle damage. Some say the nickname came from the noise the aircraft made as it crashed into the ground, but I suspect you know about the mordant humor of most fighter pilots."

"Oh, yes. It was the same in my company. Those who couldn't laugh a bit at tragedy had little reason to be in a position where it happened every day. Our very best pilots were those who decided early on that they were already dead and were merely marking time before their burial."

Jim rose to fix them another drink. He was beginning to feel light-headed and went to the large open window rather than returning to his seat. Minh joined him there. Together they stared into the soggy night.

"The day I ejected we were attacking that big bastard there," he said, pointing toward the bridge fast disappearing into the darkness. Red strobe lights flashed from its highest points. "We lost several aircraft that day. I ran out of fuel before I could get to a tanker. Damned near didn't make it to the water, either."

"That surprises me," said Minh. "Our data showed that the F-105 had ample fuel to strike anywhere in our country and still recover, at least to the refueling points."

"That's true, but this was a special instance. I had turned back in an attempt to protect other members of my flight. They were all damaged or low on fuel." Or testosterone in one case, he thought to himself. "I got into a fight with one of your MiG-21s, and by the time the issue had been decided, I was running only on fuel vapors. The MiG was from your red-tailed squadron," Jim added as an afterthought. He remained staring into the rain, not noticing Minh's head whip toward him.

"General, what happened to the enemy aircraft you were fighting?" There was a small tremor of excitement in his voice.

Jim noted the discordant tone. He turned and looked at Minh narrowly before speaking. "I shot him down as he was trying to break away. I figured he was having fuel problems of his own for he'd been gaining an advantage in the fight when he suddenly broke it off. I saw him eject but the aircraft was a flamer. A few minutes later I ejected myself—over the beach when my own aircraft ran out of fuel."

Minh was silent for a few moments before he spoke. There was a slight quiver in his voice. "General Broussard, we had no red-tailed aviation companies in our forces."

Jim turned to him in surprise. "I'm sure you did. I personally saw one of them shoot down a member of my flight, and the one I engaged that day we attacked the bridge most definitely had a red vertical stabilizer. No, we weren't wrong about that, I'm sure."

Minh shook his head slowly and for the first time seemed to be at a loss for words. He tried several combinations before he found one that he liked. "General, I did not say there were no red-tailed MiGs," he began haltingly. "I said we had no aviation company that carried that distinctive marking. To my knowledge the only aircraft so painted was my own. And that was done much against my will. I was too cowardly to have my ground crew remove it."

"Jesus Christ!" Jim said as it all sank in. "You were the only one?"

Minh nodded his head. Both men resumed staring into the darkening evening. Finally, without turning, Jim asked: "Just how many of us did you get altogether?"

"If it matters, there were twelve. But, don't forget there was one engagement in which I definitely was not the winner."

"Could that really have been us who fought that day?" he asked wonderingly.

"Probably, but I don't suppose we will ever know for sure." He smiled suddenly and the young fighter was briefly there in his face. "If it's all the same to you, I prefer to think that it was you. If you can tell the worth of a man by the virtue and strength of his enemies, I would be most pleased if it had been you."

The two pilots stared at each other for several moments, then the American took both glasses and made them fresh drinks. He handed one to Minh. "I thought I was dead meat," Jim said. "There's no way a Thud could turn with a MiG-21. If you hadn't gotten low on fuel you'd have had me in a couple more turns."

"I'm not so sure, for I was having difficulty in maneuvering for a missile shot. Our ground controller had reported a flight of Phantoms in the area and I certainly didn't want to have them join in the fight. But I was the one who made the mistake. And you took advantage of it. I gave no thought to the idea that you would stay with me so tenaciously. I knew you had to be low on fuel. Ah, well. That was the only time I had to separate from my aircraft before landing, so I consider myself fortunate."

They sat and finished the last of the bottle. Two relics of another age, rumpled and half drunk. "Minh, do you ever think about them? Those we lost? There were so many. Think of the human potential that is gone forever—genes that won't be passed to another generation from the best we had."

"It's always the best who go first," replied Minh, slurring his words a little. "They are the ones willing to do the things that everyone should, but seldom do. Let me ask you another question. Who do you suppose the Vietnamese pilots admired more than anyone? Except for Ho Chi Minh, of course."

Jim shrugged.

"We admired the American fighter pilots." Minh smiled at Jim's look of surprise. "Oh, yes. A friend of mine once accused us of emulating the Yankee pilots even though they were our enemies. She was correct, of course. Who could not admire such swaggering self-confident men who audaciously flew into a complete hell of antiaircraft defenses with so little regard for their lives? We all wanted to be exactly like you."

"Well," Jim said bitterly, "at least you won."

"Won? Look around our country. Who could call this a victory? We have no industry, our former allies have invaded us twice, we have a national debt we can never pay off, and now we're reduced to bartering bones of our former enemies for hard currency. If this is a victory, I should hate to see a defeat!"

Jim smiled. "I think King Pyrrhus said about the same thing more than two thousand years ago." He leaned forward. "Tell me though, do you miss it?"

Minh stared at him and slumped back in the chair before he spoke softly. "I miss it like hell."

General James Broussard could feel the sweat dribbling down his back beneath the class-A blue uniform blouse. He held his hand to his forehead in a rigid salute as the small American honor guard carried the caskets aboard the rear ramp of the C-141. The remains, boxes and all, had been transferred to the coffins that the Americans had brought with them. It was a small ceremony. The State Department people looked suitably somber as they stood with their hands over their hearts and in what they considered the position of attention. Jim thought it looked silly when civilians did it.

His headache from the hangover throbbed dully behind his eyes and it took a conscious effort not to squint. The Vietnamese delegation looked as though they had better things to do. Minh was not among them. The honor guard slow-stepped by Jim with their last burden and disappeared into the hold of the aircraft. The American team followed but not before going through the tunnel of out-thrust Viet hands once again.

On board, Jim removed his blouse and loosened his tie before sinking wearily into one of the reclining seats. He noted that no one was anxious to be close to him since the incident at the warehouse. Fine. He rested his head against the seatback and closed his eyes. Jesus! Did he have a head. Minh had been in even worse shape. He was disappointed that the little colonel had not been there to say good-bye.

The jet engines began their whine and the large aircraft started moving quickly across the ramp. The air conditioner fought a losing fight with the outside air being force-fed into the ducts. The pilot didn't pause at the end of the taxiway but swung directly onto the active runway and advanced power. Jim opened his eyes and watched the markers flash by. The transport rotated, and immediately after they left the ground the wheels began to whine into their wells. The air from the ducts already felt cooler.

Jim watched the city slide away. There was the Paul Doumer bridge, Bach Mai, Phuc Yen airfield. Like a time warp. The aircraft turned and the Red River valley was below them. He traced the river northwest and there it was—Thud Ridge. It looked smaller now. Suddenly, a shout from the other side of the aircraft pulled his attention away from the panorama.

"Jesus Christ! What's that crazy son of a bitch trying to do? He's going to ram us!" It was one of the young State officers.

Jim unbuckled and sprang across the aisle, ducking to peer through one of the small portholes. The small silver fighter had pulled into a tight "parade" formation, neatly tucking itself just behind the right wing of the American transport. To those unknowledgeable about the fighter pilot's world, the MiG seemed unbelievably close. Jim saw immediately that there was no danger from the other aircraft. He admired its sleek lines and the sun reflecting brightly from its scarlet tail. The face in the cockpit was indistinguishable beneath the helmet and oxygen mask.

The small interceptor held its position for several minutes, then moved slightly outboard and executed a graceful aileron roll, pulled inverted, and split for the ground.

Jim watched it out of sight. Good-bye, Colonel Minh. He returned to his seat, sank back, and closed his eyes. A small smile played on his lips.

"Let's get you on home, Andy," Cadillac Lead murmured softly to himself.

AUTHOR'S NOTE

Aerial combat operations against North Vietnam by the United States began August 5, 1964, and ended January 27, 1973. Not since our Civil War have Americans faced such a schism between policy and practicality as during this period. Foremost amongst these dichotomies were the ubiquitous Rules of Engagement (ROE), even now the thought of which is enough to drive the survivors of that combat into a sputtering rage.

These frustrating rules formulated by the civilian leadership were meant to keep the targeting options under tight White House control and prevent inadvertent air actions that might escalate and bring China into the war. The air crews were expected to memorize lengthy and frequently changing rules as to where they could or could not bomb. A valid target on one day could lead to a court-martial on the next. At varying times, enemy aircraft could be fired on only after a *visual* identification could be made, abruptly hauling the United States missile-capable fighters back to World War I tactics. Until later in the war, enemy airfields with their interceptors lined neatly in their revetments were strictly off limits.

North Vietnamese surface-to-air missile and gun sites could be struck if they actually engaged the American bombing forces but were otherwise off limits as well. Nor could the stacks of missiles just off-loaded from a ship or train be destroyed. The attackers had to wait until they were actually in place and being fired against their aircraft. Madness, thought the pilots.

The planners drew circles around Hanoi-Haiphong and along the Chinese border into which the airmen were either prohibited from flying or were restricted to specified targets. Unfortunately, these zones corresponded closely to the limits of the industrial targets found within North Vietnam. Consequently, many American sorties ended up dumping their ordnance on targets of little relative importance, a favorite being empty troop barracks and suspected truck parks.

337

Curiouser and curiouser. Strategic targets such as POL sites and iron works were struck in the north by fighter-bombers trained to deliver close support to friendly troops, while B-52 strategic bombers performed close air support in the south, demolishing huge stands of rain forest from 30,000 feet.

During the years of the war there was never a single air commander for all the U.S. forces. Lines of authority were convoluted and ambiguous, giving COMUSMACV (Commander, U.S. Military Assistance Command, Vietnam) sole authority to conduct air strikes within South Vietnam through either the Commander, Seventh Air Force, or the Commander, Seventh Fleet. This authority extended into Route Package One, that portion of North Vietnam abutting the DMZ. The commander of PACAF (Pacific Air Forces) delegated responsibility for accomplishment of the Air Force strikes out of country into Laos and Route Packages Five and Six Alpha to Seventh Air Force. Navy targets in Packs Two, Three, Four, and Six Bravo came down from CINCPACFLT to Seventh Fleet, and then Task Force 77. Nowhere were the targets coordinated any lower on the chain of command than in CINCPAC, located in Honolulu. The Marine Air Wing that traditionally responded to the needs of its own troops was only able to continue to do this until 1977 when COMUSMACV placed their in-country assets under Seventh Air Force. In essence then, one had to go as far from the actual fighting as Hawaii to find a commander responsible for all air assets and allowed to make on-scene adjustments to tactical situations involving joint activities. Even that isn't completely accurate, however, since the Strategic Air Command never relinquished control of their heavy bomber and tanker fleets. Without a superb group of aircrew and commanders in the tactical fighter and carrier air wings it's doubtful that any of it would have worked.

Decisions on targets to be struck originated in the Situation Room of the White House after receiving inputs from the secretary of defense and the State Department. Never has a bombing campaign been given such close scrutiny or detailed analysis from on high as the one directed at Hanoi. And suggestions from the working troops were not welcomed. Only at Seventh Air Force level and higher could targets even be nominated for strike. There have been numerous stories of some startled targeting officer being dragged to his knees to hunker by the President of the United States so he could point out which bridge had supported a twelve-truck convoy the previous night. In fairness to the president it was said that he usually listened attentively to the targeting officer before choosing the target. Target selection was accomplished with inputs from the various departments (see following diagram).

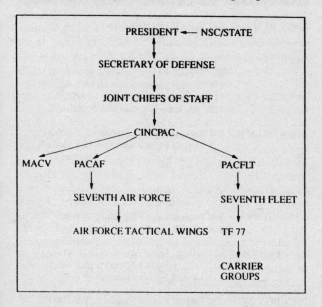

A final note. Throughout the war the president decreed an almost endless string of temporary bombing suspensions. These were obvious attempts to lure the North Vietnamese government toward the negotiating table. Inevitably they all met the same fate. The North Vietnamese government interpreted them as a sign of weakening U.S. resolve and used the periods to rebuild and reinforce their already formidable air defenses. The pilots who flew into the teeth of that system were understandably irritated when their enemies were given a respite to restore that which they had, for months, been trying to destroy or beat into submission.

AIR FORCE ASSETS IN SOUTHEAST ASIA, JANUARY 1, 1966

(Utilized all or part-time in the air campaign against North Vietnam)

UDORN, RTAFB 15 Tactical Reconnaissance Squadron 12 RF-101

UBON RTAFB 433 Tactical Fighter Squadron 18 F-4C
497 Tactical Fighter Squadron 18 F-4C

TAKHLI RTAFB 333 Tactical Fighter Squadron 18 F-105D/F
334 Tactical Fighter Squadron 18 F-105D/F
354 Tactical Fighter Squadron 18 F-105D/F
41 Tactical Fighter Squadron 14 B/RB-66
4252 Air Refueling Squadron 10 KC-135

KORAT RTAFB 421 Tactical Fighter Squadron 18 F-105D/F
469 Tactical Fighter Squadron 18 F-105D/F
Tactical Air Warfare Center, Detachment
One 4 F-100

DON MUANG 4252 Air Refueling Squadron 4 KC-135

DANANG RVN 390 Tactical Fighter Squadron 18 F-4C
8 Tactical Bomb Squadron 24 B-57B/C

CAM RAHN BAY 43 Tactical Fighter Squadron 18 F-4C
557 Tactical Fighter Squadron 18 F-4C
558 Tactical Fighter Squadron 18 F-4C

BIEN HOA RVN 308 Tactical Fighter Squadron 18 F-100D/F
531 Tactical Fighter Squadron 18 F-100D/F
510 Tactical Fighter Squadron 18 F-100D/F

TAN SON NHUT 416 Tactical Fighter Squadron 18 F-100
405 Fighter Wing 4 RB-57E
20 Tactical Reconnaissance Squadron RF-101
16 Tactical Reconnaissance Squadron RF-4C
41 Tactical Reconnaissance Squadron RB-66
522 Airborne Early Warning Center EC-121